THE GREAT TRADITION

The book opens when Hans Christian von Hohenlohe, the son of Faith Marlowe and Rudolf von Hohenlohe, the leading characters of *Christian Marlowe's Daughter*, goes back to Germany after the first world war because he wishes to unite himself with his father's people.

The Germany to which he returns is not the Germany of his romantic dreams, although his ancestral home and its devoted servitors seem at first to be part of a life as idyllic as when his mother first went there as a bride. Underneath, however, are currents which the inexperienced boy is unfitted to navigate. Defeat has brought poverty and frustration to the German people, the best are impoverished, the worst elements aggrandized. As the situation worsens, the embryo Nazi movement seems to many, including Hans Christian, the one hope of Germany's recovering her self respect and her rightful place among the nations.

THE
GREAT TRADITION

FRANCES PARKINSON KEYES

CEDRIC CHIVERS LTD
PORTWAY
BATH

First published 1939
by
Eyre and Spottiswoode Ltd
This edition published
by
Cedric Chivers Ltd
by arrangement with the copyright holder
at the request of
The London & Home Counties Branch
of
The Library Association
1970
Re-issued 1973

SBN 85594 785 3 ✓

To my son
John Parkinson Keyes
who both directly and indirectly is
responsible for large portions of this book.

Printed in Great Britain by
Redwood Press Limited, Trowbridge, Wiltshire
Bound by Cedric Chivers Ltd, Bath

CONTENTS

PART I

CAPTAIN'S TABLE

1924

CHAPTER I

"What a beautiful day we had for sailing! The sky-line clear as crystal! Like a celestial city's! . . ."

.   .   .   .   .

"Nonsense, Edith, you can't possibly be *yet*! Why! We're hardly out of the harbour, and it's smooth as a mill pond. . . ."

.   .   .   .   .

"I'll take hors d'œuvres first, and then some chicken soup, and a small piece of fish. I might as well order from the grill now too, the service on this boat is so slow; a mutton chop, *thoroughly* done! And mind you bring it to me hot! If there is anything I can't endure it's lukewarm food. I really don't care much for mutton chops, but there doesn't seem to be a great deal of choice. Now on the Italian liners—— Oh! Would you care to see the menu too? Excuse me!"

The belligerent-looking lady, wearing a severe black toque, which revealed neatly frizzed hair beneath it, closed her lorgnette with a snap. She had managed to disregard the sentimental cleric, who had remarked to the group at large that New York looked like a celestial city, and the beetle-browed man who was storming at his miserable though bejewelled companion. But something impelled her to bend her gaze upon the handsome boy beside her. He was almost too arresting a type, she instantly decided; and far too young— apparently still in his teens—to be honoured with a seat at the Captain's table. But at least he appeared to be well-bred, which was more than could be said of the awful girl sitting opposite. She was really rather pretty, with lovely pink cheeks, big blue eyes, and a bush of curly brown hair. But she was flashily dressed in a red-and-black sports suit and she had on at least a dozen bracelets, one of them strung with silly little charms that tinkled every time she moved her hands. Petunia-coloured nail polish glittered on her finger-tips as she did this, and her mouth was petunia-coloured too. Her one conversational contribution had been addressed to the dumpy, frumpy woman with an anxious air who was seated beside her

7

"Mumma, did you know I had eight corsages, besides all the other flowers? The steward was still bringing in boxes when I came down to lunch. Jimmie Nelson and Ted Sloan both sent orchids—I knew I could bank on that. But Harry Page, the skinflint, only came across with a dozen carnations. When I get home again, I'll tell him just what I think of him and his penny pinching."

Having delivered herself of this direful threat, the girl lapsed into silence, and the corners of her pretty painted mouth drooped. She had begun to smoke before the soup course was served, and she continued to do so, flicking away ashes indiscriminately and permitting them to fall on the tablecloth and the carpet. Obviously she had no manners at all.

Making a determined effort to ignore this lack, the lady with the lorgnette forced herself to smile, her comprehensive condescension taking in all her objectionable companions at once.

"As we are apparently to be fellow-guests at the Captain's table this next week," she said, "it will be much easier and pleasanter for us all, will it not, if we know each other's names at the outset? Mine is Mrs. Armistead Carruthers."

She paused, but nobody seemed to be at all impressed. The simpering clergyman and the handsome boy bowed, but the girl with the petunia-coloured finger-nails, extinguishing the scarlet-stained butt of her fourth cigarette, stared and then snickered. The charms on her bracelet tinkled more provokingly than ever, as she began to spread a large piece of French bread liberally with butter. She was not at all interested in Mrs. Armistead Carruthers, and she did not care who knew it. Instead, she was intent upon obtrusively studying the boy who sat opposite her and who had attracted her attention also, though with a different effect from that produced on Mrs. Carruthers; she thought he was just too smooth for anything, and she wished she could make him look at her. This wish absorbed her completely. Her mother, however, responded cordially to the imposing dowager's overtures.

"Can't say I ever heard it before," she remarked with heartiness. "But then I'm not acquainted much in the East, and you're *from* the East, I guess, aren't you? Boston maybe?"

"New York," said Mrs. Armistead Carruthers stiffly. "My ancestors were among the original settlers of New Amsterdam in 1640 and——"

"Well, is that a fact! I'm Mrs. Rufus Rhodes of Rhodesville, Kansas, and this is my little daughter Trixie. My husband publishes the Rufus Rhodes Farm Journals—*Contented Cows, Rhodes' Guide to Poultry Raising, The Kansas Rural Clarion*, and so on. He's prospered and he's a regular party man. But we never dreamed he'd get a political appointment, never. Not even if he did give thirty thousand dollars to the campaign fund. We were just dumbfounded

8

when the President wrote and asked if he wouldn't like to be Minister to Holland. Rufus was tickled almost to death, and he took the next boat. I couldn't go with him, because I had the house to close and all that—any woman knows how it is. And of course Trixie wanted to buy some clothes before we started. She didn't know just how the stores in Europe would suit her, so she thought she'd better be on the safe side and do her shopping in Kansas. But here we are on our way at last!"

Mrs Rhodes beamed beneficently all around her. Mrs. Armistead Carruthers shuddered slightly. Before she could frame a suitable reply, the clergyman spoke suavely.

"Let me congratulate you on your husband's well-deserved appointment, Mrs. Rhodes," he said. "I have often observed the periodicals which he publishes in the homes which I have occasion to visit throughout the length and breadth of my diocese. I know how great a force for integrity and progress they are. Perhaps I might be permitted to introduce myself also. I am Father Hastings, Suffragan Bishop of Delaware."

"Catholic, I presume?" inquired Mrs. Rhodes, her cordial voice slightly tinged with anxiety, and yet with the air of one determined to face the worst and make the best of it.

"Not *Roman* Catholic, my dear lady, Anglo-Catholic. It is a matter of deep regret to me that the word 'Protestant' has ever been used in connection with the Episcopal Church in the United States. She is a true daughter of the English Church, which has never fallen into the error of using that objectionable word. I am on my way to a great conference in London where I hope official action may be taken to clarify much regrettable confusion in regard to the word 'Catholic.' I . . ."

"I'm awfully sorry. Really, I am. But I'm afraid I'll have to ask to be excused."

The pallid lady wearing the magnificent necklace and rings had turned almost the colour of one of her own emeralds. She rose, hastily and apologetically, and, plunging down the length of the dining-room with an air of desperation, vanished from view.

Her husband made no move either to assist her or to follow her. He had been dismembering a broiled live lobster as his wife prepared for flight, and now he began to break the claws with gusto.

"My wife's a very poor sailor," he said contemptuously, picking up a cracker. "Imagination mostly. That's all sea-sickness is, in my opinion. Though I don't know as a cloud of cigarette smoke helps out a sinking feeling any." He glared at Trixie, who did not even notice his ferocious glance, for she was covertly studying the striking boy as she tilted back her head and inhaled slowly. "Well, Bishop, I feel in a way I know you already," the speaker continued, with a slight snort. "You keep a pretty good account at our bank—

the Fifth National, Wide Street, Philadelphia. I'm Elbert Fuller, the First Vice-President."

"Of course, Mr. Fuller, of course! I'm glad to meet you personally. How delightful that you happen to be taking a crossing just at this time! I hope you're off on a well-deserved vacation?"

"Well, a short one. I've no patience with people who go to Europe and stay for months on end. A few weeks is all *I* need to see everything there is worth taking in over there. Restaurants are what interest me chiefly. I like to get to at least two different ones a day. Then I do hope to get in some bridge on the voyage. That's one of the reasons I've taken a slow boat. You don't play by any chance, do you, Bishop?"

"Well, just a friendly game. Never for money, of course. I don't mind taking a hand to make up a fourth if I'm needed, just to oblige, but——"

Mr. Fuller gave another slight snort. "Well, that wasn't exactly what I had in mind! That's the kind of bridge my wife plays—ladylike and dumb. No offence, I hope, Bishop. I go in for tournaments and stiff stakes. But it doesn't matter. I'll find three other business men and we'll make up a table. The Lord knows I need some relaxation. It's been a bad year for bankers. Before this administration gets through with inquiries and reforms we'll be sunk."

"Oh, but the President is such a *kind* man! He has such a nice smile! I'm sure he wouldn't do anything to hurt the banks for the world!"

Mrs. Rhodes spoke with acute distress. Mr. Fuller regarded her with the venomous eye of one who does not suffer fools gladly, but before he could frame a sufficiently scathing answer, her daughter addressed her pettishly.

"Mumma, where's the Captain? Is that him standing over there by that post?"

"That is the Chief Steward," interposed Mrs. Carruthers icily, as she observed Mrs. Rhodes looking about her in bewilderment. "It will interest you, I am sure, to learn to recognize the different ship's officers by the insignia they wear on their sleeves. The Captain has four gold stripes. He sits at the head of this table where he has so graciously invited us to join him. But not, of course, until the ship is well out at sea. Up to that time he naturally remains on the bridge."

Trixie Rhodes seemed unaware that she was being snubbed. Without responding in any way to Mrs. Carruthers's informatory remarks, she lit another cigarette, and spoke to her mother again.

"I wonder if there aren't any young people on this boat," she said in a voice which, though curiously flat and immature, was designed to be devastating in its effect. "I can't seem to see any. I bet it's going to be an awfully dead crossing. I shall simply go bugs if it is."

10

For the first time, she looked provocatively at the boy across the table as she spoke. However, it was Mrs. Rhodes, assuming that the remark had been addressed to her, who answered.

"There, Trixie, I'm sure it'll be all right as soon as you get some acquainted," she said reassuringly. "I see two real nice-looking girls sitting over at that little table in the corner. Mercy! I shouldn't wonder if they were twins!"

"I don't see anything wonderful about them just because they happen to be twins," retorted Trixie still more pettishly. "I saw them before, anyway. I bet they're college girls or something like that, reading books all the time and planning to go and see cathedrals and picture galleries. You know I didn't mean girls, anyway."

"That little slut's mother is afraid of her," said Mrs. Carruthers to herself with scorn. Aloud she remarked freezingly, "I happen to know that young Richard Eustis, who graduated from Harvard last year, is on board with his mother. They would, of course, have been placed at the Captain's table if it had not been for their mourning—Senator Eustis died less than six months ago, and Mrs. Eustis has been simply shattered. She is going abroad on the advice of her physician. I have known Richard ever since he was a small child. He is very attractive. If you like, I will present him to you."

"Well, I don't know," remarked Trixie unenthusiastically. Her covert glance had already included Richard Eustis, and she had decided that he would do in a pinch, though he did not begin to intrigue her to the same degree as the silent young stranger at the Captain's table. "He's probably glum himself if his mother's taking on so. I heard that Terry O'Shaughnessy, the middle-weight champion, was going to take this ship, but I guess that's too good to be true. Anyhow, he trains all the time with Carlotta Carew, and I don't suppose he'd look at me. She's simply my ideal. I thought she was marvellous in 'The Double Bed.' If I could pry him loose from her, that *would* be thrilling!"

"I suppose I'm too young to fill the bill. But I'd be very glad if I could help out at all."

Mrs. Carruthers started slightly in her chair. She had had a vague impression that the boy sitting beside her had murmured a name when she had mentioned her own, but he had not spoken since, and she had almost forgotten him, so complete had been her preoccupation with the bishop, the banker, and the mother and daughter who had been catapulted into diplomatic life. Now she saw that he was leaning forward and smiling very charmingly.

"I am Chris Marlowe, from Hamstead, Vermont," he said agreeably. Although he imparted this unremarkable information to the table as a whole, it was quite evidently designed primarily for Trixie Rhodes, and the manner in which she responded to it was electrifying. Her look of blankness vanished, her big blue eyes brightened suddenly, and her painted lips parted over her pearly teeth in a way which was really entrancing. Her bracelets tinkled as she clasped her dimpled hands together ecstatically.

"I'm awfully pleased to meet you, Chris," she said sweetly. "I've finished lunch, haven't you? Let's go and give this tub the once over together. Shall we?"

"If the others will be kind enough to excuse us," he said deferentially, rising and sliding his chair back into place before an attentive steward could spring forward to do this for him.

He led the way out of the dining saloon, threading his way between the closely ringed tables without the slightest awkwardness, and lifting his hand to greet the leader, as they passed the little balcony where the orchestra was playing—a salute which was beamingly returned. As they stopped beside the lift in the corridor beyond, a diminutive blond bell-boy instantly sprang to attention. Chris Marlowe turned to his companion.

"Where would you like to go? There's a verandah café, beyond the social hall, that's very pleasant. I sat out on it for an hour or so this morning, while the ship was leaving the harbour. We might have coffee there first. Afterwards, we could shoot in the gallery on the sport deck, or play tennis. Just as you prefer."

"I'd simply adore it!"

"Which?"

"Why, all of it, of course!"

Chris gave a brief order, and the small lift began a slow ascent. When it came to a stop the blond boy opened the door solemnly, and bowed with a jerk after the manner of a toy soldier manipulated with a string.

"*Bitte*," he said, speaking as mechanically as he moved.

"He's weird, isn't he?" Trixie remarked to Chris, as the lift started down again.

"Oh, no! He's been trained to act that way."

"Why, and why does he say bitter?"

"*Bitte* means please, in German."

"But why should he thank us, when he runs the elevator?"

'It's the custom, in Germany, to express pleasure to those you serve. It's symbolic of the German spirit."

"I think it's weird myself," Trixie persisted. Then, for no apparent reason, she giggled. The sound of her laugh was not unlike the sound of her bracelets. It tinkled as she linked her arm through Chris Marlowe's, and skipped down the corridor beside him. Although he appeared to walk without haste, he took long steps and she had to scramble to keep up with him. She was quite breathless by the time they reached the open-air verandah. But such breathlessness was as of the elixir of life to Trixie. She settled herself firmly in the wicker chair which Chris drew out for her, rested her elbows on the small table which separated her from him, and leaned forward.

"It was swell of you to ask me to come out here with you. I really did think I'd go bugs if I had to sit at that table any longer."

"I'm sorry. But what made you feel that way? I enjoyed watching our table companions immensely. I thought they were interesting."

"Interesting! Why, they were all older people and horrid besides. I'll bet that grim-looking woman with the Queen Mary hat is a Tartar."

"But Tartars are awfully interesting. In their own way I mean. Don't you think so?"

"No, I don't," replied Trixie, her voice slightly sulky. She opened her bag, extracted a case and a lighter, and for several moments puffed away at the cigarette Christ lighted for her. She had been struck with admiration by the ease with which he found his way about, and the casual manner in which he gave orders; but the fear that he might be a "highbrow" had begun to consume her. None of the fellows she knew in Rhodesville pulled out chairs for their lady friends, and she was sure that none of them spoke smilingly to stewards in German. She might have known there would be a catch somewhere, that this was too good to be true. Because Chris was the best-looking thing. She had thought that his hair was brown at first; but now that the sun was shining on it she could see that it was full of copper-coloured lights. It stood out crisply from his head and she felt sure that it would have curled if it had not been cut so close. His eyes were almost the same colour as his hair and had still more light in them; but when he was not smiling, a dreamy look kept coming into them, which Trixie thought was even more fascinating than their sparkle. His skin was the sort that usually went with red hair, very white at the neck and forehead but almost scarlet over the cheek-bones; she felt as if she would like to put out her finger and touch it, as if it would be smooth as satin under her hand. She wondered how long he had been shaving. He had said himself that perhaps he was too young to fill the bill for her; there was something awfully fresh looking about his face, like a young boy's, and he was slim as a reed. Still, he was reassuringly tall, and he wore his well-tailored clothes as if they had grown on him. Besides, he did act grown-up—almost too grown-up; that was what worried her, more than his actual age——

"How do you happen to speak German, and know all about everything the way you do?" she finally inquired, in a tone of voice that was defiant rather than baffled.

"I lived abroad when I was a little boy. My father was a German. He was killed in the World War. I'm on my way to see his parents now. They live in East Prussia."

"Is that near Holland, where I'm going?"

"No, it's on the Baltic, beyond the Polish Corridor."

"What's that?"

"It's the narrow strip of land that was sliced off the German Empire when President Wilson visualized Poland as a 'united, independent and autonomous state' requiring a seaport. He made his vision into a point—one of fourteen—and it found its way into the Versailles Treaty."

A slight note of irony had crept into Chris Marlowe's voice. But though this was entirely lost on Trixie, she realized that if she encouraged Chris to continue in this strain, she would soon be out of her depth, conversationally speaking. She decided to retreat to firmer territory.

"You said your father was killed in the World War," she remarked, applying a fresh coat of white powder to her nose. "He didn't fight on the German side, did he?"

"Of course. Didn't your father fight on the American side?"

"He didn't fight at all. He got exemption because he was married and had a wife and child to support."

"I see. Well, in Germany men fought anyway. They lost, but they fought to the last ditch." Then, as if unconscious of any tension in the atmosphere, or any reason for it, Chris continued, "Those shrubs banked along the side of the verandah are beautiful, aren't they? Germans are so fond of flowers that they raise them everywhere, even on board ships."

"I adore flowers myself," said Trixie, brightening a little. She had not previously noticed the shrubs banking the sides of the verandah, and she gave them only a passing glance now; but the thought of the eight corsages reposing in her state-room, and the intelligible masculine devotion which they represented, was extremely cheering to her. For she was increasingly puzzled by Chris. He did not seem like a sissy in spite of his dreamy expression and gorgeous skin. But he certainly had a queer line. She decided to redouble her efforts at drawing him out.

"How do you happen to live in Vermont if your father was a German?"

"Oh, my mother is an American. We've lived in the United States ever since my father died."

"Is Hamstead a big place?"

"No, just a little village. My ancestors settled it. The countryside's lovely there."

"Are there many young people in Hamstead?"

"Not many. But we have good times there. And we're not far from Belford. That's a fair-sized town."

"Do you go to high school in Belford?"

"I did, before I went to Harvard."

Harvard! Well, that might account for a good deal. Trixie had not heard Harvard very highly commended among her boy friends who attended the State University. Just the same, she knew that some people thought it was tops, of its kind.

"Do you do anything special at Harvard?" she inquired with genuine eagerness.

"Nothing very special. I've managed to keep on the Dean's list so far. And I wrote a little operetta last winter that——"

"You don't play football, or anything like that, do you?"

"Oh, yes, I play football. But I like to play the piano ever so much better."

Chris was apparently inclined to dismiss football without further comment. But Trixie's cheeks had already flushed with excitement under their rouge at the magic word.

"You *do!* Would you take me to a Harvard-Yale game some time?"

"If you'd like to go, I'd be very pleased to see that you get there. I can't go with you if I am still on the squad. But I'll have eight tickets and any number of willing friends."

He spoke as casually as if he had acquiesced to a request for a banana split. Trixie, more and more intrigued, regarded him with mounting curiosity, her blue eyes growing rounder and rounder.

"Who's with you on this trip?" she demanded, an unwelcome suspicion that there might be competition for Chris Marlowe's attention suddenly permeating her mind.

"I'm alone. My mother couldn't leave her work to come abroad this summer."

"What kind of work does she do?"

"She's a senator."

"A *senator!* I thought senators were men!"

"Well, all the others are. Ninety-five of them."

"*Goodness!* Does your mother go to Washington, and see the President, and things like that?"

"Oh, yes! Mother has a nice house in Washington. It's the same house her father and grandfather lived in when they were in the Senate, very near the White House. She can run over to see the Conrads any time. But, of course, Hamstead is her real home."

"Do—you go to see the President too?"

"Oh, yes!" Chris said again. He rose as he spoke, indicating to the reluctant Trixie that he considered the first part of their date at an end. "The President has always been very kind to me, though he doesn't altogether approve of everything I do. I room with his son at Harvard. I've known him all my life. So, naturally—— Would you care to go and have a little shooting now? I'm afraid later on the gallery may be crowded."

He drew out Trixie's wicker chair as punctiliously as he had pushed it in. Then he began to assemble the various knick-knacks which had strewn themselves over the table when she opened her handbag to delve for cigarettes and make-up, and which she had shown no disposition to recapture from the places where they were scattered. These knick-knacks included a bunch of small keys, a packet of half-demolished chewing-gum, a rabbit's foot set with blue beads, some theatre-ticket stubs, a rumpled handkerchief daubed with rouge, a scent bottle, and several dog-eared letters scrawled over with collegiate handwriting. He had just gathered these into a tidy pile, and was offering them to Trixie one by one, so that she might stow them away again, when a ship's officer, looking very sleek and spruce, approached them politely, clicked his heels together as he bowed to Trixie, and then spoke to Chris in rapid, deferential German.

"What is it? What does he want?" Trixie inquired petulantly, as the officer, having spoken his precise little piece, bowed himself away again. Instinctively she sensed an attempted interference with the monopoly of Chris, which she was now determined, at all costs, to achieve and maintain. It was a sure thing that if the officer's remarks had included her, he would have talked English. Her petunia-coloured mouth drooped fretfully at the corners, and again she linked her arm through Chris Marlowe's, less playfully and more clingingly than when they had started for the verandah.

"Nothing that will interfere with our shooting," Chris said re-assuringly. Trixie was struck afresh with the nice way he had of speaking and the shining look in his eyes when he smiled.

"The Captain of this ship used to know my father," Chris explained. "So he has sent me an invitation to come to tea with him at five, alone, in order that he can get to know me also. It is natural, under the circumstances, that he should wish to arrange things this way. But the mate was careful to say that tomorrow, or possibly the day after, the Captain will begin giving a series of small parties in his quarters, and, of course, you will be invited to one of those. Besides, you will soon be seeing him regularly at lunch and dinner, all the time."

"I don't care anything at all about seeing the Captain! He's probably red-nosed and pig-headed, with a wrinkle of fat at the back of his neck, like most Germans!"

"I'm sure he is nothing of the sort, any more than I am."

"But you aren't a German!"

"Oh, yes, I am," said Chris Marlowe calmly. Trixie saw that he was not smiling any longer, and that a different look had come into his face—a look that frightened her a little, and at the same time made her feel like crying, though she could not in the least understand why. "Perhaps I should have told you that in the first place," he went on. "But I thought you were rather bored and lonely, and

16

that it would be more fun for you to feel that you were going out with an American than with a German. That is why I introduced myself to you as Chris Marlowe."

"Isn't that your name?"

"It isn't my whole name. I was named for both my grandfathers; my father told my mother, before he died, that he was glad I was, because both were men of great traditions, and that when I was old enough I could choose which tradition I wanted to follow. My mother doesn't think I'm old enough yet to know my own mind. But I do know it. I am eighteen years old, and she was only eighteen when I was born. I am going to Germany just for the summer now, but I hope that some day I am going there to live. And my whole name is Hans Christian Marlowe von Hohenlohe."

CHAPTER II

AFTER twenty-four hours, during the course of which she had not "guessed wrong," Mrs. Rhodes's spirits had begun to rise.

Her first mistake had been in tipping the stewardess before she had been aboard ship for an hour. She had been assured on every side that all continentals had perpetually outstretched palms. To her chagrin, she had found the hand of the stewardess limp and unreceptive, and afterwards she had learned that ships formed the exception which proved the rule, that nobody tipped until the voyage was over. Her second had been in asking Mrs. Carruthers, as they left the luncheon table, whether the evening would be formal. Mrs. Carruthers had crushingly replied that life on shipboard was never formal. So the budding ambassadress had appeared at dinner in a brown printed silk of the type usually known as "serviceable," Trixie charging along beside her in baby-blue taffeta ruffles. Mrs. Rhodes's consternation was great when she found that Mrs. Carruthers was wearing silver tissue, which enhanced the severe elegance of her carriage and manner; and that Mrs. Fuller, ashen but exquisite, was in moulded white satin, her neck and arms bare except for the necklace and bracelets of superb aquamarines with which these were clasped.

"There, I *am* sorry not to appear more suitable," Mrs. Rhodes had said with genuine distress, as she sat down heavily, the brown frock bunching about her. "I certainly understood you to say this wasn't going to be a formal evening."

"A formal evening? Oh! You meant to ask me whether you should dress for dinner? I am sorry that I did not understand you. In New York, we don't use the expression as you did. Of course, I took it for granted you knew that on shipboard, as elsewhere, it is customary to appear at dinner dressed for dinner."

While Mrs. Carruthers was speaking, Mrs. Rhodes glanced about her towards the surrounding tables, in the hope of finding someone else who had made a mistake. But even Mrs. Eustis's sheer sombre draperies were parted in a deep V at her throat, and her long flowing sleeves fell away from her slender arms. Even the twins' homemade pink chiffon dresses had round necks.

Mrs. Rhodes was so obviously chagrined that even Mrs. Carruthers feared she might have gone a little too far in her attempt to show this uncultured person just how uncultured she was. But she herself had a grievance. She had sent some of her own flowers to the dining saloon—some fragile white lilacs and fragrant Ascension lilies—and, instead of placing them in a graceful vase on the Captain's table, the steward had thrust them into a pitcher on the sideboard, feeling that they were too funereal of aspect to adorn a festive board. In their place rose a flamboyant gilt basket crammed with crimson roses, which some crude youth had undoubtedly sent to Trixie Rhodes—indeed, the oversized card with which they had been dispatched was still fastened to them. "Trixie, please affix me," was scrawled across it in a straggling handwriting. "And don't you fall, for Dutch at all. Stan."

Mrs. Carruthers felt that persons who permitted such vulgarities should be made to feel their inferiority, and she had certainly succeeded in creating this feeling.

But there was nothing the matter with her dress tonight, Mrs. Rhodes felt sure of that—a nice green lace; and Trixie's red velvet had come from the most expensive shop in Topeka. The shade was just like the tint in her cheeks, and Mrs. Rhodes had read in a fashion magazine once that you should "match the colour of your clothes to your make-up." Trixie had certainly done that, nails, slippers and all; and Mrs. Rhodes was puffed with pride as she addressed the Bishop.

"Well, Bishop, we've missed you, and that's a fact. It's just a shame that you should've been seasick, such lovely weather, too."

She was dismayed to find that he seemed to take her cordial greeting amiss. "But my dear Mrs. Rhodes! I assure you that I have not been seasick, not for a single minute. I had a slight cold when I came aboard, and I thought it prudent to take precautions before this became worse. Besides, I have had a great deal of work to do—in preparation for the Anglo-Catholic Conference, you know. I have been toiling away in my cabin, deprived of the pleasant company that I could have enjoyed if my duty had not kept me there. But the work of the Lord, you know—a man may not serve two masters!"

The Bishop paused rather abruptly. He was conscious that Trixie Rhodes was looking at him, her large blue eyes half veiled by the long black lashes that drooped over them, her small scarlet mouth
18 ·

relaxed, a cigarette hanging from the side of it. But there was something contemptuous in her expression. He suddenly remembered that he had seen the Rhodes' name neatly placarded on the door of the suite beside his state-room, and was uncomfortably fearful that this insolent girl might have heard certain repulsive sounds, not usually associated with the slight colds or the service of the Lord, issuing from it. He had been vomiting violently all the day before; and, moreover, several times, in his anguish, he had spoken to his steward in a manner unbefitting his cloth. He decided that possibly it might be best to divert the attention of the table to someone else.

"I'm sorry to see that Mrs. Fuller is missing from our congenial little circle," he said brightly, turning to the banker. "Perhaps she really is sick?"

"Sick as a dog," her husband answered impatiently. "Lord! Sometimes I think if she just looked at a picture of a clipper-ship hanging on the wall she'd retch. I beg pardon! But it does get on my nerves. They're not in very good shape just now, anyway."

"It must be tedious for her, lying in her cabin all day," Mrs. Rhodes said kindly. "If you think she'd like company, don't hesitate to tell me. I could go in and see her any time."

"You don't need to bother," Mr. Fuller said tersely. "She hasn't spirit enough to be bored. When she feels like doing anything at all, she amuses herself with her jewellery. She's got a lot of it, and she likes to fool with it, taking it out of the box, you know, and spreading it over the sheets. It's sort of childish of her, but the jewellery's all well insured, so there's no danger in case of loss, and I'm glad she appreciates it. There aren't many men who've made the effort I have to give their wives handsome jewellery.—Did you happen to notice her pearls?" he inquired abruptly, addressing himself to Mrs. Carruthers.

"Yes, Mr. Fuller, I noticed them."

"Used to belong to a member of the Russian Imperial family," said Mr. Fuller with satisfaction. "She's got a tiara and a pair of earrings too—diamonds and rubies—that came from the same collection. How about that, Baron? Got anything to beat it in your family?"

The exciting facts regarding the identity of "Chris Marlowe" had spread like wild-fire about the ship. Overnight he had become the chief topic of conversation on deck, in the bar, and at every table in the dining-room. Hans Christian himself appeared to be entirely oblivious to the furore which he had aroused. Now, at Mr. Fuller's brusque question, he drained the glass of Rudesheimer that he was drinking, and set it down carefully before he answered.

"My mother has never cared much about jewellery," he said. "For years she's never worn any at all, except her engagement ring and a beautiful old Spanish cross. Probably my Grandmother von Hohenlohe, whom I'm going to visit, has more. I was with her a good deal when I was a little boy, and I seem to remember that she looked rather glittering when she went to a Court ball."

"Of course, the Archduchess Victoria Luise was known as one of the most regal women of her time, throughout Europe," remarked Mrs. Carruthers, in an explanatory tone of voice.

"Is your grandmother a Russian?" avidly inquired Mr. Fuller, who had missed some of the details concerning Hans Christian's family, turning to the boy again.

"No. She's an Austrian by birth, and her first husband was an Austrian too. But she's lived in Germany ever since she married my grandfather."

"Well now, I understood the Hapsburgs had about as much jewellery, before the war, as the Romanoffs, and that they are parting with it about as fast now."

"As far as I know, my grandmother's been able to hang on to hers," Hans Christian remarked, still quietly.

"But there's no telling when this inflation is going to stop, is there? I understand people are getting harder and harder pressed in Germany all the time. If anything should arise——"

"If I find it would be worth your while to come to Schönplatz, Mr. Fuller, I will let you know. But since your time is so short, I shouldn't advise you to change any of your present plans on the chance of it." Hans Christian's glass had been refilled by an assiduous steward, and, raising it, the boy took another slow sip of Rudesheimer. Then he turned to Mrs. Carruthers. "Are you planning a longer visit abroad than Mr. and Mrs. Fuller?" he inquired conversationally.

"I shall be in Europe for several months at least," said Mrs. Carruthers, with an expression which Mr. Fuller realized was aimed at him. "But I shall not rush madly about from one country to another. I am disembarking at Cherbourg, to visit some cousins who have a château in Normandy, which fortunately has not been overrun by tourists like the Loire Valley. Later I think I may motor with my friend, the Duchess of Duchesne, to the Dalmatian Coast. I shall probably sail for home from Trieste. The Italian boats are so much the best in every respect."

"Mrs Carruthers—it rejoices me to find that you with us cross again, that you do not us altogether desert for the Italians. *Aber, gnädige Frau,* permit that I have my so small joke! . . Mrs. Rhodes—to you my congratulations on your husband's appointment, and to us congratulations that you so honour a German ship by your presence . . . *Gnädiges Fräulein,* there is nothing that brings such fine luck to the table of a Captain as the presence of one charming young lady—unless, Father Hastings, it might be

20

the benediction of an eminent divine. Mr. Fuller, it makes me grief that your lady should not well be. I take the liberty to her some Henckel Trocken to send with my compliments. . . . *Also, Hänsel, mein lieber Junge, wie geht's?*"

A tall man, solidly but not heavily built, with clear colour, dark eyes, and black hair gone gray at the temples, kissed Mrs. Carruthers's hand, and appeared to sense Mrs. Rhodes's distress lest he might kiss hers also. Placing an arm affectionately around Hans Christian's shoulder, he bowed to her instead, and then to each of the other persons whom he addressed in turn. Afterwards he seated himself, with unhurried dignity, at the head of the table. In spite of the cordiality of his manner, there was a hint of reserve in it; he was not bluff. And though his being seemed to be permeated with salt air, it had been tempered by careful grooming. The blue gloss of his uniform was lustrous; the gold stripes and gold stars on his sleeves, the double row of gold buttons on his jacket, the medals on his chest were all glistening; his linen was so white that it seemed to sparkle. On one hand he wore a massive carved ring with a huge dark stone sunk deeply into its setting. The stone glittered as he picked up the "Card of Suggestions" attached to the menu.

"Crême Nelusco," he read. "I shall have to come to an understanding with the chef not to use these French names. They confuse me. What do you suppose a Crême Nelusco might be, *gnädiges Fräulein?*"

"It's a thick carroty soup." Trixie answered, emerging, as if by magic, from the silence which had enveloped her ever since the meal began. "It's really pretty and it's real good."

"Since you commend it so highly I shall some have to try. *Also,* Crême Nelusco, steward. If it is so excellent, like you say, we must some send to Mrs. Fuller. I hope you impress on her, Mr. Fuller, that for seasickness it is always necessary that one should eat."

"Well, I've tried," said Mr. Fuller briefly, with the air of implying that it was a hopeless task to endeavour to impress much of anything on his wife. "But I finally gave it up. She won't do anything but lie with her eyes shut and moan. She won't even fool with her rings. It gets on my nerves. So I've spent most of my time in the smoking-room. Last night I ran into a man I know there— Ferris of the Chicago Loan and Trust—and I knew he played a good hand of bridge. So I asked him how about it, and he said 'Fine!' if we could get up a foursome. We gave the place the once-over, and saw a man and his wife who were sitting sort of vacant-eyed, as if they hadn't much to do with themselves. They said they'd be pleased to have a game. We played until about three o'clock this morning and then ended up with a snifter. The Hunts —that's the name of this pair, Mr. and Mrs. Harris Hunt from

Macon, Georgia—know their cards and they put up a stiff fight, but they weren't any match for Ferris and myself in the end. We cleaned them out of nearly a hundred dollars. But the Hunts took it in good part."

"It pleases me that for you all has so well worked out," said the Captain cordially. Then he turned from Mr. Fuller to Trixie, who was snapping her enamelled lighter in a vain attempt to make it work. "Please to mine accept, *gnädiges Fräulein*," he said courteously. "The steward will see to it that yours shall be fixed. That is better, is it not so? . . . This is your first trip abroad, *ja*? I hope you enjoy yourself."

"Yes, it's my first trip," Trixie replied, with another dimpling smile. "I was sort of sorry to leave Rhodesville—there's going to be quite a lot going on there this winter. And the ship seemed dead as a doornail to me at first. Nothing much going on. I guess most of the young people were seasick. Besides, I can't see much sense in shuffle-board and deck-tennis, and those were all I could find doing at first, except that I passed Carlotta Carew and Terry O'Shaughnessy walking up and down the deck together. The way they were looking into each other's eyes was just divine! I did get a thrill out of that. But they went off somewheres and I didn't see them again, so it didn't last long. I've danced quite a lot evenings, though. I simply adore to dance. I'd rather do it than anything else in the world. And I like those little wooden horses you have races with. The deck steward said I can shake the dice tomorrow afternoon. I won three times this afternoon. Chris helped me make my bets. He's been simply sweet to me. I guess I'd have passed right out if it hadn't been for him."

She shifted her smile to the opposite side of the table. Hans Christian returned it pleasantly, lifting his glass.

"*Prosit!*" he said gravely. Then, looking from the girl to the Captain, he added, "The best thing I've done has been to present 'Card' Eustis to Trixie, Herr Kapitän. He knows more about amusing girls than I do."

"*So*, the Senator's son," said the Captain, glancing quickly in the direction of the Eustis' table. "You knew him before, then, did you, Hansel?"

"Yes, Herr Kapitän. He was a Senior at Harvard when I went there. But we both play football and belong to the same club."

"That is then most fortunate for the present pleasure of all. And those two young ladies in the corner—have you met them, *gnädiges Fräulein?*"

"They were in swimming this afternoon," Trixie answered rather reluctantly. "They seem to be just crazy about sports—sports and Shakespeare. They're college girls. They talk about all sorts of things I never heard of in my life. Mostly just to each other,

22

though. I guess nobody else wants to listen. Anyway, they don't seem to know many people. I guess no one ever showed them a really tall time."

"*Ach so!*" exclaimed the Captain again. "We shall have that to remedy. Could you not show one of those poor under-privileged ladies a tall time, Hansel?"

Hans Christian smiled.

"I've been trying already," he answered. "I was dancing with one of them last evening and making some progress with light conversation when Card cut in. So I went off to smoke a cigarette and collect my thoughts for further persiflage. When I went back to the social hall I cut in on Card. The young lady looked at me coldly and asked if I wasn't sort of fresh, starting out with a line like that. I burst into a cold perspiration! I had made a mistake! I was dancing with the other twin, whom I hadn't met at all!"

The Captain laughed outright. Mrs. Rhodes and Mr. Fuller echoed him heartily. Trixie, her face gone blank again, took a lipstick and a powder puff out of her small beaded handbag, and began to apply these vehemently to her already dazzling complexion. It was evident that she had not welcomed the intrusion of the twins upon the scene, either conversationally or otherwise. The Bishop looked grave. Mrs. Carruthers, her expression severe, addressed the company at large.

"I cannot sufficiently deplore this custom of cutting in," she said. "When I was young there was still such a thing as good society left in America. Father Hastings can doubtless remember this also."

"Yes, indeed, my dear lady, yes indeed! Those were the halcyon days, though it has now become customary to deride them At present our unfortunate nation seems to have fallen into an abyss of vulgarity as well as an abyss of crime."

"Goodness!" exclaimed Mrs. Rhodes nervously. "I hadn't the least idea it was as bad as all that! Perhaps it's different in the East. In Rhodesville there's as nice a crowd of young people as you'd ever wish to see. Nice, clean, upstanding young men. Nice, quiet, modest girls. All Trixie's friends . . ."

"Oh, Mumma, don't be such a fool!"

Trixie had pushed back her plate and now sat furiously smoking one cigarette after another, flicking the ashes to the floor with her carmine finger-nails as she did so. She spat the words out at her mother without even lowering her voice. There was a moment of electrified silence. Mrs. Carruthers and Father Hastings exchanged glances. Mrs. Rhodes reddened uncomfortably, her kind ingenuous face suddenly looking like a crushed and wilted peony. The Captain rose.

"I think we have all our dinner finished," he said evenly. "It is pleasant coffee to take in the smoking-room, is it not? And if to the rest of you it is agreeable I shall also these so bewildering twins ask if they will not give us the honour of their society. It seems to me a shame that they should be so much alone, as Fräulein Trixie says, and that Hansel should not the opportunity have of learning ·to tell them apart."

He certainly must have known them apart before the end of the evening, Trixie decided. He danced first with one and then with the other, not unconsciously, as he had done before, but purposely; and there was every indication that he was not only giving them a "tall time," but having one himself, primarily with the twins. He did ask Trixie for one waltz, but she could not waltz nearly as well as she could fox-trot, and she found herself tangled up in her attempt to follow his intricate lead. Under these circumstances the performance became one of watchful technique on his part and enraged effort on hers; it was impersonal and unstimulating. Trixie was actually relieved when the encore was over, and she was quickly claimed again by Richard Eustis.

"Chris really does act like a German when he dances," Card observed, swinging her easily into a one-step. The remark was meant to placate Trixie's pride, but as she made no immediate response to this overture, either conversationally or physically, he went rambling along the same line, hoping for better results. "Usually you don't notice it—when he's around with other fellows, I mean. But he's behaved badly to his mother. So I hear, anyway. And that's another typically Teutonic trait."

"What do you mean, behaved badly?"

"Oh, she didn't want him to strike off like this, all by himself. She wanted him to stay with her. Just the way my mother likes to have me hang around."

Trixie did not fail to notice the comparison between Chris as an erring son and Card as a dutiful one, but somehow the picture did not seem convincing.

"Germans are great on keeping women in their place, you know," Card went on persistently. "And they think the place is beside a kitchen stove or hanging over a cradle. I believe even the Kaiser said something to that effect. Chris didn't raise a rumpus when his mother went into politics. In fact he acted the part she wanted him to play damned well. But he hated it—Gosh, how he hated it! And I suppose eventually she found this out and then they began to get on each other's nerves."

"Maybe his feelings were hurt first. Maybe she struck off and left *him* alone when this political bee stung her. Maybe he was lonely, when he was just a kid. Maybe they sort of grew away from each other then, and he thought she wouldn't care if he came away

24

and left her. You don't actually know that he's on bad terms with her, do you?"

"No, I can't swear to it. But everybody thinks so. You see, the general impression was, that when Rudolf von Hohenlohe told his wife he didn't care what tradition their son followed, he was making it easy for her to bring him up in the *American* tradition. That's what she thought herself. She never dreamed of anything else. And then Chris suddenly sprung this Junker idea on her. He stirred up an awful lot of talk in Washington and Cambridge when he came away. Almost as much as he has on this boat."

"Well, we might talk about someone else for a change."

Card was quite willing. Indeed, what he really wanted was to talk about Trixie and himself. It was only because he did not dare rush his fences, as his fox-hunting Southern relatives called it, that he had diverged at all from this topic. For the rest of the evening he stuck to it assiduously. The results were less satisfactory than he had hoped, however. Trixie danced with him readily and repeatedly enough. But eventually an awful truth dawned on him. She was not listening to his line. She was mastering the mysteries of the waltz.

CHAPTER III

TRIXIE RHODES sat at her dressing-table scrutinizing her face with a magnifying glass, and taking appropriate steps to transform it. She was a great believer in preparedness. Although she had chosen a sheltered spot for her date with Card Eustis—the most sheltered, indeed, which she had discovered on the ship—she had agreed to meet him first in the brilliantly lighted bar, where a large majority of the passengers were habitually forgathered, and where Carlotta Carew and Terry O'Shaughnessy regularly got drunk in each other's stimulating company. Half the thrill of having a date with a fellow like Card Eustis lay in bearing him off to cover with the consciousness that you were followed by envious eyes, and she had reason to believe that even Carlotta, when sufficiently sober, coveted Card. Besides you never knew: of course everyone else had been in bed when she and Card had finally parted the night before— or rather, this same morning around three. But possibly tonight someone would still be up at that hour. It was even conceivable that Chris Marlowe might be mooning around on deck all alone, looking at stars or sea foam or something of the sort. He was quite capable of such eccentricities.

At the irritating thought, Trixie attacked her paint pots with a certain savageness. Her original estimate that there was a dearth of young people on the ship had quickly been proven fallacious.

After a day or two they seemed to spring up from every side, and many of the male contingent promptly "fell" for Trixie. The twins, Nancy and Nora, also annexed admirers without effort, and the resemblance which had led Chris astray on the first evening out resulted in countless other baffling episodes. The character of the "crowd" thus created, at no time standoffish, quickly grew uproarious. The movies in the social hall were subject to disrespectful interruptions in the form of snickering and catcalls. A peaceful *Bier Abend* in the smoking-room developed the characteristics of a riot, as paper hats were hurled through the air and sound of wooden whistles mounted to pandemonium. When the featured entertainment of the evening was over, the unruly youngsters devised other amusements for themselves; and some of these took a form which caused both Father Hastings and Mrs. Carruthers to complain to the Captain, in addition to airing their views on the subject to other censorious travellers who lent a willing ear to tales of depravity as they comfortably consumed their morning bouillon.

At first the Captain listened to the complaints of his star passengers courteously but non-committally, and commented casually upon them to Hans Christian, the next time the boy came to his quarters, in a manner which indicated that he took little stock in such criticism. Within three days, however, the ship's discipline was so openly flouted that he called several of the ringleaders together and spoke to them with a certain show of severity.

"Well it is that young company should on a ship find itself *lustig*," he remarked in an admonishing tone, "but to be *lustig* is it then needful that the boat deck should still be cluttered with couples after all lights are out and it is the moment that the proper work of cleaning should begin? *Nein, nein,* that does not do itself, *meine junge Freunde!* The night watchman, making his rounds, must on no such scenes stumble that he will blush when he his report to me makes. He must on nothing at all stumble, a leg perhaps to break. And the sailors must room and time to holystone have. This is no French *paquebot* lightly to be brushed off once or twice a year, and encouraging indiscretions. Such are not the standards of the German Merchant Service Marine, and our guests must by our standards abide." He came to an impressive pause, and added still more sombrely, "If again anyone on deck after hours is found, he shall straight to our lock-up be marched. It is a nice clean place, but bare. And all visitors are *verboten. So!* We will no more about the matter say."

The culprits disbanded, overlooking the slight twinkle in the Captain's eye as he dismissed them, and for the most part in a somewhat shamefaced manner. But it took far more than a threat or a lecture to embarrass Trixie.

26

"Phooey!" she said, linking her arm through Card's as they went down the companionway together. "Just feature getting off that line about the blushing watchman! I don't believe even Terry O'Shaughnessy and Carlotta Carew could get a rise out of him, and I've caught them in some pretty close clinches. If the watchman never sees anything worse after dark than the little light necking our crowd has been doing, I'll say he's missing a good deal. Look at the colour of his face, anyway—raw beefsteak wouldn't match it. How are you going to tell whether a man with a mug like that is blushing or having a fainting spell? And I wish he would break his leg."

Card made no immediate answer to her persiflage. They were walking aft, and his eyes were thoughtfully fixed on two hooded ventilators which towered over the swimming pool like giant caterpillars.

"How far would you say it was, at a guess, from the top railing around the pool to the inside of one of those hoods?" he inquired.

Trixie followed the direction of his glance without excitement. "Oh, I don't know," she said idly. "Four or five feet maybe. Why?"

"There's a piece of wire-netting stretched across the funnel inside the hood. I happened to see it this afternoon when I climbed up to take a high dive. We could lay a rug across that netting and sit on it. I could climb up first and pull you up after me. I guess the night watchman wouldn't look for us there, or break a leg stumbling over us."

"Card, I do think you are the cutest thing! We could try it out tonight, couldn't we?"

All this had happened early in the week, and since then they had been trying out the convenient ventilator with great success. The only trouble was, that if she sat secluded under its shelter, cuddled up to Card, Trixie kept thinking all the time how much more fun it would have been to sit there cuddled up to Chris.

She had tried pretending that she was, but it didn't do any good. Card had a grand line, one you could hang clothes on; he was simply swell. But there was no use talking, he didn't have the same class that Chris did. There was more of a thrill, just looking at Chris, than in necking with Card. She kept saying to herself that she was a sissy and a softy, that a date was a date, that one Senator's son was as much of a match as another's. And still it was Chris that she wanted. Still it was Chris that she was determined to get——

She must have filed her nails down too far. The sharply pointed white pencil had gone straight to the quick that time. Furiously she flung it across the toilet table, pulled her dress down once more over the hips, and rose to regard herself in the mirror.

She had begun to think that ruffles were a mistake, now that she had attentively looked over a couple of New York girls whose abode conversation had revealed as Park Avenue, and whose evening wraps, draped negligently over chair backs, had revealed Hattie Carnegie's labels. So she had chosen something different to wear this time—something very slinky and sophisticated in green satin, with accessories of costume jewellery which, as far as she could see, were every bit as good-looking as all that junk of Mrs. Fuller's that everyone was making such a fuss about. The green satin was a little too tight; it pulled in places. And it was pretty low. Not just behind, of course it had no back at all, and that didn't count. But perhaps in front . . . She had an idea that Chris . . .

However, it was too late now to change. She had sat for ever at the dinner table while Mr. Fuller talked about debts and reparations and how much money he had lost at bridge, and Mrs. Carruthers had kept saying that she knew Owen Young personally and was sure he would prove the salvation of Germany, and Father Hastings had murmured that they should not forget true salvation came from only One Source, and that they must pray that the Prince of Peace would soon rule all the world. Then the stupid steward, who looked so skilful when he was serving the Captain or Chris, had spilled macaroon ice-cream on her gold lamé and that had been the last straw. Of course, he had pretended to be terribly upset about it, and she *had* reached for a cigarette just as he started to serve her. But this did not alter the fact that the lamé was a mess and that she could not possibly wear it on her date with Card. The green satin was the next best thing, and she had an idea Card would like it. She had better not keep forgetting that after all he was the person to be pleased, at the moment, anyway.

Card was waiting for her in the bar. He was sitting at a little table with Chris and one of the twins when she went in. They had big mugs of beer in front of them and a huge platter of sandwiches between them, and apparently they were having a grand time, for they were laughing and talking like anything. There was a place saved at the table for Trixie, and for an instant she had a feeling that it would be sort of cosy to stay right there in the bar and not climb up into the ventilator at all. Then Chris made a remark that queered everything.

"The Captain seems to have cheered up since you and Card stopped giving him so much trouble, Trixie. He's having a party himself tonight—aft, in that open space on B deck. He's planning music and a midnight supper and all that. He said the air was so soft and the moonlight so pleasant, he thought the ladies would enjoy it."

"What ladies?" inquired Trixie, instantly alert.

"Oh, your mother and Card's and Mrs. Carruthers and Mrs.

Fuller. And a few others I believe. Of course, he's asked a corresponding number of men."

"He hasn't asked you and Nora, has he?" Trixie inquired suspiciously.

"I'm Nancy. Nora is over there in the corner," interposed the twin who was seated beside Chris, nodding—darned smugly, Trixie thought—in the direction of a table where a duplicate girl was playing bridge with three personable young men.

"He said if we had no other plans," Chris remarked, with apparent unconcern. "It was all arranged very quickly. Your mother tried to find you and tell you about it before she went into the social hall to see the movie. But she couldn't. So she told the Captain that she thought you and Card *did* have other plans."

"Well, we have. Haven't we, Card?" retorted Trixie, rising immediately. "Who cares about the Captain's stuffy old party, anyway?"

"If you don't care, I don't see why you get all hot and bothered about it," remarked Nancy calmly, helping herself to another sandwich.

Trixie shot a glance of venom in Nancy's direction. As usual, the twins' appearance was unarresting. This evening they were wearing embroidered muslin dresses, of the type which Trixie recognized as coming in "patterns," boxed and partially made up. Neither the initial nor the final stages of this development revealed much knowledge of the art of dressmaking, and the white design, against a pale blue background, had about as much character as cambric tea. The gold beads around Nancy's neck and the turquoise bracelet encircling her right wrist were equally schoolgirlish. But it was also undeniable that she never seemed to be at a loss for words, and that her hair, which she had not had the sense to cut off, was a gorgeous colour.

"I'm not hot and bothered. I'm in a hurry to get out of this stuffy room, that's all," snapped Trixie.

"Well, I hope you'll find it nice and cool under the hood in the ventilator," observed Nancy, beginning to blow bubbles from the froth on her beer.

Trixie stalked out of the bar without deigning to answer, Card close on her heels. She was very angry. It was one thing to show off her conquest. It was quite another to leave a victorious and mocking rival in the field. Previously she had had no idea that anyone had found out about her hide-away, and she was beyond measure upset that this knowledge should have come to the ears of Chris. Nothing that Card could say or do had the effect of appeasing her. Instead, she drew as far away from him as their limited quarters would permit, sitting stiff and sulky in her own corner.

"What's the grand idea? You didn't come up here to ponder, did you?"

"I don't know what I came up here for."

"Well, I do. What's eating you, anyway, Trixie? You came up here because you've got a crush on me."

"Don't flatter yourself."

"Well, I've got a crush on you, anyway. Gosh, but you looked swell when you came into the bar tonight! That's a grand dress you've got on."

As if to further indicate his appreciation of it, Card's hand slid upward an inch or two from her waistline and came to rest, caressingly, on Trixie's bare back. As she made no resistance to this overture, or, indeed, showed the slightest sign of response to it, he concluded that he might venture on bolder tactics. Abruptly, he drew her closer to him, and tried to bury his face in the hollow of her breasts.

The effect of this action was immediate. Hampered as she was by lack of space, Trixie managed to get hold of his head and tug vigorously at his hair. Simultaneously she began to voice her opinion of him in no uncertain terms, and this opinion was far from flattering.

"Let go of me, you filthy cad! Take your dirty hands off me this instant! If you don't sit up and behave yourself, I'll start to yell!"

"For Chris to come and rescue you? When he didn't ask you to step out with you himself?" mumbled Card, without raising his head. "I don't think anyone but him and Nancy knows where we are so far. Do you want to tell the whole ship?"

"I don't care who knows where I am as long as I get out. I'm going to jump."

"Into the swimming-pool? With a big splash? And come out looking like a drowned rat?"

Trixie wasted no further words. She was past caring where she came out or what she looked like, as long as she could make good her escape. Shame, such as she had never known before, was surging through her. Card's strong fingers digging into her bare back, his hot face pressed against her bare breast, had outraged all the latent modesty of which she had hitherto been unaware, and kindled a flame of feeling hitherto unaroused. She began to writhe in his embrace, certain that eventually she could get clear of the netting; even if she could not wrench herself free, she would drag him with her when she jumped, and once they were in the air or the water he would instinctively release her. But she had hardly begun to put this plan into precipitate action, when she was seized with another sensation of horror.

The ventilator was moving. Something had happened to shake its stability, and it was turning, slowly but relentlessly. As it revolved, the swimming-pool, which had been so reassuringly close below it, disappeared entirely. For a terrific moment, its panic-stricken occupants found themselves swinging out over the ocean. Another revolution brought the ventilator to rest again. But not in the position from which it had originally started. On the contrary, its hooded form now faced the stern of the ship, jutting out beyond the short upper deck where the swimming-pool was located.

"My God!" ejaculated Card Eustis fervently. He was still gripping Trixie tightly by the waist. But he had raised his head, unconsciously, when the uncanny movement of the ventilator had indicated that something abnormal was happening; and now, as he gazed down towards the bowels of the ship, he gave a short nervous laugh.

"We'd better kiss and make up, Trixie," he said, his voice shaking in spite of its defiance. "If we try to jump at this stage—or if you try to jump and drag me with you—we'll go from the deep sea to the devil, instead of the other way around, as it usually is. And I don't mean maybe, either. Just take a good long look and see what's underneath us."

Still seething, and far more shaken than he was, Trixie followed his glance with forced fascination. At first she could see almost nothing. The light was lovely, as Chris had said. But it was the light which came from a young moon, already rocking away towards the horizon; it was not brilliant. It was moments before she was able to discern, on the distant lower deck over which they were suspended, a group of persons clustered around a table which had been convivially spread in the open and hear the strains of soft music.

"I don't know what you mean, but if you think I'm going to make up, not to mention kissing, you've got another guess coming. Well, what *is* it, Card? I can't tell from here. It might be almost anything. O my God—*the Captain's party!*"

There was no blinking the actualities of the situation. She would either have to stay where she was, under conditions which now seemed to her abhorrent, or take a leap in the dark, in a very real sense of the word. Either alternative was intolerable. But while Trixie was trying to figure some way to fight her way clear, the ventilator began to revolve again.

For one wild moment, the thought of drowning crossed her distracted mind without aversion. If she disappeared into the engulfing sea, everyone would be sorry, including Chris. Her mother would cry quarts; the Captain would read the burial service in a solemn voice; perhaps white flowers would be scattered on the waves. The picture was hardly complete, however, when she saw that it was no longer over the ocean that she was swinging; she was safely back above the swimming-pool again. But beside it two sailors with flash-lights in their hands were standing, and between them a solidly built officer whom she recognized with a sinking heart as the Chief Engineer.

"*Ach, du lieber Gott!*" he ejaculated, reaching brusquely up into the recesses of the ventilator. His stocky arms closed quickly around Trixie, the braided bands on his neat blue sleeves scratching her bare back. Having pulled her out, he set her on her feet, and stood for an instant staring at her, indignant exclamations rising in a growl to his lips as he did so. Before he could make another lunge into the depths, Card had swung himself down to the edge of the swimming-pool, dragging the shawl after him. But not in time to effect an escape. The brawny arm shot out a second time, gripping Card by the shoulder.

"*Was macht das denn?*" demanded the Chief Engineer, his voice shaking with rage. "For two nights now, the air in the engine-room, she does not move at all. And this night she is hot, so hot the men cannot breathe. So my assistant, he come to trouble me while I take a little ease at the *Gesellschaft* which the Commander he assemble. And I say, 'Turn you then the ventilator around. It is possible that he do not the wind catch.' Then the ventilator they turn him around, and still in the boiler-room it is hotter than hell. And the men howl, and my second, he come to me again, when I am on deck so pleasantly assembled with distinguished ladies, and he tell me, if the wind he does not blow now all shall suffocate, so shall then I not myself come, and find out why the wind she does not blow. And I come and find my netting covered with a thick rug, and upon it two numskulls sitting, so that honest workers cannot get their breath. *Ach, du lieber Gott!*"

"Oh, Mr. Loeffler, we're terribly sorry! We never thought about the men in the boiler-room and that they needed air. Honestly we didn't. Don't tell the Captain! Don't make us go down there!"

"*Not to tell the Captain! Not to make you go down there! Ach, du lieber Gott!*"

"Miss Rhodes is right, Sir. It was very careless of us, but we didn't mean to do any harm, and if you can see your way clear——"

The Chief Engineer was not even listening. Relentlessly he dragged his two victims along, still muttering furiously under his breath, still followed by the sailors with flash-lights, who bore up like a bodyguard in the rear. He did not so much as pause until he had reached the midst of the startled *Gesellschaft*. Then still clutching both Trixie and Card so tightly as to preclude any possibility of evasion on their part, he poured out the tale of his grievances to the assembled company.

It was terrible, too terrible for any mortal words. The Captain gave Trixie one withering glance, which left her feeling as if her last shred of clothing had been stripped off her. Then he ignored her completely, and began to talk to Card, in a tone of controlled courtesy which revealed far more formidable anger than the fulminations of the Chief Engineer.

"If you did not others consider at all, what then do you suppose would have happened to you and Fräulein Rhodes if that so light netting had happened to break?"

"Well, Sir, I suppose it would have been quite a long fall to the engine-room. But I didn't think of that at the time I planned to sit on the netting."

What a nit-wit Card was, what an absolute idiot, not to know you couldn't be fresh and get away with it, no matter whose son you were, no matter to whom you were talking, at a time like this, Trixie thought desperately. There was Mrs. Carruthers looking at her as if she was the scum of the earth, and Mrs. Eustis, too, for that matter, though it was Mrs. Eustis's son who had got her into this mess, and if he were such a paragon as his mother seemed to think, he would have got her out of it too. Her own mother was sobbing into her handkerchief, and between gulps wiping her nose, which was getting redder and shinier every moment. And that Fuller woman sat swinging a pendant as big as a hen's egg, and looking at her overbearing husband to give her the signal whether to laugh or frown. Women were cats, all of them, unless they were fools, and there was no way of getting even with them, ever, except by walking off with the men they wanted, and these women were all so old that probably——

"Would you care to dance for a little? If the Herr Kapitän would excuse us——"

It simply couldn't be true, and still it was. Chris was standing beside her, speaking to her in his nice quiet way, as if nothing at all had happened, as if nothing were likely to happen. She gazed up at him with agonized eyes, unable, for the moment, to speak.

"Nancy has a headache. She went to bed early," Chris continued conversationally. "That leaves me rather at loose ends for the rest of the evening. Unless, of course, you'll come to my rescue."

The *Gesellschaft* seemed to have melted away. Trixie did not know how or when, but then that did not matter. All that mattered was that she was alone in the stern with Chris, that they were leaning over the rail looking at the foam, in the way that had seemed so silly a day or two before, when she had seen other couples doing it, and that now seemed so natural and lovely. And she was saying whatever came into her head and Chris understood everything that she tried to say.

"I'll never get over this as long as I live. I'd like to kill Card Eustis."

33

"Oh, yes, you will. Oh, no, you wouldn't. What is there to get over, anyway? I think it's all a huge joke, and so does the Captain really. He'll be telling his guests about it—without mentioning any names of course—for years to come, amidst chortles of glee, in which he will lead. To my mind, you're a benefactor, considering all the dull moments there are at a Captain's table, and all the long pauses that need filling in. And Card is an awfully good sort, when you get right down to it. You'll find that out some day too. His technique has flaws in it, that's all."

"Flaws! It's got gaps in it as big as a crater! And did you see the awful look that snooty Mrs. Carruthers gave me? She'll waylay me the first chance she gets, and tell me exactly what she thinks of me."

"What do you care if she does? Or what she thinks? Her thoughts belong to about the same period as her hair-dressing."

"Oh, Chris, you're just trying to cheer me up! You don't mean a word you say!"

"Of course I do. And I meant what I said when I asked you to dance. Come along."

"I can't go into the social hall looking like this. I'm a mess."

"Well, I can wait for you here, if you want to powder up. It wouldn't take long, would it?"

"I don't want just to put on fresh make-up. I feel dirty. I want to take a bath and change everything I have on."

"Well, that wouldn't take long either, would it? I shouldn't suppose so, to look at you."

He was laughing at her, but he was laughing so lightly and whimsically that it did not hurt at all. It almost made her want to laugh too, though a few moments earlier she had decided that she would never be able to laugh again as long as she lived.

"No, it wouldn't take long. Will you really wait for me?"

"Cross my heart and hope to die." Apparently intent upon the foam again, he lighted a cigarette and leaned out over the ocean, his attitude seeming to imply that his patience was as boundless as the sea.

"All right. I'll be as quick as I can."

She sped down the corridor towards her cabin, mentally reviewing her resources as she ran. Her wardrobe had seemed voluminous in Topeka. But now there was nothing just right, nothing quite good enough for this date with Chris. She was still undecided, still dissatisfied, as she stripped off the green satin, and dropped it loathingly into the scrap basket. But when she emerged, tingling, from the shower, she had made up her mind.

She had a white crape dress that she had not admired very much at first. In fact, the only reason she had bought it was because it was so expensive, and because the saleslady who had waited on her had so enthusiastically told her that it was an original model, straight from Paris. It had full flowing skirt, and flat bands over the shoulders. The bands crossed in the front and the back of the bodice, but there was no trimming on the dress at all. It was just white and simple. Now, as Trixie slipped into it for the first time, she saw that it was lovely-looking, that she was lovely-looking in it. She thought, shyly, that perhaps Chris would think so too, that he might even tell her so. She was so eager to have him, that she decided not to stop to put on any make-up. She wanted to get back to him the very first moment she could. But for the second time that evening she found herself gripped by a force she did not understand, a force that was stronger than she was. She could not start right away. There was something else she had to do first.

She tried her cabin door to make sure that it was locked. Then she knelt down beside her narrow bed and hid her face in the counterpane.

"Please, God," she whispered, "let me have him. Please, *please*, PLEASE!"

CHAPTER IV

HANS CHRISTIAN stood on the bridge, watching the shifting scene with fascinated eyes, as the ship made its way slowly up the River Elbe. The Captain's invitation had not included the rest of the "crowd," so he was quite alone, except for the officers on duty. He was glad that this was so. Any other presence would have seemed to him like an intrusion at the time.

He had been on the bridge before, for the Captain had been conspicuously cordial to him throughout the voyage. But he was not mechanically minded. The machinations of the electrical steering device, the engine revolution counter, the fire detector, direction finder and emergency alarm switch, though these had been thoroughly and painstakingly explained to him, still remained so mysterious as to be slightly irritating. The fathometer, the chronometers and the sextant were slightly less baffling; but it was only in the charts, over which he had pored for hours, that he had taken genuine pleasure, untinged by puzzlement. Even in mid-ocean these had proved fascinating to him; now that the ship was approaching its destination, and he saw landmarks and water depths indicated on a large scale, he was beyond measure intrigued.

The final days aboard ship had seemed superb. He had been wakened very early the morning before by the cessation of the engines' movement; and, springing up to look out of his porthole, he had seen the lush emerald-coloured shores of Ireland shimmering in the opalescent light which overspreads the earth immediately before dawn. Dressing hurriedly, he had gone on deck to find a few passengers disembarking at Cobh, and a still smaller number taking passage. But there was little bustle and confusion, and without difficulty he had discovered a quiet corner where he could watch the quickening of the dormant harbour and the transfiguration of the heavens. Apparently it had not occurred to any of his fellow-travellers that these might be worth seeing, and none of the officers or crew had penetrated to the place where he stood. For two hours he was entirely undisturbed.

He went down to breakfast ravenously hungry, but returned to his hide-out for the passage of the English Channel. The weather was superb, and the white cliffs of Dover sparkled like glittering palisades of snow. The next day at noon the ship sped past Heligoland, near enough for Hans Christian to see the rust-red of its gaunt, grim coast line, and the bare rock called "The Monk," standing like a sentinel before the island. Dusk was descending when the Kiel Canal was reached; and by the time Blankenese came into view, little lights were twinkling along the shores, and on the dredges and tug-boats and freighters crowding the Elbe River. Music kept rising unexpectedly from these; the tinkle of a guitar, the blare of brass, the lusty melody that pours spontaneously from German throats. Hans Christian, watching and listening, began to sing softly himself.

It was at Blankenese that the Captain sent for him, clearing his throat slightly as he put his hand on the boy's shoulder.

"*Also, mein lieber Junge,* the voyage is at an end. But I hope, should a happy chance bring you ever to Hamburg when my ship is in port, that you will to see me come. We could have an evening's outing together, perhaps, and to the Zillertal go."

"I'd like to very much, sir. . . . What is the Zillertal?"

The Captain raised his hands in mock horror. "A German who does not know what is the Hamburg Zillertal!" he exclaimed. "Why, every man, from seaman to sovereign, goes sooner or later, and often both early and late, to the Zillertal to seek amusement. It is the most famous beer garden in the Sank Pauli district, where at midnight all the guests on small tables mount, to sway and sing in unison with the band. The music it is excellent, and the musicians wear Bavarian costumes and sit upon a small stage while they play their merry tunes and carol in so strange dialects. *Ja!* I am sure you will the Zillertal greatly enjoy, and greatly shall I enjoy to take you there. A tour of the Hamburg harbour in some small speed-boat we must also make, that there you may see the ships of every nation gathered in our great port—Russian and Roumanian, Spanish and Swedish, and dozens of others. And among them many-masted sailing vessels, not as numerous as heretofore, but still enough to show a doubting world that once they ruled the sea, and, if need, could do so again."

36

"It's very good of you, sir. . . . And you must come to see us too, when you can, in Berlin and at Schönplatz."

The Captain regarded Hans Christian thoughtfully, and, after a moment of obvious hesitation, spoke as if he were weighing his words. "That also would me much pleasure give," he said. "But *mein lieber Junge,* may I one word of warning to you say? This Germany to which you are making your homecoming—you think of it, you speak of it, as if it were a magic land. It is, on the contrary, a crushed and conquered country, smarting under defeat, writhing under insult, seeking, though so far vainly, the means and the man to strike back at its foes and effect its revenge. There are bright spots in Germany still, we have our cheerful beer gardens and our mighty harbours yet intact, and much besides and beyond these. I trust it may be only such *Gemütlichkeit* and power that you may see."

"But, Herr Kapitän——"

"I think I have already too much said. But I loved your father, though I was not blind to his faults, of which he had many and of which you seem unaware. You idolize his memory, Hansel, that I know, and it is well that a son should so think of one who has died a hero's death for his country. But your mother, she is a fine woman too, brave and loyal. Do not forget her or neglect her altogether, now that you have come to your *Heimat.*"

"I shan't, Herr Kapitän. But she doesn't need me, and——"

"I love your father's son too," remarked the Captain with a smile, putting his hand around Hansel's shoulder again. "I can that he is an idealist observe, and of such we have need in Germany even more than of avengers. *Nun, mein Junge!* I have no time further to talk to you. See, we shall to Altona soon come, the haven—and the heaven—of retired sea captains. We will mark them this evening, sitting on their trim little porches, watching the ships that come and go, and sighing perhaps, as they puff away at their pipes, because such ships no longer under their orders sail. Some day you will come to visit me when I live in such a neat little house behind such a trim little porch. And we will talk of this voyage we have together made, while I was still in command of a fine ship—and of many other things. But that is still a long way off, Hansel—still a long way off."

The Captain moved away, and an instant later Hans Christian heard him giving an order in a voice unusually peremptory for him; evidently he was seeking, in command, the vent for some emotion which he had suppressed. For a few moments the boy followed his forceful figure with troubled eyes; the Captain had slightly shaken his serenity. But this uneasiness was ephemeral. As the spell of the evening's beauty closed in upon him again, he took up his interrupted song where he had left off with it.

He was glad to have this time to himself, before he met his grandparents. Until he had managed to conceal himself at Cobh, the inroads upon the tranquillity which he enjoyed had been increasingly numerous. The "crowd" insisted in regarding him as its ringleader, in spite of his disinclination for such a rôle. He had won the first prize at the costume dance, at which he had appeared in a dress parade uniform worn by Kurtz von Hohenlohe, one of his ancestors, at the Court of Frederick the Great; and at the *Weisser Rössel* dinner the small silver horse—symbol of the ancient hostelry for which the festival was named—had been found embedded in his ice-cream. To be sure, he had not kept it long; Trixie, whose own sherbet cup had contained only the specialized sweet of the evening, had been so obviously disappointed that he had tossed the little token across the table to her; it was already firmly attached to her charm bracelet, which now tinkled more provocatively than ever. But it had been his in the first place, and neither his primary possession o it, nor his later transfer of it, had been unremarked.

The atmosphere of the Captain's table, inharmonious from the outset, had been supercharged with animosity ever since Trixie's "experiment with ventilation," as Hans Christian insisted on calling her escapade. Neither Father Hastings nor Mrs. Carruthers would speak to her; indeed, they went so far as to avert their eyes from the place where she sat, as if fearful of contamination if they so much as looked at it. Mr. Fuller, who had regarded the episode as a huge joke and hailed its dénouement with guffaws of laughter, had for a time bridged over the gap caused by their icy silence through becoming more boisterous than before. As long as this buffoonery was good-natured, it had a more or less beneficent effect; but when he suddenly appeared on the scene in a towering rage, an electrical storm would have been mild in comparison with the explosion.

He had been gypped, he had been fleeced, he had been done in. Mr. and Mrs. Harris Hunt, the nice quiet couple from Macon, Georgia, whom he and his friend Ferris, of the Chicago Loan and Trust, had persuaded to make up a pleasant little foursome of bridge with them, had skinned him out of two thousand dollars at a single sitting! They were professional gamblers, there was not the slightest doubt of it, plying their nefarious trade under a mask of meekness! He would have the law on them yet, he would see them penalized and jailed. What was more, he would take steps to see that he was reimbursed himself and that none of his influential friends travelled by a ship which permitted such nefarious practices. As soon as it arrived in Hamburg, he proposed to call both on the President of the Line and the American Consul-General. Between them, they would cause justice to be done.

Mrs. Rhodes, who had not fully recovered from the discovery of

38

Trixie's indiscretions, trembled and twisted her handkerchief into fresh knots, as she listened to Mr. Fuller's fulminations, which the Captain heard courteously but unresponsively. It was not until the banker's vehement voice rose to a bellow and his words became actually insulting in character that the Commander made any rejoinder, and this was brief and pointed.

"It is the first time since I go to sea that a case of this kind has to my attention been brought," he remarked cogently. "It is well known that on shipboard gamblers there are, as on land. But inexperienced players they seldom attack, since too obvious would their advantage be; and experienced players themselves are well on their guard and can for themselves fend, without calling upon maritime law and the American Government to protect them. Is it possible, Herr Fuller, that this is the exception which the rule proves, that you are yourself a novice, both at this so skilful game of chance and mischance, and in the ways of the travelwise?"

Mr. Fuller sprang from his seat and stalked out of the dining-room, swearing as he went. But in ten minutes he was back again, blind with rage.

"I tell you there's monkey business going on!" he shouted. "My wife planned to have her dinner on deck, and then, seeing that she was feeling better than usual, she went down to dress. When she opened her jewel box to get out her jade necklace it was gone. Clean gone! It's been stolen straight out of the stateroom, I'd have you know!"

This time the Captain rose. "This is very serious," he said gravely. "I will myself with you come, the catastrophe to investigate. Steps shall at once be taken this so costly necklace to trace. Though valuables, of course, should with the Purser be placed. That also you must know, Mr. Fuller."

"But damn it, my wife always keeps her jewellery with her! I've told you, she plays with it, just as a kid plays with dolls. Why shouldn't she? It's all insured——"

"For that, at least, we must thankful be. What would you say the value of this necklace might come to, Mr. Fuller?"

The banker's answer had been inaudible at the Captain's table; he and the Commander were already on their way out of the dining-room when he made it. Nevertheless, Hans Christian, turning to Trixie as if nothing had happened, and asking her, how about a little ping-pong, had seemed to hear a small insidious voice whispering in his ear. "The necklace is very well insured. It is worth a great deal. At least two thousand dollars. At least. At least."

He seemed to be hearing the same small sound now, as the ship continued to nose its way up the river. The necklace had not been found, in spite of the thorough search that had been made for it, and the ample reward that had been offered for it; and the Fullers had appeared no more at the Captain's table. But Mr. Fuller had sought Hans Christian out, as the boy stood watching the coast of Heligoland, and had spoken to him brusquely and pointedly.

"Mrs. Fuller's all upset over this terrible affair," he remarked. "I've got to do something to make up to her for it. So I've been think-ing—— You know we spoke once at the table about your grand-mother's jewellery, and you said you thought it was all intact. Well, if you should find it was, and that circumstances had changed any, so that now——"

"Mr. Fuller, I told you before——"

"Yes, I know what you told me. There's no need to get mad about it either. But circumstances change sometimes. You might do me a good turn—and I might do you one—if you'd let me know if they should."

The banker departed as abruptly as he had come. It was fortu-nate that he did, Hans Christian thought. The boy had never before wanted so much to hit a man in the face. He hoped he never would again——

He wondered if his grandmother would be wearing any of her jewellery when she came to meet him, and Mr. Fuller's covetous eye would light upon it. He thought again of the way she used to look, when he visited her, as a little boy, in Berlin, and she came in to bid him good-night before going out in the evening. He had failed to describe her adequately, in saying that she looked "rather glittering" in Court apparel. She had been gorgeous, simply gor-geous, from the top of her small regal head to the soles of her tiny, arched feet. But her coronet of gems had been no more beautiful than the wreathed braids of her hair, her sparkling necklace less lovely than her slim white throat, her radiant rings mere accessories to her rosy tipped fingers. It was her husband's boast that he could encircle her waist with his two hands, and Hansel had tried to do the same, sometimes, when she stood in all her panoply of splen-dour before him; he could still remember the stiffness of the bro-cade that was laced so close to her supple figure. She had laughed, in those days, and said that she must be losing her shape, when his small hands would not stretch as far as his grandfather's. And then she had caught him up against her breast, and kissed him, and he had smelled the sweet scent that clung to her garments and felt the softness of her delicate skin. . .

The mental vision which he had conjured up was so vivid that he scarcely noticed that the ship was actually nearing the wharf at last. The deck was crowded, but no arresting figures detached them-selves from the general throng to attract his attention. When Hans Christian finally began to look about he could not see any strik-

40

ingly beautiful woman or any tall, soldierly man of noticeable distinction, gazing searchingly towards the deck. One elderly lady, in dark, nondescript clothing, had managed to advance a little beyond the other patient waiters, who consented, with typical German obedience, to be kept within certain well-defined limits. There was a certain grace about her movements, and she was speaking eloquently with one of the guards, arguing perhaps, or pleading; at all events, he seemed disposed to permit her to press forward. She was quick to realize that he was moved, and to take advantage of his leniency. When the gangplank was lowered, she was the first person to set foot on it, and she came swiftly up it, her progress now quite unimpeded. As she stepped from it to the deck, she came unerringly to the place where Hans Christian was standing, and put both her hands on his shoulders.

"Hansel—mein Schatz—kennst du mich denn nicht?"

It was terrible, but it was true. He had not for one moment recognized, in this shabby, persistent old lady, the glorious creature his grandmother once had been. She was slender and erect still, to be sure; her dark eyes had retained some of their sparkle; her skin, though colourless and lightly wrinkled, was still soft and delicate. But her mouth had lost its merriment, her throat its lovely curves; the hair which escaped from under the battered bonnet was wholly white, the hands, encased in the worn gloves, quivering. The elegance, the glamour, the strength, which her very presence had once emanated, were gone completely; only her dignity and graciousness had remained imperishable.

"Why, grandmother!" he stammered. "Of course I know you. But I was looking for you in the opposite direction. And I didn't expect to see you alone. Where's grandfather?" he asked, kissing her belatedly.

"He is not very well just now, Hansel. Nothing serious. But it seemed better for him not to attempt the trip from Schönplatz to Hamburg. The railway service in East Prussia is very inadequate. We must first take a small local train to Allenstein, and then change for Berlin, crossing the Corridor, which is tedious and trying. And in Berlin we must change again."

"Couldn't you have come more easily in your car?"

"Well, . . . you had written me, darling, that you were bringing your own little runabout with you, and I thought we could return to Schönplatz together in that. It would be in the nature of a real lark, would it not, Hansel?"

"Yes . . . I suppose that since grandfather couldn't come with you we won't be stopping off in Berlin, will we? I'd been looking forward, rather, to going there—it was always such fun visiting you when I was a kid. But, of course, as things are, I'd rather go straight to the country."

"Yes, dear, it will be best. In any case, I mean. You see we do not have our house on the Tiergartenstrasse any more."

"You don't have it! Who does have it?"

"It has been bought by a very rich industrialist. It was an expense no longer justified, for your grandfather and myself, all alone as we have been so long now, to keep it. If we could have been sure that you would one day return to us, Hansel . . . though, no, not even then, as things have been these last years."

"But, grandmother, I don't understand. Do you mean that you and grandfather have been in trouble, real trouble, and haven't let mother and me know?"

The Archduchess slipped her arm lightly through his, and drew him forward.

"My dear boy, I fear we are blocking the passage of travellers who wish to disembark," she said gently. "And we should be getting off ourselves too, *nicht wahr?* We will talk over all these things later on, as we ride across country. Or even tonight. I knew you would be landing too late for us to start our journey this evening; so I have taken rooms for us at a small, clean hotel. Of course, it is not like the excellent *Vier Jahreszeiten* facing the beautiful Alster. But we shall be quite comfortable there. And tomorrow morning, if you like, we can have a *Rund Reise*, which costs only a few pfennigs, so that you may see the lake and its swans, so famous all over Germany And even linger for lunch at the 'Bürgerhaus' if you would like to stay so long, and are feeling enough in funds to give an old lady a great treat."

She smiled as she spoke, and as she did so Hans Christian caught a glimmer of the bygone charm which had once so illuminated her face They had already reached the foot of the gangplank, and the tall officer who had permitted the Archduchess to pass through the lines now saluted respectfully as she came by. She stopped and spoke to him.

"Let me thank you again for your kindness," she said. "This is the young man of whom I told you—my grandson, whom I had not seen in ten years. I am sure that now you will understand my eagerness."

"It was an honour to serve your Serene Highness . . . *Herr Baron, wenn ich bitten darf . . .*"

The lines had been lifted again, they were advancing quickly towards the customs. These would be only a formality, the Archduchess explained. If Hansel did not care to claim his car until morning, they could be on their way almost at once. On the other hand, if he wished to get it now, she was quite willing to wait She had made no engagement for the evening, because she had felt sure he would share her wish that they might spend it quietly and alone.

"Then if you haven't any plans, I do think I'd better get it off now, so that we can start tomorrow as soon as we care to. Though I'd enjoy the *Rund Reise* and lunch at the 'Bürgerhaus,' too, of course," he added quickly, seeing the slight shadow that crossed the face of the Archduchess, and loath to have her feel that any project of hers might seem unimportant to him.

"I will wait for you here, then. Indeed, by the time you return, I think I can promise that your baggage will be cleared, and we can drive off immediately in your own runabout, instead of taking a creaky old taxi."

Her pleasure in his presence was contagious. She already had almost succeeded in making him forget her shabby clothes and saddened face, through the magnetism of her manner. It *would* be a lark, driving her about and giving her a good time again, though the knowledge that good times were to have no centre in the stately old house facing the Tiergarten was still a bitter blow. Hans Christian tried to escape from under its impact, as he busied himself with the car. There was a certain amount of red tape about having it cleared, rather more than he had expected, from the way his grandmother had spoken; and apparently it hastened matters in the end if the port officers were allowed to take their own time, to read documents meticulously, and demand signatures authoritatively, and put stamps here and seals there. But the process was smooth, even though it was not speedy, and Hans Christian was treated with formal courtesy throughout. When at last he seated himself at the wheel, and swung around a designated circuit, he had not been moved to irritation or impatience.

As she had predicted, his grandmother was already awaiting him, and by her side was a ruddy and beaming porter, who had possessed himself of Hans Christian's bags, and who now began to stow these comfortably into the rumble seat. The trunks, it appeared, had already been dispatched to their destination. There was no cause for further delay.

"We're off then, are we?" Hans Christian inquired gaily, slipping several coins into the hand of the gratified porter, and helping the Archduchess into the car. "Which way do we go, grandmother?"

"Straight ahead first. I shall tell you when to turn."

He shut the door carefully, walked around to the other side of the car, and got in himself. He had already released the brake and reached for the gear shift, when he heard someone calling him.

"Chris! *Chris!* You aren't going away, are you?"

"Who is that, my dear?" inquired his grandmother, her gentle voice betraying slight astonishment.

"I think it must be Trixie Rhodes, one of the girls I met on the boat. I'm afraid that, in the excitement of meeting you, I forgot to say good-bye to her."

Hans Christian's voice had suddenly gone flat. There was no enthusiasm left in it.

"That was rather thoughtless, was it not? Of course you must go back at once," the Archduchess urged, still gently.

"I think she's coming here."

It was perfectly true. Trixie, still panting from the wild rush she had made, was already abreast of the car. Before Hans Christian could get out of it again, she had wrenched open the door and catapulted herself down on the seat beside him.

"Oh, Chris, how *could* you?" she exclaimed.

"I'm terribly sorry. But I expected to see you again on deck. And then I had a pleasant surprise which drove everything else out of my alleged mind. Trixie, this is my grandmother, the Archduchess Victoria Luise."

"I'm very pleased to meet you," Trixie informed the Archduchess.

PART II

A GREAT HOUSE
1924

CHAPTER V

THE first sight of the East Prussian countryside was destined to make an indelible impression on the receptive mind of Hans Christian. The straight road, lined with spaced trees, which clove its way alternately through stretches of dark forest and wide expanses of undulating field, so free and open that only the sky and the horizon seemed to limit them. The great herds of Holsteins, huge and impassive, reclining in lush pastures or moving rhythmically towards the corners of white fences where they met their milkers, and stood calmly awaiting the coming of sturdy peasant women who approached with small stools in one hand and large pails in the other. The horses, far less heavy of build than the cattle, attached in twos and fours to a single team, and dominating the highway as well as the hillsides, for neither trucks nor tractors had pre-empted their place. The flocks of black-faced sheep in the meadows, with here and there two or three storks, comic and pompous, amongst them. The ducks diving beneath the placid waters of small pools without rippling their surface, and rising again to glide across the water as if it had been made of green glass. The snow-white geese, with golden bills and feet, waddling across the cobblestones, negligent of their fate. The tiny cottages and big barns, alike bright with window-boxes and wreathed with flower gardens. The spires of village churches ascending above churchyards where all the graves were blanketed with bloom. . . .

"Do you remember that scene in Maeterlinck's 'Bluebird,'" Hansel asked his grandmother, "where the two children are alone in the cemetery at midnight and the poor little girl is so frightened? Then suddenly there comes a sound of music, and light after darkness, and every mound is transformed with blossoms, and the little boy cries out to his sister, 'There are no dead!'"

"Yes, I remember it. . . . Did the churchyard we just passed make you think of this scene? I am glad, very glad if it did, my dear boy. But alas! There are many dead in Germany. There is an old saying in my family that to every human being comes the sorrow of losing three, each one of whom means the most to him at the moment of loss. But many times three would not cover the losses which I have endured."

"You believe in resurrection, though, don't you, grandmother?"

Victoria Luise looked at him searchingly before she answered. "Immortality is one of the tenets of my faith," she said at last, "and I have always been a practising Catholic. Do you believe in it yourself, Hansel?"

"Of course. It seems as natural as springtime to me."

He pronounced the words with finality as well as conviction. They had already left another village behind them, and Hansel's gaze kept wandering from the wheel towards the fields. Apparently he was not inclined to pursue the subject of immortality, and Victoria Luise gradually recovered from the astonishment which he had caused her. His next remark was as practical as his last one had been visionary.

"You can feed yourselves and all your neighbours here in East Prussia, can't you, grandmother? Your national neighbours, I mean."

"Yes, if we are so inclined."

"But why shouldn't you be so inclined? I should't think two and a half million people could begin to consume all the butter and cheese that must be produced here, or all the milk and meat. Isn't it profitable to sell it? Isn't it wise to encourage trade?"

"We send butter to Berlin, and elsewhere."

"Elsewhere in Germany, you mean?"

"Yes, elsewhere in Germany. . . . See, *mein Schatz,* there ahead of us is the beginning of our own land."

The questing look in Hansel's eyes kindled quickly. The landscape through which they were passing was much the same as it had been already; but somehow it seemed suddenly to have become still more verdant, still more fresh and flowing than before. He spoke, shyly and excitedly, under his breath.

"I never had such a sense of space," he said, "and of freedom—and beauty. Do you suppose I can put it into music, grandmother?"

"I hope you will put it into something, my dear boy," she said gravely. And she saw that there were tears in her eyes.

They were entering another small village, saved from squalor by the quaintness of its architecture and the brilliance of its flowers. Secreted somewhere beyond it, Hansel supposed, Schönplatz itself must lie, deep in the woods or at the end of a long avenue. But they had hardly reached the outskirts, when a high wall appeared, flanked with luxuriant trees, and blank except for an unpretentious iron gate at one end. It was here that they should turn in, Victoria Luise signified, in answer to Hansel's unspoken question. The next instant the *Herranhaus* itself loomed up before them, its wide façade terminating in two towers, its tiled roof intersected with chimneys and dormers, its deep doors open to the summer sunshine.

The boy's first sensation, as he looked at it, was one of amazed relief. He had expected a monumental pile, moated and buttressed, suggestive of sieges, torture chambers, and incarceration. Instead he saw walls of rose-red brick, almost completely covered with glossy green vines, and set in the midst of a green lawn studded with shrubs and shaded with chestnut trees. The shape of the house was sturdy and symmetrical; its size was not overpowering; there was nothing grim and gloomy, nothing chilly or forbidding about it. On the contrary, it seemed to emanate not only security, but a warmth which antiquity had made the more mellow.

"Oh, grandmother, it's great!" he exclaimed, lapsing into an American colloquialism for the first time that day.

"Yes, Hansel, it is great. It has been great for nearly seven hundred years. We are counting on you to keep it so," his grandmother answered.

It appeared that the General was resting, that he would not be able to see his grandson until tea-time. One of the men-servants who took their bags out of the car busied himself with the possessions of the Archduchess. The other had already put Hansel's meticulously into place, by the time he and his grandmother had mounted the massive stairway leading from the vast hall into which the entrance led directly. In spite of the sunshine outside, the light in the house was dim; Hansel could see hardly more than the outlines of great carved chests, of tawny tapestries and sombre family portraits, as he climbed the two flights of steps so steep and winding that he marvelled at the ease with which his grandmother went over them. But she showed no sign of breathlessness when she finally lifted the heavy latch of a panelled door on the third story.

"This was your father's room, when he was a boy, Hansel," she said in her grave, controlled way. "I thought you would like to have it. Nothing has ever been changed in it. But if you do not find what you need to make you comfortable, of course you must let me know. I am not coming in with you. I have not been over this threshold in ten years now. I had lost three sons before your father, you know—perhaps you yourself can remember when your Uncle Hans was killed at the Battle of the Marne, and your Uncle Heinrich died of wounds received at Ypres. . . . My eldest son, their half-brother, had died a violent death years earlier," she went on in an altered voice, "and finally when Rudolf fell at Verdun—well, I suppose there are always limits to our weak human endurance. You must forgive me, Hansel, and try to understand, not only why I cannot enter this room, but why I feel there are so many dead in our country."

"I do understand, grandmother. I wouldn't have come to you, would I, if I hadn't?"

He was not sorry to be left alone. Beyond the panelled door, he found that the light was still dim, for the room was very deep, with windows only on one side, and these deeply recessed, many-paned.

and overhung with vines; such sunshine as filtered through did not reach more than half-way across the wide-planked floor, nor rise to the broad-beamed ceiling. Nevertheless, as Hansel's eyes became accustomed to the duskiness, he did not find the room depressing. The walls were covered with rose-coloured plaster, much the same shade as the exterior of the house, and the whitewashed beams were also rose-edged. A tall green porcelain stove reared itself impressively at one side of the room, while the round centre table, and a chest of drawers, standing between an immense wardrobe and a cheval glass which stretched from floor to ceiling, was covered with green moire antique. The rest of the colour scheme was haphazard: a divan was spread with a Paisley shawl; a davenport was upholstered in brown tapestry; and a chaise-longue was covered with figured crimson velvet, while similar varieties of decoration characterized all the chairs. Near one of the windows stood a commodious desk; in one of the corners, an equally commodious washstand. Both were surmounted with family portraits of bygone von Hohenlohes, primly presented in pairs.

"I wonder how I see to shave," Hansel murmured practically, as he glanced from the mottled marble stand, in which two large basins were embedded, to the belaced and beribboned couple who looked down at him from the place where he had expected to find a mirror and a light. Inadvertently, his hand touched a copper pitcher, covered with a crested linen towel, which stood between the big basins. It was surprisingly hot, and he drew his fingers away quickly. Then, one by one, he took up the smaller objects on the washstand, wondering what useful purpose they might serve—two little white bowls, a narrow china tray, and an empty carafe with a glass turned upside down over it.

"I shall have to learn to wash all over again," he said to himself rather whimsically, and, by way of a beginning, poured some of the hot water into one of the big basins. But there was no soap in evidence, and after a brief search for some, he sat down in one of the puffy armchairs, which proved surprisingly comfortable, and continued to look around him.

He was not depressed, but he was disappointed. He had never said that he wanted to occupy his father's room. But he had vaguely hoped that it might be given to him. Now that it was, he could find no trace of his father in it, neither of the Rudolf von Hohenlohe whom he had known as a child, and whom he vividly remembered, nor of the boy that Rudolf von Hohenlohe once had been. He had vaguely imagined that there would be a boy's books in the room, a gun or two, perhaps a collection of minerals or some stuffed birds. He had visualized it as small and Spartan, but revealing. Instead it was immense, luxurious, and impersonal. He would rather have been confronted with his father's ghost than with such nonentity.

A light tap on the door roused him from his reverie. He sprang to open it, then stood blinking, wondering if in the dusk his eyes were playing him altogether false. The girl who stood there did not look real. Framed in the dark embrasure of the door, she gave the effect of an idealized genre picture. Her flaxen hair curled around her face and was wreathed in thick braids over her small head. She was pleasantly plump, and her eyes were blue and beseeching. She was clad in a white blouse and apron interwoven with bright colours, a black bodice fastened with amber buttons, and blue skirt banded with velvet ribbon. In response to Hansel's startled exclamation, she dropped a quick curtsey which seemed indicative of fright.

"Der Herr General ist jetzt im Garten!" she breathed, and scurried down a dim corridor like a terrified rabbit.

Hansel's next shock came at the sight of his grandfather, whom he remembered—vividly, in the same way that he remembered his father—as erect, ruddy, and dictatorial. Nothing had prepared him to see a shrunken man, sitting in a wheel-chair, with a rug over his knees. Only the bristling white moustache, and the white hair rising stiffly from a high forehead, were as he recalled them. Even the General's eyes, which had once shone with a glacier-like glitter, were changed. They were less direct in their gaze, less clear and brilliant. As Hansel bent over the old man, he saw that his grandfather was simply staring at him, that there was no joyful recognition in his look.

"Here is Hansel, your namesake, come to see you, Hans," the Archduchess said gently. "Rudolf's son."

The staring eyes flickered, and the transparent hands, extended unclasped over the folded rug, twitched a little.

"Rudolf," the old man said in a thick voice.

"No, my dear, Rudolf's son. Think a minute. You have greatly looked forward to his homecoming. He is going to spend the summer with us."

A sudden smile illuminated the blank countenance, giving it charm and dignity again. One of the twitching hands began to move slowly upwards.

"He knows you. He wants to touch your cheek, perhaps to kiss you," the Archduchess whispered to Hansel. But as the boy put his face against his grandfather's the old man began to sob bitterly.

"Wait. This attack will pass," the Archduchess said, whispering again. Hansel stood still, bracing his own body against the paroxysm which shook his grandfather, appalled lest he might involuntarily reveal the revulsion with which his pity was tinged. When his grandfather finally kissed him, he managed to return the caress. But as the old man sought to wipe away the tears that had been shed, and which had fallen on both faces, with his shaking hand, the boy felt tears welling up in his own eyes.

"Talk to him. He understands more than he can express. He has really recognized you, and you must take advantage of this lucidity before it passes."

"We are going to have good times together this summer, aren't we, grandfather?" Hansel asked, resentful of his own inadequacy.

"Yes. Good times. Riding every day."

"You'll teach me to ride? I've never learned, you know. But every Prussian can ride, can't he? And I'm going to be a Prussian now, like you."

"Yes, yes. A Prussian like me. We shall ride every morning before breakfast on our beautiful white horses."

"Shall Fritz bring the horses around now, my dear, so that Hansel may see them?"

The General did not answer. He was staring into space again, his vacant gaze turned towards the dim corner of the park. Eventually he raised one of his quivering hands and pointed.

"The Russians!" he muttered hoarsely. "The Russians are attempting a new attack. They are upon us already! I can see them over there."

"No, Hans, you are mistaken! There are no Russians in our peaceful park."

"Sh-sh-sh——!" the General said warningly, painfully putting a shaking finger to his lips. "They will hear you, Luise, and then all will be lost."

"The Field-Marshal himself has assured me that they are all gone."

"Sh-sh-sh—— Hindenburg won at Tannenberg. But he is not infallible. This time he is mistaken. They are upon us again."

"Shall I send Rudolf to the park to drive them away?"

"Send Heinrich. Send Heinrich. Rudolf is not the soldier that Heinrich is. Heinrich will force them back."

Victoria Luise signalled to Hansel. He rose and went quickly down the gravel walk, between the formal flower beds and moss-grown statues. His grandmother's voice, sweet and soothing, followed him as he went. "There, there," he could hear her saying. "Heinrich has gone, my dear, as you wished, to drive back the Russians. They will not trouble you any more. Heinrich is the best soldier among our sons. Though they have all been good boys, have they not?"

The General's feeble answer did not reach Hans Christian, perhaps because he felt himself fleeing from him. Involuntarily he had quickened his pace. He had crossed the great garden and entered the park which overlooked the lake. Green trees surrounded him, sparkling water lay before him. But now he had none of that sense of space and beauty which had filled him with such joy that morning. He scarcely saw his surroundings. The pitiful wreck of a strong man obsessed his mind and formed his only vision.

He could not blame his grandmother for having failed to warn him of her husband's condition. He realized that it must be so heartrending to her that she could not bring herself to mention it. Probably she did not permit herself to face it fully, and surely she should be forgiven if this were the case. She was an ageing woman, bereft of almost everybody and everything that had made life glorious, as far as she was concerned. Her husband held the last links in the slender chain which still united her with an imperial past. When these links were severed, what would she have left? Nothing, Hans Christian knew, nothing at all that mattered. Unless, through some miracle, he himself——

A settee and some armchairs of elaborately wrought iron, painted white, were drawn up around a small round table near the place where he was standing. He sat down and began to try to think things out. In coming to Germany to claim his heritage, he had not possessed the faintest inkling that it would be like this. He knew, in a general way, that the country had suffered from the blockade and the inflation; but the details of this suffering had remained comfortably vague in his mind. He had not realized that it was intense or widespread; it had never occurred to him that his own people and his own possessions could be affected by it. His desire to return to his native land, sincere and intense as it was, had been largely due—he now realized for the first time—to his own loneliness and restlessness in the face of his mother's self-sufficiency, rather than to any strong inner conviction that his grandparents needed him.

But now that he had come, what—in the face of existing conditions—should he do? What *could* he do? His mother had kept his own small patrimony intact for him—the legacy which his father had originally inherited from the unmarried uncle for whom Rudolf von Hohenlohe had been named. But it was a modest one, entirely inadequate to clear up the wreckage which Hans Christian already saw around him. How much more there was still to discover he could not even conjecture. In any case, he would not come into un-supervised use of his small fortune for three years yet. It had been only with the greatest difficulty that he had persuaded his mother to let him cut into his capital for travel funds. It was inconceivable that she would allow him to use it towards the reclamation of a vast estate and the rehabilitation of a fallen fortune. And even if she had been willing that he should apply it to these ends, to what would it amount? A drop in a bucket of water cast over a torrential dam.

He could not then hope to help. But, on the other hand, having come, how could he turn back? His pride would not permit him to confess to his mother that his quest for contentment had been a failure; his pity would not permit him to desert his grandmother in her hour of need. For the present, at least, he must stay where he was, and mark time. And with the decision that this was what he ought to do came also the renascence of the conviction that it was what he wanted to do. This was his *Heimat,* his Fatherland; America had been only an adopted country for him at best. These were his people; his mother with her complete preoccupation in American affairs had long been alien to his understanding.

But even though this were true, in the larger sense, would there be any immediate escape for him from the nostalgia which had so long obsessed him, in spite of his collegiate success? If his mother, who was still young and strong and beautiful, had proven inadequate as a companion, for what sort of satisfying communion could he look with a tragic, broken woman and a paralytic old man? Obviously for none. He must seek for it somewhere beyond the limits of Schönplatz.

Involuntarily, the thought of the buoyant group on the boat entered his mind, and with the thought an undefined longing for its zestful comradeship. The breezy brightness of the twins, the gay impudence of Card Eustis, had been tonic in their effect. Even Trixie Rhodes, petty and provincial as she seemed, emanated superabundant vitality. He visualized her again as she had looked when the paint had been washed off her face and the ruffles clipped from her shoulders. She had lovely lips, so lovely that neither the scarlet with which they were generally smeared nor the sulky line into which they so often drooped could altogether obscure their soft natural curves. It was easy to understand why Card had lost no time in reaching the stage of "petting." If ever there was a girl whose mouth was meant to be kissed, Trixie was that girl, and Hans Christian felt resentful of his own lack of importunity, as far as she was concerned. Her eyes were beautiful too—dark blue, like a sapphire; when she laughed, they had a sapphire's sparkle. And on the rare occasions when she was thoughtful, their clarity was shot through with a shrewd gleam. Hans Christian had not forgotten the look she had turned on Father Hastings, when the Bishop had spoken of being confined to his cabin by the service of the Lord. Buried somewhere beneath her apparent triviality, there was real intelligence. She was not a blonde baby doll, with a baby doll's eyes, like the apparition that had appeared at the dark door of his bedroom that afternoon. . . .

He felt a light hand on his shoulder, and sprang up to see his grandmother standing beside him. She had come so quietly across the grass and through the trees that he had not been aware of her until she touched him. Slightly startled, he blurted out an unstudied question.

"Who was the messenger that you sent for me this afternoon, grandmother?"

"The messenger? The butler sent one of the maids. I don't know which. Why?"

"This one looked like a doll. She had flaxen hair, china-blue eyes and chubby pink cheeks. And she was wearing a dress that I suppose is the local costume—a *Tracht* you call it, don't you?"

"All the maids in the house wear the village *Tracht*. I insist upon this. It makes a very satisfactory uniform." Was his grandmother's charming voice rather cold and formal as she said this, or did he merely imagine that it was, Hans Christian wondered. "As for the flaxen hair and baby doll stare and the chubby cheeks—you may as well get used to seeing hundreds of those, without excitement, wherever you turn. They are almost inescapable, among the lower classes in Germany. I really have no idea which of our empty-headed little peasants it was who called you. But if she was almost noticeably half-witted, it was probably the second under-chamber-maid, Trüdchen."

CHAPTER VI

HANS CHRISTIAN dined with his grandmother, sitting opposite her at an immense round table in an apartment which she designated as the "small dining-room," though it was at least thirty feet square. Its white expanse, covered with a darned damask cloth into which the family coat of arms was woven, seemed to stretch out endlessly between them; its smooth surface was unbroken except for a ponderous silver epergne which stood in the centre, and the coroneted knives and forks at each place. The menservants, who had officiated at their arrival, and to whose shabby uniforms threadbare white gloves had now been added, served the substantial but unimaginative dinner. The drinking water was lukewarm and the wine sour. There was no butter, and the bread, disclosed when the large smooth napkins were unfolded, was coarse and black; but the roast goose was excellent, and Hans Christian had already begun to take boiled potatoes as a matter of course, and to dispense philosophically with a variety of vegetables. When strawberries had been offered on fruit plates realistically painted, the Archduchess rolled her napkin neatly inside a silver ring, and led the way through a succession of drawing-rooms, gliding across the glittering parquet flooring with no suggestion of slipping. When she had reached the fourth one, she signified that they would pause at this point and sip their coffee.

"Would you care to light the fire, Hansel?" she asked, nodding towards a corner mantle of hooded stone, under which logs had been laid upright above a foundation of light branches. "The evenings are nearly always cool in East Prussia, even in midsummer, and you may find the climate trying at first—there is a good deal of rain, and there are many dark days. . . . I am so glad that your grandfather knew you. I am sure he had real pleasure in seeing you.

53

He was tired afterwards, but not over-much. He was sleeping quietly when I came out to dinner."

Apparently she intended to make no reference to her failure to inform Hans Christian of the General's actual condition, before their arrival at Schönplatz. The boy, having lighted the fire and accepted the cup of coffee, which his grandmother served herself from an enamelled service, decided that it would be wiser for him not to refer to this either.

"Do my cousins come here often?" he inquired instead. "I've been looking forward to seeing them again." It was amazingly light, considering how late they had dined, and, holding his coffee cup in his hand, he walked over to one of the great windows and looked out past the garden to the park and lake, the same unaccustomed desire for young and zestful company, which he had felt that afternoon, welling up irrepressibly in his breast again. "Not that I remember them very clearly, or that we've written each other much if any," he went on. "But, you know . . . Aunt Rita's eldest son is just a little younger than I am, isn't he? Karl? It would be fun if he and I could get together. And there are seven of them in all, aren't there?"

"There were. But two of them have died. And one is a cripple, as a result of uncorrected rickets. Your Aunt Rita has had a very sad life Her husband, Friedrich von Mitweld, has never been able to reconcile himself to the abdication of the Kaiser. In fact, he seizes on every possible pretext to go to Doorn as often as he can, and to stay there as long as possible each time. I think he would like nothing better than to head a Restoration Movement, which would, of course, represent an entirely forlorn hope. Karl, on the contrary, has embraced many of those communistic ideas which are such a menace to Germany just now. So the household is torn with internal strife, that is very hard for Rita, with her peace-loving nature, to endure She hides herself at home, and I do not see her for months at a time. In any case, it is a long expensive journey from here to Bavaria."

"And my Aunt Elsa? Don't you see her either?"

"She is a nun, you know, in Cologne, and that is as hard and as costly to reach as Munich. Besides, the rules of her Order are extremely strict. Family visits are not encouraged; and, to tell the truth, I have never found them very satisfactory, when they must be carried forward on either side of a veiled grille."

"I shouldn't think they would be. But I should think you'd like to have your grandchildren come to see you."

"There is one grandchild, at least, whom I am very happy to see," said the Archduchess, with her disarming smile, as she poured herself a second cup of coffee, and motioned to Hansel to stop pacing about and seat himself beside her. "And Luischen, my name-

54

sake, was here for a time in the spring. But she is a wild girl, already bent on making a most unsuitable marriage, though she is far too young to be thinking of such a thing; her visits are too much of a strain, now that we have a semi-invalid in the house." Victoria Luise paused, and added, "I hope, Hansel, that when your fancies turn to thoughts of love, it will not be either too lightly or too wilfully "

"I don't think they'll turn in that direction at all, at least for a long time."

"Of course they will. That is inevitable. But it will mean everything to me, my dear boy, if you will try not to be headstrong, when it comes to affairs of the heart."

"I'll try not to be headstrong about anything, as far as that goes. Don't worry."

"I do not worry, I think, unduly. But a suitable alliance for you is a matter of paramount importance."

"You haven't anyone special in mind, already, have you, grandmother?"

"Well—not to any point of insistence, you may be sure of that. But some time, before too long, I hope it may be possible for you to take a trip to Spain. I should like to have you meet our kinsfolk there. They are not closely related to us, by blood; but, on the other hand, the ties which do unite us have always meant a great deal. I refer especially to the Cerreno family, of which I am sure you have often heard your mother speak."

"Why, no!" Hansel answered candidly. "She never speaks of them at all. But I remember Sebastian de Cerreno perfectly, myself. He came to Copenhagen once on a special mission—a centennial, or something of the sort—when father was German Minister there He brought me a splendid set of Spanish soldiers—museum pieces really, though I used them as toys—which I have still. I keep them set up in a part of the attic that used to be my play-room, in our Hamstead house. I thought he was a wonderful person. But his children are just kids, aren't they? He didn't have any until he had been married for a long time."

"Yes. They are just kids, as you have put it. But you are not markedly middle-aged yourself, Hansel, you know. Sebastian has two boys, Gabriel and Esteban, and two girls, Cristina and Cecilia. Their mother is a very beautiful woman, and Sebastian himself has always been known as one of the most fascinating men in Europe. Their daughters can hardly fail to be entrancing."

"Well, maybe. Ten years from now," Hansel replied without enthusiasm. "But really, grandmother, I'm not interested in girls."

"All the better. And all the more chance that you will be, ten years from now. In the meantime, I shall try to help you ward off young ladies from the middle-west, as importunate as the one who hurled herself into your car the night of your arrival in Hamburg."

His grandmother had previously made no reference to Trixie's rash behaviour, and Hansel, who had been silent on the subject himself, had secretly dreaded the moment when she might. Now she spoke with such delicate archness that it was impossible to be angry. Nevertheless, Hans Christian found himself instantly on the defensive.

"I hope you didn't get a wrong impression of Trixie, grandmother. There are lots of nice things about her."

"Perhaps. But what an awful name, to begin with! And what strange manners!"

"Her name is really Beatrice, of course, and that isn't awful, is it? I think it's rather pretty—just as pretty as Cristina or Cecilia!" he said, speaking mischievously in his turn. "And I think her manners will probably improve, among the polite Dutch. I don't believe I told you, her father has just been appointed American Minister to the Netherlands. She and her mother have invited me, very cordially, to come and visit them."

"I have not the slightest doubt of their cordiality, my dear boy. Nevertheless, I should much rather see you go to Spain than to Holland when you have the opportunity and the inclination to travel."

"Mr. Rhodes is what's called a solid citizen. He's made a great deal of money, all himself, in a very praiseworthy way," persisted Hansel, reddening at the mocking reference to cordiality. "And Trixie's adaptable, like most American girls. She'll probably learn to do things very well, in the end."

"The Cerrenos also have a great deal of money. And none of them need to learn to do things well. They have been doing them well for centuries," the Archduchess retorted quietly. "Would you care to have a game of chess with me, my dear boy? If you do not know how to play, this might be a good time to begin learning. I am sure, when your grandfather is better, that he will wish to engage you in contests, very frequently."

That was a fiction which must be kept up, Hansel recognized, as the evening wore interminably on; not even tacitly would his grandmother admit that her husband would not eventually regain his normal health and resume his normal pursuits. She referred to him several times, intermittently, in the course of their play; and when she had won three games of chess, and the board had been folded up and put away, her talk reverted constantly to him. Hansel tried to keep up his end of the conversation courteously, and he was careful to avoid any further appearance of argument. But he was very tired; the warm fire made him feel sleepy after his long day in the open air; and the varied experiences through which he had passed had been emotionally exhausting. He was thankful when at last his grandmother rose to retire.

"I hope you will sleep well, my darling. You will let me know if you are not perfectly comfortable, will you not?"

"I am sure I shall be. Thank you, grandmother. But I wonder if I might take something to read upstairs with me? A newspaper or a book? There didn't seem to be any in my room."

The Archduchess looked at him in surprise. "I am afraid it is true that there are no newspapers there," she said. "Wait, I will ring. There must be one in the house, and hereafter I will see that you receive it regularly. But there are quantities of books in your room, Hansel, which belonged to your father—the Danzig chests are full of them, and of his various collections—medals and coins and so on. I suppose you thought, because you saw no open cases. . . ." She glided across the parquetry again, and beckoned Hansel into still another room, which he had not previously seen, and in which the walls were covered with inlaid panels. "This is the library," she said. "There are shelves upon shelves of books behind every one of those doors. Feel free to browse among them as much as you like, tomorrow, and after that. Meanwhile, here is today's *Berliner Tageblatt*," she added, handing him the paper which a servant had brought in response to her summons. "I am afraid I have hardly glanced at it myself, there is so little about current events which I care to read. Besides, any good *Hausfrau* has a great deal to do when she has been absent from home for a few days, and I pride myself on my attention to detail."

Hansel took the paper and glanced casually over the unfamiliar lay-out, slightly baffled by the lack of headlines, and by the strange script to which he had not yet had time fully to reaccustom himself. There seemed to be nothing of great moment, worthy of passing on to his grandmother at such an hour of the night, especially when she had just said that current events did not interest her. But as certain half-forgotten items from the American press filtered through to the forefront of his mind, he made an idle comment and asked a casual question, his hand already on the knob of the drawing-room door.

"We've been hearing quite a little lately at college about a man named Adolf Hitler. What are people saying about him in Germany?"

"A man named Adolf Hitler? I cannot recall anything at all. Who is he, and what has he done?"

"He's an Austrian by birth, like yourself. He was a sergeant in the World War, and afterwards—or before, I'm not quite sure which —he was a paperhanger, and sold picture postcards on the side. I can't make out that he ever did anything much. But he's tried to start some sort of Reactionary Movement in Germany. And he seemed to emerge a sort of special hero after a *'Bloody Putsch'* in Munich."

"An Austrian *like myself!* I do not believe he can bear much resemblance to me, Hansel, even though he were born an Austrian, if he were the hero of something so unpleasant as a '*Bloody Putsch*'! When did this disagreeable event take place?"

"Oh, some time last winter. He and a few friends of his tried to buck the Government, and most of the friends got killed. Didn't Aunt Rita write you anything about it? This all happened in Munich!"

"She wrote that there had been some kind of a disgraceful street brawl in which Karl had been hurt. No details—I supposed because she was ashamed of his quarrelsome propensities. Did anything of importance happen afterwards?"

"I suppose it depends on what you call important. Hitler himself was clapped into prison, and people said it would be the last to be heard of him and his so-called Movement. But I happened to see a little item about him in this paper. That's what made me think of it. He's going to be let out after a while, and, meantime, he's writing a book."

"Writing a book? An ignorant man like that?"

"Yes, . . . Bunyan wrote a book in prison, didn't he? A book that made quite a stir, called *Pilgrim's Progress*."

For the first time the Archduchess looked at her grandson rather coldly. "My dear Hansel," she observed, "you certainly do make some extraordinary remarks. Several times this morning—and now—— What caused you to think of a comparison of that sort?"

"I don't know, I'm sure. I just happened to, that's all. I haven't offended you, have I, grandmother?"

He looked so earnest, he seemed so genuinely upset by her displeasure, that she melted instantly. "No, my dear boy, you have not offended me," she said with tenderness. "You will never do that, I know. But I hope you will never forget, either, that you are a Junker and a von Hohenlohe, and. act and think accordingly. In family matters, as I have said before. And in national matters also. Be true to your own class and you will be true to your own country. It is inconceivable that in the regeneration of Germany, which I hope you are to be helpful in bringing about, there could be any time or any place for an imprisoned paperhanger named Adolf Hitler."

CHAPTER VII

HANS CHRISTIAN passed a restless night. When he first went up to his room, tired and sleepy as he was, he could not resist the temptation of opening the Danzig chests, so great was his relief at finding that there were, after all, some personal relics of his father's boyhood in existence; but he burrowed through them vainly, as far as finding anything interesting in itself was concerned. He had left the dining-room still thirsty, and now his attempts at exploration made him doubly conscious of this discomfort; but the carafe with the glass upturned over it was still empty, and the tepid water in the two pitchers had a light coating of dust over it, as if it had been there for several days already. He turned from it with aversion, and got into bed, pulling the mountainous eiderdown with which it was covered firmly around his chin; as the Archduchess had said, it was cold, even though it was midsummer. The truth of the statement was brought home to him with double force when he felt his feet protruding below the eiderdown. He rose, pulled it back, and tried to tuck it in at the bottom without much success, for it kept puffing up around his hands wherever he touched it. Moreover, he found, when he climbed back into bed, that his chest and shoulders were now completely exposed; the eiderdown was so short that it could not be stretched to cover his entire person at once; and eventually he got up a second time and hunted for his overcoat in the dark, the electric switch by the door, which was the only one in the room, having eluded his search. With the Burberry for a blanket, he decided that he could manage, and, as a matter of fact, he did fall almost instantly asleep. But his dreams were troubled and fantastic, and he found no repose in them.

He seemed to be sitting in the ventilator beside Trixie. But she did not look natural. She had a mantilla draped over a high comb on her head and a glittering painted fan in her hand. She had turned from an American into a Spaniard, at least so far as her outer attributes were concerned. He decided to try calling her Cristina, which he thought would please his grandmother, and when that did not work he called her Cecilia instead. But she only sat and sulked, and he saw that he had made a mistake, that it was Trixie all the time. So then he decided not to talk to her at all, but to caress her instead. She made no resistance. Her smooth shoulders were soft in his embrace, her red mouth sweet under his kiss. At last he released her and looked at her again. To his horror, he saw that it was not Trixie whom he was holding now, but Trüdchen. . .

The loud clamour of a bell came clanging across his distressed somnolence, rousing him abruptly. He leapt out of bed, still shivering with shame, and convinced that a calamity of some sort must have befallen the household. Could there be a fire? Was this a toll for the dead? But he could smell no smoke, he could hear no hurrying footsteps. Surely if anything were vitally wrong, there would be some further indication of it.

He went to the window and looked out, his attention arrested by a strange sound of scraping. Far below him he could discern the figures of women with implements of some sort in their hands As his eyes grew accustomed to the dimness and the distance, he could

59

see that these women were raking the gravel walk in the garden, at the meticulous order of which he had marvelled the day before. Completely reassured, he turned away; they could hardly be pursuing so superfluous an occupation in the midst of disaster. As he crossed the room, however, a nearer noise distracted him, such as wood might make against wood, though slightly muffled. He flung open the door of his bedroom, and in the sombre hall outside saw a girl leaning against a long pole to which a heavy block covered with felt was attached, and which she was laboriously pushing across a hardwood floor, polishing the parquetry as she moved. With a contracting heart he realized that the girl was Trüdchen.

She had looked up instantly, at the raising of the iron latch. But this time she had not scurried away. Instead, after dropping another quick curtsey, she had stood as if transfixed, gazing at him with melting eyes.

"What are you doing here at this hour?" Hans Christian asked sharply, snatching at the bathrobe which hung on the rack near the door and wrapping it firmly around him.

"But, Herr Baron, I am always here at this hour. The great bell, summoning us all to work, sounded ten minutes ago. I was even a little late. If her Serene Highness knew this she would be much displeased; she might threaten to send me away. I beg the Herr Baron to intercede for me if she should. I need money so much."

"Don't be absurd," said Hans Christian, still sharply. "Of course she won't send you away. . . . So that was the seven o'clock whistle I heard, was it?"

A baffled expression overspread Trüdchen's rosy face. "I do not understand the Herr Baron," she faltered. "That was not a whistle, it was a bell. And it is not seven, it is only five."

"Five? And what time do you get through at night?"

"Sometimes at nine, sometimes at ten. Now that there are not many guests at the castle, it is often a little earlier. The work is not hard. It would be easy for me to do more." Up to this point she had continued to look at him meltingly, her breast rising and falling in quick little pants. Now curtseying again, she bent her head, her shoulders drooping. "Has the Herr Baron need of me in any way?" she asked submissively.

It had never before been brought home to Hans Christian that the relation between a dream and a reality might be so close. He was appalled at the revelation.

"Certainly not," he said, even more brusquely than before. Then, seeing how utterly crushed the girl looked, he added, "That is, you might tell me if I can get a bath in this house, and, if so, where."

"*Aber natürlich*, the Herr Baron may have a bath whenever he pleases. I shall prepare it for him. In the little room at the end of the corridor."

"You won't do anything of the sort. I don't need to have my bath prepared for me by anyone. I do that myself."

"But, Herr Baron, I always prepare the baths. Her Serene Highness would be very angry with me if I neglected my duty."

"I can't help it. I'll make her understand that I don't like the idea of having a girl prepare my bath. But I'll tell you what you can do, since you're the chambermaid. When you make up my bed this morning you can put a couple of blankets on it, and tuck them in at the bottom. And you can keep a pitcher of ice water in my room all the time."

"Yes, Herr Baron, both shall be done. I shall not fail in anything that you ask me to do."

Again he saw all the implications of her docility. She was almost asking for seduction. He knew that he had only to stretch out his hand to take her; and with the realization a hot gust of desire swept through him. But beneath it ran the dark thought that such subservience could not be spontaneous, that it must have its source, at least partly, in the fear that a lack of compliance might mean a lack of food. He wondered how often the girls in the village had yielded to the lords of the manor, their hearts taut with terror, while their bodies lay limp. No matter how many times this had happened before, he was resolved that it should never happen again.

"Then run along, Trüdchen, and get the ice water, like a good girl," he said cheerfully and casually. "I'm thirsty enough to drink a well dry."

The day to which he eventually descended differed in no essential detail from dozens of others which followed it. He spent hours at the piano and hours in the library; he wrote conscientiously to his mother, and, from time to time, briefly answered the letters with which Trixie showered him. He did not defer his riding lessons. His grandmother had told him that there was not a boy in the village who, before he was five years old, had not gone out in the pasture alone with a halter in his hand, and, planting his great toe on the neck of a grazing horse, swung himself up into a seat unaided, and ridden proudly home. In spite of the nonchalance with which the Archduchess had told this story, Hans Christian had interpreted it, and rightly, as a challenge. He was in the saddle every morning by seven, returning at nine to the bath, which, in spite of his protests. Trüdchen always prepared for him, and the hearty breakfast spread out in the "small" dining-room, where his grandmother awaited him.

In a way, it seemed futile to rise so early when after breakfast there was nothing pressing to do. He had offered to help with the accounts, to take over as much of the management of the estate as his grandmother would permit. But he had coupled these offers with

61

some questions about wages and some comments on the length of working hours which the Archduchess seemed to resent. The result of this tactlessness had been to close all avenues of responsibility to him. There would be time enough, later on, she assured him, for him to bother with matters like that; any day now, his grandfather would be expecting to take up the reins again; it was hardly worthwhile for dear Hansel to begin a task which he would not be expected to continue. She was accustomed to figures, she could manage quite well by herself until her husband was in the mood to relieve her.

Some of the young men in the neighbourhood came to see him. They were all well born and well bred, and they were extremely courteous to him in a formal, precise sort of way. He was made welcome, when he called upon them in return, at the various *Herrenhäuser* that they inhabited, many of which were far more imposing than Schönplatz; and he enjoyed many aspects of the East Prussian country life that these contacts revealed to him. He was especially intrigued when he found that falconry, which he had regarded as a mediæval pastime, was still considered a contemporary sport; and for a time the hooded bird which he learned to hold on his wrist, and which swooped and circled towards its prey when he released it, had a fascination for him. But, basically, the whole principle of hunting for pleasure revolted him. It made him feel sick and faint to see a harmless and defenceless bird or animal, at one moment free and joyous and vital, transformed, in a twinkling, to a mangled mass of inert flesh. His squeamishness was regarded as strange; it detracted from the popularity which he might otherwise have enjoyed. Even his excellent game of tennis and his skill as a swimmer did not wholly atone, it was soon plain, for the lack of hardihood with which his tender-heartedness stamped him.

He might have had more success with the young girls whom he met than with the young men, had his own indifference to them not been so insurmountable. Dances were fairly frequent, and he was duly invited to all those which occurred in the vicinity. But he could find nothing alluring in the sight of an insipid girl, who appeared at a party with a tweed coat slung carelessly over a dowdy dress, who ducked and kissed her hostess's hand like an automaton, and who expected to be returned to a chaperon's side between the dances through which she stepped with complete mental and physical detachment. All of these girls bore venerable names, all of them lived in historic houses and some of them might have been very pretty if they had been properly dressed, or even if they had shown more animation. Hans Christian remembered that the twins, whose dowdiness Trixie had decried, had nevertheless been excellent company. But these highly born Prussian maidens, with their flat figures and faint smiles, were wholly unstimulating to him.

The countryside continued to beguile him, and he went for long walks, usually quite alone, and for long motor rides, on which his grandmother sometimes accompanied him; a *Schwester* had now been put in charge of the General, by a doctor's orders, and the physician also insisted that the Archduchess must have occasional respite from the strain of watching beside her husband. Hans Christian was enthralled by the beauty of the Masurian Lakes, which he and Victoria Luise visited together, lunching upon *Maräne** in the open air at Nickolaien, and taking a speed-boat to Radjanyi afterwards. Every day he found some fresh phase of the landscape which charmed him. He loved to watch the windmills turning slowly in the breeze; to come, unexpectedly, upon some village festival; to see the goose girls sitting motionless in the midst of their flocks. These girls seemed to him the epitome of tranquillity; and he found grace and purpose in the gait of the older women who went at sundown, with white kerchiefs tied firmly around their heads, to milk the cows forgathered in the pastures, near the picket fences. Only when he saw some ancient crone staggering under the heavy weight of a wooden yoke laid heavily across her shoulders did he feel his heart contract; it was senseless, it was sinful, that any human creature should be so overburdened. More than once he stopped and tried to take away the water pails depending from these yokes, and carry them himself. Always he met with a blank start or a bitter protest when he strove to give relief.

Once he succeeded in overriding the objections so querulously voiced and walked triumphantly beside the aged woman whose load he had assumed, as far as her home. When he entered it, he was amazed to find how cheerless it was. The flowers which bloomed brightly in its garden, its quaint shape and thatched roof, had given it, from without, a false effect of cosiness. Inside it was dark and dingy, and pervaded with a stale smell. But the old woman's daughter, a not uncomely matron, with half a dozen children clinging to her skirts, welcomed him courteously, and thanked him, with obvious sincerity, for his kindness.

"Our Trüdchen has already told us of the Herr Baron's never-failing goodness," she said, with feeling. "And now we can see for ourselves how great it is. The Herr Baron does us too much honour."

"Is Trüdchen yours too?" he asked in surprise, looking up from the small, blonde heads which he had been impartially patting, as one by one the children left their mother and came shyly clustering around him.

"Yes, Herr Baron. She is my eldest *Mädel*. And such a good girl! I do not know what I should do without her, now that I have lost my *Mann* and that I myself must stay at home with all these others," the woman said amiably but anxiously.

* A fish peculiar to the region, similar to smelt.

"Could I help in any way? I should be so glad if I could," Hans Christian said eagerly.

"The Herr Baron does us too much honour," Trüdchen's mother repeated a second time. "But there is nothing, as long as my *Mädel* has work and does it faithfully. She brings her wages home. She is not scatter-brained or silly. She does not run about, Heaven knows where, at all hours of the night, like the daughters of many of my neighbours. She comes straight home from the castle, where I know she is safe, and goes soberly to bed. I have much to be thankful for."

Hansel walked back to the castle himself in an unusually thoughtful mood. The hall was empty as he entered it, and, crossing it, he looked out into the garden, to see if his grandfather might be there, in his wheel-chair. But the garden, like the hall, was deserted, and a light tap on Victoria Luise's door elicited no response. Apparently both his grandparents were resting. Solitude still pervaded the stairs as he mounted to the second story. But as he approached his own room he saw Trüdchen standing on the threshold in the same place she had stood when he had first seen her.

It was almost as if she had been waiting for him. Her early terror of him had left her completely; so had the fixed idea that any kindness he showed her must have an ulterior motive; and as if her trust in him had restored her hope in a harsh and harrowing world, she held herself more confidently now. Her pretty little figure was erect, her blue eyes unafraid. She did not even curtsey as he approached her. Instead she looked straight at him and smiled in a way that went to his heart.

"Come into my room a minute. I want to speak to you," he said abruptly.

She followed him without hesitation. When he had closed the door, he went up to her and put his hands on her shoulders.

"Listen to me, Trüdchen," he said impellingly.

"I am listening, Herr Baron."

"This afternoon, as I came through the village, I saw an old woman carrying two pails of water on a heavy yoke. It is a sight which always makes me very unhappy. I took the pails away from her, and went home with her. When I reached the house I found it was your house too. I saw your mother and she told me."

"Yes, Herr Baron."

"She also told me that you were a very good girl, that you bring all your wages home to her, that you help take care of your younger brothers and sisters. Well, I do not know how much your wages are, because her Serene Highness does not talk to me about such things. But I know they must be very small, and I know you must need more. So I am going to give it to you. I have a little money of my own, so I can. But you must never tell. You must not tell her Serene Highness, because she would be very angry at the idea that I was meddling with her servants; and you must not tell your mother because she might misunderstand. You must only let your mother know that from now on you will have more to give her, and she will naturally suppose that the Archduchess has raised your wages. Is that clear?"

"Yes, Herr Baron, it is clear."

"Very well. Here are fifty marks to begin with. I shall try to give you fifty marks every month. Now run along, and keep on being a good girl."

"Fifty marks! Fifty marks every month! *Aber, Herr Baron, ich verstehe nicht! Aber, Herr Baron, dass kann nicht sein.*"

Before he could stop her, before he so much as realized her intention, she was on her knees before him. She had seized both his hands, and was covering them with warm kisses and grateful tears. Terribly embarrassed, he strove to draw them away.

"Look here, you musn't do that. Listen, Trüdchen, I don't like to have you kneel to me, I don't want you to kiss my hands. Stand up this minute and behave yourself."

She paid no attention to what he was saying. When at last he did succeed in lifting his hands, he lifted her with them, because she would not let go. She flung herself against his breast, still crying happily, still murmuring her gratitude. Her soft rosy face looked up into his with infinite devotion. It was so close that his own touched it. The next instant they were in each other's arms.

CHAPTER VIII

IT was Hans Christian's habit to sit with his grandfather for an hour every morning and two hours every afternoon. The Archduchess had feared that the boy might cease to do this when the General's increasing weakness necessitated the abandonment of the wheel-chair. She realized that the atmosphere of a sickroom was more trying than that of a garden, and that the sight of a helpless man, stretched stiffly out upon his bed, was far more gruesome in its suggestion than that of a quasi-convalescent, seated, apparently at ease, among pleasant surroundings. She was therefore touched when she found that Hansel, instead of finding pretexts to neglect the tiresome tribute, became more and more solicitously attentive. She realized that he was genuinely distressed at the sadness of a situation which was now admittedly hopeless.

She had not, at first, been inclined to regard his tender-heartedness as an asset. She shared the scorn of the neighbourhood concerning his aversion to hunting; and his inopportune questions about wages and working hours irritated her all the more because she detected in them a possible desire to tamper with established custom, in an impracticable manner, rather than because she dreaded to have him discover how hollow was the structure of their house, how essential it was to stretch every resource to the last limit, in order to prop up the tottering frame. When she learned that he had taken Gertraud's water-pails away from her and carried them to the old woman's cottage, she had been so much shaken that she had spoken to him without any of her characteristic sauveness; and on their occasional excursions together, when he ceased to regard the countryside with admiration and concerned himself critically with the people instead, she never failed to resent the change.

Once they had driven out from Königsberg to the *Kurische Nehrung*, and had spent a happy afternoon there, hunting for amber and wandering over the dunes. The Archduchess was secretly flattered that Hansel should consider her an adequate companion for such outings, though she regretted that they could not extend this one as far as Memel, to the loss of which she was still unreconciled. She was still an excellent walker, and could climb and stoop without effort; but she knew that few boys of her grandson's age would have given her credit for possessing such prowess or the chance to prove it. There was colour in her cheeks, as well as laughter in her eyes, for the first time in many a long day when they started on their homeward drive along the isthmus. Then a series of episodes occurred which robbed her of all the pleasure she had felt in her adventure.

A doe emerged from the forest, and sprang fearlessly across their path, with twin fawns gambolling in its wake. Hansel stopped the motor abruptly, and gazed at them with delighted eyes. Then, as they disappeared into the leafy depths again, he turned to her eagerly.

"Wasn't that a lovely sight? Do you wonder now that I like to see them leaping like that, instead of lying maimed and bleeding at my feet?"

The Archduchess stiffened instantly. "I thought we had agreed not to bring up that subject again, Hansel," she said in a reserved tone of voice.

"Then you really don't see my point at all?"

"No, I really don't see your point at all. I want you to emulate the men in the class from which you have come in every way. They have all excelled in manly sports. They have all been good shots and great soldiers."

"Don't you think the Junkers have any faults at all, grandmother? I believe it's generally conceded that most individuals and most groups have the weakness correlative to their strength, and the vices correlative to their virtues."

"You sound as if you were talking out of a textbook, my dear boy.

I am afraid that Harvard is becoming extremely modernistic in its manner of teaching. No—I have never discovered weakness among the Junkers, Hansel. They are a race of mighty warriors."

"They lost the World War. There must have been a flaw in the system somewhere. You know, grandmother, I always thought it was strange. . . . The Prussian officers were a gorgeous *looking* lot of men when I was a kid. . . . I have never forgotten their bright helmets and their long sabres and their flowing cloaks. The first time I went to France I thought the soldiers there were a slouchy, slovenly lot in comparison. But it was the French who had the more shining spirit, after all, wasn't it?"

"Hansel! I beg of you never to speak in this disloyal manner again! Remember that your father and his brothers, who died gloriously for their country, were all Prussian officers!"

The boy pressed his lips together, and put the car into quicker motion. As he did so, he became aware of a magnificent stag, its great antlers towering above its superb head, standing motionless at the edge of the woods. Instantly he slowed down again, and looked intently at the stag. The Archduchess could see that his mouth, rigid as he tried to keep it, was quivering, that there were actually tears on his lashes. But he said nothing, and, after a moment or two, he went on again. As they neared the next village he spoke quietly and conversationally.

"I think we could get some beer or tea here, grandmother, if you'd care for it. There seems to be a little inn facing the *Haff*. Perhaps it would refresh you to get out."

"I should enjoy it very much," she answered formally.

They sat down at a small tin table, one of several placed in the open before the *Gasthaus*. It was very pleasant and peaceful. There were small sailing vessels in the harbour, and the sun, shining over the water, gave a soft reflection. It was not until Hansel happened to notice a plume of smoke rising from an adjacent promontory that anything happened to mar the restored harmony of their relations.

"Do you see that smudge over there, grandmother? What do you suppose it is?"

"I imagine that someone is smoking fish. It's done in this locality by putting flounder in a pit with fire underneath it, and covering the hole with heavy canvas. Of course it all has to be watched very carefully."

"I'd like to look at it, wouldn't you? Let's walk over there. Shall we? That is, if you've finished."

The Archduchess rose reluctantly. It was one thing to take a walk over beautiful, clean, sweeping dunes, quite another to pick one's way across rough, dirty ground, strewn with a variety of rubbish and offal. But she did not like to refuse. She went warily beside

67

Hansel to the place where the mound of blackened canvas covered the earth.

A wretched old woman was bending over the mound. She was dressed in voluminous garments, dingy and dilapidated, the remnants of a black knitted shawl knotted closely around her head. Her chapped hands and weather-beaten face were reddened by the wind, her eyes bleary with smoke. She hardly seemed to notice the approach of the strangers. She was too intent upon the painful task with which she was occupied.

Hansel touched her on the arm. "Would you let me look at your fish?" he asked courteously. "I've never seen them drying, like this?"

The old woman nodded apathetically. Then, giving a vigorous tug, she lifted a corner of the canvas. Hansel bent over to help her, but drew back abruptly, blinded by the smoke. It was some moments before his smarting eyes grew accustomed to the vapours and he was able to discern the lines of flounders suspended in neat rows over the fire underneath. He had hardly been able to take a good look at them when a gust of wind, scooping under the lines, caused the flames to soar dangerously. The next instant the canvas was on fire.

He sprang up and helped the old woman to stamp it out. It was hard work, and for a few breathless moments he feared that his curiosity, which had endangered the entire contents of the pit, might actually have destroyed it. But the old woman did not seem to share his concern. She expressed neither alarm nor reproach, and, when the fire had finally been put out, she apologized for the trouble she had caused him. He left her staring stolidly after his retreating figure, clutching, with fumbling fingers, at the coins which he had slipped into her hand.

"How long does it take to dry a batch of fish like that?" Hansel asked his grandmother when they were in the car again.

"I don't know exactly. Four or five hours, I believe."

"And that poor old creature, or some other woman like her, has to stoop over the mound all the time to watch it, with the smoke in her eyes and the wind blowing all around her!"

"Of course. The fish represents her livelihood next winter. She's thankful to have the chance to watch it. It was quite unnecessary for you to give her money. . . . I do not wonder that your mother declines to let you control your own patrimony, considering how you throw coins around."

"Well, I don't throw around many on cards or races."

"I shouldn't mind in the least if you did. That would be quite in keeping——"

"With the traditions of my class? But I musn't give a wretched old woman a mark or two to make up for the worry and trouble I've caused her?"

The Archduchess had never heard Hansel speak sarcastically before. The tone of her own voice rebuked him.

"You are not going to make an issue out of this episode, are you, Hansel, as you did with Gertraud's water-pails?"

"Oh, no. I am not going to make an issue out of anything. And as far as Gertraud herself is concerned, I shan't try to carry her water-pails through the village again, if that's any comfort to you."

"It's a great comfort to me. If only you will not do something else equally absurd."

"Don't worry, grandmother. As far as the peasants in the village are concerned, I think I am fast learning to follow in the footsteps of my forefathers."

His smile, usually so pleasant and open, had been ironical and enigmatic as he spoke. This, and the bitterness with which he had made the last remark, still troubled the Archduchess when she thought of them. But this was very seldom nowadays. She was far too preoccupied with her husband's condition to waste worry on a few wretched villagers; and she was too much moved by Hansel's constant kindness to his grandfather to harbour resentment for his occasional failure to conform to caste in either thought or deed.

It was evident that the end could not be distant now, that the General's days, vacant of coherent thought or natural motion, could not be much further prolonged. At last she brought herself to speak of this one night to Hansel as they left the sick man in the deep, drugged sleep which represented the one surcease from his mental and physical wretchedness, and went from his bedchamber into her own.

"We must begin to think of the funeral, Hansel. It is terrible to do so beforehand, but we must."

"Yes, of course. That is, I do not know much about funerals, but I suppose we must. Tell me how I can help you the most, grandmother. I want to help in every way I can, but I am not sure what I ought to do."

"If you knew of any way in which I could get hold of some money, that would be very helpful to me, Hansel. Funerals cost a great deal of money—especially State funerals, such as we must provide for your grandfather. At the moment I have no idea where I could raise any—— Everything I have is sold or pledged already. Except my jewels. I still have those. If I could find a purchaser——"

"You'd sell your Austrian Imperial jewels?"

"But, my dear boy, the von Hohenlohe jewels were all sold long ago. It is only the Austrian jewels that I have left. And those would have gone too, of course, if I could have found anyone in Germany rich enough to buy them."

She sat down at her dressing-table and unlocked a deep drawer.

69

There was a small safe inside, which she drew out and set down among her toilet articles. Then, one by one, she opened its compartments and lifted out their contents: a coronet, two tiaras, necklaces, earrings, bracelets, brooches and rings. There were great pear-shaped pearls among them, emeralds that flashed green fire, rubies that shone like newly spilled blood, diamonds that sparkled with a glacial glitter. For a few moments she fingered them thoughtfully, as if recalling all the vanished glory for which they stood. Then she pushed them back into place and closed the safe again, her blue-veined fingers trembling as she did so.

"Grandmother, I have a little money. Mother did let me cut into my capital for travel funds, and I'm still well supplied. If a thousand dollars would help at all——"

"A thousand dollars! I must have at least ten times that, immediately, and more very soon. There is not only the funeral to consider. There are other obligations which I must meet. If I do not, I may lose my husband and the only home I have left at the same time! Besides, if you gave me all you have, what would you do then yourself?"

"I don't need much, for the moment. We can go into that later on. I really spend awfully little, and mother would send me more for an emergency if I cabled. Besides, my return passage is paid already."

"Your return passage! Yes, of course. . . . In a few weeks now you will be going back to America. And then I shall be entirely alone!"

"Your Serene Highness, I regret to disturb you. But I feel that you and the Herr Baron should return to the General's room at once. I have sent Fritz for the doctor. A sudden change seems to have taken place. . . ."

The *Schwester* in charge of the case, usually a placid person, had spoken urgently. The Archduchess rose and with Hansel followed her back to the sickroom and sat down beside the General's great carved bed, shadowed with heavy draperies. His face had become livid, his breathing stertorous. Occasionally he choked and seemed to struggle. Then the paroxysm passed, only to renew itself again with increased violence. Victoria Luise turned to the *Schwester* with a cry of anguish.

"This is too terrible! It mustn't go on! Surely there is some way to prevent it!"

"The Herr General is unconscious, your Serene Highness. This is far more dreadful for you than it is for him. Nevertheless, when the doctor arrives, he may think it wise to administer further opiates, to ensure complete hypnosis."

"I cannot believe that he feels nothing. Every time he gasps it seems as if he were calling for succour! And still we are giving him none!"

70

"Grandmother, you must believe what the *Schwester* says. I am sure that it cannot be as bad as it seems. You are right, that would be too terrible."

He put one arm around his grandmother, and with his free hand touched the fingers that lay inert on the counterpane. Hans Christian had never seen death, or its approach, before; as its dread presence came closer and closer, he found that it was in the feeling of those strange fingers that it revealed itself first. All warmth went from them, and all colour; they lay like wax in his grasp. As he lifted his fascinated eyes from them to his grandfather's face, he saw that this, too, had slowly changed; the lividness had gone, a beautiful translucency had taken its place. The gasping had ceased too. Breath came more and more gently now, like a series of soft sighs. Then it seemed to cease altogether.

"Hans! My dear husband! Don't go—don't leave me! You can't —you mustn't! I have no one else in the world!"

Almost as if he had heard his wife, the General drew a deeper breath, and the soft sighs began again. But each one came more faintly than the one before it. At last there was one which seemed to have no end, even as it had no beginning. The *Schwester* met Hansel's questioning gaze and bent her head.

"Grandmother, grandmother dear, it's all over. He isn't suffering now; he never will any more. You can find some joy in that, can't you?"

Hans Christian knew that she would want to be alone with her dead in those last moments before strangers came into the house and laid their alien hands on the lifeless body to prepare it for burial. The time was so short before the acts which, inevitable though they were, must seem to her like a sacrilege, should be performed, that he had no right to intrude upon it. The only kindness he could show her, the only consolation he could give her, would be in safeguarding her solitude.

He walked out into the garden, to find it steeped in stillness. The very skies were sombre, for there were no stars in the heavens; and when he had sat beneath them for an hour or so he found he could no longer bear the sadness that seemed to sink from them. He rose and went up the dim stairway to his own room.

Unconsciously he paused on the threshold, half dreading, half hoping to see Trüdchen standing there waiting for him. He knew then that as he had mounted the stairs he had unconsciously listened, wondering if he would hear her sobbing with grief because she knew that he was sad. But for once she was absent. The same stillness which had engulfed the garden enveloped the house. There was not a step, there was not a sound anywhere. He did not have even Trüdchen with him at this zero hour.

He switched on the light and hesitated as he crossed the room. Then he sat down at his desk, opened the ink-well, and drew his pen and paper towards him. When once he had begun to write, he did not stop.

"My dear Mr. Fuller,

"You told me, before we left the boat, that if circumstances should ever change, so that my grandmother might consider parting with her jewels, you hoped I would let you know.

"Conditions are now such that she would like to do so. If you and Mrs. Fuller would care to come to Schönplatz, my grandmother and I would be glad to have you. If this would not be convenient for you, and you are still interested, I will meet you in Berlin, or in any other place you care to designate.

"Very sincerely yours,
"Hans Christian Marlowe von Hohenlohe."

He read the letter through, placed it in an envelope, and addressed it. Then he reached for another piece of paper.

"Dear Mother,

"It is very hard for me to write you as I am about to, but I do not see any way to help it, and I hope you will understand.

"My grandfather has just died, tonight. He has been sick for a long time, and it has all been hideous to my grandmother. Now she is entirely alone, except for me.

"I know our agreement was, that if you would let me come to Germany, I should stay only for the summer, and then return to college. But I hope you will release me from this promise, because I firmly believe I ought to stay here.

"I feel this way, not only because my grandfather has died, though, if he had not, I would have come back, at least for the present. But I feel this way for other reasons too, which seem to me important, and which I will try to explain to you some day, if you are interested.

"Of course, Schönplatz belongs to me now, and a great many responsibilities go with the ownership. I shall try to meet these as well as I can, though some have risen that I did not foresee. For one thing, I find that there is almost no money to keep up the place with, and if you would let me have my own, after all, before I am twenty-one, I should be very grateful to you.

"Please believe that I am not wilfully disobedient or unreliable or grasping, and that it makes me very unhappy to think that perhaps it will seem to you that I am. But whatever you think, I know that I have to stay.

"Always your loving son,
"Hansel."

PART III

"THE HEDGE OF THE COUNT"
1924

CHAPTER IX

THE baroque splendour of his hotel at The Hague had a depressing effect upon the American Minister to the Netherlands. From the moment that he entered it, and hastened past the head porter's lair, his discomfort increased apace. He did not like the large lounge, where stolid people sat perpetually around little tables in big chairs, consuming unlimited quantities of liquid refreshment. He did not like the circular dining-room, with its rococo white-and-gold carvings, its glacial mirrors and stiff draperies. He did not like the formal bedrooms, with their inadequate wardrobes and their inevitable centre tables, their curtains controlled by complicated pulleys. But when he complained about any or all of it, his wife laughed good-naturedly and told him what he really meant was that he didn't like hotels on general principles, that he found just as much fault with them at home as in Holland; he wanted to get her out into one of those great gloomy houses with damp dripping grounds in the Zorgvliet, where it would take her hours to get into the centre of things and where she would be compelled to have a dozen Dutch servants, who couldn't understand her and whom she couldn't understand, to keep the place running. She had kept house for nearly twenty years, and she had tried hard never to shirk. But now she really thought the time had come. . . .

"What you mean is, Trixie thinks the time has come," the Minister answered, laughing good-naturedly. "Well, maybe it has. A hotel's all right when you're travelling, and I don't know but what this is as good as any. I guess I've got to admit it's better than most. But just the same, now that we know we're going to be staying here at The Hague for the next few years, I do think it would be kind of nice to get settled more permanently. If you don't like the Zorgvliet, there are some handsome houses here on the Lange Voorhout, right in the heart of the city."

"They're big, and they look substantial, same as the people do, if that's what you mean. But when you get into the centre of the town, naturally there isn't much garden space. I don't know how good the heating system is in those houses either. I wouldn't call this country hot exactly, even in summertime, and I think we'd better take a look around come December, before we sign any leases on the dotted line. Just look around for a while, Rufus, if you can. It isn't like you to be in such a hurry."

The Minister insisted that he was henpecked, and said that soon he wouldn't be able to call his soul his own; but there was a twinkle in his eye when he did so, and he patted his wife affectionately on the shoulder. If his days had been otherwise more strenuous and stimulating, he might have settled down with better grace to the inertia of hotel life; but after fifty years of uninterrupted activity he was feeling time hanging rather heavily on his hands. The capital city, this "Hedge of the Count," was unstimulating to him. The court left him cold. His other official contacts were equally disappointing. He would have enjoyed getting out into the country, to see the fine herds and fertile farms, but he assumed that he should stick closely to the capital, though he did not seem to be of much use there. The Legation staff was experienced and competent; there was nothing he could do himself at the Chancery which the members of his staff could not do as well, or better, without him. They were extremely polite to him; but he was aware that their courtesy was tinged with condescension. He was the only self-made man among them and the only political appointee; the others were "career diplomats." The Second Secretary, Winthrop Ayer, especially, was a thorn in the Minister's flesh; the more so because, without even the semblance of a struggle, this apparently unsusceptible snob had "taken a tumble" for the Minister's daughter, and Mr. Rhodes did not feel at all sure what the outcome of the infatuation would be.

He had never found Trixie bewildering before. But ever since her arrival in Holland she had baffled him. Not because she preferred the publicity of a hotel to the seclusion of a suburban villa. Not because she scattered a good deal of money around. Not because she would not conform to the prim pattern of The Hague. But because, with dogged determination, she was systematically sightseeing and studying during the intervals between her escapades. She was going, apparently without enjoyment but with unswerving fidelity, to monuments and museums, and her lack of enthusiasm for these expeditions did not deter her from continuing to pursue them. She was taking lessons in French and German from the only hungry-looking man the Minister had seen in Holland, and practising for an hour every day on a hired piano, her progress supervised by a corpulent old lady who came rolling into the state suite at the hotel twice a week. Eventually she also suggested that she would like to take a course in Fine Arts at the University. It was at this point that her astonished parent betrayed his increasing amazement.

"A Fine Arts course at the University!" he exclaimed. "Why, Trixie, what's come over you? It was all I could do, at home, to get you to finish high school! And now you want to learn every language in Europe all at once, and hammer away at piano pieces that haven't any tune to them, and pace through picture galleries for hours on end. I can't make head nor tail of it."

"You ought to have made me study harder when I was a little girl. You ought to have told me how important it is to be well educated."

As she spoke, Trixie selected a bonbon from the ornate basket of chocolates, which, together with an even larger basket filled with showy flowers, occupied a place of honour on the centre table in the drawing-room of the state suite. Winthrop Ayer kept her well supplied with offerings of this sort and she seemed appreciative of them without being cheered by them. Her face was earnest, even slightly troubled, while she munched away at one piece of candy after another. Her father's mood was rapidly becoming more serious still.

"I ought—— Listen, Trixie, I couldn't have made you study hard when you were a little girl, not if I'd stood over you with a club. I couldn't have made you listen while I talked to you about being well educated, not if I'd tied you to a chair while I did it. You know you could have gone to the University of Kansas if you'd wanted to. You know your mother and I would both have been tickled to death to have you."

"I didn't want to. I'm not sorry now I didn't go either. But I wish you'd sent me to Farmington or Foxcroft or some other school in the East, or maybe to Lausanne, when I was small, and later on to the Sacré Cœur in Paris, so that my French would have been good. If I'd gone to college at all I wish I'd started in at Vassar. That's where those twins I met on the boat went. But I think hordes of girls are depressing, especially as they're all so awfully jolly in a systematic sort of way, as if they were trying to make up for not having any men around. So I think instead of going to college I'd rather have gone around the world."

Her father stared at her speechlessly.

"Of course it isn't too late for that even now," she went on. "In fact, I think you ought to make a point of getting to Java while you're Minister to the Netherlands. Someone was saying at the Waroong Djava just yesterday—the new Swedish Attaché I think it was—that no one could completely understand the Dutch people without seeing the East Indies. I'm sure you'd agree with him, Daddy, if you would just go out to the Waroong Djava yourself instead of hanging around that stupid old Haagsche Club all the time. The Javanese waiters wear the cutest things on their heads you ever saw—pieces of batik wound into turbans and finished off with knots that look like rabbits' ears. And the Reistaafel is simply marvellous. I could sit for hours mixing peanuts and coconut and chutney and chopped egg and curry into mounds of rice

75

and chicken. And just think how much better it would taste in Batavia than in Scheveningen! Do let's go there, Daddy! Afterwards we could come back by way of Hawaii. It would be simply grand."

"You don't think we ought to take in the Straits of Magellan and Rio de Janeiro before we come back to The Hague by any chance, do you, Trixie?"

"No, because we'd be specializing in Insulinde on this trip. But I do think we ought to get to South America some time. It's the coming continent."

Decidedly, Winthrop Ayer must have been putting ideas into Trixie's head. The Minister felt sure she had never heard of Farmington or the Sacré Cœur—as indeed he never had himself— before arriving in Holland, much less of international points of view and coming continents. Winthrop Ayer was exactly the sort of person who might be expected to over-emphasize the importance of these, since he had grown up in a rarefied atmosphere where they were freely discussed. But when Mr. Rhodes tried to sound out his daughter, he could find no indication that she took Winthrop Ayer's stilted opinions too greatly to heart. She devoured his Krul chocolates and wore his Van Houweningen flowers and accepted his invitations to drink cocktails and eat seafood with him at the Haack Restaurant; but she seemed impervious to his attempts to precipitate a more intimate footing. Since her emotional indifference to him was apparently so complete, her father could not believe that she would be unduly moved by him as a cultural mentor.

Even though Mr. Rhodes's deductions were not wholly correct, they served to soothe him. But as other suitors began to clutter the scene, the distracted Minister sought elsewhere for a plausible explanation of Trixie's extraordinary behaviour. For a time he thought he had found it. Richard Eustis arrived in The Hague, accompanied by his mother. She was a charming woman, and her son had inherited many of her attractive qualities. They had visited Holland several times already, and had numerous friends there; so they were not in need of the tourist information perfunctorily handed out at the Legation, nor were they bent upon closer contacts with a quaint country and its cleanly people, like the serious students who occasionally upset the Chancery's well-ordered routine with their importunities. In fact, the Chancery, which suffered from chronic fear that this might happen, made a rather unfortunate mistake as far as Richard Eustis was concerned, upon the occasion of his first call.

He presented his card to the Dutch doorman, with the casual remark that he had come to pay his respects to the Minister, and, walking into the outer office, seated himself in a large leather chair, lighted a cigarette, and picked up a dogeared copy of the *Foreign Service Journal*. The outer office was otherwise empty, and for half an hour no one else entered it. At length, however, a native clerk appeared with Richard's card in his hand, and inquired at which hotel he was staying.

"I'm not at a hotel. I'm with friends on the Violenweg," Richard replied, lighting his fourth cigarette and shifting to a Sunday supplement of the *New York Times*, three weeks old.

Another half-hour passed tranquilly by. At the end of that time, Winthrop Ayer opened the door of the outer office and looked Richard over with extreme coolness.

"Well?" he said, when he had completed his inspection.

"Well, what?" inquired Richard.

Winthrop Ayer had been unprepared for such a retort. He was extremely pained by it.

"Just what did you want?" he asked freezingly.

"I didn't want anything. I just came to pay my respects to the Minister. I told the doorman that in the beginning."

"The Minister is extremely busy. And I'm afraid I couldn't interrupt him at present."

"I'm not in any particular hurry. I've waited here an hour already. As long as I get some lunch, sooner or later, I don't especially mind how long I wait."

"The Minister will not be at leisure to receive you at any time this morning, Mr.—er—Mr. Eustis. He has a great many official appointments. They're crowded unusually close together, because he's on the point of leaving town to attend the dedication of a monument to the Founders of the van Rensellaer family, in North Holland. This is an occasion of great international significance, and naturally——"

"Perhaps you think I better come back after lunch?"

For the second time, Winthrop Ayer appeared to study Richard's card before he replied. He finally said with great detachment, "I don't think I should encourage you to do that either, Mr.—er—Mr. Eustis."

"Perhaps you think I better not come back at all?"

"Well, of course, if there is something very urgent, you might tell me what it is. Unless the trouble is financial. I must advise you that there are no provisions which enable us to assist stranded tourists. But——"

"No, the trouble isn't financial. In fact, there isn't any trouble at all. As I've said twice before, I just came in to pay my respects. If not now, whenever it would be convenient for the Minister to see me. But it doesn't matter in the least. I'm immensely intrigued to hear that he's so busy. I'm sure the Secretary of State will be too. He rather had the idea things were quiet here just now—stagnating, in fact. But apparently business is booming. Uncle Gilbert will be simply delighted. He——"

"Winthrop, maybe this is one time when I could manage things a little better than you can. I know that doesn't happen often, but suppose I take a try."

Both young men had been too preoccupied and too angry to observe that the door of the outer office had opened and shut again, and that Rufus Rhodes was standing behind them. For once, this gentle and genial man was angry also. He took Richard's card out of Winthrop Ayer's hand with scant ceremony and glanced quickly at the superscription.

"I'm very sorry you've been kept waiting so long, Mr. Eustis," he said as formally as if he were addressing a contemporary. "Especially as I've been doing crossword puzzles all the morning, hoping and praying that someone would come in to break the monotony. There was one word I couldn't get, and it rode me, so that at last I decided to give up and go home. You can't think of a four-letter epithet common among the Egyptians and ever since used to express contempt, can you? Well, neither can I, but never mind.—I was just passing along the hall, when I happened to overhear your conversation with my secretary. It was the first I knew of your being here. Unaccountably your card seems to have been delayed, somewhere between the front door and my own quarters. I apologize. A really good executive always has efficient subordinates. I'm on my way out now, but I'd be delighted if you'd come along with me. I know my wife and daughter would be pleased, too, if you'd drop in on them. How long are you planning to be with us, here at The Hague?"

They went down the Chancery steps together, leaving Winthrop looking after them with venom in his eye. Within an hour Mrs. Eustis and the friends she was visiting had been persuaded to join the Rhodeses and her son informally at luncheon. It soon transpired that the Eustises' sole purpose in coming had been to renew a pleasant shipboard acquaintance, and if agreeable to the Rhodes family to further it. With no signs of haste or impatience, they settled down at The Hague in pursuit of this purpose.

Mr. Rhodes did not need his wife's assurance, though this was swift in coming, that she was pleased and flattered by the turn things had taken. Indeed, he was inclined to be pleased and flattered himself. Mrs. Eustis was the most charming woman he had ever met, and her son was not without attractive qualities. It was with increasing bewilderment, therefore, that the Minister found his daughter disposed to give short shrift to Richard Eustis. Instead of placing the flowers and confectionery he sent her on the centre table, as she did those from Winthrop Ayer, she tossed them into the scrap basket; he himself rescued a large box of Haagsche Hopjes, the famous coffee candy of The Hague, under the impression that it had been thrown away by mistake, only to find that Trixie had disposed of it on purpose; so he refrained from rescuing dahlias and gladioli from a similar fate. He refrained also from comment when she declined to go swimming with Richard Eustis at Scheveningen, on the ground that the water was too cold, though she had disported herself in it nearly every day all summer, or dancing with him at the House of Lords, on the ground that it was too crowded, though she had been consistently helping to swell that crowd for some months herself. But when she flatly refused to spend the week-end at a beautiful estate near Doorn, which belonged to friends of the Eustises who had kindly included the Rhodeses in their comprehensive invitation for a visit, he ventured to give tongue to his astonishment, though he tried to do so tactfully.

"I think you'd enjoy those people, Trixie. I hear they have one of the finest places in the Netherlands, that they've fixed it up to look like one they had in Java, spacious and green and open and all that. It seems that lots of the estates around Doorn are owned by families who have spent a good deal of time in the East Indies, and brought back a considerable feeling for the exotic, as your friend Winthrop Ayer would say. They run their lives and plant their grounds to give 'an impression of leisure and luxuriance.' It ought to be very pleasant, staying with them. Besides, you might get some pointers on that world trip you want to take."

"I'd like to go to Doorn all right. But I'd rather go some time when Richard Eustis isn't around."

"Well now, if it hadn't been for the Eustises you wouldn't have been invited there at all."

"Not yet. But maybe later on I will. I'll take a chance on it, anyway."

There was no doubt about it, Trixie was patiently and persistently building towards some goal which she not only hoped but expected to achieve. Her father wished she would tell him what it was. But though their relations had always been cordial, they had never been close. He could not force her confidence beyond a certain point. However, he felt impelled to ask one rather leading question.

"You don't seem to care much for Richard Eustis. Have you got anything special against him?"

"Yes. He's fresh."

The Minister was completely taken aback by this rejoinder, not only by the immediacy and candour of the announcement, but by its unexpected implications. He had never unloaded prudish advice upon his daughter, or asked her prying questions; but though he shrank slightly from admitting it, even to himself, he would not have supposed that she would take what her mother called "liberties" too seriously. He knew that the "crowd" with which she had grown up took a certain amount of "petting" for granted; and Trixie's type almost automatically provoked it, in any time and place. Any young man would be likely to find his arm stealing around her waist or his hand straying over her shoulder before he was aware of it. That was to be expected. The unexpected lay in the disclosure that Trixie so deeply resented the idea of any such overture.

"Well, Trixie . . . of course I don't know how you young people run things nowadays. But in my time when a young fellow wanted to marry a girl, she didn't think he was being fresh, as you call it, if he sort of showed her how he felt."

"What did she think if he showed her how he felt, as *you* call it, first, and then asked her to marry him three or four months later, after he found out that she wasn't such an easy necker as he supposed? I don't know what she thought, but I think it's disgusting."

"Now, Trixie, I believe you're a little hard on Richard Eustis, I really do. I believe he's very fond of you and that he'd make you a good husband. I believe——"

"Daddy, I don't want to marry Richard Eustis or anyone else who just cares about—well, you know. I want him to think I'm wonderful, *every way*, just as I think he's wonderful every way. I mean, the way I would, if I . . . if there were anybody . . . so I've got to learn things, don't you see, just in case . . . because the way I am now no one would love me, really and truly, no one that mattered."

She leapt up, and left the room hurriedly, slamming the door after her. The Minister was not sure, but he thought her voice had trembled a little as she spoke. So she was troubled, seriously troubled, and she was taking Winthrop Ayer in earnest after all, because she thought he could help point the way to paths which she desired to tread. The Minister, who would gladly have given his right hand to supply his only daughter with every possible "advantage" himself, felt humbled and disheartened at the idea that he had failed her. Even the knowledge that he had done so inadvertently did not comfort him much. He had never heard the phrase *Ad astra per aspera;* but if he had he would still have said that if Trixie were going star-snatching, he would like to smooth her ascent to the heavens.

During the next few days he pondered the situation in solemn silence, and rather reluctantly he told his wife he thought they had better decline the invitation to Doorn. Shortly afterwards the Eustises took their departure from the Netherlands. Mr. Rhodes had the impression they were puzzled also, that mother and son alike had assumed that the eventual success of Richard's suit was practically assured before they had come to The Hague at all, that only details regarding it remained to be settled. His resentment at finding that Trixie had unconcernedly led two families into a blind alley, and with the same unconcern left them there, was assuaged only by the discovery that his daughter had been greatly influenced by Mrs. Eustis, even though she declined to accept her as a mother-in-law. It was due to Mrs. Eustis, in no small measure, that Trixie's sight-seeing ceased to be stereotyped. She began to find beauty beyond the museums and monuments which had imprisoned her at first. It was with Mrs. Eustis, for instance, that she first went to the butter market in Middleburg, bringing home the costume that started a collection of these, and a great deal of correlative study into the subject. It was also with Mrs. Eustis that she first went out to see the fishing fleet starting off for Iceland, its sails as red as the sunset into which it was steering. And a week or so later, she asked her father enthusiastically if he would not enjoy seeing it too.

"It's wonderful, Daddy, up there on the coast, with the coloured nets and the silvery-looking catch spread out to dry, and the fishermen's families all standing around waiting to see them go out on Sunday nights, or clumping along as fast as their wooden shoes will take them to welcome the fleet back the next Saturday. There are nearly a thousand boats, all with their own numbers painted on them and all so perky. I like boats to be perky, don't you?"

"Well, Trixie, that's another of those things I hadn't thought much about before I came to Holland. But now that you speak of it, I guess I do. They need to be perky, nosing their way up into the North, like they have to. It's cold and rough up there. And the men on them have to be pretty plucky. They lead a hard life."

"They get what they go out after," Trixie remarked cryptically. She meant more than she said very often nowadays, her father reflected, and her voice had taken on a different tone, no matter in what language she was speaking. She also appeared to enter and leave a room in a manner more studied and less spontaneous, and the arts of dress and dining had taken on a new meaning for her. Most of these metamorphoses could be laid, directly or indirectly, to Mrs. Eustis's door. The most welcome form of all which Trixie's appreciation of this lady's example and precepts took, however, lay in her change of attitude about a residence. Mr. Rhodes gathered it was largely due to Mrs. Eustis that his daughter gleaned the fact that no hotel, however smart, could indefinitely serve as a suitable setting for a dignified diplomat of assured standing. Once convinced of this, she began house-hunting with zeal, dragging her still hesitant mother along with her, and finally announced that she had found exactly what they needed: a tall house on the Javastraat, with the dining-room and service quarters on the ground floor, double drawing-rooms and a library above them, and the bedrooms higher still. Her mother was afraid the servants would "mind the stairs" and could not understand the blank looks with which the first applicants for positions turned upon her, when she asked them, through an interpreter, if they objected to this feature. Trixie's father teased her, telling her that it was only the name of the street which had decided her. But, as a matter of fact, he and his wife were supremely satisfied with the comfort of the commodious quarters in which they were presently installed.

The winter began pleasantly. Contrary to Mrs. Rhodes's expectations, the Dutch servants proved uncomplaining and the heating system adequate. They were all very comfortable in the big house on the Javastraat, and the social contacts which had been unsatisfying at first were more agreeable now that they were less strange. The Rhodeses called meticulously on all their fellow-guests, within twenty-four hours of each dinner to which they were invited, and they began to entertain themselves, finding a ready response to their hospitality. The Minister's days were not empty any longer. He had begun to establish a sense of fellowship with the Dutch, to find friends in all sorts of unexpected quarters. One of these friends was a retired priest, Father Maartens, who had spent the active years of his life in Wichita, and who now lived, with his two aged sisters, in a small house in the heart of Haarlem. Another was a highly successful business man possessing relatives in Topeka whom he had visited from time to time. Mynheer Kool was entirely self-made; and the monstrosity of concrete and glass which he had built for himself bore no shadow of a resemblance to Father Maartens' cosy and artistic quarters.

Trixie, whose conception of the artistic was undergoing transition, insisted that this house gave her the creeps, especially the staircase made of strawberry and chocolate-coloured marble; the piano lamps shaded with Spanish shawls; and the ruby-tinted dome surmounting the courtyard. But she did not deny that Mynheer Kool and his buxom wife were themselves very likeable, and that the "snowballs" which they served during the evenings devoted to table football at their house were the most glorified sort of doughnut which she had ever tasted. She also had a word of passing praise for the red wine cooked with spices, brought into the fantastic drawing-room in a big kettle, and drunk hot; but since she was even more fully and agreeably occupied than her parents, she did not often go to the Kools with them. She had begun to make her own friends among the Dutch, and had several pink-cheeked young Netherlanders among her followers now. One of these, Kleijyn van Boltzelaer, lived in Doorn, and had a sister Sophia, conveniently near Trixie's age; the girl's confident assertion that she would not long be dependent upon Richard Eustis for opportunities to enjoy the transplanted magnificence of Insulinde was quickly fulfilled. The van Boltzelaer family owned a plantation near Buitenzorg, and Trixie returned to The Hague after her first stay on their Dutch estate prepared to press still further upon her parents the desirability of a trip to Java. Surely they must agree with her that life on a tea plantation would be too romantic for words, that they ought not to miss such a wonderful chance to see what it was like. She had found turbaned Malay servants and copious Reistaafels even more intriguing in a private house than in a restaurant; cold coffee essence, served with hot milk, early in the morning, and steaming tea, sheltered by a padded cosy, late in the afternoon, had proved added attractions to the scheme of life; while initiation into the mysterious rites of Javanese dancing had been most alluring of all.

"So the van Boltzelaers have asked you to visit them on their tea plantation too, have they?" Rufus Rhodes asked his daughter, his shrewd eyes twinkling. "You're sure they included your father and mother in the invitation, are you? And you're sure it was just a visit that was suggested, by the entire family, not a permanent residence, by Kleijyn? When you begin to talk about the romantic aspects of the situation, Trixie, I can't help wondering."

"Don't be silly, Daddy," Trixie said rather sharply. It was so seldom she spoke sharply nowadays that she aroused her father's suspicions. It occurred to him, with an anxious pang, that Kleijyn van Boltzelaer was an even better match, in his way, than Richard Eustis, and that in this case it was unthinkable that Trixie could object to a suitor as "fresh." Kleijyn's love-making would certainly be circumspect and deferential; on the other hand, it might be persistent; and these stubborn Netherlanders had a faculty for getting their way in the end. It was no part of Rufus Rhodes's plan that his only child should be separated from him by half the world, and he did not like the sound of the word "romantic" in connection with the tea plantation. But after a moment or two Trixie began to rattle on about something else. It appeared that she had been invited, with the van Boltzelaers, to lunch at Doorn Haus, by the ex-Kaiser and his second wife, the Princess Hermine, who were on very friendly terms with the neighbouring gentry. Trixie was quite as excited over this actual experience as she was over the remote prospect of Buitenzorg. She described the gardens and drawing-rooms at Doorn Haus minutely, the clambering roses, the guarded moat, the mellow tapestries, the multitudinous *objets d'art*. She thought the Princess Hermine, whom everybody called "Your Majesty," just as if she had been really an Empress and not the wife of an abdicated Emperor, was "just as nice as she could be"; and she thought the Kaiser himself was "too cute for anything."

"He isn't ferocious at all," she said enthusiastically. "He's a friendly, white-haired old gentleman, very spruce and sprightly. When he came out into the hall to meet us his eyes were twinkling and he had a bouquet of sweet peas in each hand—pink for me and lavender for Sophie. He had raised them himself and he seemed pleased as punch about it all. I'm glad mine were the pink ones. I pressed some of them in my diary. Did I tell you, Daddy, that I've begun to keep a diary? Well, anyway, I have. . . . The Emperor talked to Sophie and me both in the nicest way, as if we were grown up, I mean, and important. He was dignified, but he wasn't a bit distant. I felt as if I'd known him all my life, in no time at all. He gave me his picture, autographed, when we came away, and so did the Empress. She sent Mother a tea-cosy too, like the ones the van Boltzelaers use, only bigger and more elaborate. She made it herself, out of puffy yellow silk, covered with white embroidery, and worked an 'H' with a crown on top of it in one corner. If Mother doesn't want to use it, I'd like to put it away in my hope chest. I've decided to have a hope chest. Didn't I tell you that, either?"

"No, Trixie, you certainly didn't. I should think there would be time enough for that when——"

"It's a form of preparedness," Trixie flashed back. Then, changing the subject before he could commence again, she rattled on: "You don't suppose people at home were mistaken, do you, in heaping quite so much war guilt on the Kaiser's head? There was a man visiting at Doorn named Colonel von Mitweld, who thinks the sun simply rises and sets on the old gentleman's head. The van Boltzelaers told me he spent most of his time at Doorn Haus, that he would like to head a Restoration Movement. And what do you suppose? I got to talking with this Colonel, and I found out he was the uncle of a boy I'd met on the boat coming over. He'd told me about the Kaiser too. His mother used to know him when she was a young girl, and he was awfully nice to *her*. She used to go to the Palace a lot, in Berlin, to balls and things, and she remembers how the six young Princes used to look when they came clattering out of the cobbled courtyard on horseback with their little sister beside them——"

"I'm not sure that I quite follow you, Trixie. I don't understand exactly who it is you're talking about now."

"Oh, it doesn't matter! But I hope you and Mother will go to Doorn Haus too some day, Daddy. The Emperor and Empress both said that they'd be very pleased if you would. And we could all stay in the Orangerie—that's what they call the guest-house—and have rooms with oil-paintings hanging over big double wash-stands, and sleep under feather beds made of lace and red satin."

"Is that the latest thing, Trixie, in household decoration?"

"You know it isn't, Daddy. But it looks comfortable, even if it does sound queer, and I like it."

There were more visits to Doorn as the autumn advanced, and in due course Rufus Rhodes shared in the manifold advantages of these without too much concern as to where they might be leading. Kleijyn van Boltzelaer had not been summarily dismissed, like Richard Eustis, nor did Trixie accept him quite as diffidently as she did Winthrop Ayer. But she had many other preoccupations which distracted her. The Fine Arts course had become a reality, and she went on with her music and French. She learned to skate, too, patronizing the Haagsche Isclub with as much zeal and far more enjoyment than she put into her studies. She always returned from the rink with her eyes shining and her cheeks glowing. Her father said to himself that she was getting prettier every day of her life.

He had never been more convinced of this than he was one evening in early December when, contrary to her custom, she came home alone. Her father was sitting by the fire in the big panelled library when she entered it, a glass of hot-spiced wine and a cheese platter on the table beside him, contentedly turning the pages of his latest "find" from Martinus Nijhoff, the bookseller on the Lange Verhoot, whose steady customer he had become. The sense of general well-being that comes from warmth and food and drink pervaded him, and as he glanced up at his daughter he felt this sense deepen and take on tenderness. She had never looked lovelier. A small gray fur cap rested jauntily on her brown hair, and her trimly belted burgundy-coloured coat was buttoned close to her throat under a collar of the same soft fur. She tossed the muff and gloves she was carrying lightly down on the sofa, and crossed the room to kiss him. Her cold cheek, pressed against his own, was as fresh and fragrant as a winter flower, and, warm as her lips were, there was a crystalline quality to her caress. The sparkle of snow seemed to encompass her.

"Why, look who's here!" he said affectionately, laying aside his book and drawing her down to the arm of his chair. "I didn't expect you back for hours yet. I supposed you were skating down the Molenvleit through the meadows to Leyden in the moonlight. "Didn't I hear something to that effect?"

"The rest of the crowd went. At the last moment I decided I wouldn't. I thought there might be some mail here for me."

"You didn't give up a skating party for a letter, did you?"

"Yes. Because I hoped it might be a very special sort of letter."

She rose from the arm of his chair, took off her hat and began to unbutton her coat. Underneath it she was sheathed in close-fitting red silk, cut in a V at the neckline, which accentuated the curves of her young figure and the whiteness of her throat. Re-

85

leased from her wrappings, she nestled down beside him again.

"Daddy, do you mind if I talk to you confidentially?"

"Trixie, my . . . my dear little daughter. . . ."

"I hoped you wouldn't. Because, you see, I'm in love. I have been ever since last summer. I've wanted to tell you about it, only I haven't dared. But tonight, sort of, I feel as if I could."

Rufus Rhodes cleared his throat. "Who is this boy you're in love with, Trixie?" he inquired, striving to speak casually. "Anyone I know?"

"Well, not exactly. I've talked to you about him sometimes— without ever saying I was in love with him, I mean. But you never seemed to be much interested or take much notice. Mother knows him, though. She likes him too. No one could help liking him."

For several months now Trixie had been referring to Mrs. Rhodes as Mother instead of Mumma, and until now the Minister had never failed to twit her about it. At the moment, however, he did not even notice.

"You don't mean someone else you met on the boat? There seems to be no end of the people you met on that boat! We've already had that Carruthers woman, who had even Winthrop Ayer frozen with fear when she turned up, and the banker's wife, who looked as if she'd just helped herself to Cartier's window dressing, not to mention the looks of the banker! You're not talking about that German boy—are you? Hans von Hohenlohe, if that's his name?"

"Yes, Daddy. Only I don't ever think of him as Hans von Hohenlohe. I think of him as Christian Marlowe."

"Wasn't his father a German? Hasn't he gone back to Germany to stay? Doesn't he live there now?"

"Yes, Daddy. And I know you don't like Germans much. That's why I've dreaded to tell you. But his mother's an American. She's a Senator. That makes her very American, doesn't it? It was she who used to know the Kaiser when she was a young girl. Don't you remember I told you, the first time I came back from Doorn, that there was someone? Well, anyway, you're bound to like her, and I'm sure you'll like Chris too, just as Mother does, just as everyone does."

"You're sure I'll like him! How am I going to know whether I like him or not without meeting him?"

"Well, you see, Daddy, I hope you're going to meet him. If he should happen to come to Holland, for instance, at Christmas-time, of course you would be likely to meet him. Because——"

"If he should happen to come to Holland at Christmas-time! But why should he? It's a time most people spend with their own families. And Prussia's a long way from The Hague!"

"Yes, I know. But I wrote and asked him if he and his grandmother wouldn't come and spend Christmas with us. I thought it would be terribly lonely for them on that big place in East Prussia. You know his grandfather has died, and I think Christmas must be hard to live through, don't you, when there's been a death in the family that same year? You must keep remembering——"

"But look here, Trixie . . . have you told your mother what you've done? Does she know about this?"

"No, but she won't mind. That is, if you don't. And I thought I better tell you about it without waiting any longer, because Chris has had time to answer my letter by now. I expect I'll find one from him waiting for me in my room, saying he's coming."

Her voice, which had been unnaturally shy, suddenly became unnaturally joyous. As she leaned over and kissed him again, Rufus Rhodes felt the full significance both of her shyness and of her joy. So here was the explanation at last of her determination to "improve," of her indifference to Winthrop Ayer and her resentment towards Richard Eustis, and her procrastination regarding Kleijyn van Boltzelaer. She wanted to be worthy of Hans von Hohenlohe, she wanted to find favour in his eyes. Steadily, for months now, she had been labouring towards that end. Secretly she had held that hope to her heart.

Her father did not know what to say to her. He was deeply moved, tremendously touched; but he was troubled too. It was true that he did not like Germans on general principles; though he had never known many of them personally, he had shared the opinion, common in Kansas, that they had been bullies before the War and whiners after it; instinctively he recoiled from the possibility, so suddenly presented to him, of acquiring one for a son-in-law. But his anxiety went deeper than that. A fear for the future, such as he had never known before, seemed to strike suddenly into the depths of his being, with the poignancy of a sharp pain. How could this beloved child of his find happiness and peace amidst the alien corn which seemed so fair and fruitful to her inexperienced eyes? Yet if she had set her heart upon this stranger, who would be able to persuade her that she should give him up? She had the same tenacity of purpose, the same singleness of heart, which had taken her father all the way from a poverty-stricken farm laid desolate by drouth to a luxurious legation in one of the world's proudest and pleasantest cities. . . .

"I'm going upstairs now to get my letter," Trixie said, still joyously.

The confidence with which she spoke only seemed to strengthen her father's misgivings. He watched her silently as she picked up first her muff and gloves, then her hat and coat. She did so slowly, as if she were waiting for him to speak to her. And still he found nothing to say, though he did manage a smiling salute. She left the room, and when she had gone it seemed hushed and dark. The fire had sunk to a faint glow; there was no longer any sound of licking flames and crackling wood, and the dark panelling had absorbed the light as a sponge soaks up water. The Minister picked up the glass at his side, but the wine was stale and tepid; the warmth and aroma had gone from it, and the drink had ceased to be stimulating. He had lost the place where he had been reading, and his book had slipped to the floor. All the comfort, all the cheer of the evening seemed to have vanished. He drifted back to the anxious questions which seemed so unanswerable.

He was still sitting there, half an hour later, when Mrs. Rhodes came bustling into the room. She was already dressed for dinner, with some resplendency. She had found a very good shop called Kuhne's, on the Plaats, that kept French models, and she had bought a number of dresses there. The one which she was wearing now was made of noisy green silk, and it was cut more daringly than any she had ever owned before. She had half feared and half hoped that her husband would make some comment on it. But from the way he looked at her she might have been wearing any old thing, bought back in Rhodesville.

"For mercy's sake, Rufus!" she exclaimed with unaccustomed sharpness. "Aren't you dressed yet? You don't mean to sit there and tell me you've forgotten we're having dinner with the Foreign Minister, do you?"

"I'm sorry, Julia. To tell you the truth, I'm afraid I had. But I'll hurry. I'll be ready in just a minute. Is Trixie going with us?"

"Why, no! You seem to have forgotten everything tonight, Rufus! She's gone skating, down the canal to Leyden, with a group of young people."

It was on the tip of his tongue to say that Trixie had changed her plans for the evening as completely as he had forgotten his. But something silenced him. If Trixie had not told her mother herself that she was in the house, he would not do so either. But, in spite of his haste, he knocked on the door of his daughter's room on his way to his own.

"Come in," she said tonelessly.

Trixie had made her room very charming, with furniture painted in pastel shades, and pale blue silk draperies embroidered with birds and flowers. Genre pictures hung on the tinted walls, and a little gilt clock ticked cheerily on the mantelpiece between the amorous porcelain shepherd that stood on one side of it and the coy porcelain shepherdess that stood on the other. The clock was striking eight as the Minister went in, which should have served as a further warning to him that he was late, but which failed to do so. He knew from the way Trixie spoke that something had

88

happened already to make her unhappy. The shyness had gone from her voice and so had the joy.

She was standing at the window between the pretty blue curtains, looking down at the street. She was not crying. But she did not seem to be seeing anything either.

"Didn't you get your letter, Trixie?" her father asked gently.

"Yes. I got it."

Rufus Rhodes waited, and the strange poignant pain darted through his body again.

"Chris isn't coming."

"Why, Trixie, I'm sorry, I'm very sorry. I know you're disappointed. If there's anything——"

"Of course, I'm disappointed. But I wouldn't have minded that so much if he had wanted to come, and couldn't. His letter's very polite. You can see it, if you like. But I can tell, from the way it's written, that he could have come, and that he didn't want to. There isn't anything you could give me or do for me that can make up for that."

She had managed to speak steadily, and to hold her head high while she spoke. But as she finished what she had to say, her lips quivered and a little gasping sob came through them. The next instant she had hidden her face on her father's broad shoulder, and was crying as if her heart would break.

He found his own voice at last. "There," he said cheerfully, "there. Listen, Trixie—— I've been thinking things over, about that trip to Java you mentioned and I believe you've got a good idea. I believe I'll go down to the steamboat office in the morning and see about tickets. I believe——"

"If you believe taking me to Java or anywhere else will make me forget Chris Marlowe or give him up, you're mistaken!" Trixie announced with startling clarity.

She had raised her face again, and she was already resolutely wiping her eyes with a small crumpled handkerchief as she spoke. Then she gave her father a slight shove.

"If you don't go and get dressed the Foreign Minister will probably skin you, or whatever else they do to delinquent diplomats," she said firmly. "Don't you worry about me either. I don't need to go to Java or anywhere else just now. I'm going to stay right on the spot, like General So-and-So, and fight this out along these lines if it takes all summer."

PART IV

"THE BEAUTIFUL WHITE HORSES"
1926

CHAPTER X

HANS CHRISTIAN sat in the small office at the right of the latticed entrance to the *Gestütsekretäriat*, painstakingly trying to balance the Schönplatz stud books. It was a tedious task, for he had always hated figures. Involuntarily, his eyes kept wandering to the weathervane, in the form of a prancing horse, which surmounted the tower of the granary across the cobbled courtyard and which had always fascinated him. His thoughts wandered much further afield.

He had been at Schönplatz for two years now—two years of unmarked monotony. His mother had not declined to send him his patrimony; indeed she had not so much as bargained with him for its undisputed possession. She had shown herself generous as well as just, though it would have been a simple matter for her to stipulate that the price of his independence must be the completion of his college course. She had not even referred to his failure to keep the promise upon which her consent to his temporary absence had been based; her letters had contained neither recriminations nor reproaches. On the other hand, they had been increasingly impersonal, increasingly aloof. He scanned them in vain for signs of sympathy and terms of tenderness. Instead, she wrote in a way which indicated that her life was crowded and complete without him, and it did not occur to him that she did this defensively, because she was wounded to the quick by his desertion. She did not respond to his repeated suggestions that she should come to Schönplatz during the summer, when the Senate was not in session. The Washington scene, on which she had quickly attained a prominent place, seemed all-absorbing to her. She moved proudly and powerfully from one triumph to another, her beauty undiminished, her security unassailable. Although she was the imagined figure on his horizon, and his grandmother the visible one, she was far the more vivid and vital of the two.

For Victoria Luise was also more and more withdrawn from him, and in her self-imposed isolation, which meant isolation for Hans Christian also, she sat so surrounded with the shadows of the past that at times her own form seemed indistinguishable from these. She had never discarded the heavy crape in which she had emerged from her chamber on the night of the General's death;

apparently it had been in complete readiness to assume at any moment, and to Hans Christian there was something ghoulish in this anticipation of her widow's weeds. She had directed, with a skilful hand, the details of the State funeral, and it had been a superb spectacle, sombre only in its implications; and she had shown herself completely composed during the calls of condolence made upon her by the local gentry. But though she had returned these, she had not encouraged their repetition. She had not even invited her daughter and son-in-law, Rita and Friedrich von Mit-weld, and their children to come back to Schönplatz a second time after the General's death; and she had not left there herself, either to visit them in Bavaria, or to go anywhere else in Germany. The sale of her jewellery had been accomplished without her personal supervision; Hans Christian had spared her the ordeal of an actual meeting with Mr. and Mrs. Fuller. Afterwards the direction of the estate had been turned over to him as the male heir without protest or interference on her part. But if she appreciated the sacrifice which he had made to stand by her, or recognized how trying the unrelieved tedium of the form of existence which she had forced upon him must be to a normal youth, she had never given any sign that this was so.

Hans Christian had not expected effusive expressions of gratitude; but he missed the awaited sign of its existence; and he longed, unutterably, for some stir in the sequence of days which brought him no stimulation, no variety, and no sense of progress. He had moments of feeling that the horse on the weathervane moved in a larger orbit than he did, and with more animation than he did.

Resolutely he turned back to the balance-sheets, and tried to focus his thoughts no less than his gaze upon them. In themselves they were not disheartening. The year before they had shown a deficit which he could ill afford. Not only had his inexperience been against him; there had been a series of "bad breaks" for which he had in nowise been to blame: he had found that much of the stable flooring was rotten, and he had been obliged to replace crumbling wood with fresh planks; an unseasonable storm had destroyed a large part of the crops just as they were ready to harvest; and Otto, the "apple boy," had proven unworthy of his trust, and had failed to make the daily rounds with his wicker basket at foaling time when cleanliness in the stalls was essential to the welfare of the young colts. Hans Christian had not immediately grasped the character of Otto's calling, for he had not un-naturally assumed that an "apple boy" gathered up fruit rather than dung; and later he had had several clashes with the youngster, finding him surly and slovenly as well as negligent. He had been disposed towards mercy, upon discovering that Otto's weekly wage came to less than two marks, and had tried to reform him by reminders of "apple boys" who had risen to the rank of keepers and even to stud masters. But this had been to no avail and Otto had been relegated to the scullery, under threat of still severer discipline and with no chance of advancement. But this was not until his carelessness had been disastrous.

So all in all it had been a bad year. But this year Hans Christian seemed in a fair way to do better. Though many repairs on the buildings were indicated none had been essential; there had been a bumper crop, and he had been able to sell produce beside stocking his own storehouses; and Max, Otto's successor, did his current duty meticulously and appeared to have his eyes fixed upon future advancement which would be well deserved. To be sure, Hans Christian was paying him three marks a week, which was economically unsound, considering the modest dimensions of the total budget for the stud. But, after all, Hans Christian had been told that the beautiful white horses, whose origin merged into so lovely a legend, would never represent solid revenue. That came from the sheep, in whose substantial presence there had never been anything mystic, anything symbolic. The first of the flock had been bought by Kurt von Hohenlohe, who had returned to Schönplatz after the Napoleonic Wars to find ruin and desolation reigning there. In his extremity he had appealed to the *Oberpräsident* of East Prussia for co-operation, only to be brusquely informed that it was not consistent with the honour and station of a nobleman, whatever his straits, to ask or accept help from the State. Stung by this rebuff, Kurt had ridden savagely through the woods, his distracted thoughts revolving. Where could he turn? What could he do? When his mind ceased to operate in circles, he had come to an abrupt decision and taken a desperate step. Walking into the bare cold study of the village pastor, he had demanded the immediate overturn of three hundred *thäler* from the meagre church funds. The bewildered divine, too dumbfounded to refuse, had yanked open the small strong-box, which contained the contributions which his flock had made to his salary and had poured the *thäler* into the Count's outstretched hands without query or complaint. Kurt had stalked out and bought sheep.

From the first they had multiplied and prospered. They took prizes and they made money. Their wool was sought for the manufacture of beaver hats; their lambs were bespoken by breeders everywhere; their flesh furnished unlimited food. Kurt, the incipient bankrupt, had quickly become a man of means and had bequeathed a legacy to his descendants which had continued to expand up to the time of the World War. Indeed, it had survived even that, albeit in a shrunken state. In spite of his revolt against unqualified ancestor worship, Hans Christian felt considerable

92

admiration for Kurt's resourcefulness, though he doubted if this lusty landowner had ever been troubled with scruples as to whether his conduct in holding up his pastor for Church funds had been more in keeping with the "station and honour of a nobleman" than squeezing something from the State coffers would have been. After all, there was nothing in Kurt's record to show that he had ever been a squeamish man. The Great Frederick himself, in promoting him to the rank of General, had remarked, "I am giving you the High Command because you are a rough-and-ready man. The lily-livered creature who cannot show himself coarse upon necessity does not create and keep order among the brigadiers."

The saving grace of coarseness, if such it were, had certainly manifested itself more than once, not only in Kurt von Hohenlohe, but in his antecedents and his progeny as well. True, there had been scholars and scientists and occasionally a conscientious sceptic among them; one had been a disciple of Kant, another had prepared a pamphlet against *Ausgedehntes Gottesdienst und krasses Gesangbuch.** But for the most part they had been men of brawn rather than of brain, buccaneers and breeders rather than students and celibates. Rather surprisingly, they had married wisely and well, on the whole. They were a sensual lot, but they had brought no undowered brides and none with tarnished reputations to Schönplatz; not a few of the girls who had come there had carried culture and consecration to the castle, and had shown themselves pious even in their pleasures. The ancestral portraits, neatly paired, which hung in Hans Christian's room, did not reveal a single female form or face which was lacking in grace and refinement. On the distaff side the family tree was fair as well as fruitful.

Hans Christian sighed as he picked up the balance-sheets which he had laid down again to gaze out of the window at the weather-vane, while considering the subject of the sheep, and all that their acquisition by Kurt implied. He would not have been averse to imitating this ancestor's high-handed methods, if he could have done so, instead of plodding along month after month trying vainly to make both ends meet. But the occasion to show similar resourcefulness never seemed to arise. Perhaps because the World War had not left the same sort of an aftermath as the Napoleonic Wars. Perhaps because there were no more pliant pastors left whose strong boxes could be commandeered. Perhaps because he himself was lacking in those essential qualities which had made Kurt's boldness irresistible. He did not know. It was all a problem, all a puzzle, like everything else.

For times had certainly changed. It was no longer considered inconsistent with the "station and honour of a nobleman" to have help from the State. There was hardly a *Herrenhaus* in East

* Long-drawn-out Church services and vulgar hymn-books.

Prussia, as far as Hans Christian knew, which did not take *Osthilfe* as dole; it had come to be regarded as a Junker prerogative. Some of his neighbours squandered the sums they received at expensive hotels in Berlin during the winter season, or on the balmy Riviera; others, more conscientiously inclined, spent it on the upkeep of estates which without it would have been close to disintegration. The Countess, whose immense property adjoined Schönplatz, spent all her share on her roofs, which covered acres, and which for years had been in a crumbling condition. Chris accepted what he could get, which was little enough considering his needs, along with the others. At first he had done so reluctantly and shamefacedly; but now he had come to take it all as a matter of course, though he tried to avoid thinking about it, aware that searching reflection would result in a smirching sense of degradation. And elsewhere in Germany, he knew, there were murmurings, less and less hushed all the time, against the so-called "corrupt distribution of public funds in East Prussia." At any moment these murmurings—far more bitter and menacing than any he had ever heard in America —might become protests; at any moment an open secret might become an open scandal. To avert this, it was rumoured that there was a plan to take over the large estates which could not be made to pay, and distribute them among small peasant holders, like the parents of Otto and Max. If this plan were put into effect, Schönplatz might be among the first of the great places to suffer dismemberment. There had never been greater need for prompt and efficient action on the part of the landed gentry than now.

"Bitte, Herr Baron, Sie haben Gäste."

Hans Christian roused himself from his troubled reverie, pushed aside the disregarded balance-sheets, and took the card which Fritz extended to him on a crested salver. The superscription was astonishing:

RUFUS RHODES
Envoy Extraordinary and Minister Plenipotentiary
of the United States of America

"Where is his Excellency?" Hans Christian inquired without eagerness. Much as he had longed for diversion, he would not have chosen to have it take this form.

"He is in the Great Hall. He awaits the Herr Baron's convenience. It appears that he is motoring through the countryside, and comes to pay his humble respects."

In spite of himself, Hans Christian smiled. It was evident that Fritz had been extremely ingenious in adapting the envoy's phraseology to conform to the standards which he himself considered suitable in addressing his master.

"Is he alone?" Hans Christian went on to ask.

"No, he has a chauffeur with him, dressed in fine English cloth. And the car is great and glistening. I could not see the interior from the door when I admitted His Excellency to the Great Hall. Therefore I do not know whether there are other *Herrschafften* with him or not."

"There are sure to be," said Hans Christian rather cryptically. "Say to his Excellency that I will come at once. And tell her Serene Highness that we have guests who will certainly be here for tea and possibly for overnight."

He had never considered, analytically, what sort of a person Trixie's father might be. Now, as he crossed the succession of courtyards leading from the stable enclosures to the open park, he tried to do so, without success. He only knew that, if he were asked to hazard a guess, the answer would not be enthusiastic. Therefore he received something of a shock when he entered the Great Hall. From the first glance it was evident that the man who was awaiting him there was the embodiment of kindliness. His beaming eyes, his genial expression, his hearty handclasp, all bespoke sincere and intrinsic goodwill. But there was nothing breezy or boisterous about him. Hans Christian could not conceive him as the hero of a back-slapping campaign or the professional promoter of the homespun. He was solidly but not heavily built, and he carried himself well; his manner had dignity as well as assurance. Moreover, though there was complete friendliness in the glance that he turned on his host, it was a surprisingly shrewd and searching glance, for all that.

"Well, Chris Marlowe!" he exclaimed, with obvious pleasure. "I am sure you'll forgive me if I call you that, instead of Baron von Hohenlohe. It seems to come more naturally. You see, Mrs. Rhodes and Trixie always speak of you as Chris, and I've formed the habit myself. You certainly were kind to them on shipboard. They've never forgotten it. And I appreciate it enormously myself. When I found that I was in your neighbourhood, I couldn't resist the temptation of dropping in to see you, so that I could thank you in person."

"It's tremendously kind of you, Sir. I hope Mrs. Rhodes and Trixie are with you?"

"No—no—I'm all by myself this time. A man feels, once in a while, that he likes to get off by himself, doesn't he, now? I had a little vacation coming to me, and I thought I'd like to slip over to East Prussia and see some of this fine farming land of yours I've heard so much about. Sometimes I think I'd have done better to stick to farming myself. Not but what I've enjoyed publishing, too. And now I'm enjoying diplomacy, if you can call my brand of action that. Holland is certainly a nice tidy little country, and I like the Dutch. They have good habits and sound ideas, and they can give us cards and spades when it comes to making farming on a small scale pleasant and profitable. But just the same, I hope some day I can go back to my own farm. Trixie tells me you felt the same way about this place. And now that I've come here I don't wonder, I certainly don't."

The sincere admiration evoked by Schönplatz in the breast of Mr. Rhodes was evident. Hans Christian felt himself warming to his guest's praise as well as to his personality.

"I'm glad you came to see it. We'll take a look around it after tea. Of course, you'll give my grandmother and myself the pleasure of staying a few days with us."

"Well, now, I'm afraid I couldn't do that, as much as I'd like to. And it's very nice of you to ask me, Chris, very nice indeed. But I have just a short time free, and I'd like to cover as much territory as I can. I will take a look around the place with you, though. That is, if you wouldn't be interrupting anything important you were doing to show me."

"I'm only too glad to be interrupted, Sir. Especially as I was trying to balance my stud books when you arrived. The result wasn't too encouraging."

Hans Christian laughed a little ruefully. The alert ears of Rufus Rhodes were quick to catch the lack of real merriment in the boy's tone, though his answer gave no real indication of this.

"Your stud books, eh? You raise horses, then? Wait a minute! Of course you do! I've been hearing all along the line about 'the beautiful white horses of Schönplatz.' So those are yours!"

"Yes. Those are ours. I'll take you out to see them. But first my grandmother will wish to tell you all about them. She does that much better than I do."

There was nothing forced in Hans Christian's smile now. The look he turned towards the Archduchess as she came towards them was tenderness itself, and Rufus Rhodes caught the quality of this also. His own voice was gentle as he acknowledged the greeting of the woman who wore her mourning like a regal garment and whose white hair wreathed her head like a crown. It was a grave greeting, extended with no glow; but if there were reluctance as well as reserve in her welcome, nothing which she said or did revealed this. And when tea had been served on the terrace, and her visitor reverted to the subject of the horses again, she did not decline to tell the story.

"I cannot guarantee how much is fact and how much is fancy, Excellency. I am an Austrian myself, not a Prussian; I do not know the *Märchen* of this region as well as I know those of the Tyrol. But the tale is told of a circus caravan which stopped long ago at the gates of Schönplatz in dire distress. The beautiful dapple gray which was its pride and joy had succumbed to some obscure sick-

96

ness, and it seemed about to die, for no shelter or succour had been found for it along the road. So the circus leader turned to the owner of Schönplatz 'as one sportsman to another' to save the steed. Of course, the appeal was not vainly made. The caravan came in and camped upon the grounds. It must have been a sight worth seeing, the tents and waggons and cages spread all over the park, and the circus people in their bright clothes, coming and going through the garden, and sitting at night around their fires, singing and telling fortunes and throwing dice."

"You make me see this sight too, Highness. What happened next?"

"A veterinary was summoned at once, and it was soon plain that the plight of the dapple gray was not hopeless. But it was critical; it required care and watching. The case could not be hurried. So long before the horse was finally healed the circus had gone on its way towards Königsberg."

"Leaving the dapple gray behind?"

"Yes. There was no choice, since it could not travel and the circus could not wait. But the leader left with the promise of a return and a reclamation."

"And then?"

"And then these never came to pass. The caravan vanished as suddenly and as strangely as it had come. And for ever."

"But the horse?"

"The horse remained and never sought to stray. Eventually it became the sire of countless colts—all pure white! Even when the mares to which the dapple was bred were coal black. Their descendants are white as snow to this day. The strain has never shown pollution yet."

"I think Mr. Rhodes would like to hear the complete story, Grandmother."

"I believe that the complete story has never yet been told, Excellency, because the end has not come yet. But Hansel means, I think, that our peasants are very superstitious about these white horses. The mystery which surrounds them is interwoven, in the popular mind, with magic. Some simple people insist that if a coloured colt is born at Schönplatz it will be a bad omen, that it will show the beginning of weakness in the strain, not only of the stud, but of the family."

"Grandmother, it isn't only the peasants that feel the force of something strange about the horses. You know yourself——"

"Yes, I know myself—or think I do. And my husband, in his last illness——" Victoria Luise paused and looked away towards the glen which they were facing, almost as if she expected to see something swift and snowy emerge. Then, with less reserve than she had shown before, she turned back to her guest. "I am sure your

Excellency does not wish to dwell on local legends all the afternoon," she said. "And I, for my part, should like to hear something of your Dutch impressions. I used to visit The Hague frequently myself when a cousin of mine, the Archduke Stefan, was stationed there as Austrian Minister. But it is many years now since I have been there. I hope you have found it a pleasant post? And that your wife and daughter also have enjoyed it?"

"Yes—yes—we've had a very good time there. As I was telling Chris when I first came, I like the Dutch and I like Holland. And I've learned a good deal about the things I'm interested in myself. I've tried not to neglect the social side. I realize an American Minister has a certain position to keep up, that this and that are expected of him, and properly. But I've managed to get out of the city a good deal too. I've looked into the Netherlanders' methods of making butter and cheese and marketing farm products. They're good, very good. Mrs. Rhodes has enjoyed seeing them too. She's been happy going around with me. She and the women she's met in the country understand each other, if you know what I mean. Not that she talks any Dutch. Trixie's done better at learning that. She's studied hard and it's come natural to her. She speaks it like a native. And she's taken up French and German too, and isn't doing a bit badly in them either."

Mr. Rhodes paused, his genial face revealing the satisfaction of a proud parent.

"When Trixie came to The Hague," he said, "the good people there were inclined to look at her a little askance. She drives her own car, and it's a pretty powerful roadster. It was something of a shock for some to see a diplomat's daughter tearing around bareheaded in an open motor, and I expected every day to hear she'd been arrested. But since then she's made friends with every cop in the city. They're a queer-looking lot, those Dutch cops. They're all stoop-shouldered, and they all wear great long, clanking swords, which you'd think would trip them up in a minute if they had to set into quick action. Of course, mostly they just wander around looking pompous. But they certainly have taken a shine to Trixie. And she's made no end of other friends too. The Legation just swarms with young people, tumbling in and out of Trixie's car at all hours of the day and night. That is, if they haven't bulldozed their families into giving them cars of their own, along the same lines as Trixie's."

Mr. Rhodes's smile became increasingly expansive as he dwelt on his daughter's popularity. He needed no urging to continue speaking on such a congenial subject.

"There was some talk, too, because she went around so much with young men. To Scheveningen and the Haack Bar and the Restaurant Royale, for instance, without a chaperon. Well, we don't go in much for chaperons in Kansas—beyond a certain point, I mean—and I can't see that the results are any different than they are anywhere else. So I didn't like to start drawing the line too close in The Hague either. Trixie's the sort of girl that finds her own feet, sooner or later, and the more I see of that sort, the more I believe in driving them with a loose rein. Now the talk has all died down, and Trixie isn't so much interested in restaurants, anyway, because she's invited to so many nice houses. She's made mighty welcome everywhere. Folks have got her sized up right and they like her. They like her very much."

"I don't see how they could help liking her," Hans Christian remarked tactfully, taking advantage of the Minister's first noticeable pause. "She's a grand girl. I wish you'd brought her along with you to East Prussia."

Victoria Luise and Rufus Rhodes both regarded Hans Christian attentively as he made this statement. But before the Minister could frame a gratified reply the Archduchess spoke suavely.

"Naturally Hansel and I are much disappointed that Mrs. Rhodes and your daughter did not accompany you on your trip," she said. "But I hope you can encourage us to believe that at some future time we may have the pleasure of welcoming them at Schönplatz."

"Thank you," Mr. Rhodes said heartily. "Thank you very much." He paused again, this time as if something portentous were on his mind which he hesitated to divulge, although desiring to do so. "I believe they will come here with me some time," he continued, "since you're so kind as to suggest it. Because I expect we'll be spending most of our time, the next few years, in Germany, and, of course, we'll want to identify ourselves with all parts of it, the same as we've done in Holland. You see, I'm expecting to be transferred before long. The appointment hasn't been made public yet. But the President's been good enough to name me as the next American Ambassador to Germany."

CHAPTER XI

WITHOUT much difficulty Mr. Rhodes was persuaded to change his plan of "pushing on" to Königsberg at once. It would be simple enough, the Archduchess explained, to take a side trip the following day or the day after for the purpose of visiting the *Ostmesse;* but it was unthinkable that the Minister should undertake to make the rounds of the exhibits when dusk was already setting in.

"It takes several hours merely to walk through the Fair Grounds, without pausing to inspect any of the cattle and sheep or attending the daily horse shows," she said. "And besides, you have not reached there yet. I know, Excellency, that you make light of distances in your great Middle West, but Königsberg is really a considerable drive from here. Moreover, we have a rule at Schönplatz, which we try to enforce, that every guest who comes to us must stay long enough to sleep under our roof. We shall be desolated if you force us to break this."

"Well, now, I never did believe in using force. There are so many pleasanter means to almost any given end."

"I am so glad that we see eye to eye on this question, Excellency. It leads me to believe that we shall agree on many others also, and find mutual pleasure in this harmony. Fritz will take your bags at once to the Königszimmer in the State Suite, where all the kings of Prussia have slept when they visited Schönplatz. And, of course, we shall see that your chauffeur has suitable accommodation also. Dinner is at eight-thirty, if that hour is agreeable to you, and I am sure some of our neighbours will join us for the evening when they hear how fortunate we are in having you with us. Meantime, while I spread the good news that you are here, what can Hansel show you about the place that will give you the most pleasure?"

It was evident that the Archduchess had immediately "taken a liking" to the Minister, as he himself would have said, though Hansel had feared she might look upon his visit as an intrusion. The vibrancy in her voice, which had so long been toneless, was even more telling than her warm words; and her suggestion of giving a dinner at Schönplatz, for the first time since her husband's death, was more significant still. In spite of the short notice, a sizable and distinguished company had forgathered by half-past eight in the baronial banqueting room which led from the Great Hall: the *Oberpräsident* of East Prussia, a Senior Senator from Danzig, and two Generals, all with their wives; Counts and Colonels, Barons and Burgraves, likewise suitably accompanied. Orders and decorations were greatly in evidence; so was ancestral jewellery of the more massive type. Tall candles flickered in the candelabra rising from the long table and from the sconces fastened to the frescoed walls. Mounds of fruit and clusters of flowers curved alternately above the silver epergnes surmounting the gleaming damask. Plates of rare porcelain and goblets of chased crystal, both heavily encrusted with gold, were set at every place; and the maids who supplemented the services of the butler and houseman wore the festival dresses and amber ornaments reserved for the most important occasions.

"This certainly is a handsome sight," Mr. Rhodes told the Archduchess, his observant eyes taking in every detail of the scene with appreciative thoroughness. "I wish more than ever that I had my family with me. They would have enjoyed this dinner, they surely would. Those soup plates now, with the pictures of all the European queens on them—Mrs. Rhodes would certainly have been taken with those. She used to do some china painting herself when she was a girl. But after we were married, and Trixie was born, she had her hands so full with the housework and the baby and all that, she didn't have time to go on with it. She's never lost her taste for it, though, and I'm sort of hoping, as things are easier for her these days, she'll take it up again. Trixie doesn't care so much for things of the kind. But I'm afraid we'd have had hard work to keep her from getting right up and asking one of those pretty waitresses of yours to change clothes with her. She's bought several costumes in Holland lately to wear at fancy dress parties. But they don't any of them compare with the ones those girls of yours have on. And as long as I know she's got her eye peeled for some more——"

"The *Trachten* of our village are all handmade," Victoria Luise informed him. "The women weave and spin still throughout the long winter evenings, just as they have for hundreds of years. The older ones keep only enough clothing going to supply their current needs. And those are almost unbelievably restricted. But the young girls try to put something aside each year for their trousseaux, so they generally have a few extra garments on hand that have never been worn. I believe I could easily assemble a complete costume, almost overnight, by getting a blouse here and a bodice there and so on. I should be delighted to do this, if you will permit me, and send it to your daughter as a little token of my interest in her, and my hope that she will soon come and see for herself the place where these costumes are made and worn."

"Well now, that is kind and thoughtful of you, Highness, very kind and thoughtful indeed! I know Trixie'll be delighted to have it, and I'll be delighted to take it to her. I don't know when I've seen anything so nice-looking as those coloured bands, matched up on the white sleeves and the white aprons. And I shouldn't be a bit surprised if you'd go first of all for supplies to that pretty girl who just passed us the jelly we're eating with this fine venison. I've never tasted any to equal it, if you'll let me say so. Now tell me—did I guess right?"

Victoria Luise did not even look up from the plate upon which her eyes were fixed as she delicately dissected a morsel of the venison which Mr. Rhodes had so highly praised. "I agree with you that the girl is pretty," she said smoothly. "But it happens that she is unusually stupid, even for a peasant, and few peasants are over-burdened with brains—which after all is just as well! Neverthe-less, a certain modicum is necessary and Trüdchen falls so far short of possessing this that, so far as I know, she has never had a serious suitor. I should be pleased to hear that she did—if for no better reason than that it would mean the kind of trouble her type almost automatically invites might then be averted. To tell you the truth, I have always been afraid that some day I would have a sudden call to send swaddling clothes to Trüdchen's house; but I should never think of looking there for a trousseau. Now—I mustn't monopolize you! I can see that Frau von Edelblut, who is on your other side, is eager to talk with you in her turn."

Mr. Rhodes found Frau von Edelblut a rather ponderous person. She was a heavy woman, and the brown grosgrain silk and cameo jewellery she was wearing did nothing to detract from her size. Her face was full and ruddy and framed with frizzled hair, arranged to escape slightly in front from a knotted net, though otherwise closely confined. Her English was excellent, but her voice was deep and she had a lisp. This childish defect, in combination with her bulky appearance, had a ludicrous effect.

"I thee you are intrigued with our hothteth-eth thtorieth," she boomed. "But I can tell you thtorieth too. Ghotht-th thtorieth. We have ghotht-th galore at Erntht-thtein, my cathtle. Jutht fanthy! The thide of my drething-room fell down latht Thaturday, and a long lock of flachten hair thlipped out of it, jutht like a thnake. I thcreamed when I thaw it thliding around on the thlippery floor. There wath not anything elthe with it—no thkeleton, no dreth, no thoeth, no thign of what it may mean. But I think that maketh it all the more thrange and thinither, don't you?"

Mr. Rhodes agreed that it was strange and sinister, and strove to change the subject. He was beginning to feel slightly surfeited with the supernatural. The story about the white horses really had intrigued him, and had sharpened his enjoyment of the stock and stable, the paddocks and riding rings, which Hans Christian had taken him to look over after tea. He had seen the snowy descendants of the dapple gray circus stallion for himself, and needed no urging to believe in their beauty or admit their actuality. But incarcerated curls were something quite different.

When the company had left the banqueting-room and gathered around the immense fireplace in the Great Hall for coffee and liqueurs, his eyes followed Trüdchen with renewed attention, as she circulated about, carrying a heavy silver tray. The Archduchess, beside whom he was still sitting, and whose glance was quite as penetrating as his own, did not fail to observe his preoccupation.

"Trüdchen," she said suavely. The girl stopped short, and looked at the Archduchess with frightened eyes, as she tried to balance her tray in her shaking hands. "His Excellency has been kind enough to concern himself on your behalf," Victoria Luise went on, in the same even voice, as if she had not noticed the little peasant's terror, "and to inquire about your possible prospects. I told him I did not think you had ever had a serious suitor. I am right, am I not?"

The unexpectedness of the attack was calamitous. The confusion which such a question would have caused the girl in any case was intensified a hundredfold by the suddenness with which it was asked, and the surroundings in which she stood. For one desperate moment she continued her vain attempt to keep her tray on an even keel, as she stammered something unintelligible under her breath. Then it pitched forward and fell on the floor, carrying crashing china with it, and sending a stream of coffee gushing over the carpet in the direction of Frau von Edelblut. This noble lady gave a little shriek, and clasped her pudgy fingers dramatically together.

"How thocking!" she exclaimed. "Jutht thee how that thmall thream ith thpreading and thinking into your thplendid Thirath rug, Victoria! I thympathithe with you, I thertainly do! Thervanth are thurely getting more and more careleth day by day!"

The Archduchess had risen majestically, drawing her silken skirts away from the spreading pool of liquid at her feet. The faithful Fritz was already on his knees beside her, picking up fragments of porcelain and mopping with a large damask napkin at the mess which the coffee had made. Hans Christian, who had taken the wife of the *Oberpräsident* into dinner, was pouring out a glass of *Danziger Goldwasser* for her when the crash came, with his back to the scene of disaster, and did not turn round. The guests, almost without exception, looked in every direction except the one where the accident had occurred with elaborate unconcern, and redoubled their efforts, already somewhat self-conscious, at casual conversation.

Mr. Rhodes was one of the few who did not seem to feel it incumbent upon him to ignore the accident. Having assured himself that Fritz was dealing competently with one sort of salvage, he hastened to undertake another. Though he had no idea of the direction which the terrified Trüdchen had taken in flight which followed the fall, he found his way to the obscure corner where she was hiding, and put his hand protectingly on her shoulder, patting this as he did so.

"There, there," he said in a soothing voice. "You mustn't cry. You mustn't feel bad either. Why, all of us have accidents! I've had dozens of them myself. When I was about your age I fed some mash to the hogs so hot that it killed them. And they weren't my hogs. They belonged to the man I was working for, and he was a grim old miser, if there ever was one. I had to pay him back for every one of those hogs in work before I got another cent of wages. And I'd been saving up my money for two years, hoping to get to the State University, for a term anyway. So I never did get there. I grieved over it considerable. But it doesn't do any good to cry over broken china or burnt hogs any more than it does over spilt milk."

Mr. Rhodes had spoken in English, and consequently Trüdchen did not understand a word he was saying. Nevertheless, the kindness of his manner was unmistakable. Her sobs began to subside, and between them she managed to form a few broken phrases, which Mr. Rhodes, in spite of his imperfect knowledge of German, managed in his turn to piece together.

"*Bin kein böses Mädchen . . . aber kann mich nicht verheiraten und nichts sagen . . . wenn der Herr Baron wuste, wäre alles los.*"

"There, there," said Mr. Rhodes again. Slowly and painstakingly he began to speak in German himself. "Of course, you're not a bad girl," he said reassuringly. "The Archduchess doesn't think that! Nobody thinks that. And why shouldn't you get married, if you want to? Or say anything about it for that matter? If I were you, I'd go to the Archduchess and make a clean breast of things."

"*Nein, nein! Dass ist nicht möglich.*"

"Well then, go to Chris—to the Herr Baron, I mean. He's got a very kind heart. It hasn't taken me long to find that out. Go to him and ask him if he can't fix it so you and your young man can get married right away."

Trüdchen began to sob again with redoubled force. Mr. Rhodes cleared his throat.

"Yes," he said slowly. "Yes, I think that's what you better do. You speak to the Herr Baron the first moment you can. You tell him all this has got to be cleared up. After you've had a talk with him, I may say a few words to him myself. We'll see. I'll have to think that over. But it'll probably be best. at that."

The clear mind of Mr. Rhodes was confused and his kindly heart troubled as he finally climbed into the immense *Himmelbett*, curtained in burgundy brocade, where so many celebrities had slumbered, most of them. he feared, more comfortably than chastely. Indeed, at the last moment before he parted from his hostess for the night, she had observed that it might interest him to inspect the draperies of the *Himmelbett*. It seemed that long ago a veiled lady had come to the castle one evening at dusk, when the family was absent in Königsberg, asking to be allowed to visit the State suite alone. Perhaps she had bribed the guardian, or perhaps he had merely been touched by her tears. As to that, nobody knew. But her mournful request had been granted. The next day the sad discovery was made that a great square had been cut, presumably as a souvenir, from the brocade curtains which enclosed the bed, and made it so secret a scene of voluptuous delight.

Mr. Rhodes had enjoyed this story even less than those about the ghosts; but his mind kept reverting to it as he tossed from side to side in the *Himmelbett*, unable to go to sleep. The radiance of the room was eerie. The moonlight streamed in through the windows.

for the only way to exclude this was to close the heavy wooden shutters, which would likewise have excluded all air; and Mr. Rhodes was a man who liked to have a fresh breeze, reminiscent of the prairies, flowing about him at night. So the bed draperies and window hangings, the massive Danzig chests and polished parquetry, and the painted ceiling, representing a starry heaven surrounded by sturdy trees, were all transfigured with a silvery translucence, unlike any which Mr. Rhodes had ever beheld on land or sea before. But this uncanny lambency, disturbing as it was, could not wholly account for Mr. Rhodes's uneasiness. There was more than a quality of colour involved. There was something sensual in the atmosphere, for the episode which the Archduchess had related so casually was apparently characteristic of the sort of thing which constantly happened at Schönplatz. Was he to understand that privileged men "took advantage" of youth and innocence as a matter of course? Or, worse still, that women not only succumbed to seduction without a struggle there, but treasured the memory of their subjugation? Had he been rash in suggesting to Trüdchen that she should seek out Hans Christian "the first moment she could" without qualifying his statement in any way? Was it possible that she might interpret this advice to mean that very night instead of the following morning? It did not seem to, and yet the more Mr. Rhodes thought of it, the more firmly convinced he became that it was probable. If he were right, what then? What would happen to her? What had happened to her already that she should seem so terrified? It was inconceivable that Hans Christian—sensitive, tender-hearted, high-principled—should stoop to a dishonourable deed, no matter how ruthless and sensuous a lot his ancestors had shown themselves to be. It was inconceivable, and yet—the boy was horribly lonely, inescapably harassed, almost at the end of his tether; he had no normal outlet for his emotions.

Rufus Rhodes was moved by the thought. But his pity for Hans Christian did not detract from his anxiety for Trüdchen. At last he could bear inaction no longer. He descended, not without difficulty, from the crimson heights of the *Himmelbett,* and, groping for his serviceable bathrobe, wrapped it securely around his substantial form. The parquet flooring creaked under his bare feet, and he was ashamed to feel cold shivers running down his spine as he stooped for his slippers. When he reached the next room, still another sound startled him, for this contained a glass cabinet filled with priceless porcelains and lovely lacquer-ware, which rattled as the floor shook slightly under his weight. His fingers were chilly as he placed them on the knob of the door leading from the antechamber of the State suite to the upper hall. Before he had actually grasped the knob the door swung open of its own accord.

Beyond its enclosure only emptiness and silence confronted him.

The light from the waning moon did not strike this side of the castle; there was no murmur of voices, no patter of passing feet. He thought of what Hans Christian had said, desperation in his voice, as they had followed a little fir-bordered walk from one set of outbuildings to another late that afternoon. "Pretty soon it will be dark I think the darkness is blacker here, and the stillness heavier, than anywhere else in the world." Rufus Rhodes knew now what the boy had meant. The blackness and the heaviness were upon him now, impenetrable and crushing. He could not prevail against them. He could do no possible good, and he might do great harm if he persisted in a quixotic quest which he realized had been ridiculous to undertake. He had no idea where Hans Christian's room was, and in searching for it he might well stumble into that of the Archduchess instead. He could only return to the sinister shelter of the *Himmelbett*. But though he had not heard them and could not see them, he was sure, beyond any shadow of a doubt, that somewhere, beyond the blackness and the heaviness, Hans Christian and Trüdchen were together. . . .

He closed the door of the antechamber firmly, trying, as he did so, to lock it this time. But the heavy key was rusty; it would not turn; the big bolt was broken in two. There was nothing to do but leave it as it was, hoping that this time it would stay shut. Rufus Rhodes did not care at all for doors which swung open by themselves, any more than he cared for china which clattered as he walked past it, or flooring which creaked under his feet. In fact, he did not care for any kind of unaccountable noises occurring in the dead of night. When the sound of soft but persistent knocking also came to his ears, he swore under his breath.

He could not instantly make up his mind to go and open the door. Yet he recoiled from the thought that it might swing open of its own accord again, or that the mysterious suppliant on his threshold might enter uninvited. Gritting his teeth, he retraced his footsteps, thankful that in the course of his progress he had inadvertently touched a switch and that there was now a pale gleam of electricity in the room. Feeble as it was, it enhanced his sense of security. He threw open the door with a show of boldness, and Trüdchen slipped inside it.

She was not crying any longer. Even in the dim light Rufus Rhodes could see that her round, rosy little face was now wreathed in smiles. She ducked and kissed his hand, but, having done so, she instantly straightened up again and faced him beamingly. Then she began to talk in a way which he had no difficulty in understanding.

"I saw Your Excellency open the door just after I had come out of the Herr Baron's room, so I knew Your Excellency was awake. I was watching and waiting to make sure no one was in the hall before crossing it, as the Herr Baron has taught me to do. I hope I do not intrude upon Your Excellency. But I am so happy, all because of Your Excellency's great wisdom and goodness, that I wanted to say so at once. If it had not been for such sage advice I should never have dared to tell the Herr Baron the truth."

"Has he ever been unkind to you?" Rufus Rhodes heard himself asking incomprehensibly.

"Oh, no, Your Excellency! Always he has been most gentle, most tender. He has never been rough, even in his speech. He has never used violence against me in any way, or shamed me by coming to my house and locking the door of my room in my mother's face. He has safeguarded me as if I had been a lady, and we have never met except secretly. Still, I feared he might be angry at learning that I was sought in marriage and that I wished to accept my suitor. Especially since Hermann's younger brother Otto is in disgrace at the castle—he was formerly the *Apfeljunge* and now he is in the scullery. Besides, I feared he might tell Hermann how it had been between us, and then Hermann would not marry me after all. He is insanely jealous. How should I know that the Herr Baron would not be jealous also, that he would be willing to let me go? A peasant girl cannot take that for granted, Excellency, when she has found favour with a *Grossgrundbesitzer*. But the Herr Baron has been more than generous. He has told me that I shall not lose my place as long as I wish to keep it, and that I shall come and go about the castle unmolested. Also that my mother will continue to receive the extra money he has given me for her each month."

The orderly mind of Rufus Rhodes was reeling. Before him in the treacherous light was standing the pretty little peasant who had aroused his sympathies, her pink face guileless as a baby's. That much was certainly true. Yet he could hardly bring himself to believe a single word that issued from her prim pink mouth. Surely he could not have understood her correctly, surely his imperfect knowledge of German must be causing his comprehension to play tricks upon him! No decent girl would babble blandly along in this wise to a man she had never seen before that night about an illicit love affair and a smug betrothal in one and the same breath. It was all a riddle which would have been ridiculous if it had not been revolting. But out of it emerged a scrap of salvage at which Rufus Rhodes grasped.

"Perhaps the Herr Baron is pleased to have you marry," he said. "Perhaps he has felt for some time that it was unwise for you to come to him secretly, besides being wrong, which he has known it to be from the beginning, even if you did not. Perhaps he hesitated to tell you he would be pleased, for fear of hurting your feelings, or perhaps he tried to tell you so, and could not make you understand." All this was true, and yet Rufus Rhodes knew also that Hans Christian's pride must have been cut to the quick at the disclosure that the girl whom he had treated so tenderly was voluntarily turning from him to the coarse caresses of the refractory *Apfeljunge's* brother. "I know the Herr Baron must have felt a great responsibility as far as you were concerned," Mr. Rhodes went on, trying to close his consciousness to the corroding thought which had just crossed it. "Having been led into this, he did not see how he could withdraw from it. He will be happier and better off now that you have made the withdrawal easy. Though you are hardly fair to Hermann, are you, in letting him marry you under false pretences?"

Rufus Rhodes was aware that his German was faltering, that he did not sound like himself when he tried to talk in this language. Perhaps that accounted for the fact that Trüdchen was now beginning to look bewildered in her turn. She shook her head stupidly.

"I do not understand Your Excellency," she muttered. "But I am sure that I have nothing to fear. The Herr Baron will never betray me to Hermann, any more than he has ever betrayed me to others. He has told me that the banns may be published at once, if I like. I showed him the ring which Hermann has given me—a real gold ring engraved with an arrow, to show that the heart has been pierced. I have been keeping it in my pocket. I did not even dare hang it on a chain around my neck, for fear that it might be found. But now I shall wear it quite openly. Her Serene Highness will be astonished, and perhaps she will not be pleased. She never admits she is in the wrong about anything, and, since she has said before other *Herrschafften* that I have never had a serious suitor, she will be chagrined to learn that this is not the case. But the Herr Baron will protect me from her anger. I have nothing to fear in that quarter either."

It seemed to Rufus Rhodes that Trüdchen actually shrugged her shoulders. He realized that if she could do this she had indeed left intimidation far behind.

"Well, now that you feel sure that everything has turned out so well for you," he remarked dryly, "don't you think it would be a good plan if you went home and got to bed?"

Trüdchen curtseyed and kissed his hand again. But this time the gesture was more lingering than when she had come in. She continued to kneel at his feet as she went on speaking.

"I am most grateful for Your Excellency's kindness. If there is anything I can do to serve Your Excellency——" she murmured; and waited.

Rufus Rhodes was not a squeamish man and he had not known

what it was to blush since boyhood. But when he had slammed the door behind Trüdchen's scurrying figure he strode across the floor unmindful of the clattering china and wiped the sweat from his brow as he delivered himself of a biting oath coupled with a brief epithet which he had never applied to a woman before.

"And the sooner I get that poor trapped youngster out of this old hell-hole and away from that young hell-cat," he concluded, as he climbed back into the *Himmelbett*, "the better deed I'll have done in the sight of the Almighty."

CHAPTER XII

MR. RHODES was not himself much of a horseman. Nevertheless, figuratively speaking, he knew better than to rush his fences. For the next three days he suffered himself to be led around the countryside, and docilely accepted every suggestion which the Archduchess made to him. He went with her to the woodland cemetery where General von Hohenlohe lay entombed in monumental black granite, surrounded by his three sons, whose graves were marked with elaborate iron crosses. Mr. Rhodes stood with bowed head while Victoria Luise knelt in prayer, arranged cascades of flowers, and described similar cemeteries which she proposed to show him in the near future. He went with her to Ernstein, and listened, patiently and politely, while Frau von Edelblut told him "thtorieth" about the eventful past of this classic pile. It had originally been a plain, substantial *Herrenhaus,* but it had been remodelled according to the ideas of an ancestor of hers who had spent a *Wanderjahr* in Greece, and who, in spite of having contracted malignant fever and other ailments there, had conceived a consuming passion for it. He had returned to his native land, bent on adorning the park with group after group of substantial sculpture, setting up pilasters with gilded Corinthian capitals in the *Festsaal,* and placing alabaster tables between marble busts in every corridor of the castle.

"Hith father wath not at all pleathed," Frau von Edelblut explained. "Ethpethially when he inthithted on building a pavilion in Doric thtyle whith he thaid wath a temple, and could not be uthed or made thuitable for hortheth. Hith father wanted to thtable them there, you thee."

"I see," Rufus Rhodes replied gravely. Secretly he sympathized somewhat with the outraged parent, for the chaste and chilly marble surrounding him scarcely seemed adapted to the lusty life of a typical East Prussian *Grossgrundbesitzer.* But he gathered that Frau von Edelblut herself was a champion of the son, so he held his peace. The result of his forbearance was that his appreciative attitude was admired, and he was taken off to see another castle, where a careful cult of Goethe had been maintained for more than a century, and *Werther* was enacted every spring in a sylvan theatre, by various members of the family. This cult, Mr. Rhodes learned, had its origin in the friendship which a wandering daughter of the house had formed in her youth with the great poet, and which had remained a romantic memory for her after she had been unwillingly dragged away from the delightful laxness of glowing Weimar to the stern simplicity of patrician Prussia.

"It is so easy to go from place to place in these days," Victoria Luise remarked, leaning against the comfortable upholstery of Mr. Rhodes's limousine as it glided over the smooth highway again. "In the days when the roads were full of ruts, and the Junkers went lumbering about in great coaches—unless they rode horseback—it was not such a simple matter to visit back and forth. Though some of the State equipages were very beautiful. We have several still, in the old carriage house. One is made of green lacquer. I must remind Hansel to show it to you. I am sorry that he was not inclined to come with us today. The habit of solitude seems to have fastened itself upon him. When he first came to Schönplatz, I sometimes feared that he would not be able to endure its loneliness. But lately he has shrunk from society quite as much as I have myself. I might even say more so! For I have been delighted to accompany you while you make the acquaintance of our countryside and our country life, though he has persisted in staying shut up in the *Studsekretäriat*, pouring over pedigree sheets and balancing books!"

The Archduchess spoke lightly, as was her habit, but her suavity was edged with sarcasm, which Rufus Rhodes had discovered was not unusual with her either. He decided that the time had come to make the plunge which he had hesitated to attempt too soon.

"Perhaps a different sort of company would suit Chris better," he suggested. "Just for a change, I mean. Of course, I can't imagine anything pleasanter than the sort of life you lead here—everyone more or less related to everyone else, everyone interested in the same sort of sports, everyone owning a fine place, just right for having lots of company. But along with it all, there is a good deal of stress laid on the past, now isn't there? Ancestors and history and all that sort of thing, I mean. After all, the present's pretty exciting too. I should think Chris would enjoy taking some kind of an active part in this new Youth Movement that's beginning to sweep through Germany like wildfire. I'm not sure yet whether it's a good thing or a bad one, but, anyway, it's alive! It isn't embalmed, if you know what I mean. Chris might help his country considerably. Germany's in a bad way just now, it needs young fellows like him to give it a hand up. But my main point is that it might help him considerably if he got out more with boys his own age."

"There is no lack of boys Hansel's age among our neighbours, Mr. Rhodes. And they did their best to make him welcome among them. But unfortunately he did not respond to their hospitality in any way at all."

"Well, perhaps he didn't find much in common with them. Perhaps his tastes and theirs weren't congenial."

"That is all too true. But I should regret to see my grandson identifying himself with a group of hoodlums and fanatics, and thus tacitly acknowledging his failure to adapt himself to the views and ways of his own class."

"It seems to me that you're just a little prejudiced in your views, if you'll allow me to say so, Highness. The boys in this new movement aren't all hoodlums and fanatics by any means. There's good material among them, and they've got a mighty shrewd, able leader—Grüber his name is. I believe Chris might go a good way in an organization like that. I think you're a little hard on him too, if I might say *that*. He was an American boy, to all intents and purposes, when he came here. He's had quite a lot of adapting to do. I think he's tried hard to do it. In fact, I'd go so far as to say I know he has. But his views and ways weren't Junker views and ways when he left Hamstead and Harvard. You'd hardly expect they would be, right off the bat, now would you?"

"He came of his own free will. He desired to leave Hamstead and Harvard to take up his father's heritage, to become a German."

"Ye—es, theoretically. But he hadn't a very clear idea, had he, what it really meant to become a German, to take up his father's heritage?"

"He knew when he decided to stay. The original plan had been that he should remain only for the summer, that he should return to the United States in the autumn. He was free to do that also."

"In a way, yes. But I believe he felt bound, don't you? That is, there had been a death in the family. He seems to have a very kind heart and——"

"I have never made my own bereavement a pretext to hold him, Mr. Rhodes."

"Of course not. Of course not. He stayed of his own free will, as you say. But now that he *has* stayed, for more than two years, don't you think it would do him good to get away for a while? To Berlin, for instance. Most boys of his age would get a lot of pleasure out of a city like Berlin."

"It had been my husband's hope, and my own, that Hansel would find Berlin a congenial centre. Not that we would have encouraged him to spend too much time there. The Prussians are not absentee landlords, Mr. Rhodes. They live on their own property, year in and year out, century in and century out——"

"That's just what I'm saying. I think it might be a good thing if they didn't stick to it quite so closely. It's rather far from the beaten track. In Berlin, people refer to it as the 'Far East!' The Corridor has cut it off considerably from the capital."

"It certainly has. But remember that the Corridor was created over the dead bodies of our heroes, not through the free will of a free people. What could be more cruel than to make a jest of the isolation it has imposed? Nothing in my experience! Besides, owing to the unfortunate economic situation which exists in Germany just now, we have been obliged to part with some of our property. We no longer own our house on the Tiergartenstrasse."

"But you could take a little furnished apartment somewhere, couldn't you, for the winter months? Just big enough for you and Chris? Or if you didn't care to leave Schönplatz, he could strike off alone, and dig himself into lodgings."

The Archduchess drew away slightly, as if she were trying to create of her own corner a stronghold for herself. "I am still afraid that you do not fully grasp the situation, Mr. Rhodes," she said, "though I appreciate your interest and your cordiality. We have an old Prussian hunting slogan in which we believe implicitly, and it runs, 'The pack must stay together.' There is a very great feeling of family unity and class unity among Germans. It is true that Hansel has not fully absorbed these feelings yet. But it is also true, as you have pointed out, that he is trying to do so, and that in a certain measure he is succeeding in his attempt. I am sure that having progressed so far, he would not do anything so contrary to custom as to leave his home, and his nearest relative, and 'strike off alone,' as you suggest. Believe me, he will be far more contented in the end if he remains where he is, prevailing over his own diffidence and discontent. Both will disappear, in any case, I believe, as soon as he is suitably married."

"I beg your pardon. Did you speak of yourself as his nearest relative? Isn't his mother living?"

"Yes, his mother is living. But he and she have never been very close together, since he was a child, and now they are almost completely estranged. She is a beautiful woman, but a wilful and selfish one. She has no sort of hold upon him."

Rufus Rhodes privately thought that there was more than one selfish and wilful woman involved in the case, and it was on the tip of his tongue to remark that such an estrangement did not speak well for the sense of family unity which he had just heard so highly vaunted. However, he wisely held his peace on that score, and asked another question.

"He's still rather young, isn't he, to think seriously of settling down? Most boys need a chance to have some sort of a fling before they are married."

"If Hansel feels the need of 'some sort of fling,' no doubt he will manage to have it, even at Schönplatz," the Archduchess said in the smooth tone which Mr. Rhodes was beginning to dislike so intensely. "I assure you I should not interfere with anything of that sort. I should not even give it false importance by appearing to notice it. But it is never too soon for the heir of a great estate to think of marrying suitably. In this instance, I may tell you in confidence, since you have been kind enough to concern yourself about Hansel, that the complication is not caused by his youth, but by the fact that the bride I have in mind for him is much younger still."

"*You've* selected a bride for Chris? Already?'

"I should not go so far as to say that I had selected her. He will do that for himself, of course, under proper guidance, at the proper time. But I should be extremely pleased to see him married to one of the daughters of our distant kinsman Sebastian de Cerreno'"

"*One* of the daughters? *Any* one?"

"There are only two, Cristina and Cecilia. They are both still little girls. Otherwise I might be tempted to leave Schönplatz for a time after all, and spend a winter in Spain. But I do not want my plans to miscarry because of prematurity."

The Archduchess smiled charmingly, and glanced out of the window. "How fast time flies, when one is in congenial company!" she said. "See, we are almost home! Or do you not recognize our local landmarks yet? I think we shall have time for an hour in the library before dinner. You have hardly seen that at all, and it contains many volumes which I am sure you would enjoy. For instance, we have a complete collection of sixteenth-century madrigal music. Also the manuscript of an opera, composed by a member of my husband's family and performed in honour of Queen Luise and King Wilhelm Friedrich when they made the first of their many visits to Schönplatz. But, after all, the greatest treasures are a Würtemburg Bible bound in pigskin, and a copy of Kant which is unique. There is a story about that which I must not fail to tell you."

For the first time Rufus Rhodes found a pretext for not falling in with her plans. Possibly she would be good enough to show him the collection and tell him the story at some other time, he suggested. He had eaten such a hearty lunch and such an enormous tea—in spite of the chilling effect of the classical surroundings on both occasions—that he felt an overpowering need for exercise before attacking the equally prodigious dinner which he knew was still ahead of him. He thought he would walk out over the fields, cross country. A five-mile hike would do him no end of good.

Besides, the sky was beautiful, just at this time of the evening, a queer pale colour, streaked with green and purple and orange light. He had never seen its equal anywhere else. Or birches that could compare with the long rows edging the lake. In a way, he liked them even better than the pine groves, much better than the alleys of lindens. He wanted to have a look at them, with all those flame-coloured clouds streaming out behind them. He didn't suppose he could persuade the Archduchess to come with him, part of the way, anyhow?

He knew he was safe in extending the invitation. The Archduchess had been a fine figure on horseback, in her day; but she had never strayed beyond the park and garden, or the sylvan glades immediately surrounding these. Rufus Rhodes swung off unimpeded. But as a matter of fact he had no intention of taking a solitary walk. He was firmly resolved to seek out Hans Christian, and talk with him, now that he was in the mood, as man to man.

He did not have to seek far. He had not gone beyond the first cobbled courtyard when he saw the boy, dressed in riding clothes and holding a crop, standing with his hands behind his back, and staring up at an empty nest, perched above a large chimney. He was so absorbed that he did not notice his guest's approach until Mr. Rhodes came up and stood beside him, following his gaze.

"What are you looking at, Chris?" the Minister asked. He could see the empty nest for himself, of course. But there was nothing about it, in his eyes, to rivet attention.

The boy turned, blinking a little. "I'm sorry, Sir, that I didn't see you come up. I just noticed that the storks are gone."

"The storks are gone? But that doesn't bother you, does it? They'll come back, won't they?"

"Oh, yes! They'll come back! In East Prussia the storks bring the *Fohlenkinder* as well as all other babies—we couldn't have our little white colts at Schönplatz without the help of the storks." Hans Christian smiled, and Rufus Rhodes found something touching and irresistible in his expression, just as Trixie had from the beginning. He made an attractive figure, as he stood there in his whipcord breeches, polished boots, and soft shirt. The clothes became him, and he wore them easily; no one would have guessed that two years earlier they had been strange and unfamiliar to him. "But at that, the storks are the last of all birds to return," he went on. "The village children have a song that they sing about that. They go through the streets, chanting:

> '*Alle Vögel sind schon da,*
> *Blos noch nicht der Adelbar.*'

And they're not only the last to come back. They're the first to leave. When I looked up and saw that the storks had gone——"

114

"You knew that presently you'd be picking the last rose of summer? Is that it?"

"Yes, that's it."

"And you didn't relish the prospect?"

"Well, the winters are pretty long here. Napoleon said that East Prussia was a country where there were nine months of winter and three that you couldn't call summer."

"Chris, didn't it ever occur to you that it might be a good plan to stop dwelling for a while on what Napoleon said and Frederick the Great did and Queen Luise thought, and give a little attention instead to what this man Hitler is thinking and saying and doing?"

"Yes, it's occurred to me. But it hasn't occurred to my grandmother yet."

"You might call her attention to it."

"I have. At least, I've tried. But she doesn't listen."

"She'll have to listen some day unless I'm very much mistaken. It might be a good plan for you to begin a serious attempt to make her."

"Oh, I've begun. But I haven't got very far."

"Chris, you had guts enough to break away from Hamstead and Harvard. You ought to have guts enough to break away from here."

The boy began to trace lines around the cobblestones with his crop, apparently as intent upon the futile gesture as he had been on the storks' nest a few minutes earlier. When he finally looked up, Rufus Rhodes saw that his face was quivering.

"Do you think it would take more guts to break away than it does to stay?" he asked vehemently.

For an instant Rufus Rhodes was nonplussed. He had not been prepared for this form of counter-attack. But he rallied quickly.

"Yes. In a way I do. You're lonely here and discouraged. You feel you don't fit in, and that's all the harder for you, because you expected to, because you didn't fit in at Harvard either, and you thought this would be different. But though you've made up your mind to stick it out this time, and believe that's what you're doing, what you're really doing is to follow the line of least resistance. You're letting your grandmother suck your strength and plan your life, because it's easier for you to do that than to oppose her."

"You're wrong, Mr. Rhodes. None of it's a question of what's easy. As far as my grandmother's concerned, it's a question of what's kind. I can't be cruel to her."

"She can be cruel to you. She doesn't intend that you shall stir from her side. She proposes that you shall stay here, shut up with spooks and stories, for the rest of your natural life. She doesn't even intend to let you choose your own wife. She has you as good as married to some silly little Spaniard already, instead of giving you

115

a chance to see something of a sensible modern girl your own age."

"Mr. Rhodes, I don't wish to be rude to a guest. But I can't permit anyone to speak that way about my grandmother. She's a very wonderful person, and she's suffered a great deal."

"I know she's a wonderful person, and I know she's suffered a great deal. But the same thing is true of your mother, and you went off and left her. I'm not even suggesting that you should leave your grandmother. Take her with you, if you must. But get out of this place, before it gets you."

"My mother has her own interests, Sir, if you'll excuse me for saying so. My grandmother has no one but her. And just now, I've no one but her. And nothing but Schönplatz. I don't believe I could make you understand how I feel about 'this place,' as you call it. It's true, I have been lonely and discouraged here. But just the same, I love it. Everything about it, even its spooks and stories. They're real to me, and precious. But quite aside from that, Schönplatz represents my only means of making a living. I haven't been very successful in that direction yet, I know. But I've got to keep on trying. I can't go away from here in the winter. That's the foaling season. Our foals are all born between November and April. And you see those 'beautiful white horses' are a potential source of income. So far, as I told you, it's the sheep that have been most profitable. But I believe the horses will be profitable too, some time. I'm superstitious about them in my own way, just as the peasants are in theirs. Only I have a different theory about omens."

"Well, what's your theory?"

"I believe a coloured colt would bring us good luck instead of bad. I want a dapple-gray, like the original stallion. I'm hoping to get this. I believe it's time for a new strain, or a return to the original strain, just as you look at it. But, anyway, a strong strain, not a weak one. I'm experimenting. I've made some dreadful mistakes, but I'm going straight on."

He paused for a moment, and then brought his crop, with a snap, up over his shoulder. "I haven't bred my dapple-gray colt yet," he said with a smile. "I haven't sired my own son either. When I do, nobody but me is going to choose his mother. Not any woman living. And not any man either."

PART V

"BANNERS HIGH"
1929-1931

CHAPTER XIII

THE interior of the Restaurant zum Nussbaum in Alt-Berlin was dark and dingy. The cartoons and chromos tacked on the walls gave it a tattered look rather than a picturesque one; amidst these the steel engravings of a prim Victorian couple struck an incongruous note. The settees were stained, the tables marred by the hieroglyphics hacked into them. The air was thick with smoke and the stale smell that comes from underairing and overcrowding. The place was filled, for the most part, by rather drab individuals. There were a few roisterers among them, but the majority talked in low guttural voices, or sat staring stolidly into space. Here and there a face that was sinister stood out among several that were merely sullen. One shabby man, who sat alone in a corner with the collar of his coat turned up and his hands thrust deep into his frayed pockets, glanced towards the door at the arrival of each newcomer with an expression that was searchingly sardonic.

Beer was brought in by a fat, frowsy woman who slopped it over when she set it down. But the beer itself was excellent. Trixie Rhodes bent over her mug and blew the foam lightly to one side before she took a long sip.

"My, that's good!" she exclaimed, as she raised her head. "I was terribly thirsty too. Weren't you, Chris?"

"You have some foam on the end of your nose," he remarked irrelevantly. Then as she brushed it off without concern, and buried her face in her beer a second time, he added, "Yes, I was. But I would have been willing to wait until we could get to Kroll's, or some such place, for a drink, instead of coming here."

"Oh, but I simply had to come to the Nussbaum! My sightseeing wouldn't have been complete if I hadn't seen the oldest restaurant in Berlin. You know it wouldn't."

"Well, I hope it's complete now. I'll be going back to Schönplatz on a stretcher if I let you drag me around much longer."

"But you haven't any idea of going back to Schönplatz yet!"

"I didn't have. But I may need to, in self-defence. You set a pretty strenuous pace, Trixie."

His tone was bantering, but his smile was sunny, and Trixie's heart warmed to it. She had been a long time in getting him to

Berlin, for he had stuck grimly to his self-imposed task at Schön-platz. But finally he had received his reward, though no one besides himself knew what this had cost him in determination and self-denial. The balance sheets which had caused him so much concern at last began to give him gratification instead. The reliable sheep continued to do their share and the stud slowly evolved from a liability to an asset. The day came when he sent a wire to the American Embassy in Berlin which caused the Ambassador to break into a roar of hearty approbation as he tossed the telegram across the table to his daughter.

"Well, the youngster surely has guts! I never thought he'd see it through. I wouldn't put anything past him now."

"I don't know what you mean. And I don't know what this tele-gram means either—except the last part of it."

" '*The strong strain is started. I have bred my dapple-gray foal and she is a beauty,*'" Rufus Rhodes read aloud, recapturing his dispatch. " '*Delighted to come to Berlin now, if you still want to have me.*' Well, Trixie, Chris had a notion . . . but I'll tell you about it afterwards. The main thing is to get an answer right off telling him to take the next train. Isn't it?"

Hans Christian had not taken the next train, or indeed any train, for the railroad service across East Prussia and the Polish Corridor still left much to be desired. Nevertheless he had appeared promptly, driving the same car which he had brought with him from the United States five years earlier, and wearing the same clothes. He made no apology and apparently felt no embarrassment for either, and he proved from the first a delightful guest. Mrs. Rhodes was completely captivated by him; he adapted himself so pleasantly to the ways of her household and was such an addition to it that she felt she would like to have him there indefinitely. Mr. Rhodes revelled openly in his presence with the pathetic satisfac-tion of a man who has always starved for the vigorous young male companionship which he would have found in a son. And Trixie, quite as candid as her parents in her joy over his visit, dashed gaily about with him from one end of Berlin to the other, and paraded her prize before the envious eyes of all her friends.

At first it was to the Ambassador that Hans Christian responded most freely. Rufus Rhodes having been to Schönplatz himself, he was in a position to understand the progress which had been made there; and Hans Christian, after his long lack of listeners, was eager to talk about this. He had brought with him sketches of the structural changes which he had made, or was hoping to make, in the stables, and snapshots of the dapple-gray foal; he spread these forth on a long table, and pointed out their best features in detail. He spoke of building improvements with sober pride, after the manner of a man who has planned them with frugality and care and has executed them with skill; but when he talked about the little foal, his face lighted up and his voice rang with happiness.

"I had her by Isolde out of Schönplatzstoltz," he explained. "She was Isolde's first foal. Now I don't see why that mare shouldn't have more dapple-gray foals, do you, if they were sired by the same stallion? Of course that is what I'm going to try first. But if I don't get results that way, I shan't be discouraged; I'll wait patiently until the little filly is old enough to be bred herself. I know she'll set up the strain."

"I shouldn't be surprised, Chris, but what you're right."

"Naturally I wouldn't have come away and left her, even now," Chris went on, picking up one of the snapshots and looking at it lovingly, "if I hadn't left her in the best possible hands. I haven't had a chance to tell you yet. This isn't the first time I've been away from Schönplatz. I took a trip through Bavaria and the Rhineland last fall. I couldn't persuade my grandmother to go with me. She hasn't left Schönplatz at all yet, and she didn't approve of my going either. But I decided it was about time I saw my German relatives again—the von Mitwelds, you know, who live in Munich, and my Aunt Elsa, who is a Carmelite nun in Cologne."

"I think you had a good idea there, Chris, very good."

"I think so too. I didn't get much out of my visit to the convent, and at first the outlook in Munich was pretty discouraging. The von Mitwelds certainly have a queer household. My uncle was away at Doorn, as usual, and my Cousin Karl kept trying to pick a political quarrel with me. He's an out-and-out Communist, and would like to see everything the Junkers stand for scrapped tomorrow. There's nothing I could do for the poor little cripple, or my Aunt Rita either; but I took a great fancy to the youngest girl, Luischen, my grandmother's namesake. There's something so sincere about her looks—straight dark brows, rather heavy—level eyes, clear colour. Well, I can't describe it, but the quality is there. She's been in love for years with a nice fellow her family thought was 'beneath her' and who was out of a job—like most of the other nice young fellows I met."

"Yes, I want to talk to you some time about this unemployment situation, Chris. It's serious, very serious."

"It certainly is. . . . Well, when I found out this suitor of Luischen's, Ernst Behrend, was a trained studmaster, I had a brain-wave. I asked him if he wouldn't like to come to Schönplatz to be my *Landstallmeister*. I could just see him in the *Gestudsekretäriat*, keeping the account books, and out in the paddocks, watching over the little foals. I asked Luischen if she wouldn't marry him and come along. I could see her too, letting sunshine into the house and filling vases with flowers. They both seemed so cheerful, in spite of all their troubles and disappointments, and so competent. . . . They jumped at the chance I gave them, and when I went home they went with me. Aunt Rita was furious, and so was grandmother. But they'll get over it. There's going to be a baby pretty soon now, and they won't be able to resist that, no matter what they think beforehand. And having Luischen and Ernst at Schönplatz has been a godsend to me. It's as if a fresh breeze had begun to blow through a musty place, if you know what I mean."

"I think I do, Chris, I think I do. I'm glad everything seems to be coming along so nicely for you. Now that you've got this trustworthy man, you won't be tied down so closely; and with a nice young woman and a cunning baby in the house, that'll be considerably pleasanter for you too. When a lady gets to be your grandmother's age she doesn't always remember how much sunshine and flowers mean to young folks, especially if she's seen a lot of sorrow in her own life. But I know how it is. . . ."

"Yes, you seem to. But what I wish is, that I could think up a way of solving our national problems as well as my personal ones have been solved. I've got the foundation laid for prosperity and progress at Schönplatz now, I feel sure of that. But East Prussia generally—and Germany as a whole—— We're not getting anywhere, Mr. Rhodes, the way we're going now. There's wretchedness on every side, and desperation—even under the surface smoothness of Berlin's most fashionable quarters. I turn a corner—hardly more than that—and see starvation. I turn another and find depravity. I don't think Trixie's conscious of it. The spring is so beautiful, the tulips are so bright, the trees are so green—those are the only things she sees and I'm glad of it. But more than once I've had to hurry her past a place where I was afraid she'd see more—gruesome sights, obscene sights. There must be some way out of all this, someone who could lead us out."

"Well, let's hope there is. I'd like to talk to you about that too, some time. But I mustn't keep you any longer just now. I ought to be off to the Chancery, and I know Trixie's waiting for you. I think she wants you should go with her to some picture gallery or other."

"No, Sir, it isn't a picture gallery today. We did that yesterday. I think I must be the first victim Trixie's found that she can sacrifice to her craze for sightseeing, she's making such a thorough job of it. But it's quite all right with me. I go to museums and monuments with her in the daytime, and she goes to concerts and operas with me in the evening. It's a mutually satisfactory bargain. We're off now to the Palace in Charlottenburg, and afterwards to an East End restaurant, the Nut Tree. Tonight we're going to *Götterdämmerung*."

"The Nut Tree?"

"Yes, Sir. The Nussbaum in Alt-Berlin. It's the oldest restaurant in the city. That's why she wants to see it. She's read about it in a guidebook. But the guidebook apparently didn't mention the fact that nowadays it's a pet place for Communists. I don't know just what sort of a crowd we'll run into there. But I'll look after her."

"I know you will, Chris. Well, have a good time. both of you."

They had a very good time, though neither the Palace nor the Nussbaum had quite come up to Trixie's expectations. But it was a beautiful day, and they were both feeling carefree and content. The avenues in the park at Charlottenburg were feathery with fresh green, and everywhere the tulip beds were bright. Trixie said that it gave her a lift just to look at them, and Hans Christian began to sing little tunes under his breath. Even the restaurant was partially redeemed from squalor by the red geraniums in the window-boxes under its gables and the verdant boughs of the ancient tree which stood in front of it. Besides, the beer was certainly very good, and they were undeniably thirsty after their long tramp through the State apartments and among those endless alleys winding around the blue-domed mausoleum. They sat relaxed and sipped unhurriedly, smoking cigarettes and badgering each other with great good humour.

"About that stretcher, Trixie. I think I better call up the Elizabethan Krankenhaus and make arrangements for it when we get back to the Embassy."

"Nonsense! We can improvise one for you ourselves, if you really want it. And I'll go along with you to Schönplatz as your nurse. You don't need one of those demure little deaconesses."

"What do you know about nursing, Trixie?"

"It doesn't take much knowledge to sit beside a bed and smooth a sheet. Any girl would be glad to do it—that is, if there is someone in the bed who had what it takes. I could put on a cap and apron, if you think that would help out, of course. I'm sure I'd have a very soothing effect upon you."

"Are you? I'm not so certain."

His tone had lost none of its lightness. Momentarily, the basic depression which he had revealed to Rufus Rhodes had been lifted. His release from long loneliness, the stimulating society into which he had suddenly been thrown, the heady atmosphere of spring and sunshine—all these had been intoxicating in their effect. But underneath his badinage he was vaguely disturbed. He was in the mood for merrymaking, almost for love-making. From the beginning he had enjoyed Trixie immensely as a companion, now he had begun to visualize her vaguely as a sweetheart. Although he did not deeply desire her, he recognized all her desirable qualities. He knew that it would take very little to ignite a spark between them, and he saw no reason for refraining from playing with such pleasant fire. Moreover, the typical male aversion for trespass upon any possible preserves of his own had begun to possess him. Trixie seemed to have a good many suitors, and he did not know how seriously she might take any one of these at any moment. He asked a casual question, which was actually less inconsequential than it sounded.

"Do you ever hear from Card Eustis nowadays?"

"Oh, yes. He turns up regularly every summer."

"Do you drag him through picture galleries too?"

"No. That isn't Card's idea of a good time."

"It isn't mine either."

"Well, I'm afraid I'm not very successful at pleasing either of you. Card keeps complaining too. You know what his idea of having a good time with a girl is just as well as I do."

"And what's your own idea, Trixie? About having a good time with a man, I mean?"

"It depends an awful lot on the man. For instance, I'm having a good time with you this minute. But if I were here with Card instead of you, I don't believe I'd think the old Nussbaum was so hot."

She smiled engagingly, and her blue eyes sparkled as she spoke. But as if forestalling any special response to her candid declaration of enjoyment, she picked up her gloves and handbag and got to her feet.

"Just the same, no matter how good a time I'm having, I suppose we ought to be cruising along if we're going to the *Götterdämmerung*. Talk about your endurance tests! I'd say an opera that lasts five hours and doesn't have a single tune in it from beginning to end was enough to lay anyone out! But you don't hear me whining about stretchers and strenuous paces."

Hans Christian laughed in his turn, paid their infinitesimal *Rechnung*, and followed her out into the street. The man with the sinister face, his hands still buried in the pockets of his shabby overcoat, looked up at them as they passed. But he did not speak to them or try to stop them. The other patrons of the restaurant appeared to be as oblivious of their departure as they had been of their presence. Unalterably drab, they continued to talk in low guttural voices, to carve their initials in the benches, and to drink the excellent beer which the slatternly *Stubenmädchen* slopped over as she set it down in front of them.

Outside, the sky was still bright and beautiful, and a fresh breeze gave a quality of stimulation to the soft air. It blew in fitful gusts down the narrow street, between the tall, blank houses lining this on either side. But the sunshine overhead did not stretch to the sidewalks; it was swallowed up in the gloomy recesses of the colourless thoroughfare Except for a few slinking and scuttling

122

figures, Fischerstrasse was empty. There were no children playing exuberantly on the pavements, no groups of labourers swinging home from work, no crowds pushing good-naturedly into little open shops. The normal bustle of business and pleasure was completely lacking. A solitary whistle, undefinable of origin, and mysteriously echoed, vibrated through the air. Then everything was silent again. The vacancy and stillness were eerie in their effect.

"I'm afraid we ought to have come in my car after all," Hans Christian said. A queer little quiver was forking its way through his body, and he looked searchingly up and down the street. "But since neither of us knew our way around the East End . . . we might at least have kept our taxi. I was a fool not to realize that it might be hard to pick up another."

"Don't worry. I'm sure one'll be along in a minute. We might walk on down towards the canal. There's probably more traffic there."

"*More* traffic! I don't get the comparison, Trixie."

"You ought not to mind emptiness, after East Prussia."

"The country never seems empty to me. But a city street with no one in it is weird. That whistle was queer too. Don't you think so?"

"Sort of. But I'm not going to let it get me."

As she spoke, a sharp spitting sound crackled through the air. She jumped back, instinctively clutching at Hans Christian's arm

"What's that, Chris?"

"I can't imagine. I don't see a soul anywhere."

"It sounded like a shot to me."

"How could it be? There's no one around to do any shooting."

"It must have come from one of those houses."

"But they look empty too."

"Well, I guess they're not."

As if in confirmation of her remark, several windows were suddenly flung open and an uproar arose from within them. At the same moment a second report rang out. It was louder than the first, and longer, and was followed by an ugly snarling outcry.

"*Es muss etwas geschehen! So geht es nicht weiter! Nieder mit den Nazis! Nieder mit der S.A.! Nieder mit dem Horst Wessel!*"

Tightening his hold of Trixie's arm, Hans Christian quickened his pace. "This is a bad quarter," he said under his breath. "Some kind of trouble's up. We've got to get out of it if we can."

"Yes, I know. I can run, Chris, if you think we better. But I'm not afraid."

They could hear tumultuous shouting now and the sound of rushing feet. Before another shot had rung out, so suddenly that they could not see from whence the crowd came, the empty sidewalks were swarming. They were hemmed in on every side by a mob that had apparently gone mad. Escape was completely cut off.

123

Ducking down, and dragging Trixie along with him, Hans Christian fought his way through the rioters towards a doorway. Twice he was knocked down, falling over her as he fell himself. Someone stamped on him before he could get to his feet again, and, when he dragged himself halfway up, someone else kicked him over; but he could still feel her clinging confidently to him. When at last he reached the doorway, he managed to push her behind him and crouched in front of her, warding off hit or miss blows with his arm. Most of the men around them were fighting with their fists. But some of them had rubber clubs, and a few revolvers. He was sick with fear lest a stray shot should whiz past him. The next time the crackling started there was no telling where it might end.

"I'm all right, Chris. I'm not frightened. Please don't worry."

Somehow, above the din, she made him hear her. But he could not answer her. The mob was milling towards the doorway now. At any moment they might be crushed by it, unless it receded, unless it scattered and disappeared as quickly as it had come. A moment before he had been cursing at his own folly for bringing Trixie into this hotbed of violence, but from cursing he went to prayer. Let me get her out, don't let any harm come to her because I've been such a bloody fool, keep her from being hurt. . . .

"Really I'm all right, Chris. I think it's going to be over in a minute, anyway."

Something snapped. The impact of struggling bodies against them slackened. The blows, the crackling, the shouts and stamping abated. The electrified air began to clear. The rioters were surging forward now instead of pressing backwards; then they separated, charging in different directions and calling out as they went. Hans Christian, still bent defensively over, heard Trixie speaking to him a third time.

"Someone is trying to talk to you, Chris. I think he means to be friendly."

Hans Christian slowly straightened himself up. A young man—hardly more than a boy—dressed in brown twill, was standing over him, looking down at him fixedly. His blue eyes were keen, but they were hostile. He was breathing hard and perspiration was streaming from his face; his clothes were badly dishevelled. In spite of these evidences of conflict, however, his manner was completely controlled.

"*Also,*" he said peremptorily. "*Was ist denn los? Warum sind Sie hier?*"

"You may be very sure it isn't from choice," Hans Christian retorted. He was still greatly shaken; it was more than a matter of a moment to regain his self-control. "This lady and I were walking quietly down the street when a mob appeared from nowhere. We got hemmed in by it," he added by way of brief explanation.

Then he turned to Trixie. "How much hurt are you?" he asked anxiously in English.

"*Sind Sie Engländer?*" inquired the young German, regarding them with still greater attention.

"We're Americans," Trixie interposed quickly. Her German was faulty but fluent, and she had no more trouble now than Chris in shifting swiftly from one language to another. "I'm not hurt, except that someone seems to have given me a sock on the jaw My cheeks's bleeding a little."

She had been dabbing at her face with a small square of cambric. Hans Christian, accustomed to her constant manipulation of make-up, had hardly noticed the unobtrusive gesture. Now he saw that the handkerchief was soaked with blood.

"I should think it was! . . . Is there a Red Cross station or an apothecary shop anywhere around here?"

"I am afraid there is not. But my own quarters are in this house. If the *gnädiges Fräulein* would be so good as to step inside, I think I can stop the bleeding myself. I know the principles of first aid. *So, wenn ich bitten darf——*"

The young German twisted an iron ring hanging from the great studded door against which they had been leaning, and it opened creakingly down the middle. Beyond it there was a dim courtyard, where a dark carved stairway curved upwards amidst hanging vines. It was beautiful but battered, and a noisome smell rose from the dank ground about it. Everything connected with the place bespoke bygone splendour sunk to decadence.

Their host produced a latchkey and unlocked a door at the right of the entrance. Then, with grave politeness, he ushered them into a room lined with ancient panelling and sketchily equipped with cheap modern furniture. Offering the one armchair to Hans Christian, he told Trixie to lie down on the couch while he fetched cold water and clean cotton from the kitchen, and, briefly disappearing into an adjacent room, he returned with a small tin basin and other supplies and capably began to bathe her bruised cheek.

"We are very much indebted to you for your hospitality and help. But perhaps you'll also explain to us what this fracas was about," Hans Christian remarked. He had not taken the proffered armchair, but stood beside the couch, watching the proceeding with anxious interest. He still spoke rather curtly, and his host, without betraying any resentment of his manner, answered with slightly satirical stiffness himself.

"It was nothing serious. Only a group of the K.P.D. carrying out orders from Karl Liebknecht Haus: '*Schlagt die Faschisten wo ihr sie trefft!*' A comrade of mine, who lives with me here at the Bomb Palast, was coming peacefully home when he was set upon. He was alone for the moment, so the opportunity was favourable. But other comrades managed to join him, and fortunately he was not hurt at all. I saw him pursuing the last of the aggressors just before I spoke to you. He will probably be along in a few minutes. In fact I do not think any of us were killed this time."

"You're not one of those wicked S.A. men they talk about, are you?" inquired Trixie excitedly, sitting bolt upright.

"Yes, *gnädiges Fräulein*. Oskar Kraus, at your service. It goes better now, *nicht?* But I think it would be well if you would lie still for a few moments yet, until I can be sure that the bleeding is entirely stopped."

"It's practically stopped now—— Why do you call this house the Bomb Palast?"

"It is only a nickname we give it, *gnädiges Fräulein*, because the Communists have sought so many times to destroy it with bombs since my comrade and I have been living here. It was formerly the residence of a great prince. Now, as you see, it is only a tenement. But it is the best we can do at the moment."

"Do you mean to say you live here in these dirty slums on purpose? When you don't have to? With bombs going off over your head all the time? And that you go around shooting up the streets and think nothing of it?"

"Your pardon, *gnädiges Fräulein*. It is not the S.A. who 'shoot up the streets,' as you say. It is the K.P.D. We only defend ourselves from them, as best we can. And I must beg of you to lie down again, as I said before."

"But what does all this street brawling *prove?*"

"Trixie, please stop talking and do what Herr Kraus tells you. This isn't any time for argument."

"I shall be delighted to explain our party principles to the *gnädiges Fräulein* later, if she is really interested. And for that matter to you also, Herr——?"

"My name is Beatrice Rhodes," Trixie announced, bounding up again before Hans Christian could answer. "And this is my friend Chris Marlowe."

"Miss Rhodes is the daughter of the American Ambassador to Germany," Hans Christian remarked drily. "I certainly hope, for everyone's sake, that she isn't much hurt."

"It is my sincere hope also. But only because I should regret that she should suffer. I am sure the American Ambassador, whom we hold in high esteem, would not make an incident out of an accident."

"Do you know my father?" inquired Trixie, still more excitedly.

"I have not had the privilege of meeting him personally. But he has done us the honour of coming to one or two of our meetings —unofficially, of course, as an onlooker. He did not make himself known to anyone. But he was recognized, and with gratitude. It is not often that a foreign envoy takes the trouble to observe what is really going on about him. . . . You would also be most welcome if you would care to attend a gathering of ours, Herr Marlowe."

"I'd like to, some time. And perhaps I can come back here some day, and hear about your party principles, as you suggest. But now, if you think Miss Rhodes is all right, I'd like to try to get her home as quickly as possible."

With the assuagement of his anxiety, and his recovery from the shock of assault, Hans Christian's natural courtesy had begun to reassert itself. He was already secretly ashamed of his incivility in the face of the young Nazi's considerate kindness. His change of manner met with immediate response.

"Of course. I am afraid there are no taxicabs near here. But as soon as my comrade comes back he will get one. I would go myself were it not for leaving you alone here in my Bomb Palast. Not that I think there is any real danger. But sometimes, after an encounter like the one we have just been through, there are slight reprisals."

For the first time, Oskar Kraus smiled. Then, tentatively, he touched Trixie's cheek with his fingers. The bleeding had stopped entirely. He opened a small jar of salve, and applied the ointment meticulously to the bruise. Then he picked up his bottles and basin and the wet cotton and stained towels which he had discarded, and carried them carefully back into the kitchen again.

"May I help you? I seem to be awfully useless! Or I could go out and find a taxi myself, couldn't I, and leave Miss Rhodes with you?"

"Thank you. There is nothing more to do. And I think it would be better that you should not go out, Herr Marlowe. I see that your German is excellent, but after all you do not know your way around this quarter, and, as you have seen, it is apt to be disorderly. However, I am sure it will not be long before my comrade comes. And meanwhile you are most welcome. Perhaps I could offer you and Fräulein Rhodes some slight refreshment. My larder is rather bare, because I have not yet bought my provisions for supper. But such as I have——"

He was interrupted by the sound of knocking. It came firmly, though not aggressively, in a succession of swift strokes against the door, repeated like signals. Oskar Kraus turned quickly.

"That cannot be my comrade. He has his key. But do not be alarmed. I know the knock. It must come from some other member of our troop, arrived to assure himself that all goes well with us."

He opened the door cautiously, saying something that sounded like a watchword as he did so. This was instantly repeated, and it was followed by a murmured greeting and one or two quick questions and answers. Then another fair slim boy stepped into the

127

room. He looked even younger than Oskar Kraus. Indeed, his
face still had the ingenuous aspect of adolescence. But he carried
himself with assurance, notwithstanding the slightness of his build,
and there was an indefinable air of authority about him. He clicked
his heels together and bowed to Trixie.

"I am sorry you have had so poor a welcome to Alt-Berlin,
gnädiges Fräulein. But happily you have come to no real harm.
And now that I am here, Comrade Kraus will go at once for a
taxi, and at the same time telephone the American Embassy so
that there may be no anxiety about you." He bowed a second time,
looked searchingly at Hans Christian for a moment, and held out
his hand. "I am sorry, too, that you should have come to us first
in such a way," he said. "But it is better that you should have come
to us thus than not at all. May I present myself? I am Horst
Wessel, Storm Leader of Troop Number Five. It is a privilege to
greet you—Freiherr von Hohenlohe."

CHAPTER XIV

"Für Deutschland das Leben zu wagen,
Wo andre greifen vergeblich an,
Da zieht man den fünften Sturm heran!"

"Good, comrades! That time it went better—much better! Next
troop night it must be snappier still! In the meantime you will be
practising, in your separate groups. You know how to do it: one
song at the beginning—for instance, *'Kameraden, lässt erschellen.'*
A second after intermission—*'Wer will mit uns zum Kampfe zie-*
hen.' At the end—*'Hoch die Fahne!'*

"No smoking! This isn't a social club! Troop night means
service night! Later on everyone may smoke as much as he likes,
and of course if anyone wants a drink—— But now, every man on
his toes—chests out, heads high! Why, there's not a paunch among
the lot of you. It's plain you're not with the Communists any more.
When you went to their meetings you sat this way, with your head
propped on your elbows, and your hands on your cheeks, and your
mouths wide open!"

The speaker paused long enough to slump into a slovenly slouch.
Momentarily his alert face assumed a vacant expression. Then
echoing the roar of merriment with which his by-play was greeted,
he sprang to his feet again.

"Beginning with our next meeting, I'm going to take a quarter
of an hour each evening to talk to you about politics. It's true that
we're not a debating society, any more than we're a social club.
But a Storm Trooper must be able to stand up for his side. He
can't convince Marxists by mouthing phrases; what he says has

got to have meat in it. We're going to put it there. But for tonight we'll let that slide. We'll talk about the subject that means the most to us—the *Sturm Abteilung*. What does it mean—S.A.? What does it mean to be an S.A. man?"

The *Lokal Zur Möve* in the Grosse Frankfurter Strasse was packed with people. Most of them were Storm Troopers, but there were also a number of onlookers. The meetings were not secret, and outsiders were welcomed, for among them many recruits were made. Within the last month seventy had been added to the ranks, and the question of a meeting place had become something of a problem. It was not too easy to find an accommodating host in Friedrichshain, and *Heinrichs Festsaale,* where Horst Wessel had directed his first troop night, had long since overflowed with his followers. But finally a landlord had been discovered who was not afraid of what the Karl Liebknecht Haus might do to him, and Troop Five had forgathered in his largest hall.

"Loyalty. Obedience. Self-control. Reliability. Honourable conduct in the service and out of it. *Kameradschaft*—these are the qualities demanded of an S.A. man," the speaker went on. "The leader of my old *Standarte*—most of you know him—never tired of hammering these fundamental principles into his troop members, and especially into the leaders he had under him. I am going to take time this evening to explain these fundamental principles which underlie the training of an S.A. man."

"LOYALTY is the greatest S.A. virtue. The S.A. man is loyal when he stands by the vow he made when he gripped his leader's hand. Along with loyalty to his leader goes loyalty to his comrades. A man is a faithless coward who leaves his comrades in the lurch at times of need, who fails to rush to his comrades' need when alarm is sounded."

"It is said of Horst Wessel's father that he was not only a good pastor, but a great preacher," Oskar Kraus whispered to Hans Christian. "You see that his son has inherited his talents. In all Berlin there is no one more in demand as a speaker. I know of fifty speeches which he has made within the last three months. Listen!"

"Next after loyalty comes obedience," Horst Wessel was saying, "and obedience always calls for self-control. Together these two constitute discipline. DISCIPLINE is the foundation on which co-operation between the S.A. man and the S.A. leader rests. A person may be a fine orator and a great organizer, a political authority and a trained athlete, with courage, energy and presence of mind. But if he does not know how to obey, he has not the marks of merit. In spite of his brown shirt, his cap, his *Koppel*, his shoulder straps and his party insignia, he is no true S.A. man. A troop may have imposing strength, it may be commanded by a

129

capable leader. But without discipline it is still nothing but a heterogeneous group.

"The S.A. man who is impressed with these truths shows his leaders the respect which he owes them because of their position. Deportment is always the expression of an inner attitude. Therefore the S.A. man, like the soldier, salutes his leader when he greets him, standing erect and facing him squarely. But he bows his head only before the majesty of God and the majesty of death."

He was only twenty-two and he looked younger still. But as he spoke the men around him, many of them old enough to be his father, paid him the tribute of their deference. There was something Biblical in the simplicity of his language and the composure of his bearing; but there was force behind both. This force made itself felt, like an electric current.

"Let me sum up what I have said so far: If loyalty is the most outstanding of the S.A. virtues, discipline is their most important attribute. Without forgetting this, we must not forget the great quality of trustworthiness—the quality which makes a man 'faithful unto death'—or the great requisite of honourable defence. But among comrades questions of honour are not settled by fighting. Remember this when you are confused and angry. Never strike a comrade, for in doing so you break the bonds of *Kameradschaft*. As my last point, shall I speak to you on this subject? I should do so if it were a problem in the S.A., but, thank God, such is not the case. The brown battalions may have lacked every other great quality of which I have been speaking. But *Kameradschaft* is the one which has been theirs from the beginning.

"The feeling that in a world full of hate and infamy we are bound together for better or worse, in life and in death—this feeling has always inspired us every one, the leaders and the led. That spirit of *Kameradschaft*, based upon valour and discipline, that spirit which gave to millions at the front the strength to serve and to sacrifice, must also animate the S.A. For it is now in the hands of the S.A. that the future of Germany lies!"

"*Sturm* Five—Attention! Quiet! I declare this meeting adjourned!"

> "*Die Fahne hoch! Die Reihen dicht geschlossen!*
> *S.A. marschiert mit mutigfestem Schritt,*
> *Kameraden, die Rotfront und Reaktion erschossen,*
> *Marschier'n im Geist in unseren Reihen mit.*"

It was over. The ranks were breaking, the men were leaving the hall or gathering together in little groups at the doorway. They were lighting cigarettes now as they laughed and chatted. But Hans Christian continued to stand as if he had been transfixed. Oskar Kraus touched him lightly on the arm.

130

"Would you like a glass of beer? Is anything the matter?"

"No . . . but I have the strangest feeling. As if I could hear thousands singing that song, not just this small assembly."

"There's a lilt to it. It's easy to sing. I imagine it will take on."

"I don't mean just that—I can't explain. Do you suppose I could talk to Horst Wessel myself?"

"Tonight?"

"Yes, now."

"I don't know. He's generally very busy. He's got a lot on his mind. But we can find out."

They went on to the back of the hall. Horst was still standing there, talking earnestly in a low voice with two or three others. Kraus approached them and saluted.

"*Mein Führer*, Freiherr von Hohenlohe is here. The man you met in my quarters with the young American lady."

"Yes, I remember. He is very welcome."

"He says he would like to have a talk with you."

"He would be welcome to do that also. I will tell him so."

Horst Wessel himself saluted. Then he turned and looked cordially towards Hans Christian. When he smiled he seemed younger than ever. And the smile was irresistible. Hans Christian was drawn to him as if by a magnet.

"Good-evening. I'm so glad you came to our meeting. I hoped you'd come to one, some time, after I saw you the other night. Did you enjoy it?"

"Yes, very much. That is . . . I want to talk to you."

"So Comrade Kraus tells me. Would you care to come to my quarters? I live with my family. I'd like to have you meet them some time. . . . My mother, my brother Werner, who's in Troop Four, and my sister Ingeborg. You'd admire her, she's very talented. But I have some small diggings of my own, besides, close by here in the Grosse Frankfurter Strasse. If what you want is a quiet conversation, we could go there. That's why I keep it—for just such conferences, I mean. I have a good many."

He smiled again. If there were any element of irony in the remark, Hans Christian did not catch it. He grasped eagerly at the opportunity which had been offered him.

"Thanks a lot. Shall I wait till you're through here?"

"I'm through now. We can walk along together."

There was rain in the air when they went out. Horst Wessel lifted his head as if he welcomed the freshness of it on his face.

"I love weather like this. In my part of the country we call it `ein richtiger, erbärmlicher Landregen.` Do you have the same expression in East Prussia? *So!* . . . Sometimes I wish my grandfather had never come to the city. I like the land. While I was still in Standard Four, my brother Werner's troop, I used to get out there once a fortnight at least over the week-ends. Now I'm too busy. But there's a farm not far out, owned by a man who's friendly. He always lets· the S.A. come there. He has a big barn, three hundred can sleep in it. I've often acted as sentry there. Sometimes the nights seemed pretty long, if I'd been doing guard duty and drilling all the week. But there was something about it . . . the stars and the silence. Or on the evenings like this the haze and the mystery. I could feel their beauty as if it had been alive. And I was never tired the next morning. Perhaps because of all this sombre splendour. Or perhaps a sense of responsibility is always a stimulation. Or perhaps just because cold water out of a pump, dashed over your head at five in the morning, and coffee made in a field kitchen, are even better ones!"

He laughed pleasantly. Hans Christian laughed too, but he asked an earnest question.

"Could I go out into the country with the troop, too, as well as coming to the meetings?"

"But of course! Werner would be delighted to take you if I cannot. And in August you should come to Nuremberg with us, you should see the great celebration of our *Parteitag*. I promise you it is worth it! . . . Well, here we are at my lodgings. You must tell me whether you like it as well as the Bomb Palast."

Horst Wessel unlocked the door of a bleak house, stale-smelling after the fresh misty air they had been breathing, and Hans Christian followed him up two flights of steep slippery stairs, covered with brown linoleum. At the top of these Horst ushered him into a small dormer room overlooking the street and furnished in nondescript fashion. Magnetized as it was, its furnishings did not matter.

"May I offer you some refreshment? No? Then tell me what it is you have on your mind."

"I want to tell you first of all that I didn't intentionally conceal my identity from Oskar Kraus that night at the Bomb Palast. I'm tremendously proud of being a German—in fact, I'm one by choice. I'll tell you about that too. But Fräulein Rhodes was terribly over-wrought, and she was injured. Every time I tried to say anything she interrupted me. She's obsessed with the idea that I'm essentially American. I didn't want to seem to argue with her before a stranger or do anything to make her worse."

"Of course. I understood perfectly. And so did Kraus, afterwards. At first, since he didn't know who you were, it didn't matter, any-way. But it is my business to be informed on such matters. Any prominent guest whom the American Ambassador might have for a prolonged period . . . may I ask if his daughter, the pretty young lady I saw, is your *Braut*? On this particular point I am not in-formed!"

"No, she is only a friend. But a very good friend. I'm extremely fond of her—of the whole family."

"It appears that they have made a very favourable impression in Berlin. That is fortunate. We have not always been so pleased with the officials which the United States has seen fit to send us, and it is better this way. We need something to counteract the trouble made by this cursed Young Plan. What Dawes did was bad enough. It never could have worked, a substitute had to be found. But what is this substitute? A policy of humiliation, a plan for bondage! The Reichspräsident is defending it and the Reichstag will accept it—but to their own cost as well as Germany's!"

He spoke with mounting fervour, and for the first time Hans Christian was conscious that there might be a strain of vindictiveness in his valour. But there was cause enough for vindictiveness in German hearts; even the most lofty natures could hardly escape it. And Hans Christian was eager to speak of Germany's wrongs himself.

"I'm glad you mentioned politics. I especially wanted to talk to you about these, since you didn't mention them in your speech. Things are in a bad way in East Prussia."

"You could do a great deal to make them better, if you cared to."

"I? I've succeeded as a horse breeder, but for all the prestige I have, I might as well be the *Landstallmeister* in my own *Herrenhaus*. All my neighbours look down on me! They think I haven't got the true Junker spirit."

"Then show them that you have the true German spirit—the spirit of the new Germany, the resurrected country! Who could be so supremely suited to do so as yourself? A man who has voluntarily left luxury and leisure behind him in America to cast his lot with our hard one, to perpetuate a proud name and revive an ancient house!"

His praise was stimulating. Hans Christian felt his self-assurance returning. But his mind was still in a state of upheaval, and until his mental processes had undergone adjustment and steadied themselves, he knew he could achieve no clarity of vision, no strength of purpose. Reluctantly but resolutely he steered the conversation back into the political field, and Horst Wessel followed his lead with enthusiasm. Hans Christian could not imagine how so young a man could have mastered so much or how he could impart what he had learned with such skill. He embarked fluently on the subjects of unemployment and reparations, as if he were intimately acquainted with them. He spoke with assurance of the characteristics of Stresemann, Streicher, Hanfstängl, Hess. From policies and personalities he passed on to the discussion of principles.

"Have you read *Mein Kampf*? It's so expensive, most of my men can't do so. I pick up a copy, here **and** there, as I can, to lend to leaders; and I read aloud, key sentences, at most meetings. By and by there'll be a popular edition that will help a great deal. But probably you haven't needed to wait for that."

"No, I've read the book. My grandmother was bound there shouldn't be a copy in the house. But I bootlegged it, and since then I've hidden it."

"Your grandmother? *Ach ja*, the Austrian Archduchess who stands in so well with the Church. . . . You have no Catholic leanings of any kind yourself, I suppose?"

"No. . . . My grandfather von Hohenlohe was a Lutheran. His sons were baptized Catholics, like the children of all mixed marriages, but when my father was old enough to choose for himself, he became a Lutheran too. I was raised as a Protestant from the beginning. But probably you know most of this already."

"Yes, but it is gratifying to have your confirmation of the facts. Your grandfather was a great general. I hope you may follow in his footsteps, as far as leadership is concerned."

"That was my own hope, when I came to Germany. But so far I've done nothing."

"I should say you had done a great deal and that you will do much more. In regard to the Austrian question, for instance. It is a ticklish one, and you must be in a position to know a good deal about some forms of feeling concerning it. We will talk that over some other time. I have spent six months in Vienna myself, and I think you would enjoy going there, which would be a natural thing for you to do, considering all your connections. . . . A pity the first *Anschluss* movement was a failure. But, after all, these adjustments do take time. We must not be impatient or allow ourselves to become discouraged. . . . So your grandmother does not approve of our Party! That is very interesting. And your mother, what about her? What do they think about Nazis in America?"

"I haven't been back there in five years. But my mother sends me some clippings. I gather they think the club-foot and cleft-foot are pretty close together—not to mention the affiliation between dope fiends and perverts."

"*Ach*, that freedom of the press of which Americans are so proud! What a channel for chicanery it can become! When you meet the men who have been so slandered, your gorge will rise with indignation."

"Do you think I'm likely to meet them?"

"Of course, if you wish. Nothing could be easier. Unless your own time is fully filled with functions—or unless, lacking a *Braut*, you have a sweetheart."

"No, I haven't a sweetheart yet."

"Well, they do sometimes lead to complications! On the other hand, they add to the zest of life. In any case, since your time is so free, I must help you to fill it. Shall we arrange for another meeting?"

It was not a dismissal, it was an invitation. Nevertheless, as he accepted it, Hans Christian rose to leave. Horst Wessel straightened his shoulder-straps and reached for his own cap.

"I'll walk with you a few blocks."

"But then you would have to come home alone!"

Horst Wessel laughed again.

"And quite right that I should. Right and entirely safe. Nothing'll happen to me. Other comrades are occupying our friends the Communists just now. I know the orders that have gone out from Karl Liebknecht Haus. '*Den Horst Wessel den lässt zunächst Mal in Ruhe. Das besorgen wir schon. Der kommt auch noch 'ran.*'"

"But then any time——"

"No, not any time. Not for a long while yet."

A strange shiver passed through Hans Christian. Again, as in the *Lokal*, he seemed to hear multitudes singing Horst Wessel's song and the tramp of millions of marching feet. But the dark street was still as they went into it, and they went down it together in silence. At the canal Horst Wessel stopped.

"Now I know you will be unmolested as you go on your way. I thank you for your visit. Remember your promise to repeat it."

"Indeed I shall. *Auf Wiedersehen.*"

Horst Wessel saluted. "Since we are now friends, suppose we part in the modern fashion. In the new Germany we do not say either '*Grüss Gott*' or '*Auf Wiedesehen.*' We say '*Heil Hitler*'!"

It was a long way to the Tiergartenstrasse; but something impelled Hans Christian to go on walking. The spell that had been cast over him during the meeting had deepened while he had been talking in the quiet room. He could not bear to break it now; he wanted it to close more and more tightly in around him. The electric currents which had been unleashed were still coursing through his body; he wanted to go on feeling their mounting magnetism, their invincible power. Cold caution and rigid reason were both quiescent within him, lulled or drugged—he did not ask which—by wonderful words and matchless fervour. He had never felt so much. He had never reflected so little. His high mood sustained him as he swept on through the night, sure that he had seen with his own eyes and touched with his own hand the force which was to save Germany.

CHAPTER XV

HANS CHRISTIAN had fitted easily and well into the Embassy set. He was made instantly welcome in the circles where the Rhodeses moved, and was soon accepted as a permanent part of these. But after a fortnight's visit he announced that he was moving into a bachelor flat; he had been fortunate in finding one furnished which he could take over temporarily from a young diplomat who was going home on leave. He did not wish to trespass too long on her hospitality, he told Mrs. Rhodes; he must look up some more of his German relatives and his father's and grandfather's old friends, he explained to the Ambassador; he was encountering so many black looks at tea dances that he was afraid of what the suitors whose style he cramped might do to him, he said to Trixie. They all protested vigorously. Nevertheless, at the time he himself had appointed, he drove buoyantly away in his battered car. After that, though he dropped into the Embassy frequently at all sorts of odd hours, he declined to return to it on the still more intimate footing of a house guest.

The spring continued to be balmy and beautiful, and, as the season advanced, every week-end witnessed an enormous outpouring of pleasure-seekers from Berlin. Camping, tramping, bicycling, swimming, racing, tennis tournaments—these and kindred diversions lured the youth of the capital out into the suburbs and the country, to lakesides and mountain-tops. Sometimes they went in gay, heterogeneous groups; sometimes in sober, purposeful bands; sometimes in amorous, isolated couples. Hans Christian, once he was ensconced in his own flat, occasionally disappeared entirely from Saturday to Monday without giving any very definite explanation of his absence afterwards. He was sorry he had not been accessible by telephone, he had been dashing about here and there, he had wanted to get off entirely by himself, some friends who were rather retiring had invited him to join their quiet outing. . . . These were the unsatisfactory explanations which were all that Trixie could get out of him. His elusiveness irritated her intensely, but her attempts to overcome it were vain; the more she teased him, the less he told her. Repeatedly she declared she would never ask him anything again, only to break her vow the next time she saw him. Repeatedly she declared she would never invite him to go out with her again, only to urge him eagerly to do so at her first opportunity. For the most part he accepted her invitations with sufficient show of pleasure to salve her piqued feelings. His periods of withdrawal were the exception and not the rule.

One Sunday morning, as they went down the steps of the Embassy together, Trixie noticed a girl wearing an elaborate costume and carrying a baby covered with a long lace veil, who was parading slowly up and down the avenue opposite. With the rich green of the Tiergarten as a background, she was an arresting figure. Trixie touched Hans Christian's arm.

"Look, Chris! What sort of a fancy dress do you suppose that is?"

"It's the Spreewald *Tracht*," he said smilingly. "When I was a little boy the Tiergarten used to be dotted with them. The Spreewald nurses were supposed to be tops, as you put it. In fact, I should probably have had one myself if my own mother hadn't proved so adequate. Now you hardly ever see those costumes—except in the Spreewald itself, of course. Babies are fed with formulas, aren't they, out of bottles, when there isn't any natural source of supply? Not that I know much about it——"

"Chris, you do put things the craziest way!—Where is the Spreewald, and *what* is it?"

"Dear, dear! Haven't you picked up any information at all since you've been in Berlin, Trixie? You must have crossed the Spree thousands of times. It's the self-same stream that flows through this very city. About sixty miles from here it divides into natural canals and intersects a forest. That's the Spreewald. There are a few villages in the region, and clearings of farmland, too, along some of the canals, which the people use for streets. They speak a queer dialect of their own called Wendish, and the women still wear costumes like those you just saw, with a special *Tracht* for christenings, and another for Communion, and so on. The *Spreewalderinnen* are very religious. But apparently they're clothes-conscious too. As soon as a girl leaves school and begins to make money herself, she starts buying all these different outfits and putting them away in a big chest, so that when she's married she'll have a complete assortment. Her husband never has to replenish it. Not such a bad idea at that."

"There you go, crazy again! Why didn't you ever take me to see this Spreewald, instead of talking to me about it as if you had just studied a geography lesson? You know how wild I am about costumes."

"Well, you hadn't told me before that you wanted to go there. You've wanted to go everywhere else—to all the museums and monuments and shows and races and music-halls and beer gardens. But you never——"

"How could I ask you to take me there when I'd never heard of it? But I'm asking you now——"

"Very well, there's no reason, as far as I know, why we shouldn't start for the Spreewald this minute instead of going to Karlshorst or Hoppegarten."

Trixie hesitated. She had not expected to be taken quite so literally, and she adored the excitement of Hoppegarten, as Hans Christian was well aware. But after all, he had called her bluff, as he had such an uncomfortable way of doing. If she were to save her own face, she really had very little choice.

"All right. Shall we go in your car or mine?"

"Oh, I think we'd better go in yours. It's speedy as well as resplendent, and mine is such a forlorn old derelict. If we broke down we'd have a very dull day. The towns between Berlin and Luebbenau are all pretty dreary."

"Are we going to Luebbenau?"

"Well, it's the usual starting-point for excursions through the canals. But I think we might go to Burg first. That's where the most stylish show is staged, at church. We may be in time to see it if you step on the gas."

"Are you expecting me to drive?"

"Of course. I'm not in your class, Trixie, when it comes to speed—or in anything else, for that matter."

He opened the door of the car and offered her his hand, looking at her in the whimsical way which she had always found so winning. For the first time it angered her; behind the smiling surface of his face she sensed a slight sarcasm. To be sure, she had often done so. But never before had this ironical element been so disturbing. She sprang into her seat unaided and pressed her foot down savagely. The car leapt forward, lurching as it turned a quick corner.

"What you really mean is that I'm not in *your* class at all," she said vehemently. "Why don't you tell me so, Chris?"

"I've never had the least idea of telling you so."

"No, but you've always thought so. I'd rather you came right out with it, like that snooty Carruthers woman we met on the boat, than have you keep hinting."

"So Mrs. Carruthers did speak to you about your little experiment with the ventilating system! What did she say?"

This was the last question which Trixie would have chosen to have Hans Christian ask. Her rage mounted at the consciousness of the trap she had set for herself.

"She said everything you think."

"The conversation must have been fulsome and lengthy. Just how did she embark on it?"

"Spitefully. Just as you're doing now."

"Trixie dear, you're not going to spoil this beautiful day by quarrelling with me at the very beginning, are you?"

Trixie's heart missed a beat. Hans Christian had never before spoken to her in that tender tone; he had never before called her "dear." Instantly her anger evaporated. Her pulses still pounded, but not with rage. The electrified atmosphere was transformed. It was all she could do to keep her eyes on the stream of traffic pouring out past the airport towards the country. Yet one grievance still persisted. Why had he chosen such a moment to give the first sign that he was not utterly indifferent to her, that he did not inwardly deride and despise her? If he had only waited until they reached that strange forest of which he had told her, she might have been in his arms by now. While as it was——

"We'll have to go into all this more thoroughly later," Hans Christian remarked. His voice was whimsical again, as if he had read her thoughts and were gently teasing her. But now his banter did not seem to hurt—not with the sound of "dear" still ringing in her ears. "Meanwhile I wouldn't run down that group of bicyclists if I were you. The consequences of that might be even worse than a quarrel," he concluded, still jestingly.

"They're a highway menace," observed Trixie, dodging the pedalling youths expertly, with no slackening of speed.

"*That* from a young lady travelling at a hundred and twenty kilometres an hour? People in glass houses, Trixie——"

"I'm in a hurry. I want to get to this Spreewald of yours."

"You're always in a hurry. You always want to get somewhere."

"Yes, and I do too! I got from Kansas to The Hague and from The Hague to Berlin, didn't I?"

"You certainly did. Where are you bound from Berlin?"

"I told you, to the Spreewald."

"You may find it a step in the wrong direction."

"I don't expect to."

Hans Christian had been right, as usual. The towns through which they were passing were certainly dreary. There was a famous church in one of them; a famous man had been born in another. But Trixie shook her head when Hans Christian asked if she would like to stop anywhere for sightseeing.

"You said yourself we had barely time to get to Burg before church let out."

"You're right. I did. Drive on, MacDuff!"

He settled more comfortably in his seat. As he did so, however, one of his arms strayed, as if by accident, across the back of it, and presently it slid easily down over Trixie's shoulder. After that she ceased to notice the dreariness of the towns. Electric currents seemed to flow from the fingers that rested so lightly on her sleeve. She could count all five of them, coursing in different directions through her body. Hopefully, eagerly, she wondered if the delight were mutual, if Chris were conscious of her ardent response to the magnetic forces he was releasing. But if he were, he gave no sign of it.

"Oh—you should have turned left there," he said suddenly. "This is Vetschau. You'll begin to see women in costume any minute now."

He had scarcely spoken when two girls on bicycles wheeled past their backing car, both equipped with umbrellas tucked expertly under their arms, and both wearing the huge triangular head-dresses, gay aprons and voluminous skirts of the Spreewald. Closely in their wake a child came trudging along, her small face encircled with wide-spreading silk and lace, her small feet emerging from under bright bands. Encumbered though she was with her petti-coats, she was evidently hurrying; presently they saw that she was trying to catch up with her mother, a solidly built woman whose *Tracht* was made of unrelieved black.

"Oh, Chris, I think they're too quaint for anything! This is going to be good!"

"I hope so. Look out! There's another sharp turn here, and the road's awfully narrow."

The bicyclists were rapidly increasing in number, and all the women Hansel and Trixie saw were in costume now. They went clattering over the cobblestones of another small village and across another stretch of pleasant countryside. Then again they ap-proached small clustering houses and an open square flanked on one side by two taverns, and on the other by a red brick church. The place was crowded with people coming and going, with large carts and small shabby motor-cars standing side by side. There was a sound of music in the distance, and in the foreground the jovial noise arising from a jesting, jostling crowd.

"This is Burg," Hans Christian said somewhat superfluously. "Look, Trixie! Do you see that little procession going into the church? I believe it's a christening party! Let's hurry and catch up with it."

They parked the car quickly, disregarding the admonitions of a grumbling guardian, who tried to indicate exactly where they should place it, and went rapidly across the park. Trixie had not declined Hans Christian's proffered help this time; and they were still hand in hand when they went into the church, which was gaily decorated with tissue-paper festoons. Apparently the regular ser-vices were already over. Only the first rows of pews were occupied, and at the left of the altar a group of costumed women were facing a grave young pastor who wore the long black robes and white-tabbed collar of the Evangelical Church. One of the women was carrying the white bundle which had first attracted Hans Chris-tian's attention outside, and as layers of embroidered net and thin silk were gradually lifted from this a small pink face and swaddled form were at length disclosed. A faint protest had risen at intervals from the wrappings, but as the pastor began to pray these outcries were stilled. The sturdy arms upholding the baby swayed gently back and forth, soothing it. Except for the pastor's voice the little church was hushed.

The sponsors began to recite the Lord's Prayer slowly with the pastor. They all together advanced toward the small font, surmounted by a brass ewer and basin, which stood midway between the altar and nave. The swaddled bundle was held over it, the names "Margarethe Martha" pronounced to the sound of trickling water. Music issued from an unseen organ. The layers of silk net were carefully replaced. Smiling, the procession went down the aisle and out of the church.

"It was sort of sweet, wasn't it, Chris? I wonder why there were no men in the group around the altar, though, don't you? I should think the baby's father——"

"I don't know why, but perhaps we can find out. Let's go across to the *Gasthaus* and get some coffee and pound cake. . . . It's hours since breakfast! Besides, the christening party may be taking place there. But even if it isn't, probably the landlady can tell us something about local customs."

The tavern was as crowded as the square. In the room at the left of the front door men were gathered around the bar, and seated, with their families, at small tin tables, drinking early beer and morning coffee. In the room on the right two christening parties were assembled, with the young pastor, looking less grave now, but still bearing himself with dignity, standing impartially between them; apparently the ceremony which Chris and Trixie had witnessed was the second to be performed that day. One of the babies was lying on a pillow in the centre of the table around which its admiring relatives were gathered; they were sharing their creamed coffee with it. The other baby—Margarethe Martha—was now reclining in an elaborately decorated carriage, a rubber pacifier in her mouth. As wine began to circulate, her mother removed the pacifier, dipped it in her own glass, and restored it to the baby, who sucked at it with renewed relish.

"I guess those formulas you were talking about haven't got to Burg yet," Trixie observed, lighting a cigarette. As she sipped the hot coffee Hans Christian had ordered, she continued to watch the babies, while she talked with the landlady, who had answered cordially when they asked her if they might sit in the *Festsaal*. Trixie could understand German very well now; indeed, if Chris had not been with her, she would have talked to the landlady herself. She knew that she still made a great many mistakes, but usually she did not hesitate on this account. Now she felt suddenly shy, listening to his flawless flow of ready idiomatic language. It was one thing to have other people hear her horrible grammar; quite another to have Hans Christian do so. Especially since—— Once more she seemed to feel the pressure of his fingers against her shoulder, their warmth and strength penetrating the stuff of her sleeve.

The landlady was explaining that it was usual for fathers to remain at home on the day of a christening, to oversee the preparations for the feast. It appeared that the drinks which were now being circulated were only by way of preliminary, that the real celebration came later. Chris was listening to her with absorption, but Trixie's interest was beginning to wander. She had taken in the situation with characteristic swiftness. Now she wanted to move on, to see more. Above all, she wanted to feel Hans Christian's fingers locked in her own again or pressing against her shoulder.

"I liked the sound of that music we heard before we came in here, didn't you, Chris?" she asked. "Let's go and see where it comes from."

He nodded, but he finished his cake and coffee and went on talking with the landlady as he counted out coins. Trixie could have risen, of course, at once and gone to the door without him, to make her impatience plain. Once she would have done so. Now she knew better, knew that Chris did not like to be hurried about anything, that she must let him take his time if she were to get good results, whatever they were doing together—even on the day when he had first made a gesture which could be interpreted as a caress and had called her "dear" for the first time.

Her restraint was rewarded. As they finally went out of the tavern door Chris took her hand and tucked it into the crook of his arm. All the other fellows who were out with their girls were walking that way, he said gaily; she had only to look around her and she would see. She had seen already, and the rite lost some of its significance because it seemed to be so generally observed. But not all of it. Nothing could rob her of the sense of comfort and security which it gave her to walk like this with Hans Christian. Nothing could render his touch so casual that it did not thrill her.

The cobblestone street was lined with booths, at which all sorts of Spreewald souvenirs were sold. As Chris and Trixie passed the third one, a small black puppy lying beneath the counter wriggled out and wagged its tail in friendly fashion. Hans Christian paused.

"I really think we ought to buy something to assure future dog-biscuit for that puppy, don't you? What about one of those costume dolls? You could name it Margarethe Martha, after the baby we saw baptized. . . . Or a miniature Spreewald boat? See how the settees stand on two bars, with nothing at all to hold them down, apparently! Well . . . I seem to be rambling on. . . . Perhaps you think it would look too touristy to go around carrying little packages."

"I don't at all. I'd love to have you get me a doll and a boat."

Damned white of you!' I promise I won't take advantage of your mood to sit down and dash off a few fond messages to absent friends on postcards."

"I wouldn't care if you did that either."

It was perfectly true. Chris had never given her a present before,

142

had never suggested that he might. She knew that until lately he had been terribly hard up, and she had not expected anything from him, both because he was so pressed for money and because he was so indifferent to her. That is, because he had seemed so indifferent. He couldn't be any longer, or he wouldn't be carefully counting out those coins into the thin hand which the vendor extended with such pathetic eagerness. The large doll and the small boat were nothing much in themselves. But as symbols they had vast importance.

"If you like, we can leave the packages here and get them later on, after we have seen the *Heimatsfest*."

"No, I want to take them with me. . . . What is a *Heimatsfest*? I heard the vendor say there was one, but I didn't know what it meant."

"It's the German version of Old Home Week. We're in great luck to have got here for it."

They were passing a big open-air pavilion now, which, like the tavern, was crowded with guests seated at little tables. Beyond it was a band, the source of the hitherto unexplained music; beyond the band stood a series of wide wooden platforms, where country dances were in progress. The girls' dresses were gayer here than any that Trixie and Chris had seen before, their aprons made of pleated lace, their headdresses embroidered, their white stockings spotless. As they whirled about, snowy lace-edged petticoats were revealed beneath their bright skirts. Trixie gazed at them entranced.

"Could . . . Do you think we could dance too?"

"Those are all special steps, harder to do than you'd think. And I wouldn't like to intrude, to give them the idea that we were trying to crash their party. After all, it *is* their party. Don't you think we'd better just watch for a while and then go back to the pavilion for lunch? We must have eels with Spreewald sauce, and white beer with raspberry syrup floating on top of it, in big goblets that look like champagne glasses run riot, that hold about a quart."

"Chris, I couldn't eat an eel, even to please you!"

"Nonsense! Pretend you're a German *Mädel* today, out with her *Schatz*. You'd eat whatever he suggested if you were. You'd lap it up immediately, gloating over it."

"Yes, but I am not a German *Mädel*. And you're not my *Schatz*."

"Couldn't you pretend that I was?"

There was nothing which Trixie would have been so glad to pretend. In her intermittent pursuit of the German language she had learned that the literal translation of *Schatz* as treasure was entirely inadequate. She knew that the word was also used to designate a very special sort of sweetheart. There was a quality of entreaty in the look she turned on Hans Christian.

"Yes, I could. But that wouldn't make it true."

She was deeply chagrined, so deeply that she was almost angry

143

again. Her voice trembled as she spoke. She hadn't been able to keep it under control. Now large unwelcome tears came welling into her eyes, and she turned aside furtively to hide them.

"*Aber Liebchen! Was thust du denn? Du weinst—heute? Unser frölicher Tag?*"

It *had* been a happy day. But it had also been a day of startling surprises. One had followed so closely upon another that Trixie, for all her vaunted swiftness of thought and action, had not been able to keep pace with them, either figuratively or literally. Now two supreme shocks had come together: Hans Christian had spoken to her instinctively in his mother-tongue instead of in English, which showed her that he was deeply moved himself. And not only that. He had used the familiar form of speech—the *du* reserved for intimate relationships. He had addressed her as *Liebchen*, a lovely term of endearment which had no exact equivalent in any other language, but which came under the same general classification as *Schatz*.

The sequence of events after that was never quite clear to Trixie when she tried to disentangle these from the maze of mysteries in which she had been caught. She did remember, however, that entirely without self-consciousness Hans Christian had wiped her eyes with a large handkerchief and kissed her gently on both cheeks. Then he asked her to wait for him a minute—as if she would not have waited endlessly!—and had gone over and spoken to one of the couples standing near them. There was a lull in the dancing just then, so it was easy for him to do this. The Spreewälder looked at him as if they were surprised too, but they were very cordial to Chris, and when he came back to Trixie he told her that it would be quite all right for them to dance after all, even if they didn't know all the steps, that they would be very welcome. So they had joined the revellers on one of the wooden platforms, and had been taken into a figure, and danced for a long time. It was not hard to catch on, after all; it was easy. And it was the greatest fun of anything that Trixie had ever done in her life.

Finally, she and Chris realized that they were tired and hungry, so they went back to the pavilion with some of the other dancers and had their dinner. They did have Berlin white beer in big goblets, with raspberry sauce floating on top of it, just as Chris had told her that they would; but they did not have eels at all. Instead they had some nice little white fish called *Schlei*, which looked and tasted something like smelts, though they were boiled instead of fried; and the Spreewald sauce was a good deal like any other kind of cream sauce, except that it had more butter swimming on top of it. They also had quantities of boiled potatoes, and afterwards some flat pasty little cakes with pale cherries embedded in them. And coffee, and then more coffee, because they had had lunch so late that before they had finished it was really time for afternoon refreshments. And finally, when they could not swallow another drop or consume another morsel, Chris said they could take one of the funny boats at Burg just as well as at Luebbenau, if Trixie would like to . . . the "harbour" wasn't quite so big, that was really the only difference. And when she said she would like to very much, he went off to see about getting one, tactfully remarking that she might like to powder her nose or something while he was gone, which was unlike the usual German.

Presently they were gliding along over a smooth dark canal, sitting side by side on one of the queer settees, while the boatman poled in the stern. They passed a few picturesque little cottages, which all seemed to have small private canals leading up to them, houses with bright scalloped window-frames and latticed window-boxes and clean lace curtains draped inside the glass. They saw scarred targets fastened to the sides of the houses and ducks swimming primly in rows up and down the private canals. They heard dogs barking and cows mooing. At a sudden bend they came across a man seated alone in a boat drawn up at the water's brink, playing an accordion, and tossed him some coins, as they saw the passengers doing in another boat coming from the opposite direction. After that they did not pass any more boats. It was growing late, and besides, they were leaving the main arteries now. As the boat slid under one little arched bridge after another the farmlands began to disappear. There were fewer fields and more swamps beyond the banks. And finally the forest closed in around them, the curving branches of the trees reflected in the polished water below.

"Trixie, I want to tell you something."

He had not spoken to her in a long time. Like her, he seemed to have fallen into the spell of their surroundings. Now, at the sound of his voice, her heart contracted again.

"It's something that means a great deal to me. I didn't mean to tell you so soon, but we've had such a happy day together, you've seemed so close to me, that I can't wait any longer. . . . I've joined Horst Wessel's Troop. I'm an S.A. man."

The rhythmic motion of the boat had ceased. The beautiful green forest had turned black. Trixie spoke in a smothered scream.

"Chris, you're joking; you're teasing me again. You don't mean that. It isn't what you started to say."

"Of course it is. Why should I start to say one thing and end up by saying another? I haven't told anyone else. I wanted you to be the first to know."

Far off in the distance Trixie could hear soft singing. Passionately she rebelled against the intrusion of song upon her anguish.

"Chris, you *can't* mean it. You've got too much good sense to let that slick agitator hypnotize you with his gift of gab!"

She shouldn't have said that; no one should say anything against a man another man revered. It was almost as bad as insulting his mother or his religion. Chris would be terribly angry with her, and he would have a right to be. But now that she had started she could not help going on. The words came rushing to her lips of themselves.

"He's never taken my father in, not for one minute. I don't see how he can take you in either. He's supposed to be a 'student,' isn't he? Why doesn't he go to classes at the University? Why hasn't he any friends there? Why does he spend all his time in the slums? What does he live on? What did he live on all the time he was in Vienna? Why did he go there? *Who sent him?* I can't see that the Nazis are any different from the Communists, except that they're cleaner and better looking and better drilled. They're both stirring up trouble, they're both bent on destruction and despotism, they're both ready to go to any lengths to gain their ends!"

"Trixie, you don't know what you're saying. Horst Wessel is a great leader, a great idealist. Some day he'll be regarded as a great hero. He's not destroying, he's creating. I want to help him if I can. By and by you'll understand what he's tried to do, what he's done already. I thought you'd understand now, if I talked to you about it. That's what I meant to do, what I looked forward to doing. I thought it was something we could share. And if we could share that . . . I'm sorry I made such a mistake."

"Oh, Chris, don't—don't speak to me like that. You know how much it means to me to have your confidence! You know how much I care! Only——"

It was a cry straight from the soul. Startled, the boatman ceased to paddle, and stood motionless in the stern, permitting the tide to sweep his craft further and further down the stream. He had been out many times with lovers, and often he did not understand the words which they spoke. But he understood their dreams and their desires. The fragrant forest might shelter them in its depths and screen them from his eyes; but it could not shield them from his knowledge of their urgent need for each other. Never had he heard this need more poignantly expressed. After that cry he must not look, he must not listen. . . .

A hand was resting firmly on his shoulder. Startled afresh, he sprang to his feet, rocking the boat. The young Herr who had hired him and who was now standing over him helped him to steady it.

"I think we will not go any further," the stranger said quietly. There was not a trace of passion in his voice; it was merely civil and toneless. "Please start back to Burg as soon as you can turn the boat around. The *gnädiges Fräulein* is very tired. We shall not go walking in the woods after all. Of course I will pay you the same as if you had waited while we did so."

CHAPTER XVI

AFTER Hans Christian was shot in the shoulder there were endless hours when he lay wakeful and rigid, reliving the series of episodes which linked his new life and his old one together.

The break with Trixie had been a greater blow than he had realized at the moment. Afterwards he remembered how casually he had accepted her companionship on the boat, only to long for it later, amidst the silences of Schönplatz. This was a similar experience, but one which meant much more. He had been horrified at her reception of his tremendous tidings. That she should have denounced his allegiance to a compelling creed and insulted the prime prophet of the New Nationalism seemed to him nothing short of a sacrilege. That she had spurned his tender of the confidential relations which he had assumed she was eager to establish humiliated him so deeply that he could conceive of no compensation which would assuage his hurt pride.

He could see her as she looked throughout the dreadful drive home, defensive and defiant, with her shoulders straight and her head held high. He remembered now that her cheeks had been unnaturally red, her eyes unnaturally bright; but that he had not seen at the time. For the sake of surface civility, he had tried, at infrequent intervals, to bridge the uncomfortable stillness between them with trite remarks; but her monosyllabic replies had rendered this effort futile. They had covered the last part of the way back to Berlin in stony silence. By the time they reached the Embassy, he was past caring for any conventional gesture; and when Trixie brought the car to a sudden standstill and made a precipitate appeal to him, it required no will power to steel himself against it.

"Chris. Please—please don't do this awful thing!"

"If by this 'awful thing' you mean joining the National Socialist Party, I've done it already. It can't be undone now."

"Are you sure?"

"Certainly I'm sure. In any case I don't want to undo it. I believe this movement will be the salvation of Germany. And God knows it needs saving."

"Well—— If you feel that way absolutely, so that nothing could change your mind, couldn't we just agree that we wouldn't ever speak of it? I mean, we be friends, the way we have been, but avoid certain subjects? Like Horst Wessel and Party politics and——"

"I don't see how it's possible to be intimate and guarded at the same time. You can't talk freely to a person if you keep saying to yourself, 'There, I almost mentioned something that wouldn't be pleasing, something that might be misinterpreted.' There has to be mutual confidence and respect between real friends."

"But, Chris, I am your friend, I think the world of you. I——"

"I thought you did. But as I said once before tonight, I realize now that I made a mistake. I'm sorry. Good-night, Trixie."

He did not see her again for a long time, not until after he had been shot, not until he no longer remembered clearly how they had quarrelled. But he saw the Ambassador. Mr. Rhodes sent for him to come to the Chancery and gave explicit orders that they were not to be disturbed. He settled himself securely in a deep leather chair, and motioned to Hans Christian to take one also.

"Chris, I'm sorry to gather that you and Trixie have had a kind of falling out. It does seem to me as if something could be done to patch it up. Especially, since as far as I can make out it wasn't in the least personal—it was all about politics."

"But politics are the most personal thing in my life right now, Mr. Rhodes."

"Well—I can understand that, in a way. But you can't expect a girl like Trixie will. She wants a young man to take a personal interest in *her*."

"I did take a personal interest in Trixie, Mr. Rhodes. You knew that. I wasn't in love with her, but I was very fond of her. I'm very fond of you and Mrs. Rhodes too, if you don't mind my saying so. But I can't keep on caring for Trixie now that she's denounced a great cause and slandered a great man. I feel dreadfully about it myself. But it just isn't possible."

"Now, Chris, I wish you wouldn't take what Trixie said quite so hard. I think myself she was a little too harsh in her judgment. I can see some mighty fine things about this New Movement. It's a good thing to take young people into consideration as a political factor. Most of the energy and selflessness and idealism in the world is concentrated in young people, and stodgy old statesmen usually forget that. This man Hitler doesn't. . . . It's also a good thing to teach the doctrine that every kind of work is worth while, as long as it's well done, to make a day labourer feel just as proud of what he's accomplished as a student, say. The world hasn't got very far along those lines, and in most places it hasn't even seriously tried to. In this part of the world a man is trying. And he's trying to give a feeling of unity to a lot of different groups that can't any of them get anywhere because they're all pulling in different directions."

"I'm awfully glad you can see all that, Sir. Now, if Trixie had only seen it——"

"Maybe she will, maybe she will, if you give her a chance. But there are a lot of other things she sees too, and that I see, and that you don't seem to, Chris. This attitude towards religion, for instance—— Not that Trixie's especially religious, but she does like to see fair play. How can you swallow this fanaticism, hook, bait and sinker? Here you grew up in New England, which never would

148

have existed, if freedom to worship God according to their consciences hadn't meant more to a forlorn little sect than safety or comfort or anything else in the world! You're a descendant of those Pilgrims yourself, on your mother's side. You've seen what came out of their courage and their convictions. I don't see how you can shut your eyes to intolerance long. Pretty soon the Catholics will be in for the same kind of treatment, more or less, that the Jews are having now. Next the Protestants will begin to get it in the neck. Then you'll feel differently about it—after it's too late for the way you feel to make any difference."

For an instant, something seemed to click in the back of Hans Christian's brain, something that came as a warning. He remembered that there had been a note akin to veiled satire in Horst Wessel's voice, when he had spoken of the Austrian Archduchess "who stood in so well with the Church," a light warning in the question. "You've never had any Catholic leanings yourself, have you?" But the alarm was stilled, almost as soon as it was sounded, by other arguments that came crowding in.

"I don't mean to seem disrespectful to you, Sir, but what you're saying is absurd. Why, Germany's a third Catholic. No leader would ever buck one-third of a country's population, much less the other two-thirds! Besides, Protestant or Catholic, it takes its religion seriously—much more so than we do—than Americans do, I mean. The pastor is a power among his people as well as the priest. I see that all around me in East Prussia."

"Exactly. And when a man's after power, Chris, he likes to keep it pretty well in his own hands. He doesn't like interference with it. He——"

"After *power!* You think our leaders are after power! Why, they're after unity, as you said yourself, after vigour and decency, after national self-respect and national salvation."

"I guess there are several thousand boys in this country today, Chris, who feel just the way you do, who believe that with all their hearts and souls. I guess in a few years there'll be several million of them—— It looks that way to me, anyhow, from the way things are going, more's the pity!"

"More's the *pity!*"

"Yes, because things aren't going that way just of their own accord. They're going by force. You're tender-hearted, Chris, unusually so. You're sensitive to suffering of every kind. Why, even falcons and fawns get you down, and if you think a woman's overworked you're so crazy to lighten her labours that you're easy prey yourself. I don't believe you'll be able to take it when it comes to seeing men brutalized and abused. It's going to be hard for you not to look the other way when acts of violence are committed—so hard that I don't know but what you'll do it, but what you'll try hard

149

not to see everything that's going on around you. I think maybe you'll try to close your mind as well as your eyes. And I don't know how long or how well you'll succeed. And when it comes to committing acts of violence yourself, I don't know how you'll ever bring yourself to that."

"I shan't see men brutalized and abused. I'll see them trained and hardened. I'll be trained and hardened myself. You're quite right. I need it. I've been a pretty soft specimen."

"Now, Chris, I didn't say that. I said——"

"I know what you said and I know what you meant. Anyhow, I can assure you that I won't be easy prey for any woman again, whether she's overworked or under-disciplined, and I'll never try to take another completely into my confidence."

The Ambassador opened his lips and closed them again, pressing them firmly together. There was a long pause. The drab curtains at the window flapped, the leather chairs creaked slightly. At last Mr. Rhodes cleared his throat.

"Well, I guess there isn't anything more we can say to each other, Chris. I guess maybe you're right, that we can't be friends any more. And I'm sorry. Let's not try to talk any more about it now. Only some day, when you're in the mood, I want you to explain something to me—not to argue with me about it, you understand, just explain it. How it comes that a horse breeder like you, who spent years trying to introduce a new strain into old stock to make it stronger—— Well, we won't go into that right now. I'll say good-bye to you, Chris, much as I hate to do it. I think a lot of you. I think there's fine stuff in you, as fine as in any young fellow I ever knew. Some day it'll come out. I hope I live to see that day, Chris."

Hans Christian had never gone back to the Chancery again. In the memories which preoccupied him, as he lay on his hard hospital bed, there were none of Trixie or of Rufus Rhodes that reached further forward than that tragic trip to the Spreewald, or to that futile discussion in the Chancery, when he and Mr. Rhodes had sat in the deep leather chairs with an ugly wooden table stretching out beside them, and dark window shades flapping on the curtainless casements behind them.

As the image of Trixie receded, other images began to take its place. Very few of them were feminine. To be sure, there was Agathe, that girl he had met in Nuremberg, where he had gone in the early fall, as Horst Wessel had suggested, for the celebration of the *Parteitag*. He had heartily enjoyed the tramp down with his troop. They had gone to a fair in Leipzig and a musical festival in Bayreuth on their way south, both of which had delighted him; so had the verdant countryside through which they passed, at the zenith of its late luxuriance. Most of all, he had revelled in the exhilaration of good companionship and strenuous exercise, of songs sung on the march and snacks devoured by the roadside. He had told the truth when he said to Mr. Rhodes that he would be trained and hardened himself. His easy mastery of horsemanship at Schönplatz, his unsupervised hours in the saddle and the *Studsekretäriat*, had been in no way comparable to the discipline of the planned programme which he was forced to follow now. He was no longer his own master, and occasionally his mind and his muscles both revolted. At first he was so stiff and sore by night that he could not relax, and he had to bite back retorts and smother argumentative answers. But gradually his body responded to the treatment it was undergoing; it took on new vigour, new elasticity; at the same time, his mental processes became more tractable. Evening found him ready to drop in his tracks and sleep wherever he could bunk without self-analysis or inner rebellion. In the morning he waked refreshed, eager to the effort which lay ahead of him, ready to accept command unquestioningly.

When he reached Nuremberg the sight of the mediæval city, with its gables and towers, its grim fortresses and tall façades, all decorated with floating banners, had a still more animating result. He had not realized that these flags would be so red in their general effect. The black swastika on the white circle which formed their centre was obscured when they fell in folds; but their scarlet streamed from the housetops, and—except for that accidental encounter with Agathe—gave him the greatest thrill he had experienced. The speeches were long and dull; the Party chiefs preoccupied; the clashes with Communists much the same as in Berlin. Even the great parade, in which he participated, and the presence of sixty thousand men, impressive from the numerical viewpoint, did not provide the uplift he had expected, nor the same excitement as the march. Reaction seemed to set in, and he realized that he was still smarting from the after-effects of Trixie's rebuff. Then, going into a crowded beer garden above the bluffs to snatch a hasty bite, he had slid into the last vacant place at a long wooden table, and found himself face to face with a pretty girl, in a Red Cross uniform, sitting opposite him, wedged between two laughing groups of kindred spirits, but herself quite alone.

It had been natural enough to speak to her, after the friendly fashion of any continental café. And when it evolved that she had been separated from her friends in the crowd, and did not know where to find them, it had also been natural enough to linger along, chatting with her. Hans Christian's duty for the day was done So, it appeared, was hers. Eventually he asked her if he might not return with her to her lodging. He did not leave it until it was time for him to report again to his troop. And after that there were several intervals when he found it possible to return to her. They were both lonely, having missed something of the holiday spirit which others were so amply enjoying. They were both young, eager and ardent. There was enough, in these attributes, to draw them forcefully to each other, and neither made any attempt to withstand the attraction. They packed an extraordinary amount of robust pleasure into a few broken days and nights.

Hans Christian looked back upon this affair without either regret or repentance. He had neither seduced the girl nor bribed her. She had known how to look out for herself, and she was not mercenary; she was simply overflowing with lust for life, and she had stimulated and strengthened his. During his moments of rebellion against the helplessness and incapacity imposed upon him after he was wounded, he thought hungrily of Agathe. He did not recoil from her image with disgust, as he did from Trüdchen's, and he bore her no deep-seated grudge, as he did Trixie. Though he had never tried to see her again, while he was still up and around, he was inclined to feel that perhaps he had made a mistake. If he had gone back to Nuremberg, he could probably have persuaded her to come to Berlin. As Horst Wessel had said, a sweetheart might create complications. On the other hand, a girl like Agathe, who was strong-limbed and light-hearted, could contribute an immense amount of good cheer and good feeling to a bachelor's existence.

In spite of this normal viewpoint, the episode of Agathe had been an isolated one. For the most part, Hans Christian had been wholly absorbed in his novitiate as a Storm Trooper, and most of his memories centred around this. A few of them still made him wince. He never had reconciled himself to all of Horst Wessel's orders. For instance, he had never been able to bring himself to act as an informer on a friend in spite of the admonition that a man who failed to do so was an offence to the Party, that loyalty to its leader transcended loyalty to a comrade. He had never been able to accept the theory that "sensitivity was not in order," that a harsh element was not an obnoxious one, or to view cruelty in the light of vigour. But he tried to dismiss these disturbing principles from his mind, to keep his memories unmarred.

He loved to dwell, for instance, on the thought of that abnormally cold day, when he had first taken part in a drill himself. It was in the Neuern Markt at seven o'clock on a Sunday morning. Only a few windows in the houses round about had shown signs of life, for on Sunday people slept later than on other days. A street-car, just coming around the corner, was almost empty. The motorman and the conductor had a long way to go; they did not concern themselves with what was immediately before their eyes. They were still drowsy, and, after all, it was no unfamiliar picture that confronted them here: two hundred and fifty S.A. men, formed in two ranks. Five *Stürme* altogether. At intervals on the right wing the *Sturm* flag. One flag-bearer and two men. Three steps ahead of the flag-bearer the *Sturm* leader, distinguishable by his three stars and the black-and-white braid on his collar and around his cap.

A police-lieutenant, in company with several sergeants, was observing the formation of the *Stürme* more attentively than the motorman and the conductor, though without seeming to do so. Hans Christian thought that he was probably full of private approbation for what he was witnessing. It would be easy for him on duty today. There was not a sign of disturbance anywhere. It was not as if he had a later watch or a longer beat. He knew that these S.A. men would make no trouble for him, and he on his part would make none for them either. He was doubtless saying to himself that he would make no search for arms today, that there would be no point to that. After all, this was just drill. The youngsters had discipline in their bones. . . . Hans Christian felt sure this was what the policeman, whom he had been observing with interest, was saying to himself when the order to fall in came.

"Close ranks—line up with the man ahead—dress ranks!"

Everything was done silently, each man looking at the leader of his standard, at the front with his adjutant.

"S.A.—'Tention!"

The command came like the crack of a whip. The men sprang to obey it. They loved this voice of authority, a clear, ringing voice, dispelling weariness, warming the heart, stirring the soul: the voice of Horst Wessel.

"Standard Five—left wheel—in step—march—sing—'Banners High'!"

After the drill was over, Hans Christian had started for the Bomb Palast to have a chat with Oskar Kraus and his comrade Max Müller, with whom he had become very friendly. As he walked briskly along, something familiar in the face and figure of a man slouching behind him arrested his attention. He slackened his pace, looked at the shabby individual more closely, and stopped short.

"Karl! What on earth are you doing here?"

His cousin came forward, disregarding his outstretched hand, and spoke in a surly voice.

"Why should it be any stranger that I should leave Bavaria than that you should leave East Prussia? I thought you went in for nothing but breeding—horse breeding, I mean. It seems you're taking another sort seriously too."

There was no mistaking his sneer, but Hans Christian tried to disregard it, though this was doubly hard in view of the similar comment from Mr. Rhodes. Karl certainly looked down at the heel; he must have run into hard luck.

"I don't devote all my time to it, anyway. I'd like to see something of you. Can't we get together?"

"I'm afraid not. We seem to be on opposite sides of the fence."

"You don't mean to say you're under orders from Karl Liebknecht Haus?"

"Not too strictly. We leave strict orders to you Nazis." Karl laughed unpleasantly. "But I'm voluntarily associated with it and I take helpful hints from it. This morning it was suggested that I might see what you were up to."

Hans Christian could not believe his ears. He spoke his stupefaction.

"A von Hohenlohe—a von Mitweld—throwing away his birthright! Conspiring against his own flesh and blood!"

"Those funny little vons don't mean as much as they used to, Hansel. You know that yourself. Your own doctrine teaches you to pour all men into the same mould, to put princes on a par with paupers. Why should you quarrel with me if I do the same thing? I don't call myself von Mitweld any more, by the way. I'm more consistent than you are. Karl Welder, your humble follower. Very humble and very much your follower."

"But, Karl, your mother must be broken-hearted!"

"Well, what about your own mother? I suppose you've been a source of unmitigated joy and comfort to her these last five years! The United States Government is looking at National Socialism with its tongue in its cheek, I can tell you that! And when a high Government official thinks of her only son fraternizing with panderers and prostitutes——"

Hans Christian had never knocked down a man in his life. But he did so now. Karl fell so swiftly to the sidewalk that he did not know what had struck him until afterwards. Hans Christian left him lying where he was, and went on to the Bomb Palast, seething with such rage that he neither knew nor cared what the consequences of his rash act might be. Afterwards he realized how much he must have changed already that he could have done such a thing; also that from that day he himself had been a marked man.

When the young diplomat whose apartment he had temporarily taken over returned to Berlin, Hans Christian rather hesitantly asked Oskar Kraus whether he and Max Müller could make room for a third person in their quarters. They hailed the suggestion with enthusiasm, and Hans Christian moved without more ado from the select surroundings which he had enjoyed in the Margarethestrasse to the dubious shelter of the Bomb Palast. The transition was surprisingly easy for him. He was genuinely attached to both Oskar and Max, and he was far less lonely bunking with them than he had been living all by himself. Besides, since the break with the

Embassy set had come, he preferred that it should be a clean one. He cared nothing about hanging on the fringes of a milieu into which he felt he no longer fitted. Indeed, as far as he was himself concerned, he would have been willing to postpone his return to Schönplatz indefinitely. He could not get up and walk away from his grandmother if she grieved or angered him. He could not turn on her and berate her either, and certainly he could not convert her. But he knew that his present course would be as obnoxious to her as it was to Trixie. He dreaded the rebukes and recriminations with which he foresaw the stately old house would ring. Yet there was a point of delay beyond which he could not go. When it came, he braced himself for his encounter with the Archduchess in much the same spirit that he would have met a major operation.

As a matter of fact, his grandmother rather reminded him of an officiating surgeon. She did not so much rebuke him as dissect him, and she used no merciful anæsthetics meanwhile. The process was painful throughout, and in the moments when she spoke scathingly of birds that fouled their own nests, she made it clear that she considered him no less a traitor to his class than Karl. Indeed, she coupled their names in referring to what she called dishonour. There had been mutual recriminations. She had asked him how he could justify the assault upon the station agent at Insterburg, who, according to reliable report, had been set upon by Nazis and taken to their *Heim*, where he had been stripped and beaten with riding whips until he had collapsed. Was that the sort of sport in which the cavaliers forgathering for their annual contests now specialized? He had retorted by asking her if she had heard about the Nazi who had been stabbed in the neck by a Communist, and who had died as a result of a severed artery, in Königsberg the day before the Insterburg incident. There had been a heated argument over the ensuing episodes, which included attacks upon a Communistic councillor, shot in his bed, upon the editor-in-chief of a Democratic paper, and upon a former *Regierungpräsident*. Reverting once more to proverbs, Victoria Luise had spoken of the old adage about the pot which called the kettle black, and had made the caustic comment that perhaps now the pot was brown and the kettle red.

He left her presence writhing. But Luischen, whom he had dreaded to see almost as much, was far kinder, far more tolerant and understanding.

"I don't know whether you will want Ernst and me to stay here any longer, Hansel, after the stand Karl has taken."

"Of course I want you to stay. I wouldn't be free to go on with my work in Berlin if you weren't here to look after my grandmother, if Ernst weren't in charge of the stud."

"I know you trust us. And we're doing our best for you, our very best. We—we love you, Hansel, and we're grateful to you. But, after

155

all, Karl is my brother. I love him too. I think he's misguided and mistaken, but I love him."

"Do you think I'm misguided and mistaken also?"

"Ernst doesn't. Ernst thinks you're right about everything. He thinks you're marvellous. He says, when the time comes, when you say the word, he'll help you all he can in East Prussia. He thinks there's a fertile field for the New Movement. I don't know anything about politics myself, I don't care anything about them. But when I listen to Ernst I want to agree with him. Isn't that a natural way for a married woman to feel, Hansel?"

"Of course it is. It's the natural way and the right way, the way that will make Ernst happy, that will keep him close to you. Every woman who's alienated me has done it because she meddled in politics of some kind, in some way. First my mother, now my grandmother. And in between——"

"I'm sorry there was someone in between, Hansel. I was afraid there might have been."

"Don't let's talk about it, Luischen. It didn't amount to anything really. I wasn't in love. When I marry it will be a girl like you, a girl who will leave public questions to her husband's judgment, who'll keep house for him and look after his children."

"When you marry it will be someone much more beautiful than I am, Hansel, and much more wonderful. And she'll adore you. You'll be very happy, you'll forget this hard period you've been through. It will all be over by that time."

She had comforted him and encouraged him. He still remembered her loving-kindness with gratitude as he lay wounded in the hospital. But when she asked him to go out to the paddocks with her and see the dapple-gray colt, he shook his head. The words which Karl and Rufus Rhodes had spoken were still rankling in his heart. Whatever joy might lie ahead of him in his stable, he had lost all sense of it now. He did not even visit it during his short stay at Schönplatz.

There was reason enough, quite aside from his personal grievance, for him to hurry back to Berlin. Things were in a bad way in the Friedrichshain district. The Communists seemed to be gaining strength. A Storm Trooper, walking alone, was brutally attacked; after twenty-four hours had gone by he was still lying unconscious, battling with death. Then another surprise attack occurred. Again a solitary man was assaulted and knifed. His injuries were not as serious as the other's; it seemed unlikely that he would lose his life; still, the matter was serious. The following week there was a third assault, and after that a fourth. There was system in this; that was plain. The question was how the malefactors were to be stopped.

Hans Christian knew that Horst was pondering about this, then that he had formed a resolution, finally how it was to be carried out. There were great doings in the beer shop where the Communists generally held forth. A representative had been sent from headquarters in Moscow to express to his Red comrades in Friedrichshain the appreciation of the Bolshevist leaders. All the revellers were in high spirits. Otherwise they might have been somewhat distrustful of two young workmen who stood beside the bar, taking no part in the general jubilation. They had come in quietly, ordered a beer apiece, and lighted their cigarettes. Then they did nothing further. They did not even bother to say *Prosit* as they lifted their glasses and buried their noses in them. Those who noticed them at all concluded that they must have further plans for the evening, for one of them kept looking at the watch fastened to his left wrist with a broad leather strap, as if he were watching the time. The landlord, who alone troubled to observe them closely, noticed that they were powerful fellows, and decided that any Nazi they got by the neck would have a hard time. But having reached this point, he did not continue his reflections. At that moment the door of the *Stube* was thrown forcefully open and twenty men burst into the room with Horst Wessel at their head.

The Reds were completely surrounded with such suddenness that none could escape. Only one, alert in emergency, managed to bound towards the telephone, intent on giving the signal of alarm for an attack. He reached it at the same time as the landlord, but the booth was already blocked—by the two young workmen who had been so stolidly drinking beer: Hans Christian and Oskar Kraus.

Horst made short shrift of what he had come to say. His clear voice was not heart-warming tonight; it was death-dealing. There was more than a threat in it; there was a sentence. From that day on, for every S.A. man assaulted, two Communists would fall. It was as trenchant as that and as final. He added a single word of warning: "I believe that my meaning is clear. You pay double for all that you take. And there is no escape. If you crawl into holes in the earth we shall still know how to find you. Remember this, for it is the last notice I shall give you!"

He was gone as he had come, suddenly, stormily, surrounded by his troopers. Weeks passed without further assaults. There were still threats, there was vile abuse, there were fist fights now and then. But there was fear, and with it something like respect. Men from the Red Front who had been in the beer *Stube* at the time of the strange apparition came crawling to apply for membership in the Troop. There were other signs too that the tide had turned. Christmas would have been joyful for them all, if great personal sorrow had not come to Horst: Werner, his brother, who was in Troop Four, went on a holiday excursion to the Riesengebirge and was lost in a snowstorm. When he was found, he was dead. There was a funeral instead of a festival, and in the mourning that followed the Communists were temporarily forgotten by most of the Wessels' friends.

Hans Christian was one of the few who did not succeed in dismissing them from his mind. This was not because he feared them. It was because he was still secretly smarting from the charge, made first by Trixie and later by his grandmother, that ethically there was little to choose between Communism and National Socialism. He had not yet succeeded in triumphantly refuting this, and he knew he would never rest until he had.

His own resurgent sense of fairness and logic was his greatest handicap. He was no longer convinced that all the men who had fought a losing fight to save Germany from the first post-war chaos were traitors, or that all those who now succeeded them were heroes. The first thrill of his participation in the New Movement was gone, the first blindness concerning its principles beginning to clear. When he was under the spell of Horst's oratory or swayed by the excitement of vigorous action, the *Hakenkreuz* seemed to emanate radiance. But when he was alone, or when he tried to give form to his faith, he groped towards a glow which eluded him. False notes seemed to have crept into the melodious gospel of progress, unity and austerity which had first been preached. He heard these threats about heads that should roll and others that should be placed on pikes, after the Party came into power. In spite of reiterated assurances that the Movement was legal, that nothing should be done unconstitutionally, he knew now that vengeance and violence were an integral part of its plan. He heard hints about the absorption of Austria, the reclamation of the Sudeten, the abolition of the Polish Corridor; he learned that acts of aggression and repudiated promises were not considered inconsistent with the new code of honour. He tried to quiet the "still small voice" that spoke to him of all this; sometimes he succeeded, reminding himself that the means justified the end and that no pattern was perfect. But there were other moments when he wondered, wildly, if the miracle which he had seen as saving Germany were, after all, to prove a mirage.

Most of Hans Christian's periods of reflection and rebellion, strangely enough, were associated with the humblest tasks which he was called upon to fulfil. He had more natural culinary skill than either Oskar or Max, and he had unconsciously learned a good deal about making homely fare appetizing as well as wholesome during his New England boyhood. When he suggested that he might take over the domestic direction of the tenement in the Bomb Palast, his offer had been hailed. From that time on he was chief cook, although his comrades always helped as bottlewashers. While his hands were busied at the stove and sink, his thoughts flew far afield. It was at such times as this that he found them hardest to control.

While he was getting supper one cold night in January, he analysed the new "Ten Commandments" of National Socialism. Some he could wholeheartedly follow—"Your Fatherland is called Germany, love it above all and more through action than through words!"—"Be proud of Germany; you ought to be proud of a Fatherland for which millions sacrificed their lives!"—"Make your actions such that you need not blush when the new Germany is mentioned!"—"Believe in the future; only then can you be a victor!" But then there were others—"Germany's enemies are your enemies; hate them with your whole heart!"—"Strike a rogue more than once! When one takes away your good rights, remember that you can only fight against him physically!" Would hate not breed further hate, bloodshed further bloodshed?

As he asked himself these troubled questions, he heard Oskar tearing into the courtyard and pounding on the door of their lodging, without waiting to use the latchkey. Hansel dropped the skillet he was holding and rushed forward.

"Hansel, you must come at once. The worst has happened.'

"The worst——"

"Horst has been attacked!"

"You mean——"

"No, he isn't dead. Not—not yet. But he's dying——"

"Where?"

"He was in his own room on the Grosse Frankfurter Strasse when he was shot—through the half-open door!"

Oskar strangled as he spoke, then he went on chokingly. "He's been taken to the hospital. We can't see him, of course. But we can go there."

They could always go there. The hospital authorities were kind. But the small pavilion where Horst had been taken was not large enough to hold them all at once. Only a few could take shelter there at the same time, in the corridor between the small room where Horst lay and the general ward. The others milled around in the little park that separated the pavilion from the larger units of the plant encircling it. Occasionally some of them stamped their feet or swung their arms in an effort to stave off the biting cold; but for the most part they tried to march in orderly formation. That was the way Horst himself would have wished it. ("Now every man on his toes—chests out, heads high! Why, there's not a paunch among the lot of you!" . . . "Close ranks. Line up with the man ahead. Dress ranks. S.A., halt!" . . . *"Sturm* Five—attention! Quiet!") Marching men, as many as the park would hold, from the very first; and yet, miraculously, it seemed to hold more and more all the time. Waiting men, standing guard. The death watch of a hero.

They could always go there. And finally the day came when they could see him. He himself had asked for them, and the doctor had told them that they might go in, that it would not matter any more. . . . Still, they tried to be quiet. As they entered the pavilion they sat down on the bench in the corridor, and pulled off their heavy shoes. They prepared to enter Horst's room in their stockinged feet, not because anyone had told them to do so, but because they themselves did not want to make any noise, they did not want to disturb him.

His room, at the right of the entrance as you went in, was small and very white. The walls were white, and the narrow bed, and the dress of the *Schwester* who stood behind this, and Horst's face, upheld by a wide pillow. Whitest of all, that uplifted face. From time to time his eyes closed quietly, as if he were too tired to hold them open any longer. But for the most part, he looked at his men as they passed, recognizing each one, cherishing each one. Occasionally his lips moved, he murmured their names: "Heinrich . . . Oskar . . . Ludwig . . . Max . . . Gustav . . . Hansel!" Then he fell silent again.

His men went through in single file, stopping just long enough to salute. And Horst saluted them. Even when his eyes were closed, even when his lips ceased to move, his right arm rose rhythmically from the snowy spread, rose and fell, and rose again. The men, coming out of the narrow room, saluted each other, with tears streaming down their cheeks. Then they went back to the bench and sat down, and pulled on their boots, which were stacked up beside it, and went outdoors again, to make room for other men who had not yet seen Horst and saluted him.

Every man who was in the garden that night saw Horst and saluted him. But the last that went in he did not see, he did not salute.

Horst himself had told them that a trooper bowed his head only before the majesty of death and the majesty of God. The troopers in the garden bent their heads now.

On the day after Horst Wessel's death, Hans Christian heard Joseph Goebbels speak. He had never before been able to overcome a certain instinctive aversion to the "Little Doctor"; the man's grotesque appearance, and the malignancy of mind which seemed to complement his deformity of body had always roused Hansel to repugnance. Now, as he listened to the moving words which poured from the Minister's lips, he forgot everything except his thankfulness that Horst's eulogy should have been so proclaimed.

"Horst Wessel has gone to the Great Beyond. After storm and stress the mortal part of him lies here, mute and motionless. But I feel, almost as though assured by the evidences of the senses, that his risen soul reaches down towards us all. He himself believed that this would be so. He bore witness to his belief when he said he would march on in spirit within our ranks.

"In coming years when in a Germany redeemed workers and students march together, they will sing his song, and he will be among them. Already they are singing it everywhere, the soldiers in brown. Ten years from now the children in the schools, the workmen in the factories, the soldiers along the highways will be singing it.

"In spirit I see columns of marching men, endless—endless. A nation once humbled rises up and sets itself in motion. Behind the standards he marches with us, keeping step.

"The banners wave, the drums roll, the fifes announce the jubilee, and from a million throats rises the song of the German Revolution: 'Banners High!'"

So that was the meaning of the vision Hans Christian himself had seen, of the sounds he himself had seemed to hear, the first time he saw Horst Wessel. Now that Horst was dead nothing would stop the spread of his song, nothing would halt the march of his men. If, as an individual, he had possessed human failings, these were already forgotten. As a leader, he had been peerless. But as a martyr he became invincible.

It did not matter that two months after Horst's death the Reichstag accepted the Young Plan, which Horst had held in abhorrence; the acceptance was bound to be short-lived. It did not matter that Brüning, the pale-faced, thin-lipped leader of the Centre Party, against which Horst had fought, became Chancellor of Germany; he would not be Chancellor long. These facts Hans Christian accepted as certain, and his faith was justified. In the September elections the Nazis polled six and a half million votes. Two years earlier they had managed to muster twelve deputies. Now they had nearly ten times that many. A startled world suddenly became Nazi conscious and a powerful English newspaper owner printed a statement that set forth the tenets of Hansel's own belief:

"These young Germans have discovered . . . that it is no good trusting to the old politicians. Accordingly they have formed a parliamentary party of their own. . . . We must change our conception of Germany. . . ."
"If we examine this transfer of political influence in Germany to the National Socialists we shall find that it has many advantages for the rest of Europe. It sets up an additional rampart against Bolshevism. It eliminates the grave danger that the Soviet campaign against civilization might penetrate to Germany, thus winning an impregnable position in the strategical centre of Europe. . . ."

"Were it not for the new direction given to the energies and ambitions of a youthful Germany by the National Socialists there was a grave likelihood that the cause of Communism might have made a sensational advance and even become—who knows—the first party in the state . . . I repeat that the dramatic success which the German Party of Youth and Nationalism have just won should receive the closest possible attention. . . ."

Hans Christian, poring over these words, paused in his reading long enough to buy extra copies of Viscount Rothermere's paper which had contained them, and to send these, marked, to both his mother and his grandmother. But, after all, words were cold and lifeless things. It was actions that counted, and there was plenty of action for him in those days. He was a troop leader himself now, organizing, directing, planning, perfecting. His physical world had shrunk to the East Side of Berlin, where his duties lay; his only companions were the comrades working with him and under him. But his mental world embraced all of Germany, and he saw himself surrounded, on every side, by the legions of liberated German youths. He no longer shrank from any means that might serve this end, and his purpose had never been so pressing, his concept never so clear, as the night he himself was shot down as he left the Cemetery of St. Nicolai, where he had gone to spend a few moments of restful silence in the sanctuary enclosing Horst Wessel's grave.

He was alone when the assault occurred, and he told Oskar and Max and the others who questioned him closely afterwards that he never saw his assailant, that he could not swear who had shot him. This was true enough. And he was suffering so greatly—he was so exhausted from loss of blood—that his comrades did not press him. They knew he must have complete quiet, complete rest, if the same thing were not to happen again that had happened to Horst Wessel and so many others. They did not need the warnings of the grave surgeon and the grim *Schwester* to cause them to leave Hans Christian in peace. But for all that they knew he was sure, in his heart, that it was his cousin who had done the deed, and they meant, when the time came, to deal with Karl Welder themselves. But not now, not when Hans Christian might ask them awkward questions, when anything they said or evaded saying might upset him. They were too overcome by his anguish to add to it in any way.

It was a long time before they could keep their anxiety out of their eyes when they came to see him, and therefore they did not look straight at him as they sat in his room, although he was their leader now, although both duty and discipline bade them face him. But he did not seem to care. He lay still and white, as Horst had lain before him, in the same hospital, in the same pavilion. They

162

could not help thinking the same thoughts, as they looked at him, that they had thought before. They could not help dreading the end. Often they did not stay very long, because it did not seem bearable to go all through this a second time.

Late one afternoon, when Oskar was tiptoeing out of Hans Christian's room, leaving him seemingly asleep, he saw that a young lady was standing at the door with flowers in her hand. He did not recognize her; he only observed that she was very pretty and beautifully dressed, in rich furs that enveloped her slim figure and framed her rosy face. To his surprise, she stepped forward and held out her hand, smiling although her face was sad.

"Don't you remember me, Herr Kraus? I came to the Bomb Palast once with Hans Christian, about a year and a half ago. I think it was the first time he went there himself. My name is Beatrice Rhodes."

"*Aber ja, gnädiges Fräulein!* You were Hansel's great friend! But then you never came to see him after he lived at the Bomb Palast himself."

"I would have been glad to come, but he didn't care to have me. Because we had quarrelled. You see, I don't believe in all your Party principles. But when I heard he had been hurt I had to come, at least to inquire. I hope I may see him now."

Oskar had stiffened slightly. He resented the reference to disagreement with Party principles. But the young lady disregarded his change of attitude.

"You'll see a very sad sight."

"I'm not afraid of sad sights."

"And he is very weak. He is not allowed to talk."

"I won't talk to him. I'll just go in and sit beside him for a few minutes. The *Schwester* at the desk told me I might do that, after you came out."

"Then, of course, it must be all right. The *Schwester* is very careful. She has to be."

"I'll be very careful too, Herr Kraus."

He watched her enter, with eyes that were more anxious than ever. He saw her seat herself very quietly, and he caught her expression as she looked towards Hans Christian. Momentarily he could not harbour resentment against her, and he went away. Because he knew she had not meant that anyone else should see this look.

When he came back the next day Hans Christian was better, and the flowers that Fräulein Rhodes had brought were attractively arranged in a vase which stood by his bedside. A week later he heard them talking earnestly together when he came in, and he knew that peace had been made between them, probably without any words of explanation, since Hans Christian was still too weak. But surely, if Hansel had seen the same look that Oskar himself had seen on Fräulein Rhodes's face, he would have known that no explanations were necessary. However that might have been, it was only a few days afterwards that they greeted him laughingly, and Hans Christian said Fräulein Rhodes had been asking why he did not treat himself to a trip to Spain when he was able to travel, and that he himself was inclined to think it was a very good idea.

Oskar Kraus thought so too. He knew now that there would not be another black cortège winding its way to the St. Nicolai Cemetery, another black polished stone marking a new grave. He knew that instead of dying Hans Christian was going to get well, and Oskar was very grateful to the lovely young lady who, in some mysterious way, had helped where all the rest of them had failed. He admired her very much, and at the same time he felt sorry for her. He could not imagine why, since she was so pretty and so pleasant and since she and Hans Christian were obviously such good friends again.

PART VI

"THIS IS THE DAY"
1931

CHAPTER XVII

"You are sure I can be of no further service, Señor? Anything at all that I can do——"

"It's more than kind of you. But I'm quite sure. And there'll be someone at the station to meet me, I know."

Hans Christian's smile was reassuring and his voice confident. Nevertheless, the stocky Spaniard who had shared his compartment from Irun to Madrid continued to regard his travelling companion with troubled eyes. He knew that the delicacy of skin and slenderness of build which characterized the young stranger often gave a false effect of fragility, that actually persons of this type sometimes had great resilience; but this boy was half helpless as well as woefully weak. It was incomprehensible that he should have been permitted to travel at all, much less that he should have undertaken a long journey alone.

"Please don't be so concerned. My grandmother felt just the same way that you do about having me strike off by myself. But I told her I knew I should meet a good Samaritan along the way. And, you see, I did. I met you!"

There was no doubt about it, this youth was *muy simpático*. The Spaniard found himself regretting the imminence of their arrival in Madrid, not only because of solicitude, but because of attraction.

"If your friends should not meet you——" he began again.

"If they shouldn't, I'll be immensely grateful if you'll let me come home with you—long enough to telephone and find out what the hitch is, anyway. And maybe to have a cup of coffee. Coffee always tastes extra good after a night in a train, doesn't it?"

"You are right, Señor! Because I am of that opinion myself, there is always an extra supply prepared for me when I have been absent. And if the absence has entailed a sojourn in France, where—so save us—coffee in the true sense does not exist, the supply is tripled instead of doubled, as in the case of ordinary journeys! So there will be enough for you also, and to spare. My house is yours. And permit me to offer you my card. If you do not come home with me now it is my hope that you will seek out my address at some future time."

Hans Christian accepted the small white square, glanced at the superscription, and nodded.

"Thanks again, Señor Ramirez. I'm afraid I can't reach my own card-case, but if you've got a scrap of paper in your pocket maybe you'll scribble my name down on it yourself. Von Hohenlohe—Hans Christian von Hohenlohe. I'm on my way to visit some Spanish kinsfolk of mine, the Cerrenos. Perhaps you know them?"

The pause before the stocky Spaniard answered was almost imperceptible. Hans Christian barely caught it—that and the slight stiffness that crept swiftly into the courteous voice to be as swiftly suppressed again.

"All Spain knows the Cerrenos, Señor. If you are to be their guest, there is indeed nothing I can do for you. But I shall still hope that some day you will be mine."

There was no time for further conversation. The train had already begun to slow down while they were talking. Now it had come to a standstill. Hans Christian, leaning his sound shoulder against the window casing, saw that this framed a face and figure which he recognized instantly, though he had not seen them in over fifteen years. He tapped on the glass and called out.

"I'm here, Sebastian. Right in front of you."

"So I see. *Se bienvenido!* And stay where you are; I'm coming in to help you out myself."

Sebastian de Cerreno had pulled down the window as he spoke, and instantly he felt the man's magnetism flow out to meet him, like a sparkling stream. Remembering the tragic disillusionment of his reunion with his grandmother, he had shrunk from the possibility of a second such experience, as far as this distant kinsman was concerned. When he was a little boy he had idolized Don Sebastian, who had come to Copenhagen as a Special Envoy of the King of Spain, and who had been frequently at the German Legation; he had feared that now he might find his idol's feet were clay. His family, he dimly remembered, had always been cool and constrained in manner towards Sebastian; his mother had been constrained too, though in a different way. He had never understood why, or sought to do so at the time. His own sense of admiration had acted as an anodyne to anxiety on the subject. But afterwards he had remembered the strain. If there were not some flaw in Sebastian's seeming perfection, would his parents have acted towards him as they did? The question had often risen out of the past to trouble him. Even more than his grandmother's insistence that he should go, it had deterred him from coming to Spain. Now that he was here it was instantly submerged. The feeling that flooded his being as he looked at Sebastian was still closely akin to hero worship. In the extremity of it he entirely forgot his travelling companion for the moment. When he remembered Señor Ramirez again, and turned from the window to say good-bye to him, the stocky Spaniard had vanished.

Hans Christian felt a genuine pang of disappointment. The rather coarse-looking man had gone out of his way to be kind, helping him to undress and to dress, even rising more than once in the night and descending from the upper berth to see that Hans Christian was well covered and that his pillows were comfortably arranged. And now he had been swallowed up by space, before any adequate words of appreciation had been spoken. Well, Hansel could always write—that is, as soon as he had the use of his writing hand again. And meanwhile he would ask Sebastian to telephone. Sebastian, who was himself the personification of courtesy, would, of course, be only too glad to undertake such an office. Though now he thought of it, there had certainly been something very strange in the look that had gone over Señor Ramirez's face the minute the name of Cerreno had been mentioned. Had he unaccountably hit upon constraint again, as far as Sebastian was concerned?

For the time being he had no chance to give the matter more than a passing thought. Sebastian supported him from the *wagon-lit* so casually that it seemed as if they were walking arm in arm merely for the mutual pleasure in so doing; then he had been eased into a wheel-chair that stood just outside, and they had chatted gaily together as this wove its way along the station platform between the unhurried passengers and the laden porters and the push-carts, where luscious fruits and fluttering periodicals were being pleasantly offered for sale.

"The train connections between here and the south are deplorable. But I have a glorified gypsy-waggon waiting for you outside. If it appeals to you, we might push along to Granada in it at once."

"A glorified gypsy-waggon! You mean a motor caravan?"

"Yes. It's my latest toy. Do you dislike the idea?"

"No—no. But I couldn't help thinking it was strange you should have one too."

"Too?"

"Yes. My mother thought of the same thing the first time she ran for the Senate. She even called it the same thing that you did, a glorified gypsy-waggon. I used to travel all around with her in hers. It was a great drawing card, and really helped her to win the election. Since then lots of people have taken to using what they call 'trailers' in the United States—a supplementary cart with living quarters in it that can be attached to an ordinary motor-car and towed, instead of being all in one piece like a truck, as hers was. But when my mother got her green caravan it was such a novelty that it created a sensation."

"Yes? A curious coincidence, as you say, that she and I should have had the same idea. But mine has never taken definite form till now. Well, you can see how you like it. There is no reason at all why we should not stay in Madrid if you prefer. The Azucena Palace

167

here is open and fully staffed. But I have a feeling that our Andalu-sian sunshine——"

He broke off, his smile seeming to complete the sentence which his words had left unfinished. In repose Sebastian de Cerreno's face would have been sombre had it not been for a certain blade-like quality which gave it luminescence as well as keenness. But when he smiled it was transfigured. For the first time it crossed Hans Christian's mind that this smile of Don Sebastian's must have made him almost irresistible to women, when he was younger, in spite of the disfiguring scar across his left cheek. When he was younger? Was there, after all, any occasion to place his fascination in the past? His hair had turned iron-gray at the temples, but that had only en-hanced his general air of distinction. There were a few lines etched around his eyes, but Sebastian's eyes, Hans Christian remembered, had always "crinkled when he smiled." Recalling his own childish phrase, Hans Christian smiled himself.

"Here we are, *amigo*. Tell me what you think of my glorified gypsy-waggon."

It stood backed up against the kerb, its small rear platform half concealed with bright potted plants. Beyond them, through an open door, Hans Christian could see a narrow bed at one side, its snowy sheets turned down invitingly. Beside this two easy chairs were drawn up near a little table, set with a silver service. The scent of coffee mingled with the perfume of flowers. Two men in spotless linen suits stood at the foot of the descending steps, their dark, lean faces anxiously attentive. Sebastian de Cerreno motioned towards them.

"Leopoldo and Leonardo have come with me from Granada to greet you," he explained. "They used to drive for your mother, so I thought you might like to have them drive for you. We will have breakfast here in any case. I am sure you must be starving. Then you can decide whether we shall push on to Granada or whether we shall stay in Madrid."

"I've decided already," Hans Christian answered. "In fact, there's only one thing that isn't quite clear in my mind. I can't understand why I've been such a stubborn fool not to do what my grandmother advised, why I didn't come to Spain years ago!"

"What man wants to take his grandmother's advice? None that has red blood in his veins! You have lost more of that than is good for you lately; but I am sure you still have plenty left! To me the surprise is not so much that you have come tardily as that you have come at all."

Leopoldo and Leonardo had helped Hans Christian expertly from the wheel-chair to the platform. As he sank down gratefully into one of the cushioned seats, Sebastian took the other, lighted a cigarette, and went on talking as if there had been no interruption.

"But I am gladder to see you than I can say. And to relieve your mind at once on a certain score, may I tell you that my two little daughters are not at home, that they are both safely installed in an excellent convent school, where the rules about receiving young male visitors, even under close supervision, are exceedingly strict? I doubt whether you will catch so much as a glimpse of them. Which is just as well. Were it not for the absence, I might have hesitated to introduce so appealing an invalid as yourself into my peaceful home! Though one of these children has already decided more or less that she wishes to become a nun, a plan which harmonizes admirably with her mother's wishes, something might happen to disrupt this. You never know."

Sebastian de Cerreno's voice was still merry, but a note of light mockery had crept into it. Hans Christian felt himself flushing.

"Oh, but I'd be terribly disappointed——"

"Nonsense! You are terribly relieved, and you know it. Well—we do not really need to dwell on that subject, do we, now that I have clarified it for you? So you think that you are going to like Spain?"

In the face of Sebastian's perfect ease, it was impossible to remain long embarrassed. Hans Christian answered enthusiastically, his flush fading.

"I've been here about fifteen minutes, and I feel already as if I'd lived here all my life, up to now, and as if I wouldn't mind if I lived here the rest of it. Do you know, Sebastian . . . if I hadn't been a German, I think I should have rather liked to be a Spaniard?"

" 'Every man has two countries, his own and Italy,' " Sebastian quoted gravely. "There are many who paraphrase that statement, and say 'his own and Spain' instead. I hope and believe it may be so with you. Make yourself at home in the caravan, *querido*. It is all yours."

Hans Christian woke to the pleasant consciousness that he had been asleep for a long time, and that if he so desired he could turn over and sleep indefinitely again. He lay still, enjoying the soothing sensation that this gave him. His bed was very comfortable, the handwoven sheets cool and coarse, the mattress soft and springy; Leopoldo had helped him to bathe and shave before he settled down, and the refreshment this had given him still prevailed. The movement of the "glorified gypsy-waggon," which had been Sebastian's tactful substitute for an ambulance, was rhythmic and quiet, causing neither disturbance nor pain. Rather, it seemed to invite complete relaxation, prolonged slumber. There was no sound beyond the muffled one made by its wheels. He had almost drifted off again when the instinctive feeling that he was being watched caused him to open his eyes so suddenly that Don Sebastian, whose gaze had been riveted on him, did not have time to glance away before the boy had caught sight of the strange look of tenderness suffusing the blade-like face.

As usual, however, Don Sebastian did not betray the slightest embarrassment. "*Que tal?*" he said. "You have had a long sleep—so long, in fact, that you slept straight through the luncheon period, and it is now late in the afternoon. Will you have some tea? Or will you join me in a glass of red wine, with bread and ham and olives, which is what old-fashioned Andalusians like myself still prefer to take at this hour?"

"I'd like it too, then. And I'd like to know, if it isn't awfully rude to ask, what you were thinking about, just as I opened my eyes?"

"I am glad to have you ask me anything you wish, *querido*. I was thinking how uncannily you look like your mother, when your face is in repose, as it was then. When you are speaking there is occasionally something in your manner and expression which reminds me of your father's family. But caught off your guard, so to speak, you are essentially American."

"Essentially American!"

"Perhaps I should say essentially Marlowe. Would you like that better?"

"I'm afraid I shouldn't. You see——"

"Oh, I know how you have spent the last seven years. Sacrificially, which is much to your credit. Successfully, too, on the surface. But I have a feeling—I might almost say a hope—that your Prussian attributes are only skin deep. After all, why should you wish to obliterate that Puritan heritage of yours so completely? It is a good one—or at least your mother thought it was. She has patterned her whole life after it."

"Yes. Perhaps that's why."

"Why you revolted from it, as in the case of your grandmother's advice? But that was natural, whereas this—— You are inconsistent, *amigo*. Your father was Prussian to the marrow of his bones, so you determined to pattern yourself after him, or rather after what you imagined him to have been. Your mother is a Puritan, so you determined to shatter the New England mould if you can. I warn you that I do not believe it can be done. And certainly I do not see the logic in your course of action."

Don Sebastian rose, not restlessly or irritably, but as if bringing an amiable argument to an easy end. He pulled back the soft orange-coloured curtains from the window facing Hans Christian's bed, so that the caravan, which had been in darkness while the boy was sleeping, might be flooded with mellow light. Raising himself on his pillows, Hans Christian could see the landscape through which they were gliding. Save for the dazzling sky above, it bore no resemblance to the arid plain, rough and rock-strewn, which had met his eyes when he wakened that morning near Madrid.

Golden wheat fields and silvery olive groves sloped all around him. He noticed that ploughing and planting and harvesting were all taking place simultaneously and resolved to question Sebastian about this later on; for the moment he was too entranced for curiosity. Long lines of oxen, sleek and shining, were plodding away towards the sunset; there were mules in evidence too, with gay tassels on their bridles and bells around their necks, driven two abreast; and here and there a clustering flock of goats. Occasionally they passed a cloaked horseman, who swept off his hat with a flourish, or a peasant driving a small laden donkey, to which he talked volubly, and which twitched its ears in response, and though there were no signs of human habitation except a few scattered farmhouses, placed far apart, the fields were full of labourers. Hans Christian had begun to wonder where all these workers turned for food and shelter at the end of the day, when without warning the caravan drove into a tight little town and wove its way through a narrow cobblestoned street, with brown-roofed white houses on either side. They were out of it almost as quickly as they had entered it; and when the hills which had concealed it parted on either side of it, Hans Christian saw that it was crowned with a stronghold of tawny stone.

"So castles in Spain are real, are they?" he said to Sebastian, who was still standing by the window.

"Certainly. You may have one of them, for the asking, whenever it suits your fancy."

He walked forward, and gave an order to Leopoldo, who was seated beside his brother at the wheel. Then he returned to his lounging position again.

"I want to talk to you about your mother very soon," he remarked, picking up the thread of conversation where he himself had broken it off. "Though I gather you have seen almost nothing of her during these last few years. That is correct, is it not? . . . For the moment, however, I want you to talk to me about yourself, if you feel rested enough now to do so. You have had a rather bad time, I gather from your grandmother's letters. So you got shot in the shoulder?"

"Yes, from a Communist sniper on the Fischerstrasse. The Berlin Streets are full of them, you know. Of course the bandages were taken off long ago and the wound seemed to heal well. But the nerves must have been severed, for my arm is still pretty painful. That's why I still keep it in a sling most of the time. And I don't seem to have made a very quick convalescence generally. So grandmother was determined that I should come south, and the surgeon backed her up. I had no trouble at all in getting indefinite leave."

"Your grandmother was quite right, of course. As for your surgeon and your superiors, naturally the sooner you are in shape to do some shooting yourself again, the better they will be pleased. Perhaps you were not in the best possible condition nervously, even before you had this accident?"

"Would you expect a fellow to be in the best condition nervously who keeps seeing his comrades killed before his face and eyes? There have been fifteen of us so far, besides all the wounded. Of course, much the greatest loss and the hardest to bear was Horst Wessel's death,"

"You cared greatly for him, then?"

"Cared greatly for him! Why, Sebastian, there was no one like him! He was the greatest leader, the greatest organizer we had, among the Storm Troopers, and the most beloved. And the way he could talk! It was like that phrase in the Bible, don't you remember, about the 'tongues of men and of angels'?"

"So there is a little of the Puritan still left in you after all, Hansel. You haven't forgotten that your mother taught you to read out of the Bible."

Again Hans Christian felt himself flushing at the light mockery in Don Sebastian's voice, and again the older man went on as if oblivious of his confusion.

"I should like to have you tell me everything you will, Hansel, about the Storm Troopers in Germany and about Horst Wessel himself. You are convinced, are you not, that National Socialism is a good thing? You think that Wessel himself was really a patriot and a martyr? Some stories have filtered through——"

"Those dirty Communistic lies, smearing his memory! Don't tell me you've listened to those, Sebastian!"

"Oh, yes, I have listened. When you get to be as old as I am, you will know that it is generally a very good thing to listen. One learns a surprising amount that way, both of what is true and of what is false, and how to distinguish one from another. I did not mean to infer that I believed anything to Horst Wessel's discredit. Though, as a matter of fact, a young hero would be no less a hero in my eyes because he knew a pretty girl when he saw one. Would he in yours?"

"It isn't a case of saying he knew a pretty girl when he saw one! It's a case of saying he was killed in a quarrel over a light-of-love, instead of saying that he was treacherously shot from behind when he sat quietly studying alone in his room!"

"I know that is what he was supposed to be doing, according to the Minister of Propaganda, who has used the episode to magnificent advantage. But sometimes I find the 'Little Doctor' almost too clever to be convincing. Since you were not present at the time, how do you know Horst Wessel was studying in his room?"

"I know his habits! I know his ideals!"

"It is the habit of most young men, idealistic or otherwise, to fall

172

from grace now and then. Have you not found that out for your-self? Never mind, do not look so upset. I was not asking for a con-fession. Only for the admission that this young leader of yours was a creature of flesh and blood and not a plaster image moulded by a cunning hand to suit the need of the moment. Ah—here is Leo-poldo with our so-called tea. Now you will have a chance to tell me how you like this, Spanish style."

Hans Christian had been hungry, he had been looking forward to this strange repast with eagerness. Now his hand shook as he extended it to take the bread and olives which Leopoldo offered him, and he could feel tears stinging beneath the surface of his lids. When he tried to sip his wine it choked him. He did not want to talk to Don Sebastian any more. The sense of communion which had seemed to bring them so close together was shattered. Only pride prevented him from bursting out crying, like a baby. When the caravan came to a quick lurching stop, he was thankful for the excuse it gave to ask a commonplace, steadying question uncon-nected with controversy.

"Is something the matter? Have we had an accident?"

"I do not think so. But I will go and see. Lie still, I shall be back in a moment."

Hans Christian was glad to be alone, and even in his resentful state he realized it was probable that Sebastian, with his uncanny intuition, had divined that this would be the case, and had pur-posely left him, instead of quietly waiting himself to be told what had happened. When he reappeared, Hansel had pulled himself together again.

"There is nothing the matter," Sebastian said reassuringly. "We were hailed by the driver of another caravan, going in the opposite direction. He has run out of petrol, and has asked us to lend him some. As a matter of fact, he probably has no money to buy any more, and simply went as far as he could on what he had—then swung across the road to block it, so he could hold up the next passer-by for more. Leonardo is going to pump a fresh supply out for him. I want you to catch a glimpse of this outfit, if you can. It is not drawn by one large white horse, as your mother used to insist all real gypsy-waggons should be. But it is typical, for all that—perhaps more so because it moves, when it does move, by engine power. Even gypsies must keep abreast of the times! Here, let me help you up so you can look out of the doorway."

It was impossible to withstand Don Sebastian's persuasiveness. Hans Christian suffered himself to be wrapped in a dressing-gown and supported to the entrance. From the small platform the vehicle which had blocked their progress came into view—a queer cartlike structure with a top not unlike that of the Western covered waggon. From under its shelter a dark, shawled woman with gold hoops in her ears and a gay cloth on her flowing hair looked rather anxiously out. She had a baby at her breast, and beside her nestled a chubby child with large liquid eyes and a seraphic expression. The woman's face brightened as she caught sight of Hansel, and rousing the sleepy baby she held it up for him to see, while the man who had accomplished the hold-up came forward to say thank you, his white teeth gleaming, his shabby cap in his hand. Then he climbed up on the seat, and they started on their way again, waving bright handkerchiefs and shouting "*Adios!*" as they disappeared in a cloud of smoke and dust.

"The ideal way to travel," commented Sebastian, "with the high-wayman's spirit, and a pretty woman beside you. Ours is a dull journey compared to theirs."

"It doesn't seem dull to me. I'm finding a fresh thrill in it every minute," Hans Christian protested. He spoke sincerely. Nevertheless, Sebastian's suggestion proved provocative. Left to himself, it would not have occurred to Hansel that a nomadic existence could be attractive, or that feminine companionship would enhance the charm which it might have in any case. Now he began to consider the question; and surprisingly, when he did so, the image of Trixie rose buoyantly before him as it had during his first desperate days at Schönplatz. Against his will, he visualized an open road enlivened by her gaiety, in the same way that he had seen her re-animate the dying embers of his ancestral hearth. He could almost hear the tinkle of her bracelets in the breeze and feel the fluff of her hair blown across his face. Gold loops in her ears and a gay cloth on her head would become her. . . .

He drifted off to sleep again, and, when he woke, found he could not distinguish fact from fancy. For a time he lay still, striving towards clarity. Finally he gave it up, and appealed to Sebastian, who was still sitting quietly beside him.

"Did those gypsies really exist or did I dream them?"

"Oh, they really existed! You can see plenty more of them, on the Sacro Monte, near Granada, any time you choose. I will take you there to have your fortune read, as I did your mother." Don Sebastian looked musingly out at the landscape for a moment, then back to Hans Christian. "Why not eat our interrupted meal out here, on the platform?" he inquired. "The air is very pleasant at this time, and it will rest you to have a change of position." And as Hans Christian acquiesced eagerly, he went on, "I cannot help reflecting how history repeats itself. I met your mother when she first came to Madrid, on the *train de luxe* from Irun, just as you did. She felt instantly as if she had always lived in Spain, or would like to, as you did. And shortly afterwards, when she came south to Andalusia, the place put a spell on her, just as it has already on you."

"She was married then, wasn't she? I must have known, but I have forgotten."

"She was just married. She came to Spain on her wedding journey."

"And you—you were married too, weren't you?'"

"Yes. I had already been married a number of years. But my wife was an invalid, living in isolation among the Pyrenees. In fact, it was not until long afterwards that she was restored to health, and during those years of her retirement, the march of progress passed her by. She is still a lady of the old school, completely absorbed by her Church and her children. Her recovery is largely due to your mother. It was she who persuaded me to permit an American doctor, an old friend of hers, to operate on Doña Dolores. The result was an almost miraculous cure."

"It was David Noble who operated, wasn't it? Of course, it must have been! He's a great surgeon—and a grand person besides."

"Yes, that is very true. I do not underestimate the part he played. But still, the major part of the credit is due to your mother. As David said of her himself, she is a very gallant lady." Don Sebastian looked out over the *vega* again, and then added inconsequentially, "By the way, your Spanish is very good. I noticed it at once, when you spoke to Leopoldo, and again when you were talking with the gypsies. Did your mother teach you that?"

"Yes. That is, she taught all the children in the local school, after my father was killed and she went back to Hamstead to live, you know. I think you're right. I think she must have been very gallant. Anti-German feeling was pretty strong then, in New England. But she never let it touch me or mar my father's memory. Children can be awfully cruel, you know, to other children, and I suppose she must have had to shield me from a good deal. She was terribly busy too, teaching, and managing a day nursery, and running a farm, but somehow she always managed to have a free hour just before supper. She read aloud to me every night. And I slept beside her, in an old-fashioned trundle. So if I were frightened or wakeful or sick, I could always climb into her big bed. And lots of times I did."

He paused, reminiscently. They were approaching another small, compact village, and from the tower of a nearby church the Angelus sounded softly. As the music melted away into the encircling stillness, Don Sebastian laid his hand on Hans Christian's arm.

"I am tremendously interested in everything you are telling me, Hansel. It is a long time since I have heard anything about your mother."

"There is a lot more I could say, of course. She seemed to have time for everything and everybody. She used to mean the world and all to me, too. I think it was politics, in the first place, that caused the estrangement between mother and me, Don Sebastian. She became so absorbed in them that after a while she forgot everything else. Well, she didn't forget exactly, but everything else seemed to fade from the forefront of her mind. Do you know what I mean? She was so efficient and executive and successful it didn't seem human or—or womanly. I wouldn't have minded half so much if she'd marry again. In fact, I hoped she would. For a little while I thought she was going to. But she never has. I know now she never will. Her life's complete just as it is."

"*Querido*, I wish I thought you were right. But I am afraid you are mistaken. I am afraid her life is very, very empty. That is why she has permitted politics to absorb her. To take the place of all she hoped would fill it and which has not."

Again Hans Christian was conscious of the pressure of Don Sebastian's hand on his own and of the tenderness of his touch.

"You have told me much I did not guess at all before, and much that I had only half-guessed. As I said, I know I owe a great deal to your mother. But I am beginning to believe that the debt is even greater than I thought. However, you will see the harmony of the family life which is due to her, as soon as you get to the *caseria*."

"The place where my parents spent their honeymoon?"

"Yes, close to Granada. It is very old and primitive. Ordinarily I do not spend much time there—more often I am at Ventosilla, near Toledo, which is much more of an estate. But just now I am at the *caseria* so that I may be near my brother Gabriel, the Archbishop of Granada. He is not well and he is much older than I am, old enough to be my father—which makes him a veritable patriarch, does it not? Well—I am glad, as things have turned out, that it is to the *caseria* you are coming, and not to Ventosilla. Your mother used to call it 'a magic house,' so I believe you yourself may find happiness and healing there. And Gabriel will be glad of a chance to welcome you—as we all are. Ah, we seem to be stopping again. But this time I think it is only the *consumista*, who must assure himself that we are not carrying contraband provisions from one locality into another—you were asleep the last time we went through the local customs. This time you should take a look at our smart *Guardia Civil*."

Hansel glanced admiringly at the natty uniforms and upturned black hats and raised his own hand in response to the salute of "Go with God." But he was growing very drowsy again, and after saying to Sebastian, rather shyly, that he felt as if they were doing just that, he did not try to talk any more. He had been reflecting with a happy glow around his heart that everyone did indeed seem very glad to see him, that even the man on the train had gone out of his way to be courteous and considerate. He had meant to speak to Don Sebastian about his travelling companion, to ask if he knew anyone named Bautista Ramirez. But somehow he had never asked

176

the question because the conversation had been switched into other channels, and he had rambled on, without asking any questions at all, because it was so easy to confide in Don Sebastian, who sometimes mocked him and sometimes made him angry, but to whom he was drawn as he never had been to an older man before. Then he realized that he was not rambling now but dreaming. He was dreaming that the setting sun had changed into a great crimson bowl from which liquid colour was being dipped to spread out over the *vega*, and that the stars which had come out were not like the stars at Schönplatz, small and cold and distant, but big and warm, and so close that he could not only touch them, he could gather them, as if they had been sparkling flowers, and make them into a garland. But after the garland was made he did not know what to do with it. After all, you could not give a starry garland to anybody. Only to an angel . . .

"*Querido*, I am sorry to waken you. I think your dreams must be very pleasant. But you can dream again soon, as long as you like, in your own room. We have come to the end of our journey."

Hans Christian rubbed his eyes and sat up. The caravan had stopped in front of a tall blank wall, intersected only by one immense iron-hinged door. As this swung open from within to admit them, the caravan rolled slowly into a large outer patio, containing hedges and flowers and trees, and stopped a second time before a grilled gate.

"We shall have to walk now. But I do not think you will find it too hard. The inner patio is paved and the *galeria* which surrounds it leads straight to your room. Lean on me, *amigo*. It will take but a minute."

There was a fountain in the paved patio. Hans Christian could hear the water flowing over the form of a small stone cherub in the centre of it and dripping down to the stone cockle-shell on which the statue stood. The sound it made was sweet and soothing, and the scent of the flowers surrounding the fountain seemed subtly mingled with this sound. Overhead was a sapphire sky, star-spangled like the one in his dream, and almost as close as at hand; it seemed to form a dome over the patio, mysteriously enfolding it.

"Is it real like the gypsies? Or am I dreaming this time? I was just now, as you guessed. I dreamed I gathered stars, and then I grieved because there was no one to whom I could give them. I wanted to offer them to an angel . . ."

Certainly he had heard no other sound in the patio than that of the flowing fountain, no footfall, no opening or closing of a door. Yet suddenly he saw that he and Sebastian were not alone there. A white form was gliding among the shadows of the *galeria*, its nebulous movements only half-detached from the encircling gloom. As Hans Christian watched it, fascinated yet frightened, his heart seemed to stand still. The apparition had come closer, and the outlines of a young figure were visible under its flowing draperies; the moon shone full on a flowerlike face, framed by dark hair smoothly parted over a pure brow and falling in long plaits across a budding breast.

"That is not a ghost, Hansel. It is a girl," he heard Don Sebastian saying reassuringly. "How she escaped from school I do not know, but I suppose she will tell us all in good time. Apparently bolts and bars slip sometimes, even on convent doors, and I have never been able to cure her of a childish habit of stealing out to meet me when she is at home, no matter at what hour I come in myself. Perhaps I have not tried as hard as I should." He stepped forward, and kissed the girl's white forehead. Then with one arm still around Hansel, he put the other about her. "*Querida,* this is the young kinsman of whom I told you," he said. "He has been very ill and needs good care. You must help your mother and me to see that he gets it. Hansel, as you have probably guessed by now, this is my daughter Cristina."

CHAPTER XVIII

The whitewashed walls of Hans Christian's room were high and blank. The tiled floor was bare. One large metal lamp hung suspended from the distant ceiling. The great carved bed in which he lay was set into a shallow recess, with a long narrow window across the top. It faced the double doors leading into the *galeria.* In addition to the bed the room contained, for furniture, a *bagueno,* a chest, two tables and two chairs, also exquisitely carved. There was a prie-dieu, surmounted by a crucifix, beside the bed, and, in the niches on either side of the doors leading into the *galeria,* small wooden statues with silver crowns on their heads. The brocade coverlet and window curtains were gold-coloured; so were the top-heavy, full-blown roses which stood in a silver vase on the *bagueno.*

How quiet it was, he thought contentedly, how cool and restful and spacious! He tried conscientiously to make no mental comparisons between its superb simplicity and the inharmonius clutter of his room at Schönplatz. He tried to argue with himself that the latter was comfortable, even though it was hideous. He was unsuccessful. He knew, down deep in his heart, that he had never, in all the years he had spent in East Prussia, found as much comfort as he had already experienced in this beautiful bare Andalusian chamber.

There was an old-fashioned bell-pull by his bed, and at length, idly, he tugged at it. The answer was not instantaneous. Apparently there was no spurred service here. But presently he heard firm footsteps padding across the patio and the sound of panting and puffing in the *galería*. Then the square of sunlight made by the doorway was blocked out and a beaming peasant woman of prodigious size entered the room.

She was carrying a breakfast tray, which she set down on the bedside table with a flourish before she leaned over to possess herself of Hans Christian's pillows, prop them up behind him, and lift him bodily higher in the bed. All of this she did without the slightest effort. Afterwards she folded her arms and stood staring at him, her smile becoming wider and wider as she broke into voluble and excited speech.

"Anywhere I should have known the Señor Baron, anywhere!" she exclaimed. "His eyes—his hair—his skin—in all of them do I see again our beloved Baronesita. Have I not watched over her again and again in this very room? For as the Señor Baron must know, it was here that his lady mother came as a bride. I can see her still as she lay where he lies now, *la preciosissima,* so little and so lovely that she looked like a rosy child. But that was only at first. Her roses faded fast enough. She had her husband to thank for that, if the Señor Baron will forgive me for saying so of his father, who, I understand, now rests with God. It was little enough he rested then, or let his young wife rest either. Bridegrooms are much the same when it comes to that, so I mean no disrespect to nature, but this man was like one possessed." The peasant woman paused to cross herself and draw breath before she rattled on again. "He sapped strength away from your mother, so that when she began to make her baby she was very sick. Remembering all this, how could I but dread the outcome, Señor Baron? I feared that some mark of your mother's suffering might have been made upon you. But now, beholding you, I know that all is well!" She turned towards the *galería* and called lustily. "Felipe! Come at once! The Señor Baron is awake and has need to be served, and still you see fit to tarry, indolent creature that you are!"

"Be still, Catalina! Felipe has gone out to gather pomegranates. I am coming in to see the Señor Baron myself. If you have brought him everything he needs for the moment, you may go."

The square of sunlight by the door was obscured again, but only partially this time. Radiance still streamed in on either side of the lady now approaching, for her slim figure did not suffice to block it out completely, as Catalina's substantial bulk had done. She was wearing black silk, made with a fitted bodice and full skirt, and finished with flat bands of lace at the neck and wrists; though exquisitely fashioned and finished, as if it had been made by a master hand, the dress had the old-time effect of one painted in an ancestral portrait, and it was fastened at the throat with a jewelled cross of antique design. A bunch of silver keys fell on a ribbon from the lady's small waist, tinkling lightly as she walked, and her long earrings tinkled too, though with an even softer sound. A sprinkling of white showed in the shining black of her abundant hair, which she wore parted in the middle and drawn down over her delicate ears to form a large knot behind; but her face was still as smooth as a girl's. It had the serenity of a woman, temperamentally calm, whose life has always been sheltered and softened, and the same sort of pure beauty which Hans Christian had seen so startlingly revealed in her daughter's the night before. She came over to the bed and held out a white hand, which was cool against Hansel's lips as he kissed the long, tapering fingers.

"*Se bienvenido*, Christian," she said, seating herself in one of the large carved chairs. Her voice was cool and pleasant too, and the smile which parted her perfect lips, though a little grave, was gracious. "Pray drink your coffee while it is still hot—I see you have hardly begun on it. No, no, if you do not continue, I shall be obliged to leave you until you have finished your breakfast. I am glad that you have been able to sleep so late—the house is not as quiet as usual when my daughters are at home. Not that Cristina makes any noise—my husband tells me that she actually startled you, she came into the patio so quietly last night. But Cecilia makes enough for two—more than either of her brothers! She has gone into town this morning with her father to see her uncle, the Archbishop. When she gets back you will hear her singing and romping from one end of the *caseria* to the other."

Doña Dolores took a scrap of net from a small silken bag which had been hidden by her keys while she was standing, and which, like them, hung suspended from her waist. "Perhaps Sebastian told you that our sons are at school in England," she said, drawing a fine thread through the gossamer-like fabric. "We agreed that they should be educated there, as he was, in the modern manner, but that our daughters, on the other hand, should go to the old convent where I went myself. It seemed a well-balanced arrangement, and it has been satisfactory to everyone. Indeed, it is so satisfactory to Cristina that I doubt whether she will ever wish to leave the convent. I believe she has a true vocation."

"Isn't it too soon for her to be sure?"

"Vocation is a matter of instinct, not of age," Doña Dolores replied. "As all the world knows, the little Saint Theresa was so sure of hers that as a mere child she obtained special permission to enter the Carmel of Lisieux when she was only fifteen."

"But you wouldn't be willing to have Cristina do such a thing, would you?"

"I should rejoice to have her become the bride of Christ. It is very evident that Cecilia will never be suited for a cloistered existence. And it has always been my prayer that one of my daughters might devote her life to worship, in order that through her my own prayers of thanksgiving would rise the more effectively to the Throne of Grace. God has shone His divine mercy in giving me four beautiful children, after all hope for them had been lost, and my husband seemed destined to be the last of his line. Can I do less than give one back to Him?"

Hans Christian could see that Doña Dolores was supremely sincere in what she was saying, that she earnestly believed such a sacrifice should be made. Respect for her piety prevented him from arguing with her further, though her logic seemed to him as unsound as her faith was great. He could not understand why anyone should feel that the incarceration of a beautiful young girl should be pleasing to God, or why a daughter should be doomed to celibacy because her mother had proved fruitful. Besides, he had heard horrible tales about convents. He recoiled from the thought of fasting and flagellation in connection with the radiant vision he had seen the night before. Cristina's mother, he could see, was thinking of her as she would look in the candlelight at a glorious festival, veiled with white lace for her investiture; he seemed to behold her, instead, kneeling on bare stones, with a knotted cord in her hands. . . .

"Well, I am very glad she is here now, anyway," he managed to say at length, hoping that his voice would not betray overmuch earnestness. "I hope I shall see a great deal of her."

"Inevitably you will see her," Doña Dolores replied. Her manner had become more reserved, and it seemed to Hans Christian that there was actually a note of regret in it. "Unfortunately, several cases of severe illness have occurred in the school, and the Mother Superior decided that it was best to send the pupils to their homes and keep them there until all danger of further contagion is passed. But I shall make arrangements to have my daughters study regularly here, of course. And you will require a great deal of rest, for the present. Do you not think, on the whole, that it would be prudent for you to remain in bed today?"

Nothing could have been less appealing to Hans Christian than such a suggestion. He had slept long and heavily, but now he felt restless—the more so because so many of the remarks to which he had been listening were disquieting to him. Of course, Catalina was only an ignorant, coarse-mouthed peasant; he had no idea of taking her seriously. Still, it was upsetting to learn that the very servants at the *casería* had failed to respect his father and had thought his mother ill-treated. . . . And, of course, Doña Dolores would not forcibly induce Cristina to become a nun; the girl would be allowed to follow her own mind in the matter. But it was disturbing to wonder whether she would have a chance to know her own mind.

He was eager to be up and about, to rid himself of such troublesome ideas; and when Doña Dolores saw that he was uneasy, she did not insist that he should remain in bed. She rose, refolding her embroidery and placing it in the small silk bag again, and said she would summon Leonardo to serve him, since she understood from her husband that the men had been satisfactory to him the day before. Then she left the room in a rustle of silk, remarking that she would see Hansel at lunchtime, and adding again that he was very welcome, as if she feared he might have misinterpreted her growing reserve. A large tin tub, which in due time was filled from buckets with tepid rainwater, was brought into the room, and Hans Christian bathed and dressed with comparatively little help. His shoulder pained him less, his right hand and arm were not so stiff. He felt much stronger, much less listless. He penetrated to the patio without undue exertion, and there the sound of dripping water, which had been so soothing the night before, seemed stimulating now; so was the song of the birds fluttering among the yews and myrtles. The perfume of the flowers had a pungent quality; there were spicy geraniums among the scented roses. And he had never seen such sunshine. It gilded the very stones with its lustre and penetrated to the innermost depths of his being with its warmth. In the full flood of it, all his apathy, all depression was suddenly submerged.

He was hesitating whether to linger beside the fountain or to wander about in the extraordinary sunshine when he saw that the patio was not empty. A table, heaped with roses, was drawn into the shade of the *galeria;* and Cristina, with Catalina beside her, was sitting behind it. The girl's small feet, encased in black kid slippers trimmed with stiff little bows, were crossed demurely in front of her; but her fingers, fluttering among the flowers, were as swift as they were sure: unerringly she selected the loveliest of these, freed them of thorns and foliage, and added them to a garland which had already taken fragrant form. Her dark head was bent over her task, in which she seemed wholly absorbed; and Hans Christian could see, more clearly than the night before, the sheen of her dark hair with the white parting running through it, and the fluid grace of her young figure. She did not look up, and he felt uncertain whether he ought to stop and speak to her. But Catalina, meeting his eye, smiled broadly and gave a hearty exclamation of welcome.

"Señorita! Here is the Señor Baron, come to help you with your labour of love! Wait but a little minute; I will fetch another chair."

"If I won't disturb you, I should like immensely to stay for a little while," Hans Christian answered, seizing upon so pleasant a solution for his indecision.

"You will not disturb me, but will you not find it rather dull? If we were making a *nacimiento,* we could all work on it together, assembling and arranging the different figures. But garlands are different. Two persons cannot very well twine the same one. Though perhaps you would like to start another yourself?"

"I'm afraid I'd be very clumsy at twining. But possibly I could hand you the roses," Hans Christian answered, suiting his action to his words. He had no illusions about his helpfulness, but it occurred to him that in the course of handing roses to Cristina their fingers would almost inevitably meet, and the idea seemed to him singularly pleasant. He also hoped that she might look him full in the face; while her eyes were downcast he could not determine their colour, and he was consumed with curiosity concerning them. Logically, he should expect them to be brown; but he had an instinctive feeling that they might be gray instead.

"What is a *nacimiento?*" he inquired conversationally, as Cristina, though accepting his rose, neither touched his hand nor met his gaze in doing so. "Is it the Spanish equivalent of our German *Krippe?*"

"I have never been to Germany, you know. But I think it must be. We are generally in Madrid at Christmas-time, and we all go together to the old market on the Plaza de la Santa Cruz to choose the figurines for the *nacimiento*. My little sister Cecilia especially enjoys doing this; but the entire family takes pleasure in it."

"Tell me more about it," Hans Christian said encouragingly, holding up another rose.

"There really is not much to tell. There are booths and stalls all around the Plaza, and in the middle of it too; and each stall has its own speciality for sale. For instance, there are drums decorated with paper flowers and long streamers, and there are tambourines and *zambombas*."

"*Zambombas?*"

"Yes. They are musical instruments also, made of pottery jars with parchment stretched across the top. A straw of wheat or barley is inserted in the parchment, and the musicians who play on the *zambombas* wet their hands and rub them up and down the straws. They really produce quite a variety of tone. After the midnight Mass—the *Misa del Gallo*, the Cockcrow Mass, we call it—the *zambomba* and tambourine players go through the streets singing *villancicos*, which, I believe, you call carols. They represent shepherds searching for the Christ-Child, and, since Spanish shepherds use just such instruments as these, what could be more fitting?"

Cristina asked the question artlessly. Hans Christian, though his thoughts had not been diverted from his original purpose in helping her to weave garlands, was genuinely touched with the simplicity with which she spoke, and eager to have her continue her recital.

"And what else can be bought at the Christmas fair besides *zambombas?*"

"Let me see—well, there are some stalls which specialize in tiny three-branch candelabra with pink candles. I have never understood exactly why the candles must always be pink, but they are very pretty in that colour. Then, of course, there are the figures for the *nacimiento*, the Blessed Virgin and the Holy Child and St. Joseph and the shepherds. Also the animals that are appropriate to go with them. And the houses and stables to fill out a village scene. And a windmill."

"A windmill?"

"Why, yes. No Spanish *nacimiento* could be complete without dear old Don Quixote and his windmill, could it?"

Hans Christian put back his head and laughed, spontaneously and joyously, as he had not laughed in a long time. The idea of Don Quixote in connection with the Nativity seemed to him irresistibly amusing. But though he heard Catalina echoing his merriment, he was aware that Cristina had not. He checked himself swiftly, and glanced towards her, so quickly that she did not have time to avert her eyes, which she had lifted at last. With a triumphant thrill, Hans Christian saw that they really were gray, large and limpid and fringed with long black lashes.

"Why are you making fun of me?" inquired Cristina. She continued to look at Hans Christian, and in spite of her slightly puzzled expression, her gaze was one of clarity and candour. More and more moved, Hansel hastened to reassure her.

"I wasn't making fun of you, Cristina. I wouldn't, for the world. I was amused—in a pleasant way, I mean—at something you said, that was all. I couldn't quite picture Don Quixote at the Nativity in the beginning. But, as you explained, it was a Spanish village scene you were creating, so, of course, he would have to be there to make it complete and typical. Just as the carollers had to play the *zambomba*. I can see that now."

"I am very glad," Cristina answered gravely. But she bent over her flowers, and seemed disinclined to talk any more. Hansel, cursing himself for his maladroitness in silencing her, was wondering how on earth he could make amends for it, when Catalina came to his rescue.

"Señorita, you have not told the Señor Baron how I choose the *turrón* and the turkey for the *Noche Buena* dinner, at the same time that you are selecting all the pretty figures, and how I oversee the preparation of the feast while you and the little señorita are arranging the *nacimiento*. He will like to hear about that too."

"Indeed I shall. Please tell me, Cristina."

"I do not wish to tell you too much, all at one time. You would end by thinking I was a bore or a chatterbox. Besides, I am not getting ahead very fast with my wreath."

She looked up again, and for the first time she smiled. There was the slightest suggestion of archness in her look. Hans Christian's heart bounded again.

"I do not think you are a bore or a chatterbox. I think you are a darling," he said fervently. Then as Cristina became quickly pre-occupied with her flowers again, and Catalina's broad grin developed into a chuckle, he decided that the time was hardly opportune to continue in such a vein. Instead, he asked, with an attempt at non-chalance which he was very far from feeling, "And when do you have your presents?"

"Our presents? Why? on Three Kings' Day, of course!"

"You don't have any presents at all on Christmas Eve? Or any tree?"

"No, we have our dinner—a special feast, with turkey and *turrón*, as Catalina has told you, and many other good things besides—and then we go to the *Misa del Gallo*. Of course, we have all made our Christmas confessions, so we take Holy Communion, and then, after the benediction, we go again to the altar rail and kiss the foot of the image of the Christ Child which has been placed on a table just behind it. By that time it is very late—or very early, just as you choose to say!—and we are glad to have a long sleep and a quiet Christmas Day. We do not have any merrymaking until Innocents' Day, on the twenty-ninth, when we play all sorts of pranks on each other. Then on New Year's Eve we each take twelve grapes, and go out to the Puerta del Sol, which is not far from our Palacio, to eat them as fast as we can while we watch the big clock and listen to it strike the hour of the New Year. And, finally, on January fifth, after we have been to see the procession of the Three Kings parade through the streets, we come home and open our presents."

"It seems to be a long time to wait for them. You must come to Schönplatz next year, and have them on Christmas Eve, as we do! And a special tree, festooned with stars and lighted candles, which I shall decorate myself, on purpose for you!"

"Cristina, I have been waiting for you in the library nearly half an hour! Have you forgotten that we were to read *L'Histoire d'une Ame* together at eleven? Never have I known you to be so slow in making a wreath!"

Cristina and Hans Christian sprang to their feet simultaneously. Catalina had disappeared with a speed surprising in one of her size, and Doña Dolores was standing directly behind them. Even when she did not seem to be moving, her black silk dress rustled slightly, and it was inconceivable how she could have come into the patio unheard and unobserved. But somehow she had managed to do so, perhaps because the trio at the table had been so deeply absorbed in each other that they had been unperceptive to any other presence. Her beautiful face was still characteristically calm,

185

her cultured voice still characteristically controlled; but the annoyance that she evidently felt, though actually invisible and unexpressed, was nevertheless unmistakable. Hansel hastened to apologize and to explain.

"I'm afraid it is all my fault, Doña Dolores. I saw Cristina sitting here when I came into the patio, and I asked if I could not help her with her garland. But I have hindered her instead. I dreamed last night that I was making one myself out of stars; but in reality I do not seem to be able to make one out of flowers! I do hope you will forgive me for being such a nuisance! Because I have enjoyed myself so much and have learned so much. Cristina has been telling me about all sorts of Spanish customs."

"And you have suggested showing her some old German ones in return? It is very kind of you. But, as I believe Cristina has told you, we generally spend Christmas in Madrid—and possibly by next Christmas she will not be leaving the convent at all. Be that as it may, I think possibly I had better help her finish her garland, if we are to get in our French lesson. And I am sure that instead of staying all the morning in the shade, you should get out into the sunshine. It is very beneficial after an illness. We will excuse you while you explore our garden, which we think is a pleasant one."

For the second time that morning Hans Christian's freedom of choice had been taken from him. He knew that he was definitely dismissed, and he feared that in the future Catalina's supervision might not be considered sufficiently rigid for Cristina. Nevertheless, he could not manage to feel completely crushed. He had just been handing Cristina another rose when Doña Dolores had revealed her presence; and in their start of mutual surprise their fingers had met. Both the wishes he had made, in seating himself beside Cristina, had been fulfilled. He had looked into her eyes and found them full of clarity; he had touched her hand and found it soft against his own. Since so much had happened in one morning, why should he despair as to what another day would bring forth?

Uplifted by this thought, he sauntered out between the fragrant box and graceful pomegranate trees. Though unconcerned at the prospect of solitude, he was almost instantly hailed. Don Sebastian was coming towards him, dressed in tweeds. He always wore his clothes casually, after the manner of a man who can afford to be indifferent to what he wears, both because he has the means and the taste to secure the best, and the face and figure to set this off. But Hans Christian was aware of a subtle difference in his appearance; the day before he had been debonair and detached, almost adventurous of aspect; now he looked the part of the important and responsible landowner bound by family ties. At his side a little girl who was obviously his younger daughter tripped along. Her only resemblance to her mother and her elder sister lay in the fact that she, too, was dark and beautiful. Her hair was not smoothly parted, as theirs was, but hung in a full fluffy bang across her brow, like a pageboy's; her face, instead of being pale and oval, was round and rosy. Her rather old-fashioned white dress was demurely cut, but she wore it with undefinable dash, and she had on a red sash and a coral necklace. Hans Christian had a feeling that Doña Dolores had undoubtedly chosen the dress and insisted that it should be worn, but that the vivacious child had added the sash and the necklace, after a successful struggle for self-assertion, in which she had perhaps been surreptitiously aided and abetted by her father. Just now she was swinging a large hat by its ribbons, and she managed to make this simple action seem like a defiant gesture as well as a gay one. She had a small neat box tucked under one plump arm, and she was humming happily beneath her breath. If her father had not caught her back, she would have sprung ahead of him and run up to Hans Christian alone.

"*Momentito*," he said, laughing, as he looked down at her restrainingly. "Our guest is not going to escape, *querida*, if you do not succeed in reaching his side in one bound. . . . *Que tal*, Hansel? I am happy to hear you had such a good night. Permit me to present you to the firebrand of the family. You saw the flower of it last night."

"I should say you had two flowers in your family—one white rose and one red one."

"Very pretty. It would be more correct, however, to say that we had a Madonna lily and a blossoming thorn."

The little girl paid no attention to her father's bantering remarks. She gave a quick, quaint curtsey, and then, smiling contagiously, offered the box she had been carrying to Hans Christian.

"I have brought you some *mazapán*," she said. "It comes from Toledo, and it is very good. If you would open the box now, we could all have some."

"A very good idea. Thank you, Cecilia. I have always been very fond of *mazapán*, and it has been a long time since I have had any. Besides, I was just beginning to get hungry. Weren't you, Sebastian?"

"*Mazapán* does not happen to be among my many weaknesses. However, I will have a piece—if for no better reason than to reduce the amount on which my daughter will gorge herself. And now, Celita, since you have had the meeting with Hans Christian that you have been plaguing me all the morning to arrange, suppose you go and find out what your sister is doing."

"I know what she is doing without going to find out. She is making a wreath for the Virgin."

"Then suppose you help her."

"Oh, *padre mío*, you know that I hate to make wreaths, and I see

187

so much of Virgins in the convent. I would much rather see a young man, for a change."

In spite of himself, Sebastian joined in Hans Christian's laugh. Almost instantly, however, his face grew grave.

"No doubt. But your mother will be waiting for news of your uncle. Run and tell her that we found him better today than I have seen him in a long while. Then if she has no task for you before lunchtime, you may come back."

"*Por favor!* She always has a task for me, unless you are with me. So let me stay with you, *padrito*. You are always saying that no news is good news, when mother tries to make you write letters and you are seeking for an excuse. So she is sure to guess that nothing is wrong with *Tío* Gabriel. . . . He asked after you," the pretty child went on, addressing herself more directly to Hans Christian again, "and said he hoped you would come to see him soon. He was very fond of your mother. Everyone in Spain was very fond of her, because she was so gay."

"What nonsense are you talking now, Celita? People were not fond of Doña Fidelidad because she was gay, but because she was good."

"I do not believe it," the little girl objected, skipping forward again. "Catalina has talked to me a great deal about Doña Fidelidad, but it was her gaiety Catalina admired, not her piety. She thought you admired it too. She said she used to enjoy hearing you and Doña Fidelidad laughing together in the patio, after her horrid German husband had gone away. Do you really believe, *padre mío*, that ladies are ever loved just because they are good? I know *madrecita* says so, when you can get her to talk about love at all, which, of course, the nuns never will, no matter how hard you try to make them. But somehow she swallows her words. Is that the reason why you married *madrecita*, that she was good?"

"Of course."

"And the way she looked had nothing to do with it at all? You know I have seen the pictures taken of her, when she made her First Communion and when she was a bride, and she was very pretty. You mean you would have wanted her just as much if she had had buck teeth and squinty eyes, just so long as she was good?"

Sebastian laughed again. "You are absurd, Celita. If you do not do as I tell you, and go to your mother now, I shall be really angry with you." Then as the little girl tossed her head and went laggingly away, looking backward with almost every step she took and still swinging her hat and chewing *mazapán*, he asked, "Well, what do you think of her, Hansel? She is a little baggage, isn't she?"

"She's bewitching. I'm glad scarlet fever, or whatever it was, broke out in the convent."

"I wouldn't put it past Cecilia to scatter germs herself, if she only knew how, in order to get out. She is in a state of constant rebellion at all restraint. Sometimes I think a different sort of school—— But my wife and I had an agreement. . . ."

"Yes, she told me. But couldn't you over-persuade her? If you really felt it would be better for your daughters, I mean."

"I didn't say my daughters. I said Cecilia. I think Cristina is perfectly placed where she is. Suppose we sit down for a few moments," he said. "Perhaps it would be just as well if I tried to tell you, at the very start of your stay here, how men feel about women in Spain."

"Is it so different from the way men feel about women in other parts of the world?"

"In a sense, I think it is. Seclusion of every kind has almost passed out of the picture elsewhere, and naturally the seclusion of women has been part and parcel of this disappearance. Theoretically we have kept up with the march of so-called progress too. For instance, institutions of higher education have been open to women in Spain longer than they have in the United States. But as a matter of fact very few men of our class have encouraged their daughters to seek the freedom of university life, and all that goes with it, and very few well-born and well-bred young girls have tried to take matters into their own hands in this or any other respect. Though question ⸳ of the sort are never discussed in their hearing, they subconsciously associate liberation with laxity, and the wall between the Spanish lady and the Spanish light-of-love is impregnable. In republican and radical circles, of course, there is much more feminine emancipation, and some individuals, like Concha Espiña, the writer, and Isabel de Palencia, the feminist, are respected both for their talents and their integrity. I must also admit that the young barrister, Victoria Kent, was very adroit in her defence of certain notorious revolutionists at their recent dramatic trials. It is unfortunate that her cause was unworthy of her talents. Even if it had been, however, most gentlewomen look upon such evidence of emancipation askance and the viewpoints of their husbands and fathers is the same. Very often Spaniards do not even admit the existence of change. Have you never heard the classic story of Fray Luis de León, who was dragged away from the University at Salamanca by the Inquisition?"

"No, never. What happened?"

"After four years' imprisonment he was permitted to return to his school. He walked into his former classroom, where students had continued to forgather, and remarked calmly, 'As I was saying yesterday, gentlemen——'"

Hans Christian laughed. Sebastian's charming smile flashed momentarily across his face. But he continued seriously.

"I thought you would consider that amusing. As a matter of fact, it is typical of our immobility. We cling, in a closed circle, to the ancient customs inherited from the Moors as well as the Christians. It is not wholly a matter of religion. The patio, surrounded on all sides, is almost as remote as the cloister.".

"But not as futile."

"I cannot argue that point with you, because I am a Latin and a Catholic, and you are a Nordic and a Protestant, and we could never agree, or come close to agreeing. All I am trying to make you understand is that for centuries in Spain well-born women have lived in voluntary seclusion, and well-born men, in both civil and clerical life, have safeguarded this seclusion for them. Such a career as your mother's would be inconceivable in Spain, and since we did agree, yesterday, that this has not been without its disadvantages, both for herself and for you, perhaps you can bring yourself to believe that our system has its merits after all."

"In spite of everything you've just said, I can't see much merit in a system based on the assumption that a girl can't be happily married!"

"But there is no such assumption."

"Isn't that what you said, to begin with, before you got started on the general theme of seclusion?"

"I was speaking only of Cristina at the moment. Girls for whom marriage is the manifest destiny are entirely different. Indeed, Doña Dolores and I will select a suitable husband for Cecilia in a very short time now, for obviously she should marry early. But Cristina is very different. Marriage would be a martyrdom for her unless she were treated with supreme tact and tenderness."

"But she might be."

"Not by any man I can visualize."

"Isn't it possible you're lacking in vision?"

"I think not. I know a good deal about men."

"In other words, though the wall between the Spanish lady and the Spanish light-of-love is so impregnable, the *caballero* feels free to take his fun where he finds it—provided he can scale the wall?"

"Yes, and in spite of the other differences I mentioned, in this repect the Spanish *caballero* is no different from the German Junker, as you know very well! Except that the Junker is more brutal in his methods!"

Hans Christian had spoken satirically, almost insolently, considering that he was addressing a man old enough to be his father; but Sebastian de Cerreno answered with a degree of intensity that had in it elements of fury as well as scorn. The boy felt himself flushing painfully, as if every act of impetuous folly which he himself had ever committed had been laid bare before Sebastian's searing glance; but the barb with which he had been struck also seemed to dart through him into the past. The memory of what Catalina and

190

Cecilia had said concerning his father forced itself again to the forefront of his mind. It was on the tip of his tongue to ask a question which he would instantly have regretted; only his embarrassment and confusion halted him; and fortunately Sebastian spoke again before he had found any words in which to form a retort.

"Forgive me, my dear boy," he said gently. "I had no right to speak to you like that. But neither—if you will pardon me for saying so—had you any right to goad me into it. Let us stick to safer subjects . . . though if you will permit me the last word on this one I might add dispassionately that I not only know a great deal about men, little of which is reassuring when I consider them as suitors, but also that I know a great deal about women. Unfortunately most of that knowledge is more to my discredit than theirs. So perhaps you may think that it is the voice of the guilty conscience that has been speaking rather than the voice of wisdom. And alas! you would not be far wrong. But one thing I am glad to be able to say with some certainty: I have safeguarded my wife, according to the old Spanish custom of which I spoke, and in spite of many departures from grace, that would cause her anguish if she knew of them, which pray Heaven she never may! And I mean to safeguard my daughters also. That is all—I believe we understand each other now and need never quarrel again. . . . Shall we go up to the house and have some *refrescos* after this very serious discussion? I am sure it must be almost lunchtime."

CHAPTER XIX

AT the end of three weeks Hans Christian was convinced that a deliberate conspiracy existed to keep him from being alone with Cristina.

He saw her constantly, of course: at luncheon and dinner in the patio, at tea on the terrace which led from the turreted library at the top of the house, in the garden where the boxes and pomegranates grew. When callers came he was always summoned to see them, with the family, in the *salita*, containing the dark screens painted with flowers and the great crimson velvet chests studded with metal. He sat in a tall gold-and-black chair, and sipped pale sherry, and conversed civilly with these visitors, trying to keep his eyes and his thoughts off Cristina. She also sat in a tall black-and-gold chair, her dark head bent, her white hands clasped, her small slippered feet crossed in front of her; and she was invariably separated from him by the length of the room, just as she was always separated from him by the breadth of the family board and the depth of the patio pool.

Not that these visitors bored him, or that he felt the same antagonism and contempt for them that he had for many of his neighbours at Schönplatz. On the contrary, they greatly intrigued him, and if Cristina had not fascinated him even more, he would have been charmed by them. Their manners were suave and sophisticated. The men were well turned out in English country clothes or natty uniforms which they set off to advantage by their svelte figures and their rich colouring. The women, who fanned themselves incessantly, opening and shutting their fans with a swift little click, invariably wore dark silk dresses and black mantillas drawn across their creamy brows. They were beautiful in a smouldering distant way, and gradually Hans Christian began to feel the force of what Sebastian had told him about their voluntary seclusion. They had elements of unreality about them, and he could not reconcile their remoteness to the easy affability of their husbands. Yet he recognized that these men and women were closely linked together by powerful ties. Their lives might seem strange, but they were not without splendour.

Some of these callers came in sleek Hispano Suizas or *nuevo modelo* Fords; but for the most part they arrived in red-wheeled open victorias, very spruce and smart, and emblazoned with coats-of-arms to proclaim their noble ownership. Occasionally they actually swung into sight in a coach-and-four, flying a ducal flag, the men on the box wearing bright cockades and dashing livery. Andalusia and East Prussia had at least one point in common: the horse had not been driven out of his kingdom in either place, though the uses to which he was put were not the same. As a connoisseur and a breeder, Hans Christian revelled in the beauty of the satiny creatures that came prancing into the outer patio. He thought how much he would like to see Cristina seated on one, and he finally asked her one day at luncheon if she never rode. Her mother answered for her.

"Certainly Cristina knows how to ride," she said evenly. "When we are in the Pyrenees, we all ride together, a great deal."

"*Mamecita* and Cristina and I wear red bodices and long white skirts and *padrito* wears a scarlet coat," interposed Cecilia. "We dress up exactly as if it were carnival time, or as if we were going to a masquerade."

"Not at all. We merely keep up the customs of our ancestors, in the style of our riding habits as in other respects," Doña Dolores said with a touch of asperity. "There is nothing fantastic about that. It shows that we do not feel obliged to slavishly follow every new fashion. But that is vacation time, as it is when we go to Biarritz for the bathing. This is not. Merely because the school schedule has been interrupted by a catastrophe, there is no reason for taking a holiday, especially during Lent. Cristina and Cecilia both go to Mass with me every morning, Hansel, while you are still asleep, and begin their studies before you are up and dressed. By the time they have finished these, for the morning, it is too warm for them to dash about in the sun; it is better for them to sit quietly over their needlework. After luncheon, of course, comes the siesta period, and then, if we have no visitors and are not driving out ourselves, I like to have them resume their studies for a time, and set apart an hour for evening devotions. Thus the day is very full, without further diversions."

"But riding is such good exercise," objected Hans Christian.

"I rather agree with Hansel," Sebastian remarked, uninsistently. "Perhaps by the time his arm is better, so that he could join us, we might do some riding here, Dolores, in the early morning. It would do no great harm if you and the girls skipped Mass occasionally, or even if they missed a few study periods."

"*Padrito*, you always have such nice ideas!" exclaimed Cecilia. "And if we missed the needlework too, I do not see that it would make much difference either. And you know you promised me that I should have a horse this year. My poor pony is so fat and wheezy. I want a spirited steed. Don't you think I should have a spirited steed, Hans Christian?"

"Yes, and I think Cristina should have a gentle palfrey," he answered, rather absently. His thoughts were preoccupied with a mental picture of Cristina, dressed in a close-fitting red bodice and a flowing white skirt, coming on horseback down the steep incline from a moated castle. The mediæval vision fascinated him.

"Ah . . . I fear that when Hans Christian's arm is well again he will find the quiet of the *caseria* irksome," Doña Dolores said, addressing her husband and disregarding the others entirely. "There is really so little for an athlete to do here. Even you complain that you cannot keep occupied, Sebastian, and say you would much rather be in Madrid or Toledo. How can you imagine that a young man would fail to be restless? Besides, I believe the girls will soon be able to return to the Convent. I had a note from the Mother Superior this morning, saying that no more cases of illness had broken out, that the epidemic was certainly subsiding."

The manner of Doña Dolores was characterized by its customary graciousness, but Hans Christian was not slow to catch the inference in her words. She had already remarked that he should get away from the *caseria* as soon as he felt able, that he must not leave Andalusia without seeing something of the countryside. She had also urged him to accept an invitation for a visit which had reached him from Don Jaime de los Rios.

"You will find Malaga a delightful city and Don Jaime a charming host," she had said persuasively. "Perhaps you remember him? He was the Spanish Minister in Copenhagen when your father was stationed there. They were very good friends."

"Oh, yes, I remember him. He was at the German Legation a good deal," Hans Christian answered rather shortly. His curtness was based on the fact that, while he did remember Don Jaime perfectly, he also recalled that it was his mother's society rather than his father's that the Spanish Minister had seemed to enjoy, and that he was tiring of reminders concerning his parents' comparative popularity. But he also could not help wondering whether this recent invitation from Don Jaime had been wholly spontaneous, whether the elderly diplomat had not extended it because the Cerrenos, or more specifically the Duquesa de Cerreno, had intimated that it would be to the benefit of all concerned if such hospitality were suggested. He had experienced similar misgivings every time he had seen Sebastian's brother Gabriel, the Archbishop of Granada. The gentle, white-haired old man, whose dark eyes were so kindly and yet so piercing, had repeatedly told Hans Christian that he would be more than welcome to stay at the Episcopal Palace; and his invitations became increasingly urgent after Hans Christian had escorted Cristina there, to see the Holy Week processions from one of the Archbishop's wrought-iron balconies.

They had, of course, been amply accompanied. Don Sebastian had declined to leave his library; but Doña Dolores had gone with them, and so had Cecilia. However, it was Hans Christian who had precipitated the expeditions, in the same persuasive way that he had spoken of riding horseback; and there had been little in his manner to suggest that he was primarily interested in sightseeing, or that he was much moved by religious ceremonies. On the contrary, his attitude from the beginning had been that of a gallant, and as the week wore on it became more and more definitely that of a suitor. After the ladies and the prelate were seated on the balcony, he invariably turned his own chair in such a way that he could see Cristina much better than he could see the procession; and though Doña Dolores kept icily recalling his attention to superb floats preceded by military escorts and followed by hooded *penitentes*, his errant glance quickly strayed from the wooden figures in the street to the warm figure of the girl at his side. True, he asked her to tell him what all the richly robed images represented, and listened to her explanations with the same eagerness that he had shown when she talked about *zambombas* and *nacimientos*. But when she fell silent his own interest waned. A bejewelled Virgin, a bleeding Christ, a galaxy of saints in stiff brocades—none of these thrilled him except when he saw them through Cristina's admiring and awestruck eyes. The sound of shuffling feet, made by the bearers concealed beneath the draperies of their burdens, intrigued him momentarily. But when he saw the men set down their loads, and emerge from hiding to wipe the sweat from their swarthy faces and

194

turn their task over to another shift, while they went rollicking off to drink beer, he was perilously close to laughter. What was far worse, he made Cecilia laugh more than once. He kept upsetting the solemnity of the occasion. It required a grave word from the Archbishop to remind him that what he was seeing was traditionally sacred.

He had not been deliberately sacrilegious, and he genuinely regretted his apparent lack of respect. At the same time he was now past keeping either his eyes or his thoughts off Cristina. She looked enchanting in a mantilla; and every now and then, when her mother was momentarily preoccupied, she spoke to him with the same suggestion of archness that had charmed him when she had been weaving her wreath. She dropped her fan, and though he stooped to retrieve it, he did not forestall her own quick motion. Their fingers met again, and this time he managed to press hers as he placed the fan in them. It was after this fell to the floor the second time on the same day that the Archbishop's invitations to Hans Christian took a new tone, and shortly they became actually urgent. Apparently the importunate guest's adroit but complete removal from the scene was under general contemplation.

He was irritated beyond measure that this should be the case. He had not come to Spain on his own initiative. Both his grandmother and Sebastian de Cerreno himself had been urging such a step for years; and he had finally succumbed to their importunities because he had been weak and ill, and not because he had any idea of paying court to Sebastian's elder daughter. It was unjust to suspect him of any such intention—or so he hotly asserted to himself. Yet at the very moment of doing so his own essential fairness compelled him to admit that, while he had indeed been possessed of no such intention in the beginning, he was now. He had fallen in love with her at first sight, on the night of his arrival at the *caseria*, when he had dreamed about offering a garland of stars to an angel, and she had come gliding out from the shadows of the *galeria* to meet her father.

He argued that it must be madness to want to marry a girl with whom he had never even spoken alone, and yet instinctively he knew that it was not, except in so far as that all lovers are obsessed with madness. He did not need to talk to her alone to know that her face was beautiful, that her voice was sweet, and that her heart was guileless. All this he saw and heard and felt every time he was in her presence, no matter how many other persons were gathered around her. In fact, he had gradually acquired the faculty of ignoring alien elements which crowded in upon them, of pretending that he and she were alone, of imagining what communion with her could become. He knew it would mean more to him to put his hand on her hair. or to feel her fingers clasped in his, than to take largesse from anyone else. The memory of Trüdchen's easy subjugation was horrible to him now; the thought of a mercenary marriage with a self-willed heiress scarcely less loathsome. He wanted nothing, for the moment, except Cristina's gentle companionship. He was confident that in time her tenderness would blossom into love, that the day would come when she would be ready for his kiss and come to rest within the circle of his arms. But he would never seek, or take, more than she would willingly welcome.

It would have meant much to him if he could have said all this, frankly and freely, to Sebastian; but a barrier seemed to be rising between him and his Spanish kinsman almost as insuperable as the one that divided him from Cristina. It had not existed at first. Sebastian had really been glad to see him, he felt sure of that; the older man had been kindly and understanding in his attitude, he had treated his guest as a kindred spirit, expansively and sympathetically. But from the moment of Cristina's unexpected appearance he had changed. He had continued to be courteous and considerate, but he had become defensive; he neither invited nor offered confidences. If there had been a whimsical quality in the initial remarks he had made on the inaccessibility of his elder daughter, it had completely vanished in the course of his argument about the sheltered life; he was in deadly earnest now when he said she was destined for the cloister. Hans Christian would not have put it past him to clap her into a convent at the first intimation that his guest was seriously interested in her.

Under the circumstances Hans Christian did not know what to do. Obviously he could not linger on indefinitely in a house where he was made welcome as an individual, but considered superfluous as a suitor. On the other hand, he could not accept defeat on the terms which were being dictated. Later, after Cristina had taken the veil and was lost to him for ever, Sebastian would be quite capable of illogically taunting him with having left the firing-line before the battle had half begun, and asking him what he expected to have happened in that case. He did not know what he expected to have happened. His thoughts went round and round in a vicious circle. At last he decided upon a course which seemed to him ingenious. He determined to go and talk to Gabriel.

No one made the slightest objection when he asked if it would be convenient to send him into Granada. Sebastian assured him that Leonardo would be at his disposal at any hour he would like to start out. Doña Dolores told him that he should be sure to see the Capilla Real and the Virgin of the Augustias. Cecilia said he would have much more fun if he went up on the Sacro Monte, where the gypsies were, and had his fortune told, and intimated that she would like to go with him. Cristina, addressing him spontaneously for almost the first time, asked him if it would be convenient for him to stop at the Palace for a moment, as she would like to send a little note to her uncle. . . .

Relieved to find everything made so easy for him, he answered them all gaily. He would really like to try driving himself, if Sebastian did not mind. . . . Though he could not manage a car, he thought he could drive a pony-cart without straining his arm. . . . And for the very reason that he was in such an unsociable mood, he wouldn't advise Cecilia to take him on as an escort, though he hoped some other time both she and her father would go with him to see the gypsies. He hardly thought he would get as far as the Sacro Monte that afternoon. . . . In fact, he would rather wait until they could all go together. But he would certainly plan to see the Capilla Real and the Virgin of the Augustias, and possibly part of the Alhambra as well. He would also be glad to take a note to the Palace. It would give him an excuse to say *"Que tal?"* to Gabriel himself. . . .

He set off in an old pony-cart, his spirits actually higher than they had been at any time since his arrival. Leonardo, in handing over the reins to him, had told him proudly about certain points of interest for which he should watch on his way into town; and he found so many of these along the dusty road that the turrets and domes of Granada came into sight almost too soon to suit him. Conscious that he would be questioned about his movements on his return, he asked his way to the Capilla Real. Then, after a hasty glance at the tombs of the "Catholic Kings," he left the pony-cart in charge of a willing street urchin and mounted the incline towards the "door of justice" leading to the Alhambra gardens. When he reached the plaza overlooking the *Albaicen,* he sat down to rest for a few moments on a bench beside a blind man who was tinkling away at a guitar, and watched some *seminaristas,* in black and scarlet, walking slowly up and down; then, succumbing to the importunities of a garrulous guide, he suffered himself to be led past the baroque monstrosity built under Charles V into the courts and courtyards of matchless beauty lying immediately beyond this. A quarter of an hour later he astonished his conductor by giving the man a liberal tip and asking to be led out of the Alhambra again, before he had seen a fraction of it or listened to any details about dates and dimensions; and fifteen minutes later still, having enriched the waiting street urchin with even greater liberality, he presented himself at the Palace gate and asked to see the Archbishop.

He was instantly admitted and conducted to Gabriel's study, where the prelate was alone, occupied with a collection of medallions on which he spent much of his leisure time. The old man laid down the one he had been fingering, and held out his hand cordially to his caller.

"This must be mental telepathy," he said, smiling, as Hans Chris-

197

tian kissed his ring and straightened up again, "or perhaps, since I am a Churchman, I should say instead it must be an answer to prayer. I was just thinking about you and wishing I could have a talk with you."

"Cristina asked me to give you this note," Hans Christian said, producing a small white envelope from his pocket.

"Ah . . . well, I am always glad to hear from Cristina. She is a great favourite of mine. I will see what she has to say, if you will excuse me." The Archbishop opened the envelope, extracted with care the small sheet of paper which it contained, and glanced over it, a pleasant expression hovering around his mouth as he did so. Then he laid it down on the desk beside the medallions he had been arranging when Hans Christian entered. "This is a very interesting letter," he said, still smiling. "I am extremely grateful to you for bringing it to me. But I hope, now that you have done so, you are not going to run away immediately. It would give me great pleasure if you would stay and dine with me."

"I'd like to, if you still want me after you hear what I've come to say."

"So you had a special reason for coming? Aside from acting as messenger for Cristina?"

"Yes. I came especially to tell you that I've fallen in love with her, and to ask you what you would do about it if you were in my place."

"I am very much touched at your confidence. And when it comes to a matter of good counsel, I should certainly advise you to do what is most natural and fitting under the circumstances. In other words, if I were you, I should ask Cristina to marry me, with the hope and expectation that she would accept me, and then I should hasten back here to urge the cleric of the family to perform the wedding ceremony without delay."

"You'd ask her to marry you! When you'd never had a chance to be accepted, when so far she had hardly glanced in your direction!"

"Why, yes. The situation seems complicated, I know. But perhaps it is simpler than it looks. Sit down, my dear boy, and let us talk this matter over quietly. It makes me uneasy to have you stand there, as if you might disappear at any moment." Then, as Hans Christian seated himself on the edge of a chair, the Archbishop shook his head. "No, I did not mean like that," he remonstrated; "I meant that I wanted you to really settle yourself. What about a cigarette and a glass of sherry? Or perhaps you are tired of sherry by this time? I can give you *Lacrima Cristi* or *bastardo* instead, if your taste runs in either of those directions."

"I'd like very much to smoke, if you'll let me. But I don't care about anything to drink," Hans Christian answered, somewhat astonished at the Archbishop's light satire, but deciding to disregard it.

"Please follow your own inclination—and now for my little homily.

Part of the trouble, my dear boy, lies in the fact that you have been rather a laggard in love."

"*A laggard!* Why, it is only three weeks since I came!"

"Yes. But you were a long time coming. And you made it quite clear to your grandmother why you did not wish to come. She passed this information along and Dolores was piqued."

"So you think if I'd come sooner——"

"I think your delay has made matters much worse for you, primarily for the reason I have just mentioned. It is always better for a young man to ingratiate himself with a girl's mother than to antagonize her You have made precisely this mistake. And, in the second place, if you had come before Cristina's thoughts began to turn towards a cloistral life, such contemplation might have been avoided altogether. It is part of the normal picture for a Spanish girl, who is naturally devout, and who is beginning to be conscious of emotion without understanding it, to feel she will find her best outlet for this in religion, that she has a vocation to become a nun. Sometimes she is right, of course. Only time can tell. There are exceptions to every rule, as in the case of the Little Saint Theresa, which I believe Dolores cited to you. Under usual circumstances, however, I should say that no girl should be prevented from taking vows if she still wishes to do so when she is twenty-five, but that no girl should be encouraged to do so before she is twenty-one. As the Archbishop of this diocese I should certainly do everything in my power to prevent Cristina from taking such a step earlier than that."

"You would!"

"Yes. I do not feel at all sure that she has a vocation. Her mother and I disagree about that, as we have on many other points, though we are devoted to each other. On this one I feel very strongly. It is far more likely that Cecilia might follow such a course triumphantly. She has nearly all the qualifications for a successful abbess."

"Cecilia!"

"Yes—vitality, determination, endurance and intelligence. I think we may take her faith for granted—she takes it for granted herself, without dwelling on it overmuch, as her mother is inclined to do. However, you did not come here to discuss Cecilia, but Cristina. Well, as I was saying, it is unfortunate you did not come sooner, for several reasons. But I do not think your delay has necessarily been fatal to your hopes. Especially since Cristina herself does not seem to have been as much piqued by it as her mother."

"What difference does it make whether she was piqued or not, if she's so determined to become a nun?"

"I'm not sure she is so determined. In fact, I am very doubtful of it. Her mother is determined, which is quite a different matter."

"But you said——"

"I must beg you to listen to me more carefully, Hansel. I said, to

199

begin with, that you had unnecessarily antagonized Dolores by your procrastination, and that this same procrastination had been unfortunate as far as Cristina was concerned. If she had met you for the first time two years ago, she probably never would have thought about becoming a nun, because almost certainly your image would have filled her thoughts instead. Consequently she would never have mentioned such a plan, on her own initiative, to her parents. Of course, they might have taken the initiative in mentioning it to her. Dolores is excessively pious, in the more restricted sense of the word; I have no doubt that she honestly believes her attitude is prompted entirely by piety in this instance, instead of partly by pique. Sebastian is fearful, with reason, of the extremes to which passion can carry a man. In the end I do not think their determination can prevail against yours and mine, if Cristina is on our side."

"But how can we hope that she is?"

"Well, she came in to see me the other afternoon—the day following your arrival, I believe it was—accompanied by Catalina, who remained in the kitchen while she was in my study. The ostensible purpose of her visit was, I believe, to inquire for my health. But after telling me that she had greatly enjoyed your company while she was making a garland, she continued to talk about you the rest of the afternoon. Since then she has been back here twice, and the subject of my health has not even been mentioned. And now she has written me a letter, saying she is in the deepest despair because she never has a chance to see you alone, and asking if there is not something I can do to help her out of her difficulties. You may read the letter if you like."

Without waiting for a repetition of this suggestion, Hansel seized upon the small piece of paper which the Archbishop shoved gently in his direction. The very sight of the script, flowing lightly across the crested sheet, sent a thrill through him. But as he read the unbelievable words, the handwriting in which they were formed faded into complete insignificance. For a moment he was too much moved to speak. Then, still holding the precious paper, he looked across at the Archbishop.

"What—what shall I do?" he asked, striving in vain to keep his voice steady.

"In the end you will do what I advised in the beginning. You will ask Cristina to marry you and you will invite me to perform the ceremony. We will both accept. But I am afraid there must be a few preliminaries. First of all, you must talk to Sebastian."

"I wanted to do that, anyway. But I was afraid he wouldn't listen. I'm still afraid he won't."

"Possibly you are right. No one can ever foretell what Sebastian will do. But if he should decline to listen to you, he will then come rushing in here, and eventually he will be obliged to listen to me. I can prevent him from clapping Cristina into a convent, and I can advise him to let her marry you. I shall certainly do both."

"I can see how you might make it impossible for Cristina to become a nun. But I don't see how you can make it possible for her to marry me if her father won't consent."

"Suppose we face one difficulty at a time. As long as she does not become a nun, there is no insuperable barrier to her marriage. I admit it may take patience to win Sebastian over. But Cristina is still very young. I myself think it would be just as well if Cristina did not marry for several years yet."

"You want me to wait *several years!*"

"Yes—partly on general principles and partly because of Sebastian's aversion to early marriages. In this regard, I should consider you bound to respect his viewpoint. There are tragic reasons for it."

The Archbishop sighed softly and looked away. Hans Christian, who would ordinarily have been curious as to the causes for Sebastian's viewpoint, was far too preoccupied with his own pressing problems to give it a thought.

"There is another aspect of the case which I think I should mention," the Archbishop went on after a moment. "That is the question of your nationality. All things being equal, I think Sebastian would have been glad to have an American for a son-in-law. He admires Americans very much. But he has never cared greatly for Germans—again on general principles. He insists that he has never known one who would admit he was wrong about anything or who had a sense of humour. And his natural antipathy for them was intensified, a number of years ago, by several unfortunate circumstances. I know it was a great shock to him when you decided to remain in East Prussia."

"But why should my decision to stay in East Prussia have made any difference to him? I should think it would have been just the opposite! After all, I'm related to him through my father, not through my mother."

"You are related to him through your Austrian grandmother. She and his own mother, whom he adored, were both originally Hapsburgs. You do not need to be reminded how long, or how closely, the Hapsburgs have been allied to Spain. But the Junkers have not. There are no binding ties there. Quite the contrary."

"Are you trying to tell me that Sebastian disliked my father?"

"I have tried not to tell you. I have hoped against hope that it might never be necessary for you to know that. But I am afraid, as things have turned out, that it is. He disliked your father intensely. In fact, he hated him. And he is obsessed with the fear that you may come to resemble him. You look like your mother—the resemblance is very striking. But you are moulding yourself after the Prussian pattern which is so obnoxious to Sebastian. Your course of action makes him think of you as a wolf in sheep's clothing."

"But why should he put it that way? Why shouldn't I want to follow in my father's footsteps, even if I do happen to look like my mother? They were glorious! He died a hero's death. Why should everyone here hate him so?"

The question, so long suppressed, came surging out to his lips. Gabriel looked at him with pity.

"My dear boy, everyone here did not hate him. I did not, for instance, if that is any comfort to you. I was infinitely sorry for him. I regret that some servant's gossip or childish prattle has disturbed you. I know how Catalina and Cecilia are apt to run on."

"Yes, they do run on, and I've tried not to listen to them. But how can I help being disturbed by things they hint, by things they let slip? If nothing they say matters, why did Sebastian hate my father, why were you sorry for him?" Before Gabriel could answer, Hans Christian had sprung to his feet, and confronted the Archbishop with blazing eyes. "You were sorry for him because you knew another man was making love to his wife!" he cried. "And Sebastian hated him because he wanted my mother himself! That's why he won't trust his daughter to any man—because *he* wasn't to be trusted! And, besides, he means to have his revenge—that's why he won't let me marry Cristina! Not because of anything I've done or haven't done!"

The Archbishop rose in his turn, and laid his hand on the boy's shoulder. Frail as he looked, his fingers were like steel. He forced Hans Christian back into his seat, swung his own chair around, and faced the boy imperiously.

"Listen to me," he said sternly. "I'm going to tell you the whole truth, because nothing on earth is so deadly as a half-truth, and that is what you are battling. Sebastian did love your mother—they loved each other. But they were both already married when they met. They had been married so young that they did not know their own minds. Perhaps you will begin to understand why Sebastian is opposed to early marriages when you hear the history. His own was arranged, by his family and his bride's. He saw that Dolores was beautiful, he sensed that she was docile and devout. He thought nothing else mattered. Like many other men, he was prepared not to take his marriage vows too seriously. He did not dream, at twenty, that he would hunger and thirst for a mind to match his own, for a radiance that would dazzle him, for a courage he would find invincible—in short, for all the qualities he found in your mother. He thought that Dolores de Romera would adorn his house and bear his children, and that he would continue to find light diversion wherever he looked for it. He was mistaken on both scores. Within a few months of her wedding Dolores began to act strangely; within two years she was violently insane. She tried to kill her husband, and she very nearly succeeded. That scar on his cheek was made by a dagger she threw at him. After that she was shut up in the Castello Viejo under guard. She remained there for years, a raving maniac. And meanwhile Sebastian drank his cup of dissipation to the dregs and found it bitter brew."

"Good God—what a ghastly story!"

"It is a ghastly story. But it would have been ghastlier still if it had not been for your mother. It was she who declined to make Dolores' condition a pretext for escape—escape for Sebastian or for herself. Though she was very unhappy. At sixteen she visualized your father as a sort of shining St. Michael, just as you do. She married him with that illusion and it was cruelly shattered. She was sensitive, idealistic and immature. Instead of acting towards her with gentleness and loving-kindness, your father treated her with ruthless selfishness. That is why I was sorry for him—because I saw him destroying the innocent trustfulness of a young girl, and knew that for such a sin as this there can be no forgiveness either on earth or in heaven. And that is why Sebastian hated him. He could not endure the spectacle, or the thought, of your mother's persecution. But she endured it. She is one of the bravest women I have ever known."

"Yes," Hans Christian said in a choked voice. "I have always known she was brave. But, of course, I did not know of this. Only that it was she who insisted that David Noble should operate on Doña Dolores."

"If the malignant tumour which was pressing on Dolores' brain had not been successfully removed, she would never have been restored to sanity. She never could have lived a normal married life. She never could have achieved maternity. She owes all this to your mother—who could so easily have stolen her husband instead of restoring him to her. Dolores is not blessed with keen intellect or great vision, but in her limited way she realizes this and is grateful. I believe I can make her see that this gratitude should express itself in a changed attitude towards you. But it will take time and tact."

"And—and Sebastian?"

"Ah, Sebastian—I suppose you would not consider saying, when you talk to him, that you might go back to America after all?"

"And leave Germany!"

"Your father is dead, Hansel, and all that he personified has gone too. But your mother is still alive, and what she stands for is vital also. Go back to her. Go back to America."

"Abandon the Fatherland when it needs every one of its sons!"

"I believe your mother needs you too. I believe you are needed in America. A terrific collapse has taken place there this last year. Perhaps you have been too preoccupied to give it much thought."

"A stock market crash! What does that amount to, compared to the rebirth of a crushed country?"

"It amounts to a good deal more than a stock market crash, my dear boy. However, I am not trying to persuade you against your will to do something you do not feel is right. I am only trying to ease your path, if I can."

The Archbishop leaned back in his chair. The tenseness of the hour had passed and he was very tired. He hoped that Hans Christian would not argue with him any more at present, that the boy would go tranquilly away and ponder on what had been said already, before attacking any more problems. He was unprepared for the almost irrelevant remark, coming quietly after the outburst that had preceded it, with which Hansel broke in upon his reverie.

"Even if my father is dead and everything that he stood for is gone, my grandmother is still living. I mustn't forget about her. She's all alone in the world except for me. My mother at least has a career. Even though I see now that it doesn't mean to her what I thought it did, it represents some sort of fulfilment."

With a great effort, the Archbishop roused himself once more. "Your grandmother!" he said musingly. "No, of course you must not forget your grandmother. I have never forgotten her for a single moment. . . . You have listened to so much ancient history tonight, Hansel, that perhaps you could bear it if I told you a little more. You know that I was the eldest of a large family and Sebastian the youngest. All our brothers and sisters died long ago, leaving this gulf of age between us—for I am old enough to be his father. Consequently your grandmother and I are about the same age. I met her shortly after I had taken Orders. . . . I had delayed doing so for a long time, until after Sebastian's marriage, in fact, when I thought our heritage would be secured. But I had many bitter moments of wondering whether I had delayed long enough, after all. Partly because of the dreadful debacle of Sebastian's marriage and partly because if I had not forced myself with anguish to be mindful of my irrevocable vows, I should have been sorely tempted to break them, for the sake of your grandmother."

As he spoke, Gabriel bent his head and clasped his hands in front of him. His attitude might have been one of fervent prayer, or merely of overwhelming exhaustion. As a matter of fact, it was both. Hans Christian, still mindful of the great ring glittering on the Archbishop's finger, of the richness of his robes and the splendour of his room, saw him for the first time as a sad and sacrificial figure. He slid from his own seat and knelt beside his kinsman, bowing his own head. The old man placed a hand gently on his hair.

"So you see," he whispered, "that through two generations already there has been sorrow in surrender to the will of God. I pray it may be part of His plan that in this generation there may be joy instead.

We are told that like as a father pitieth his children, so the Lord pitieth them that fear Him. I hope He may show pity on you and on Cristina. Go in peace, my son. We are all in His keeping."

CHAPTER XX

Hans Christian went down the palace steps in a state of tumult. The astonishing revelation of Cristina's tenderness towards him dominated his distracted mind. But underneath the beatific assurance this gave him, surged doubt and dread in a hundred forms. Now that he knew his love was returned, how could he await fulfilment of it for years? The mere suggestion of such a delay was unreasonable and intolerable. On the other hand, unless he accepted every condition with which Sebastian chose to hinder and harass him, how could he dare to hope that he would ever win Cristina at all?

When weariness overcame him, the Archbishop had evidently forgotten his invitation to dinner, for it had not been renewed; and unaware of the enervating after-effects of an upheaval such as he had just experienced, Hans Christian was surprised, and slightly ashamed, to find that he was hungry and thirsty. The street urchin to whom he had entrusted the pony-cart outside the Alhambra had pursued him to the palace, and insisted upon mounting guard over it there; and telling him to continue his vigil, Hansel crossed the street, and sought out a sidewalk café.

He did not have to look far. There were several within the next block, and he sat down at a small table and asked for beer. The thin Spanish brew which was brought to him was a poor substitute for the rich foaming *brau* he got at home; but he could think of nothing else to order; and at the moment he did not even notice that it was sweet and tepid. He drank it down uncomplainingly and motioned for more, grateful for the tempered refreshment it gave him.

The café was crowded and people pressed all around him, though none of them bothered him. Many were alone, as he was; they sat staring into space as they rolled their cigarettes and sipped their sherry, neither moving nor speaking. He had the feeling that they had been there the day before, and that they would be there the next day. A small shabby man, with a mild bearded face, seated at the table next to his, seemed especially quiet and detached. Other men, in convivial couples, exchanged innocuous remarks about the passers-by, and gesticulated as they conversed volubly with each other. Hans Christian himself was too abstracted to pay any attention to what they were saying. So Sebastian and his mother had been in love, and before them, Gabriel and his grandmother! And Doña

Dolores had not always been pious and precise, but had hurled daggers and inflicted deadly wounds! It was all unbelievable and unreal, and yet, now that he knew it was true, many mysteries were clarified for him. With clearer vision, he would be able to act more tolerantly and intelligently. If only there were not that aversion from Prussia and all that was connected with it to combat! If only Sebastian would not make the renunciation of these a condition! If only he would not harp on an American note which to Hansel himself was inharmonious. . . .

A soldier with his arm around a pretty girl, his blue chin close to her glossy head, sauntered past, oblivious of the café and its occupants. A water vendor loitered by, calling in a sing-song voice as he went, *"Agua, agua! Quien se quiere refrescar?"* No one paid any attention to him, and he did not have the air of expecting trade or notice. A photographer and a flower woman stopped at the sidewalk with ingratiating smiles; but though they seemed a little wistful, they were not intrusive, and presently they too went quietly along the street. At their heels came a newsboy, who threaded his way among the tin tables, and the occupants of some of these bought the paper which he rather diffidently offered. Among them was the small bearded man sitting beside Hansel; and mechanically, the boy's eyes followed the black headlines that were so close to him. There were some items about the elections which had been held the Sunday before. The Republicans had made a surprisingly strong showing in most of the major cities. The Government was withholding comment for the moment. But Zamora, and the other leaders who had been imprisoned with him the previous December, were all ahead by large majorities. Hans Christian, who had been far too preoccupied in Berlin to pay intensive attention to anything that had happened in Madrid, did not know whether this was significant or not. He did not suppose it was. What was even more to the point, he did not care.

A peculiar rustling finally caused him to look at the paper with attention. He saw that the hands of the small bearded man were trembling, and that the reason the paper was making such a strange noise was because it was so unsteadily held. There was something fascinating to Hans Christian about the sight and sound. For the first time since leaving the palace he ceased to isolate himself with his own thoughts. As if aware of being under observation, the small bearded man lowered his paper, folded it with fingers which still quivered, and returned Hansel's look with a solemn gaze.

"This is the day," he said portentously and without preamble.

"I am afraid I do not follow you, Señor. What day?"

"The day for which we have been working and waiting. The day for the great change."

"The great change? What change?"

The mild-looking man raised his shoulders, after the customary manner of Spaniards wishing to emphasize what is being said, and to imply more than the spoken word actually indicates. His voice betrayed greater and greater exaltation.

"I am not sure. It is still too early . . . If you will excuse me, Señor, I will return to my home and read this paper to my father. He cannot read himself, and he will be anxiously awaiting me. He also hoped this would be the day."

Hans Christian returned the queer little man's polite bow, asked for his bill, and after a moment's hesitation, left the café himself. No one else seemed disposed to speak to him or to share a paper with him, and, as the newsboy had disappeared, he could not buy one himself. For the second time, he tipped the street urchin who had stood guard over the pony-cart, and drove carefully out of the city, his mind reverting to his impending conference with Sebastian.

Hans Christian heard no more gossip and felt no further stir of excitement. He stopped to dine at a *ventorrillo* set high up on a hill, and built in a succession of arbours, overhung with purple morning glories. The place was almost empty, for it was very late; and the *patrón*, though courteous, was uncommunicative. But the food was excellent and abundant, and Hans Christian rose from his rustic table soothed and refreshed, and took to the road again in a tranquil mood. When he reached the outer patio of the *caseria*, he found Leonardo waiting for him with a lantern, scanning the landscape anxiously.

"We were becoming anxious about the Señor Baron," the faithful servant said, with unconcealed relief in his voice, giving a poke at the pony's well-covered ribs. "Not that this fiery animal would have run away! But that something else untoward might have happened. Has Your Excellency dined?"

"Yes, and very well."

"Ah—Catalina has continued to keep food hot. There was a fine sucking pig for dinner tonight, Señor Baron."

"I had some too. It was very good."

"It is always very good, but this is the best season of any for it," Leonardo remarked with a certain importance. Then he yawned behind his hand. "Has the Señor Baron further need of me?"

"No, thank you. And thank Catalina for keeping the roast hot too, but tell her I could not swallow another morsel tonight."

Leonardo closed the grilled gate leading to the inner patio carefully behind him. The *galeria* and the rooms surrounding it were all in darkness. But in the turret a light was still burning. Hans Christian hesitated for an instant. Then, following an impulse, he mounted the stairs leading to the terraced library.

He immediately saw that he had been right in obeying his instinct. The library door stood invitingly open, and Sebastian was alone there. He sat reading in a large chair drawn up beside an old-fashioned student lamp. The light which streamed from under its green glass shade made a single circle of radiance in the shadowy room. As Hans Christian approached, he looked up from his book with a smile.

"*Que tal?*" he said, in his usual agreeable way. "I was beginning to wonder what had become of you."

"Leonardo said you had been anxious. I'm very sorry. I'm afraid you sat up on purpose for me."

"Yes. But I was glad to do so."

"I did not realize it was so late, and of course I had no way of sending you a message. I did some sightseeing and then I had a long talk with *Tio* Gabriel. Afterwards I went to a café and stayed longer than I intended. There seemed to be more or less excitement there, and I was intrigued. Have you seen today's paper by any chance?"

"No. Haven't you discovered that Monday in Spain is always a day without newspapers until the evening, in compliment to the principle of the *descanso dominical*, the Sunday rest? Is there some special news tonight?

"The men sitting around me at the café seemed to attach a good deal of importance to the result of yesterday's elections. One of them, a pale bearded little man, kept saying 'This is the day!' in a very solemn manner. It seems the Republicans have won by a very substantial majority."

Sebastian shrugged his shoulders. "I am not sure that the King was wise in permitting these municipal elections to take place," he remarked. "There have been none since 1922, and there was no sound reason why there should have been any now. You may have noticed that I did not take any part in them myself. This is the main reason why I suggested that we should all go off on a picnic yesterday. It gave me a valid excuse not to vote. I was not among those who advised Alfonso to have the elections held. Personally, he is very liberal minded. I see no reason why he should pay the penalty at this time for the suffocation of popular expression which Primo de Rivera enforced years ago."

"The King permitted that too, didn't he?"

"Yes. And I fear he was ill advised then also."

"Are you worried—about what may happen now?"

Sebastian closed his book and laid it down on the table beside him. "No," he said slowly. "I am not really worried. Yesterday's elections do not obligate the King to inaugurate a republic. As matters stand now, parliamentary elections will not be held until next month and senatorial elections not until June. There will probably be time enough to worry then, for those who are bent on doing so. Personally I have ceased to worry very much about anything.

When I was younger I went about beating my head against stone walls, and raging because I could not batter them down. I no longer do so. I accept the fact that they are there. Sometimes they crumble of their own accord. Sometimes they prove even more impregnable than I supposed. In either case they do not infuriate me.'

Hans Christian, to whom this declaration of fatalism was more significant than it would have been twenty-four hours earlier, considered it without replying to it. Sebastian went on talking of his own accord.

"Almost anything may happen to Alfonso. Almost everything has already. He is immensely popular. People call him 'El Rey Valiente,' and he merits the title. Besides being valiant, he is debonair, tactful and extremely able. He is an excellent scholar and a fine sportsman. I really must arrange to have you meet him. You would be captivated by him. Everyone who comes in contact with him is affected by his magnetism, and even to those who do not know him he is fascinating as a figure and a symbol. Yet he has bitter enemies also, and he has always been the victim of murderous attacks. Some time when you are in Madrid you must go to the room at the Royal Palace which has been converted into a museum for the weapons, or what is left of them, that have been used against him. One of them is a milk bottle, with which an attempt was made to poison him when he was a baby. So you see the attacks began early. Even on his wedding day he did not escape. Twenty-seven persons were killed in an explosion which he mercifully survived. But he and his bride were bombed in their carriage. He turned to her quite calmly and helped her to wipe the blood from her lace veil, with the remark that he regretted she should have been subjected to an 'accident of his trade.'"

"So Spaniards are not always able to safeguard their wives after all? Not even the King of Spain?"

Sebastian laughed. "*Touché!*" he said humorously. "I knew that conversation of ours would rankle in your mind and that some day you would have the last word in it after all. Your retort is exactly the sort of thing your mother used to say, and still does, I hope. You are extraordinarily like her, as I have told you before."

"Does that predispose you a little in my favour?"

"It has always predisposed me in your favour. I thought you knew that. But why do you ask?"

"Because I want to ask you something else. I want to ask you to let me marry Cristina."

The words which he had supposed would be so hard to say, and which he had meant to string into so many formal phrases, had come tumbling out haphazardly of themselves. He drew a deep breath, and waited for the impact of the volley with which he felt sure they would be returned, determined not to flinch or falter under it. By the time he was fully braced against it, he incredulously realized that no volcanic explosion was taking place. Sebastian said nothing at all for a moment. Then he rose, and put his arm around Hans Christian's shoulder, in the same friendly way that had marked his manner at the beginning of the boy's visit.

"I am very happy that you should have spoken to me in this way, at this time, *querido*," he said kindly. "I knew, of course, that you had fallen in love with Cristina. But I hardly dared to hope you would come and tell me so, quietly, of your own accord, before you spoke to anyone else on the subject. I was afraid you would rush in upon Cristina some day, when she was quite unprepared, and try to tell her exactly how you felt."

"I never wanted to do it that way. I wanted all along to speak to you first. But I didn't dare. I thought you had taken a dislike to me. As a matter of fact, though, I didn't speak to you first. I spoke to *Tío* Gabriel first. And he encouraged me. He told me that through two generations already there had been sorrow in surrender to the will of God. He said he prayed that in this generation there might be joy instead. I thought possibly you might feel the same way about it, if you could come to look at it fairly. So when I saw the light in the library I came straight up. I hoped I'd find you here."

"The hope was quite mutual," Sebastian said, still kindly. "I did not suppose that your conversation with Gabriel was political, no matter what you discussed in the café. I thought you had probably gone to talk with him about the matter nearest your heart. It is the way of many persons in perplexity, and it is a good one. I have often gone to him myself under circumstances somewhat similar to these. Personally I have never known him to be quite so candid as he was with you. But since he has seen fit to confide in you, that brings us all closer together, does it not? . . . Besides, when I said I was glad you came to me before anyone else, I was not thinking of Gabriel. I was thinking of Cristina—and of her mother."

"Well, now that I have spoken to you, can't I speak to Cristina? And won't you speak to her mother?"

"I shall certainly speak to her mother. And I am sure she will appreciate your attitude. But you know her plans for Cristina. She will not be easily persuaded to change them."

"But you could persuade her, couldn't you? I should think you could persuade almost anyone to do almost anything!"

Hans Christian's voice rang with sincerity. Sebastian smiled, but he shook his head.

"I have not always been so successful at persuasion as you seem to imagine. Besides, you also know that I have shared my wife's viewpoint regarding Cristina's vocation. It was because you became so vehement on that subject that you and I nearly quarrelled. Not because I disliked you. I could never do that."

There was something so tender in Sebastian's tone that Hans Christian was deeply touched. The poignancy of the moment, instead of silencing him, gave him courage to go on.

"Then, if you don't dislike me, couldn't you consider me as a son-in-law? Couldn't you change your viewpoint about Cristina's vocation? Especially if you found out she had changed hers?"

"*Querido*, I found that out some time ago. Perhaps before she was aware of it herself—certainly before she went to Gabriel about it. I am right in assuming she has also been consulting Gabriel, am I not? You see, it is quite the family custom. *Bueno!* It is possible I might change my viewpoint about Cristina's vocation. It is even possible I might consider you as a son-in-law. But that is not equivalent to saying I am ready to have the banns published next Sunday, or even that I am willing to have you propose, unconditionally, to Cristina. There are more complications to the situation than you realize. Suppose we go outside on the terrace and talk them over. It is very cool and pleasant there, and I always think a sense of space and darkness is helpful at such moments as these."

Sebastian moved away from the circle made by the student lamp and walked toward the double doors leading to the terrace. They stood wide open, and, arm in arm, he and Hans Christian went through them together. The groves and gardens, the wide plains and distant mountains were all dimly visible in the starlight. But there was no moon, and the night had a mystic quality. Slowly approaching the parapet, the two men leaned over it in silence

"I had a double purpose in asking you to come out here," Sebastian said at last. "I want to talk to you, not only about Cristina, but about your grandmother. I had a letter from her today, after you had gone to town. I am afraid, from what she writes, that she is not at all well. And it is evident that she misses you very much, that she is extremely dependent on you. I really feel you should return to Germany immediately. I hesitate to say this to you because I am afraid you will think I am using her illness as a pretext to send you away at this time. But that is not so."

"What do you mean by 'immediately'?"

"I mean exactly that. I have had your bags packed. There is a train leaving early in the morning. If you feel well enough yourself, I think you ought to take it."

"Without seeing Cristina at all!"

Sebastian did not answer at once. When he did so, he spoke as if he were weighing his words carefully.

"Since you have had a long talk with Gabriel, I see no reason why you and I should talk at length. You probably know by this time that I do not approve of early marriages, and why. You probably also know that I like Americans much better than I do Germans—and why. You cannot leave your grandmother just now, I can see that. But if your grandmother, who is already a very old lady, should die—what then? Would you go home then?"

"Germany is my home, Sebastian."

"Are you sure? Remember I have told you that you seemed to me essentially American."

"Yes, I do remember. But I'm very sure."

"You wouldn't leave it—not even to pay your mother a visit? You wouldn't go there—on a wedding trip, for instance?"

Hansel caught his breath and clutched hard at the parapet. He tried to answer quietly.

"Yes. I'd go there to visit my mother. If there were no misunderstanding about it. That it was just for a visit, I mean. And, of course, I'd go there—on a wedding trip."

"Very well. I want you to promise me that if your grandmother should die you will go to see your mother—at once. And, whether she dies or not, I promise you that you may take Cristina there on her wedding trip two years from now."

"Two years!"

"Yes. It is a long time, I know. But do you realize how young Cristina is? I do not believe you do, because Spanish girls seem so much older than Germans or Americans at the same age. She will still be under twenty, Hansel, two years from now. That is early enough for any girl to marry. After all, what are two years? They will be gone before you know it, the passage of time is so swift! And meantime, of course, you may see Cristina. You may see her now, for that matter. I am perfectly sure that she is not asleep. I am certain she is lying awake, wondering what you and I are saying to each other."

Sebastian leaned over the parapet and gave a low whistle, which penetrated the air between the soft notes of a nightingale's song. He waited for a moment, and then repeated it. Almost instantly there was an answering call.

"We have had that signal ever since Cristina was a little girl," Sebastian said. "She will be here in a minute. You had better think fast. Because when she comes I'm going to speak to her myself on the subject we have been discussing. So it will be necessary for me to know whether you are willing to meet my conditions. Ah—here she is now."

Hans Christian turned sharply from the parapet. Cristina was coming through the doorway and across the terrace, dressed in white, with her long braids hanging over her breast, as she had been the night he first saw her. Sebastian went to meet her and took her hand.

"Alma de mi alma" he said fondly, "Hans Christian and I have been having a long talk together. I have been obliged to tell him

212

the sad news that his grandmother is ill, that I think he should go to her at once. Therefore he is leaving very early in the morning, and you may not see him again in some time. But he has told me something too, something that has caused me to send for you, since I felt you should hear of it before he goes. He says that he loves you, and has asked my permission to tell you so himself. Do you feel you would be happy in accepting him as a suitor?"

"Yes," answered Cristina without hesitation.

Hans Christian gave a quick movement. Sebastian spoke warningly.

"Just a moment," he said. Then he turned to Cristina again. "You know it had been your mother's hope, and mine, that you would become a nun, *querida*. We understood that it was yours also. In fact, you have repeatedly said so yourself. Have you changed your mind?"

"Yes," said Cristina again.

"I have told Hans Christian that I am not willing you should be married for two years. If you do not stay in the convent, you will inevitably have many other suitors. But if you give him a promise tonight you should be prepared to keep it. You must not change your mind about this too. Do you feel sure you can be loyal to him, so that his long wait will not be in vain?"

"Yes," said Cristina a third time.

Sebastian was still clasping her fingers. But with his free hand he reached out, and, taking Hans Christian's, placed Cristina's in it.

"Are you ready now to accept my conditions, Hansel?" he asked. "If you are, I will leave you to talk to Cristina for a few moments yourself. Do not keep her too long. It is very late. But I will go into the library and wait for you there. And while I am waiting I will repeat Gabriel's prayer that in this generation there may be joy instead of sorrow in surrender to the will of God."

CHAPTER XXI

CRISTINA did not withdraw her hand from Hansel's. Instead, after a moment, he felt her fingers flutter lightly against his palm. Then she interlaced them with his.

"Shall we sit down?" she asked softly. "We are free to say anything we wish to each other now, you know."

He nodded, and moved with her towards a stone bench. But still he did not speak. The miracle had come to pass so swiftly that he could not believe, even though he beheld. It was Cristina who went on talking after they had sat down side by side.

"I have kept trying to be calm. I have kept saying to myself,

'Something will happen. Something will make it possible for us to be together after all.' And I was right. You see that it has."

"Yes," said Hansel hoarsely, "I—I see that it has."

He was powerless, for the moment, to go on. But Cristina, who had been gazing lovingly toward him, continued to regard him with large trustful eyes, undisturbed because his emotion did not take articulate form. Exultantly he became aware that in spite of her youth and inexperience she had divined the reasons for his restraint, and that since this was so there would never be any need of explanations between them. The joyous conviction that they would always understand each other had a steadying effect. He leaned towards her, speaking more naturally.

"I want to hear you say that you love me!"

"But, *querido*, that is something you must say first! And so far you have said nothing at all!"

"Only because I was so stunned that I couldn't. You know that!"

"Yes, I know that. But now you seem to be recovering from the shock of finding out that my father is not an ogre after all and that I——"

"That you——"

"That I am just like any other young girl, *querido*."

"But you're not! There isn't anyone like you in the whole world."

"I am glad you think so, even if it is not true. But what I meant was, I am just like any other young girl when it comes to falling in love."

"And I was so sure you wanted to be a nun!"

"You mean you were so credulous when *mamacita* told you so. You never talked to me about it. If you had I should have told you at once that I stopped wanting to be a nun the morning that we wove garlands together."

"If I had guessed anything of that sort, of course I would have done so long ago. I would have found a way somehow. But I am not going to do so now. I am going to talk to you about being a bride instead of a nun. Oh, Cristina—Cristina—since I know you love me, how can I wait for you two years?"

"But how unreasonable you are, *mi corazón!* Will it not be much easier to wait for me, knowing that I love you, than wondering whether I did or not? And, after all, what are two years?"

Unconsciously she had repeated her father's question. Then she began to count off the calendar on her fingers, which were still interlaced with Hansel's. "This is 1931," she said, with a light tap. "One year will be up in 1932. Then comes '33! That is all that there will be to our waiting. It will be over just like that!"

She blew into the air and tossed her head slightly, dismissing time as a trifle. One of her long, glossy braids, which Hansel had so desired to feel, brushed against his cheek. He took hold of it, and of its twin, and drew her closer to him by her own plaits.

"And then we shall be married," he said, as she came nearer and nearer, "and live happily ever after!"

"Yes. Then we'll be married—and live happily ever after!"

He had sworn that he would always treat her with that tact and tenderness of which her father believed no German capable, and he meant to keep his vow. Indeed, he might have left her with no caress beyond their long handclasp if she had not raised her lips to him as trustfully as she had raised her eyes. Then he kissed her gently, without taking her in his arms, and she did not turn her head away until she had kissed him in return.

"I must go back to my room," she said, with a little sigh, which was half sadness and half ecstasy. Then after a moment she added: "And you must talk to my father in the library. Come! We will walk across the terrace together, and then we will part—for the present. But some day there will be no more partings between us. Do not forget that, *vida de mi vida.*"

They had reached the steps leading into the library, and once more she raised her lips. "Go with God," she said softly. "And come again—to me."

Had he made a mistake in claiming no embrace? he asked himself repeatedly the next day as the slow train jolted northward. He did not think so, though he had longed for it so unutterably. He knew that Cristina would not have shrunk away if he had attempted it. But he himself shrank from the thought of mere acquiescence in connection with Cristina. Having beheld her eyes lighted with love and felt her lips warm beneath his own, he wanted more than ever to see her arms spontaneously outstretched before they were passionately pinioned. And she herself had not indicated that she was ready for an embrace. Perhaps the next time he saw her—oh, certainly the next time. . . .

He had tried to persuade Sebastian to set a date for this when they said good-bye to each other. But on this point Sebastian had been somewhat evasive, and Hans Christian had decided that it was wiser not to press it, especially in view of the fact that otherwise Sebastian had been very liberal. He had promised to speak to both Doña Dolores and Gabriel the next day; he had raised no objection to correspondence; it was evident that he recognized the existence of a definite though informal betrothal. Indeed, he raised one question of his own accord which had not once entered Hans Christian's mind.

"You have said nothing at all about a dowry. Did you have any special sum in mind?"

"A dowry? *Money?*"

"Why, yes. Of course, Cristina will have a very substantial dowry.

You have seen us living so simply here, perhaps you have forgotten that this is not our usual mode of existence, that we have a place in Madrid, and several castles besides the one in the Pyrenees and the one near Toledo. Had it slipped your mind that Gabriel and I are sole heirs to one of the greatest fortunes in Spain, and that Gabriel has no children?"

"Yes. That is, I never thought about it at all. I'd rather not think about it now, if you don't mind."

"But, my dear boy——"

"Yes, I remember it's customary, now that you speak of it. But I've thought of heiresses—differently. You see, I know another. And sometimes I've thought—for the sake of Schönplatz——"

"Oh, so you know another heiress, do you?"

"Yes, a very rich American. She's a nice girl too. But I don't love her. And I do love Cristina. I can take care of her, Sebastian. Not lavishly, but suitably. If you'll only trust me——"

"Strangely enough, I have considerable confidence in you," Sebastian remarked rather dryly. "Well, we will let the matter of a dowry rest for the moment. Though I hope very much you will not object if I give Cristina the *caseria* for a wedding present. It was originally built by one of my ancestors as a bower for the lady he loved. It seems to me appropriate that you and Cristina should have it, since you have met and are happy here. I shall not need it when there is no reason why I should stay close to Gabriel. And I am afraid there will be none very much longer." He broke off abruptly, and after a moment went on in a changed voice: "There is still another reason why I should like you to stay from time to time at the *caseria*, Hansel. I—once offered it to your mother as a gift, and she declined to accept it. Not because she felt she could never take presents from me. I am glad to say she did so honour me from time to time. She declined it because she felt, if she owned it, she might come to regard it as her home, and she wanted Hamstead to be her only home. Since you do not share that feeling, perhaps you——"

"I'd like to have you give the *caseria* to Cristina and me, Sebastian. And—thank you for telling me about the other too."

Yes, Sebastian had been surprisingly generous, all things considered, and Hans Christian had so much cause for contentment that he knew it should be possible for him to possess his soul in patience as far as seeing Cristina again was concerned. After all, summer-time was not very far away, and meanwhile his yearning for her was mercifully numbed by fatigue. The day before had been supercharged, in every sense of the word. He had exerted himself far more than at any time since his accident; and he had experienced doubt, despair, reassurance and joy within the space of a few short hours. He was both physically and emotionally exhausted, and he might even have gone to sleep sitting bolt upright on the hard seat of the compartment, if it had not been for the conversation of the two men who were sharing it with him.

They had both greeted him courteously when he had entered, and both had offered him a share from a laden lunch-basket, a gesture which he had duly returned. They had also made a conscientious effort to draw him into their talk, and it was only after he had indicated that he was a stranger in Spain and knew next to nothing about its internal affairs that this conversation became a duologue.

It was wholly political in character, but at no moment did it become heated. The two Spaniards did not lose their tempers, as Hans Christian had repeatedly seen both Americans and Germans lose theirs in the discussion of similar subjects. Indeed, it did not seem to occur to them that there was any reason for doing so. They were absorbed, not angry. In their possession were newspapers, printed later than those Hans Christian had seen in the café the afternoon before, and these they spread out, reading aloud to each other, and commenting on the news items therein contained. The march of events had apparently been very swift. There had been an emergency meeting of the Cabinet the night before, and the possibility of setting up a military dictatorship had been considered. Now it was already announced that the Cabinet was about to resign, in the face of a Republican threat to use force to make the King heed the Republican victory, and the word "heed" was being interpreted in terms of abdication. Moreover, the Labour Party was prepared to paralyse public utilities if any attempt were made to resort to force. The Civil Guard had already killed two persons. A few agitators had been shot in Madrid and Seville, and many other persons hurt in the course of unbridled revelry. On the whole, however, the demonstrations, though riotous, had been harmless.

"But it is impossible! The King will never abdicate!"

It may be impossible, but it is true. See, Señor, he is quoted as saying he knows he has lost the love of his people, that therefore he is prepared to resign in favour of the Infante Juan."

"Yes, he is so quoted in one paper. But in the other he states that he has no intention of renouncing the throne, and asks that this assertion be published. What, then, can one believe?"

"I believe, Señor, that the King is sincere in saying he knows the country is angry with him. Has it not been angry ever since the fiasco in Morocco? He is right about that. But he is wrong when he says the people are monarchistic at heart."

"And I believe, Señor, he is right in this also, and that the throne may yet be saved. The King has acted in strict accordance with the Constitution. If a new Cabinet is formed, conservative-monarchistic in character, with Cieva at the head, it will be empowered to use military forces to quell a revolution and a general strike."

"*Empowered!* What power could such a Cabinet have in the face of everything else that has happened? The Republican Committee has been in session all night, and when Maura left the meeting at dawn he remarked: 'There is no news now, but there will be after Anzar visits the Palace today!' And Anzar himself, on being asked whether a crisis existed, replied: 'When a monarchistic country turns republican within twenty-four hours, that is crisis enough for anyone!'"

"And I still say it has not so turned! When did the election of a few aldermen ever change the political complexion of a country? Listen to this dispatch from Barcelona: 'All the Captains-General in Spain have been ordered to Madrid. This was interpreted as indicating the Government's implicit faith in the Army.'"

"It may be so interpreted. The loyalty of an army numbering eighty thousand, where one man in ten is a general, may perhaps be taken for granted. The Army, like the Church, is well subsidized. But how shall it prevail against the nation as a whole? How could it even prevail against Catalonia alone, now that you speak of Barcelona and bring that issue to my mind?"

"There, Señor, I see we are agreed. Those cursed Catalans! One never knows what they may do! Francisco Cambo has left for Madrid as well as the Captains-General. That also may portend almost anything!"

The duologue went on and on. Even the siesta hour was forgotten in the intensity of it. Hansel only half heard it. Recalling the prevailing air of apathy in the café the day before, and Sebastian's philosophic attitude, it caused him no alarm, though it roused his interest intermittently. He was actually much more concerned because it had tardily occurred to him that nothing had been said about a ring for Cristina the night before. He should have found out what she would like, he should have asked Sebastian for permission to present her with one immediately. He was comforted with the conviction that Cristina would not be offended at his oversight; the complete harmony of her spirit with his would cause her to understand that she had not been wilfully neglected, that he had overlooked a minor point because he had been occupied with a major issue. Yet would she consider the question of her betrothal ring a mere detail, as he did? He knew the feminine penchant for jewellery; he had never forgotten Mrs. Fuller's passion for gems, or his grandmother's prostration over the loss of them. And Cristina had reminded him, playfully, that she was just like any other girl! Well, amidst the wreckage there must be still one ancestral ring of the von Hohenlohes that he could offer her. And yet, after all, he thought he would rather give her one he had planned and purchased himself. He did not think that massive designs or flamboyant stones would be suitable for her. Pearls, lightly set in platinum, and perhaps surrounded with small diamonds, would be far more fitting. And a pearl cross, set like the ring and hung on a long, flexible chain, would be lovely for her to wear with it. He hoped he could afford to get her both. Yet someone had told him there was a superstition that pearls were unlucky for brides. He wondered if Cristina shared this——

The train slowed down at a station, and one of Hans Christian's fellow-passengers got out, after bowing gravely to the other occupants of the compartment and expressing the hope that they would continue to have a pleasant journey. The second man succeeded in securing an afternoon paper from a vendor who was besieged for them as he rolled his push-cart down the platform; and by this time Hansel was eager to listen to the news. It appeared that excitement unparalleled in fifty years was reigning in Madrid. Upon a report that the King had abdicated, a mob had surged through the Puerta del Sol, shouting, "Viva la Republica!" Shots had been fired into the air as the Cabinet change was cheered. Benches had been smashed, streets closed, traffic paralysed. Meanwhile the King had remained secluded with his family in the Palace, reputedly seeing a moving picture show. But the Socialists, after a meeting of the "Directive Committee," had "given him only until night to make up his mind. . . ."

"I thought the King was greatly beloved. I'm very much confused."

"Señor, we are living in a confused world, and as yet we have seen only the beginning of its confusion."

"If the Church and the Army and the aristocracy all stand by the King, doesn't that still give him the balance of power?"

"No, Señor. For when you say the Church, you can count only on the cardinals and the bishops. You will find many simple priests with Republican leanings. And when you say the Army it is the same. It is top-heavy with monarchistic generals and colonels and captains, as our Lord knows. Even so, there are some sixty odd thousand enlisted men and non-commissioned officers, and many of these are Republican also. As for the aristocracy—well, it is true enough that there are a thousand grandees in Spain, that the gentry owns more than ninety per cent. of the land . . . as it did in Russia, Señor, before 1918. God grant that what happened there may not also happen here!"

At the word "Russia" a small quivering fork of fear darted through Hansel's body for the first time. He found that he dreaded the answer to his next question.

"These Spanish Republicans—they're not Communistic, are they?"

"Heaven save us, no, Señor! But there are Communists and

Socialists in Spain as well as Republicans—not to mention Carlists and Separatists and Catalans and all the other groups. In a crisis like this it is hard to tell which will prevail. Politics make strange bedfellows."

The Spaniard picked up the paper again and began to read aloud from it. " 'Nobody who is not wilfully blind or crazy would deny that these elections are the most important political act in our history. The national will has been expressed, and, since we want peace and order, we hope everyone will make the necessary sacrifice to reach a peaceful solution.' . . . I am a lawyer, Señor, as well as a patriot, and I concur in that hope. I rejoice that the will of Spain has been expressed within the law. . . . 'We ask the King, who frequently has shown his patriotism, and to whom we offer our respects, not to demur about taking the action which his conscience as a good Spaniard must inspire——' "*

"But how can his conscience as a good Spaniard inspire him to do something so unpatriotic as to leave his country? I thought you called him your 'Rey Valiente'."

"A thousand pardons, Señor. I see you are still very young. When you are older, perhaps you will feel, as I do, that sometimes it takes more courage to retreat than to advance, to disappear from a scene rather than to dominate it. . . . I wish it were possible to continue this conversation with you, by which I have greatly profited. But we seem to be approaching my own station. *Felix viaje, Señor! Vaya con Dios!*"

He was gone, his flowing cape wrapped around him, his soft black hat still held courteously in one hand. He had insisted on leaving his lunch-basket behind him, lest Hansel's own supply should not be adequate for his needs until he reached Madrid. Dusk was creeping over the landscape, and the small dingy globe in the ceiling of the compartment emanated little light; since he could no longer see to read, Hansel tried to eat. But he found he could not choke down the food. He was angry with himself now because he had not listened more attentively during the earlier part of the day, because he had not scanned every line in an effort to understand what was happening. He was angrier still because he had left Granada at all, because he had not stayed with the Cerrenos in this crisis. What would happen to Gabriel, who was so frail and aged, if there were a forcible separation of Church and State? What would happen to Sebastian, who was so charming and so nonchalant, if the aristocracy were dispossessed of its lands? What would happen to Cristina if—if—if—— At one moment he resolved to take the next train he could catch back to Granada. At the next he was convinced that since he had started north he should go on to his grandmother, since she needed him so desperately, and then, as soon as she was able to

* *Informaciones*, April 14, 1931.

travel, that he should bring her back with him for the prolonged stay which it would be impossible for him to make without her, now that he knew of her critical condition. His reason told him that Sebastian would resent his return. His heart prompted him to speed to Cristina's side.

Tardily, as he had thought of a ring for Cristina, he wondered why he had not asked to have his engagement to her formally announced at once. From every point of view this seemed to him desirable. His grandmother would be immensely pleased; in her complacency over the turn things had taken, she would doubtless gloat over him a little. Well, he was willing enough she should remind him that she had been right all along, if this would give her satisfaction. There was little enough joy in her life. On the other hand, there were persons who would be less pleased, but to whom he owed candour on such a subject. He could not imagine why the thought of Trixie should give his heart a queer twist just then; but it did. Illogically his conscience smote him at the idea of telling her that he was in love with another girl. He could see exactly how she would look when he did so—slightly startled, slightly defiant, her cheeks redder than usual, her eyes momentarily bewildered but her head held higher than ever, as she had on the drive back from the Spreewald. As darkness descended the image became increasingly vivid.

When the train finally jerked into the Madrid station he was appalled by the abnormal quiet. There were no push-cart vendors on the platform, and no porters; the absence of their cheerful importunities left a strange void. With some difficulty Hansel shouldered his own bags and stepped out of the compartment, striving to suppress his sense of the uncanny, which increased as he walked through the vacant waiting-room and passed the blank ticket windows. His arm still hurt him if he put much strain upon it. But he felt he should at least be able to reach a cab unaided. To his increasing dismay he found no taxis outside. The station plaza was as empty as the station itself. Shifting the position of his heavier suitcase, and gripping the smaller one more firmly, he set out across the vacant space on foot, incredulously searching for a street-car or a subway station. Neither was anywhere in sight.

He was overwhelmed with a feeling of unreality before he came upon a few scattered pedestrians. As one after another hurried past him, he strove to stop them to ask his way to an hotel where he could spend the night. No one regarded him with animosity, but no one offered to help him, and no one gave him any information.

"Ah, Señor!" one man paused long enough to exclaim. "To think that you should have to carry bags on such a night as this!"

"It is a rather disagreeable thing to be doing," Hans Christian replied. "But unless——"

"No gentleman should ever carry anything!"

Again Hansel agreed, asking the way to an hotel with the same futile result.

"No one will have to work any more."

"That will be a happy state of affairs. How will it be arranged?"

"The new Government will arrange it. The new Government will arrange everything."

The man scurried on again, as if regretful of having wasted so much time in explanation. The *new Government!* So that was it! There was a new Government already! As Hansel went blindly on, still undirected and still without sense of location, he came upon clustering groups which slowly thickened into a milling mass. Flags were fluttering all around him, from the staffs of big buildings, from the iron balconies of houses, in the hands of the pressing people. Nearly all were crudely put together, as if they had been made hastily or surreptitiously. Most of these flags were striped, purple, yellow and red; but there were a few black ones also, carried aloft between pictures of "martyred" patriots, and many which were wholly red. Indeed, a weird note of red was repeated in different forms on every side. Automobiles flaunting red posters, inscribed with the words "Republican Socialist Union," were coursing through the crowds, unmolested by a police wearing red armbands. Taxicabs flying red flags seemed to be spreading some kind of news, and excited throngs, gesticulating, gathered in their wake. Above the entrances of shops workmen were hurriedly covering the royal coat-of-arms with red paper. Hansel saw that little boys were wearing red bow ties, little girls red hair ribbons, that men had long red caps on their heads and that women were carrying red roses. One stepped out of her red petticoat and waved it over her head, crying aloud as she did so, "The petticoat of the Queen!" The noise, like the crowding, was overpowering. Amidst the shouts of "Long Live the Republic!" and "Death to Alfonso!" rose the strains of the *Marseillaise* and the *Internationale*.

Hansel had long since ceased trying to find out where he was going, or saving himself from being swept along in the general direction of the mob. He could see plenty of street cars now. But they seemed to be going around in circles, almost like merry-go-rounds, for the purpose of pleasing revellers, rather than of taking passengers to any fixed destination. Their small platforms were packed, and even their roofs surmounted with teeming humanity. The advertisements on their sides were completely covered with moving arms and legs, heads and bodies. Every now and then a man who had been riding inside, swung himself out through a window and was quickly hauled upwards by helpful hands. As he climbed he continued to sing, and to wave the flag which he still managed to hold tightly clutched.

There was no possible point in trying to board any such demoralized street-car, provided it could be reached at all, which was doubtful. As Hansel approached a great archway, which he supposed must be the Puerta del Sol, the throng became denser than ever. His shoulder was becoming increasingly painful, his exhaustion annihilating. But if he could do nothing else, he decided, he might be able to take shelter in some doorway, as he had in his first Berlin street brawl. Many of these had deep embrasures, and the crowd, pushing ahead, shouting and singing as it went, was not pausing in any event. When his vague idea had become a fixed purpose, Hansel found a way of carrying it out. By forging his way slowly further and further from the kerb, and nearer and nearer the blocks of buildings, he reached the sort of indentation he was seeking. He struggled into it, and the mob roared past, leaving him behind.

He set down his bags and leaned against the wall, thankful for its support. For a moment he slumped; then he took out his handkerchief and wiped his streaming face. As he put it back into his pocket his eye lit upon a row of neatly lettered plates, placed one above the other near the bell beside the inner doorway. Reading these mechanically, something stopped him before he reached the last one. It occurred to him that he was looking at a name which he had seen or heard before.

With increasing bewilderment he tried to remember where and when this could have been. At last, surprisingly, he did so. He put his hand back into his pocket and drew out his wallet. When he had opened this he saw, still slipped into its depths, the card of the man he had met a month earlier, on his way to Spain.

CHAPTER XXII

Hans Christian had very little hope that his tug at the bell would be answered. The porter's cubby-hole, inside the vestibule, was empty. He was almost certain that the quarters above would be vacant also. Judging from the size of the mob outside, it looked as if every habitation in the city must have disgorged its occupants. But since another miracle had happened to him, he could not disregard the significance of this. He seized the iron handle attached to the end of a long jointed metal bell-pull, and drew it down with all his might.

There was no answering click at the latch, no sign of a slight swing setting the door ajar. But after a moment he heard steps descending the stairs, not with a sudden rush of feet, but with a slow, cautious tread. Apparently whoever was coming had been almost at the top of the house, for the sound continued for some time before Hansel saw anyone. Then a man's figure, blurred by the

obscurity, appeared around the bend of the mottled marble staircase. He came to the door and opened it a crack.

"Good evening, Señor," he said. "Were you seeking somebody?"

His manner was neither surly nor suspicious. He merely showed
the hesitation that any sensible householder might display at finding
a total stranger on his threshold at midnight.

"I was looking for Señor Ramirez. I see he is listed as living here."

"Then Bautista Ramirez is a friend of yours, Señor?"

"I can't say that exactly. But he has certainly been very friendly.
We shared a compartment on the Paris Express a month ago and he
told me I would be welcome at his home any time. At the moment
I am feeling very badly in need of a welcome."

Hans Christian extended the card he was holding for the
stranger's inspection. The man barely glanced at it.

"If that is the case I am sure that he will wish to see you now. I
gather that you yourself are not a Spaniard, Señor?"

"No, I'm a German. But I have Spanish kinsfolk whom I've been
visiting in Andalusia, while recovering from a bad wound. Now I've
had word that my grandmother is very ill, and I'm on my way back
to East Prussia to see her."

"Ah . . . I am afraid you may find the trains to the frontier full
to overflowing. But in the morning we must see what we can do for
you, since such an emergency exists. In the meantime I know my
friend Ramirez will wish you to consider his apartment yours for
the night. You are correct in assuming that he lives here. A little
meeting is taking place in his quarters, which I happen to be
attending. But you will not disturb us, if we do not disturb you.
Follow me, Señor, that I may show you the way. The stairs are
dark and rather winding. Pardon me, but I see you are burdened
with baggage. Permit me to relieve you of part of it."

The stairway had the cold stale smell which Hans Christian had
often noticed in continental apartment houses, and the pale bulbs
of electricity which cast an intermittent glimmer on it were few
and far between. He mounted slowly and painfully, still carrying
his smaller suitcase. From time to time his guide paused, and spoke
to him encouragingly.

"I'm afraid you will find this a long climb, Señor, since you have
been ill and are now very tired besides. We still have no lifts in our
old houses, as you see—in Germany I believe everything is much
more modern. Did I understand you to say you had come from
Seville today?"

"No, from Granada."

"Granada! Everything is quite quiet there, is it not?"

"It was yesterday. But a good deal seems to have happened since
yesterday."

"You are right. Much has happened since yesterday, and much

more will happen tomorrow. . . . We are almost at the end of our ascent, Señor. Before we reach our destination, permit me to tell you my name. It is Pedro Valeza."

"And mine is Hans von Hohenlohe, Señor."

Valeza had stopped, and knocked on a dark door. It was opened after an almost imperceptible delay, and in the narrow corridor beyond Hans Christian saw the man who had befriended him on the train.

"An old acquaintance has done you the honour of coming to see you, Bautista," Pedro Valeza said immediately. "Señor de Hohenlohe tells me he met you last month, when you were returning from Paris."

"Of course! We compared notes on French coffee and I invited him to come and try mine at any time. And felicitously a fresh pot has been brought to me at this very moment. Come in, Señor. Come in! *Esta es su casa!*"

The man's manner was completely cordial. Hansel had been drawn inside the door, and this had been closed again, before he himself had been given a chance to speak.

"I must apologize for intruding on you like this, Señor," he managed to say at last. "I was afraid you wouldn't even remember me. And apparently I've come at a rather disturbed time. But I'd been looking for shelter over an hour before I found your name in the doorway."

"*Lástima!* But I am glad you saw it at last! Let me lead you to a little room where I hope you will sleep well tonight. Then when you have arranged your belongings you must come into the *salita* and meet the friends who are holding a conference with me."

"You're sure I won't be in the way?"

"But how should that be possible, Señor? A guest—in the way?"

Hansel was far too exhausted to protest. His host led the way into a tiny bedroom, barely big enough to contain a ponderous wooden bed of the Isabelline period, and a marble-topped night table, washstand and chest of drawers to match. In order to set down the baggage it was necessary to shove two small chairs around. The rest of the massive furniture loomed large and dark against the drably papered walls, enhancing the general air of gloom.

"I am going to bring your first cup of coffee in here," Ramirez said kindly. "You can drink it while you're getting oriented." He disappeared, to return almost instantly with a steaming drink. But short as his absence had been, Hansel had already sunk down on the big bed before his return, his shoulders bowed, his body sagging with fatigue. He looked up to acknowledge his host's thoughtfulness, and Ramirez saw that his face was pallid.

"Why not go to bed at once?" the man suggested solicitously. "It will be time enough to meet my friends tomorrow. They will be in and out all day. I will explain all that has happened to you then also. I suppose you are eager for news. But it can wait."

"Not all of it. . . . Is it true that the King has abdicated?"

"Yes. He left Madrid secretly this afternoon. He is now speeding along through the night to some undisclosed destination, probably Cartagena. It would not have been safe for him to attempt to reach Portugal or pass through Northern Spain."

"Not safe! Has his life been endangered?"

Ramirez hesitated, but only for a moment. "Not in Madrid, since he did not delay. But elsewhere there has been more disturbance than here."

"More disturbance than here!"

Ramirez smiled. "I can understand that you should feel, after your experience, that there has been considerable disturbance here. But nothing serious has happened in Madrid. Yesterday there were a few clashes between the students and the police. The latter did some disciplining with the flats of their swords, and the youngsters finally retreated, rather vociferously, to the subway. But they were not pursued there, and no one was really hurt. Today the atmosphere has actually been characteristic of a fiesta rather than of a revolution. A flowing stream of joy and light and music is rippling over the city of Madrid. Her people are intoxicated with its splendour. If you were not so tired, I would suggest that you should go out again later on, and join in the jubilation yourself. But you can do that tomorrow instead."

"Tomorrow! Tomorrow I must be on my way back to Granada . . . or off to Germany."

"I doubt whether you should attempt either. There is such an exodus of Spanish nobility that northbound travel is completely choked. When I went out to get your coffee, Valeza told me that he had tried to explain this to you already. As to returning south . . you know best, of course, but are you sure it is wise, all things considered? Would it not be better to wait over a day, and see what develops? Since your grandmother has need of you, I assure you we will bend every effort to getting you on the first train where there is an inch of space."

"You don't understand—any better than I do. I'm almost beside myself with anxiety. I don't know what I ought to do; I don't know who needs me most!"

Hans Christian had struggled to his feet. Ramirez took his coffee cup from him and put it quietly down on the night table. Then he laid a restraining hand on the boy's arm.

"You mean you're almost beside yourself with fatigue and emotion," he said. "There is no cause for anxiety—unless your grandmother's condition is critical, which I doubt. I have observed that elderly ladies are apt to summon their young relatives to their bed-

226

sides long before there is any question that these may become deathbeds! I will explain everything you wish to understand tomorrow, and you shall explain to me whatever you wish me to understand—no less and no more. Meanwhile, I can assure you that as far as the Cerrenos are concerned, they are wholly unmolested."

"You can assure me! But how can you be sure?"

Ramirez smiled again. "Because I am very thoroughly informed," he remarked. "It is my business to be. Come, perhaps I had better tell you. If you have seen the papers today, you have perhaps read that several exiled Republicans are on their way back from France— Indalecio Prieto, who will probably be the next Minister of Finance, and Ramón Franco, the famous flyer, among them. Well, I have been in exile also, but I succeeded in getting back sooner than some of my fellow-Republicans. I was just returning when I had the honour of meeting you before. Since then I have been extremely busy, as you will understand, Señor. But your comment that you were on your way to visit the Cerrenos interested me so much that I have kept a watchful eye on that family, in spite of my preoccupations. I shall continue to do so. They may find themselves, by tomorrow, with fewer titles than they had yesterday—than they have had for centuries, as far as that goes. And eventually Sebastian de Cerreno may find himself with somewhat less land. One of the first problems of the new Government will be how best to break up the great estates, though property rights will have such respect as they merit."

"You are a Communist—you!"

The friendly expression of Ramirez's face did not change. "I understand that Communists are not popular in Berlin at present," he said gravely. "However, they are not always characterized by horns and a tail, or even by bloodthirsty behaviour and churlish manners. As far as I am concerned, however, you do not need to be in the least alarmed, Señor. I am not a Communist, and neither are any of my immediate associates. Of course, there are Socialists in Spain, as elsewhere, and no doubt those who hold radical views and who nevertheless merged their votes with ours on Sunday will demand some recognition in the new Government. But that does not mean it will turn red overnight."

"Perhaps not overnight, but sooner or later! I know the breed! I know the way they work! I've lost almost everything worth having because of them! And now——"

He was so close to tears that he could not control his voice. A terrible sob choked him and a great wave of nausea swept over him. The last thing he saw before he fainted was the face of Bautista Ramirez, the kindliness of its expression transfigured by its solicitude.

It was also the first thing he saw when he came to himself again.

227

At first he was not sure where he was, and the thought flickered across his mind that his stay in Spain was ending, as it had begun, with strange and fitful sleep, that he should never be able to disentangle truth from trance when he thought about it afterwards. The crowded little room was still engulfed in obscurity, for its one window was closely muffled by drab woollen curtains, tightly drawn over Venetian blinds. However, Hans Christian had a feeling that it was day again, and as his eyes became accustomed to the dim light, he could see the outlines of the ponderous furniture, and the objects with which this was ornamented, most of them ludicrously fragile by contrast—brittle bric-à-brac, unfurled paper fans, family photographs framed in hand-painted silk and velvet. He noticed, with passing surprise, that there was no crucifix beside the bed, and no pictures of religious character on the walls; but the fact struck him as curious rather than portentous. And, after all, it was not half so curious as the fact that a self-confessed revolutionist who was a complete stranger to him should have given him comforting shelter.

He fixed his gaze more firmly on the seated figure beside the bed, and again he was struck, as he had been on the train, by the kindliness of this swarthy, stocky man. Something about his thoughts was apparently telepathic in its effect. Before long his host, who had been staring into space, as if completely absorbed in his own reflections, turned his head without moving his bulky body, in an evident attempt to avoid making the slightest sound which might disturb a sleeper. Then, seeing that Hansel's eyes were open, he rose creakingly and lumbered over towards the bed.

"*Que tal?*" he asked, not after the casually charming fashion of Sebastian, but with real concern in his voice. "You gave me a bad turn last night, *amigo,* with your fainting fit! Fortunately there was a physician among my comrades who were conferring with me in the *salita* and he brought you out of it. Then he gave you a good strong sedative before you could do any more worrying or ask any more troublesome questions. Now you have had a fine sleep, and all will be well with you again—if you do not immediately attempt another long journey, or try to drag heavy baggage for miles through a mob! I am sorry my city seemed to give you so indifferent a welcome. . . . Shall we let some sunshine into the room? And what about coffee? I am sure you would like a cup at once!"

He manipulated the cords controlling the heavy curtains, and rolled up the blind. Then he departed, to come back carrying a tray laden with coffee, hot milk and soft sugary rolls.

"I am a widower, Señor," he remarked as he set down the tray, and plumped up Hansel's pillows with a capable hand. "I live alone, except for an old servant, whose name is Antonina. She is a good woman and a good cook, which perhaps is even more to the point under the circumstances. You will find her glad to be of service, and

228

you will see her when you get up, for such plumbing as there is in my apartment is behind the kitchen. But I hope you will not be too greatly inconvenienced. She would have brought in your tray had I not preferred to serve you myself for the moment, so that we could talk undisturbed."

He reseated himself, making the same creaking sound as when he had risen, and drew a telegram from his vest pocket.

"I took the liberty of wiring your grandmother last night. I also took the liberty of opening her reply, so that I might know whether it was necessary to arouse you. I am sure you will be relieved at the good news this telegram contains."

He handed the flimsy piece of paper to his guest: RESTING COMFORTABLY AFTER RECENT HEART ATTACK (Hans Christian read eagerly) DESIRE BUT DO NOT REQUIRE YOUR IMMEDIATE PRESENCE. V. L. von HOHENLOHE.

"How did you know the address?" he asked in astonishment, looking up from the dispatch.

"But, *amigo*, I naturally keep an *Almanac de Gotha* on hand for easy reference! My library is unpretentious, but that volume is indispensable to me. If I had not possessed it, I should naturally have telephoned the German Embassy. I am rather glad, however, that this was not necessary, since Germany has not yet recognized our new Government. A statement to the effect that she has will doubtless come in at any moment, but it has not come yet."

Hans Christian, who was still torn between revulsion and gratitude, took refuge, for the moment, in silence on this subject, though he found his admiration for his host's ready resourcefulness mounting rapidly.

"Nevertheless I have telephoned to Granada," Bautista Ramirez went on, "and I have learned that everything at the Episcopal Palace is quite as usual. His Eminence, the Archbishop, has stood the shock of recent events remarkably well for a man of his age and convictions, and he has not seen fit to ask the Government to permit him to move his residence, as it is rumoured his colleague, the Archbishop of Seville, has done."

"*Tío* Gabriel would die first!" Hansel exclaimed heartily.

"I do not doubt it. But let us hope no such calamity will occur. I have always had great admiration for Gabriel de Cerreno. If all Churchmen of rank were like him the present situation would be considerably simpler. However, there will be no complications as far as he is concerned, as I tried to tell you last night."

"But the rest of the family——" began Hans Christian.

"As you know, there is no telephone at the country place where Sebastian de Cerreno is staying with his wife and daughters. However, I have asked for a report on them at once. Merely to ease your mind. Let me assure you again that they will be quite unmolested.

229

But it might be interesting to know whether they will join the general exodus. I understand that no fewer than thirty-six families are leaving today with the Queen, and I could not tell you how many have gone already."

"*Today* with the Queen! Didn't they go yesterday with the King?"

"No—no. He went by motor, accompanied only by the Duke of Miranda and two Civil Guards. He has always been a rapid driver, but I understand that this time he broke all speed records in reaching Cartagena. Now he has embarked on the cruiser *Principe Alfonso,* presumably for Marseilles."

"He left the Queen behind him when he fled? And that poor sick son of his, suffering with hæmophilia? *El Rey Valiente!*"

"Drink your *café con leche, amigo,* before it becomes completely cold. If you will pardon me for saying so, you should learn to take life more philosophically. You must not let the crash of your illusions overwhelm you so, when they are shattered; otherwise you will end by being shattered yourself. . . . Doubtless the King realized that the Queen would be entirely safe with the good Republican guard which was placed all around the palace to watch over her. As for the suffering of the Prince, that may be laid to Victoria's door, not Alfonso's. The bleeding sickness was not among the diseases which are part of the Hapsburg legacy, though those are not pleasant ones either."

Hans Christian flushed angrily. "My grandmother is a Hapsburg," he said curtly. "And therefore I am part Hapsburg myself. These stories about Hapsburg diseases are all slanders."

"Your pardon, Señor. We will let them pass as such. And since I spoke unwittingly of your own family, let us return to a discussion of the Cerrenos. I understand they are kinsmen of yours at least, if not near relatives."

"They are much more than that now. I'm engaged to Cristina, Sebastian's elder daughter. He's stipulated that we shouldn't be married for two years. But that's all got to be changed. That's why I want to go back to Granada at once."

"Again your pardon, Señor. Of course, I did not guess anything of that sort. As you said, there was much I did not understand. But I am beginning to understand better now."

Ramirez removed the tray from Hansel's knees and carried it carefully over to the bureau. When he turned back again his face was troubled.

"If you would prefer to move at once to the German Embassy, Señor," he said slowly, "I shall take no offence. I will send you in a motor-car as soon as you are dressed, and you can make all arrangements for your future movements from there. Of course, the Ambassador and his staff would be delighted to receive you—or I will send you to the Azucena Palace. The family servants are in residence; they could look after you; and, of course, the place is properly guarded. Not that it would be harmed in any case. It will be respected, in the same measure that the Royal Palace has been. Perhaps you would consider the Azucena Palace even more suitable than the German Embassy under the circumstances."

"I'd like to go and see it. Not that I doubt your word. But I'd like to see it for myself."

"Of course, Señor. As soon as you like."

"But I wouldn't want to stay there unless Sebastian invited me. You see, it was he who thought I ought to go away. He has consented to my engagement, he's been very fair, but he's not enthusiastic about it. And it doesn't seem possible, but it was only night night before last——"

Again Hans Christian felt himself flushing, not with anger this time, but with remembered ecstasy. Bautista Ramirez continued to regard him gravely.

"In that case, Señor, perhaps I might go on with what I was about to say when you told me of your betrothal, on which please accept my congratulations. I asked my comrade in Granada with whom I spoke on the telephone to inform both the Archbishop and Señor de Cerreno——"

"Señor de Cerreno!"

"The decree has already been issued, Señor, abolishing titles of nobility . . . to inform them both, as I was saying, where you are, in order that they might communicate with you rapidly, should they wish to do so. If you feel you can be contented and comfortable with me, I should be honoured to have you remain here until some message comes through. If you do not, I will send you wherever you may specify, and dispatch a message after you with as little delay as possible."

"Of course I can be comfortable, and of course I'd rather wait for the message here so that no time will be lost. You've done everything in the world for me, Señor; I can't ever thank you enough. But how can I be content—anywhere?"

"That is a question of character, *amigo*, not of conditions. I hope that some day you may achieve contentment. And for my part, of course, I cannot see why you should be more contented in Germany than in Spain."

"I could have been contented enough in Germany if there had been no Versailles Treaty and no communistic consequences!"

"Someone has said there are no ifs in history, Señor. Be that as it may, I have been doing what I could to facilitate your return to Germany, for I know you feel your duty lies there, even though I now understand that your heart does not. I think I may promise you that you can leave by plane, either tomorrow or the day after, just as you prefer. In that way you will arrive as quickly as if you had gone by train today."

"As I said before, I can't begin to thank you——"

"Pray do not try, Señor. I will leave you now while you dress, if you feel able to do so. Afterwards perhaps you would enjoy sitting in the *salita* and listening to the radio. It has done much to clarify the issues of this election, for the proclamation of the Republic was broadcast and the voices of our leaders have been heard by all the people. They had not been obliged to depend wholly on rumour, or on an unreliable press, as heretofore. How I wish you might have heard Zamora's great speech last night, in which he said, 'The Republic does not represent happiness, but it shall be my endeavour to have it represent law and order!'"

"Zamora is already elected President?"

"He is our provisional President, Señor. He will serve until elections can constitutionally be held."

"And meanwhile, how is the country to be governed?"

"By decree. All official orders will be issued by decree."

"Then isn't Zamora a dictator, just like Primo de Rivera?"

"No, Señor, for he will act only with the advice and consent of the cabinet, and not without the advice and consent of anyone." The Spaniard still spoke with the utmost politeness, but a slight note of forced patience had crept into his voice, as if he were speaking to a child, who either could not understand or would not try to do so. "You will find the morning papers as well as the radio in the *salita*," he went on. "On the whole, they have been fair and accurate. Stay to lunch with me in any case. And afterwards, if you feel able, go out and see the city, while it is still in holiday mood. Tomorrow it will be back at work again, as if nothing had happened. By evening you will probably have had a message from Señor de Cerreno. If not, you can decide for yourself what you had better do. I must leave you for a time now to go out myself. But I will see you a little later. *Hasta luego!*"

Ramirez smiled and left the room, closing the door quietly after him. Hans Christian, pushing back the heavy linen sheets and hand-woven blankets, swung out of bed and rummaged in his suitcase for his dressing-gown. Then, toilet articles in hand, he set out to find "such plumbing as there was." It did not take him long to find it, for the apartment was tiny. A second bedroom, similar to his own, opened from the other side of the *salita*, which apparently served as both living-room and dining-room. The inevitable centre table was now covered with a dark woollen cloth and strewn with papers. The radio, which was in action, stood in the centre of it. The curtains at the windows were thick and clumsy, and the chairs were finished off with antimacassars. Directly behind was the kitchen, where an elderly woman of formidable proportions was standing over an old-fashioned range, intersected on top with openings in which there were live coals. Her back was towards Hans Christian as he entered, and it was quite evident that she did not hear him, for she was engaged in singing the *Marseillaise* at the top of her lungs. Even so, she was not wholly successful in drowning out the notes of the national anthem of Royal Spain, which rang forth with equal vigour, from an adjacent apartment. It was evident that the maids of the two establishments were engaged in a vocal duet designed to announce to the world their sympathies with the political views of their employers!

The plumbing was certainly archaic, and, without the personal service which had been a satisfactory substitute for modern conveniences at the *caseria*, Hans Christian felt that his toilet was rather sketchy. But in spite of himself he was intrigued by his surroundings, and after he was dressed he followed the suggestion of his host, and settled down in the *salita* with the radio and the newspapers. He searched in vain for a statement from the fugitive King, justifying his position; there was only a brief announcement with an indirect quotation outlining the inevitability of his course. On the other hand, Zamora's radio address, to which Ramirez had referred, was given in full, and Hans Christian learned that the first decree signed by the new Government had been one granting complete amnesty to all political prisoners. He also noticed, with some surprise, that the provisional President had sent special greetings to America "as the leader of democracy in the world." It had never occurred to Hansel that the historic revolt of the Colonies against the Crown could possibly have set any precedent for the sort of uprising he had just witnessed; and as he laid down his paper, he tried to recollect fragmentary episodes in the American Revolution. Later, when he picked it up again, he happened to see, tucked in an inconspicuous corner, a brief dispatch from Berlin, stating that the Blücher Palace, bought by the United States for an Embassy at the cost of two million dollars, but never yet occupied as such, had been gutted by fire.

He knew how greatly Trixie had looked forward to living in this prodigious establishment on Unter den Linden, even more pretentious than the French Embassy on the other side of the broad street. She had told him some of her plans for the renovation and decoration of her own quarters. Her experiments at The Hague, though these had been carried out on a small scale compared to what she now had in mind, had whetted her appetite for that sort of thing. She had planned accommodations for private parties of her own, to take place while large official functions were going on in the great gilded drawing-rooms; she had even gone so far as to ask Hansel to help her with a housewarming. Well, she would be disappointed and he was sorry. She strove so sincerely to give other people a good time that it seemed too bad she should ever be thwarted in plans for a good time herself. But, after all, Trixie's personal disappointment was an infinitesimal matter, in the midst of the cataclysm of world events. He forgot it almost as quickly as he had thought of it. . . .

Antonina came in from the kitchen, placed the radio on a side table, cast most of the papers on a sofa in the corner, and laid a white linen cloth, which was evidently not being used for the first time, over the dingy dark one. She spoke to Hans Christian with the unembarrassed goodwill which seemed to be such a characteristic of Spanish servants and which was so different from the menial subservience to which he was accustomed in East Prussia. She was afraid the patron might be late, she told him. If he himself would like something to eat or drink she would bring him a snack at any time. He assured her that he felt as if he had hardly finished breakfast; but still she seemed to feel uneasy about him. Presently she brought him some variegated hors d'œuvres, a long loaf of bread and a bottle of sherry, and set them down in front of him with a triumphant flourish.

It was nearly three o'clock before Ramirez returned. He apologized for having kept Hans Christian waiting, and after briefly brushing his hair before the long glass in the bedroom which led from the *salita*, joined his guest at table. The meal which Antonina set before them was elaborate as well as excellent; Hans Christian did not see how she could possibly have prepared it, with only the primitive equipment which he had seen in passing through the kitchen; but her hand was evidently as light as her tread was heavy. There was a well-flavoured omelette, followed by fried fish, veal cutlets surrounded by vegetables, roast chicken served with green salad, fruit, cheese and her justly famous coffee. The wine that went with the meal was sweet and sound. When Hans Christian praised her efforts she lifted her great hands in an appreciating gesture.

"It is nothing, Señor, nothing! I was taking part in the carnival most of the night, and this morning I have been too drowsy to do myself justice. But after the siesta I shall be refreshed. I shall prepare small white eels and a sucking pig. Will those please the Señor?"

"I haven't eaten any small white eels yet, in Spain, Antonina, but I'll take your word for it that they are good—as good as the big black ones we have in Germany! And I know I shall like the sucking pig—it was wonderful, in Granada."

"It is always better in Madrid," remarked Antonia, giving another triumphant flourish and closing the door of the *salita* after her with a skilful thrust of an immense foot. A moment later the strains of the *Marseillaise* floated vociferously through the air again.

"If Antonina was drowsy this morning I think she will be deafening this afternoon," Hans Christian said with a laugh. "She sang all the forenoon—apparently in keen competition with a neighbour. If she starts in again, after she is 'refreshed,' we shall have to put on ear muffs."

Ramirez smiled in his turn. "She's a good creature, as I told you," he said, lighting a big black cigar. "You notice she spoke of going to the 'carnival' last night. That is the way she and most of her kind think of this—episode. The ill-feeling is remarkably short-lived. By the way, the Queen has gone. She left the Palace quietly by the Puerto Campo Moro, and was rushed out to the Escorial, where she took the train for France. I understand that she went first to the Mausoleum, and knelt in prayer before the tomb of her mother-in-law. Now there, Señor, was a woman for whom it was impossible not to feel respect."

"Another Hapsburg!"

"Yes, another Hapsburg. There are flowers in every family, Señor. . . . Well, we must not get into another discussion. Would it interest you to go out to the Cuatro Vientos Airport with me this afternoon? Ramón Franco is expected to arrive by plane from Paris, and there will be a great demonstration."

"If you don't mind, I'd rather stay in the house. I saw enough demonstration last night to last me for a long time! And I can still see a good deal, just by looking out of the window. Besides, if I'm here, I'll get the message from Granada the minute it arrives. Then I'll know better what to do next."

"You are right, Señor. And I am more happy than I can tell you that you have decided to stay with me. I myself must go out again. But I shall be in, if all is well, for an early dinner, not later than ten o'clock."

He departed, leaving Hans Christian to his own devices again. Surprisingly, considering the boy's impatience to hear from Cristina, the afternoon did not drag. He took a siesta himself, when the cessation of Antonina's song indicated that she was beginning hers. Later he carried a chair out on the small iron balcony and watched the crowd. It was still shouting, still singing, still milling about, as it had been the night before. Hans Christian felt it had not once stopped; he could not bring himself to believe Ramirez's quiet assertion that the next day everyone would have gone back to work. Such ill-feeling as the mob continued to harbour was apparently vented now on royal statues. Hansel had already seen the crown unscrewed from the head of one of these; now he saw another pulled from its place and hammered to pieces. Here and there a miniature guillotine appeared high above the head of some reveller, who held it as if he were showing off a toy. Aside from such grim exhibitions, the prevalent note was still one of hilarity rather than bloodthirstiness.

Antonina came out on the balcony to offer him some *refrescos*

235

and her glance followed him as he watched the mutilation of the royal statue. There was no venom in her gaze, but it was evident that she was intensely interested. Having set down his drink, she leaned back against the wall of the house and volunteered various items of information.

"My brother told me a week ago that I should see such sights as these, Señor. I laughed at him then, but now I perceive that he was right. Therefore I do not doubt that he is right about other matters also."

"What other matters, Antonina?"

"About the matter of the churches. These will have the next attention of the people."

"What kind of attention?"

"The people will take from them what is rightfully theirs, Señor. They will strip the altars of their pretty dolls and gilded flowers and take these home to their children. Other things they will burn."

"Burn! Beautiful old statues and paintings! Surely they wouldn't destroy treasures like those! Especially if they feel such things are their own property. They'd preserve and respect them, just as they have the Royal Palace."

"Perhaps, Señor. I only know what my brother has told me. He says he already has a list of ten churches which the people are planning to enter very soon now. And that the police will not interfere with anything the people want to do. All the people are going to be happy and rich and free in Spain, now that we have a new Government. So my brother says."

She picked up her little tray, and disappeared into her own regions beyond the *salita*, her manner still confident and calm. Hansel, striving for calmness himself, tried to keep his mind fixed on the scene before him, without looking too far into the future.

The sunset was extremely beautiful. The sky changed colour, as if its brilliant blue were a mere overlay to the fiery rose behind this; then it seemed to glow like a great opal. Against it, a huge square tower, looming solidly above its lesser surroundings, shone as if it had been made of black onyx. Lights began to appear in the blank windows above the heads of the populace, which went on exulting in its frenzy of sound. The noise that it made rose to the house-tops; it drowned out the radio, which continued to function in the *salita*, and the song which Antonina had resumed in the kitchen. But at last, above its din, Hans Christian thought he could hear someone knocking at the door. Sure that the awaited message had come at last, he leapt up, overturning his chair as he did so, and rushed to open it himself. When he flung it wide he saw Sebastian standing on the threshold.

CHAPTER XXIII

For a moment he stared at his kinsman speechlessly. Before he could recover himself, Sebastian stepped inside, and spoke with concentrated fury.

"This is the last place on earth I should have expected to find you!"

"It's the last place on earth where I would have expected to find myself. But if you've wandered around lost for two hours, carrying two heavy suitcases in the midst of a mob, and see a familiar name on a strange door, you're pretty apt to take shelter."

He was amazed at his own coolness. Sebastian, on the contrary, seemed to be still further infuriated by it.

"With a Communist! After you've seen your own country nearly wrecked by them! After your best friend's been killed by them and you've nearly lost your own life by one of their bullets! If you have no respect for Alfonso as King of Spain, have you forgotten that he's also an Archduke of Austria? A kinsman of yours no less than I am? Is blood so much thinner than water as far as you're concerned?"

"I haven't forgotten anything, and there's nothing the matter with my blood. Besides, when I rang Ramirez's doorbell I didn't know anything about his politics. I only knew he'd been kind to me on the train, which was the only place I'd ever seen him before. I thought he might be again. I was right. He has been."

"And you were willing to put yourself under obligations to a man like that! If you had told me you'd met him on the train, I could have given you a *dossier* that would have left no doubt about him in your mind. Why didn't you speak to me about him?"

"I meant to, but to tell you the truth I forgot. He disappeared as soon as we got into the station, and I was absorbed with you right away, and then afterwards with Cristina. I suppose if a man falls in love at first sight he forgets a good many things. I've never done it before, so I don't know. But I even forgot to write and thank Ramirez for looking after me so well between Paris and Madrid."

"When he was on his way back to the country he'd been plotting abroad to betray! I can well understand that he might have found it convenient to vanish, especially if you told him who was coming to meet you! How much real difference do you suppose there is between a so-called Republican and a self-confessed radical? Moscow and Madrid are a good deal nearer together than you imagine!"

"I can imagine that in some respects they aren't far apart. But, Sebastian, what could I do? I couldn't get out of Madrid today. And I had to wait somewhere for word from you. I thought I would get

237

it quicker here than anywhere else. And apparently I was right. Though, of course, I never dreamed you'd come yourself. How did you do it?"

"I understand that Alfonso's enemies are already saying that he broke all the time records in trying to escape. Well, I have broken some records too, though not for that reason. If anyone else has ever covered the ground between Granada and Madrid in less time than I have, I should be interested to know it."

"You drove!"

"Yes, I drove. I started almost immediately after I got your message—or rather the message from that man Ramirez! Though, as a matter of fact, I meant to come in any case. I was not thinking primarily of you. I wanted to see the King! And I got here too late! Because first of all I had to put my wife and daughters in a place of safety before I could leave them."

"What do you call a place of safety?"

"They are all at the Convent of Our Lady of Perpetual Sorrows. Cristina and Cecilia have returned there as pupils, and Dolores is installed as a guest. I suppose a convent is safe, even in the midst of anarchy."

"Well, let us hope so. . . . Sebastian, please come in and sit down. I want to hear all about Cristina, how she is, how she's taken all this. And about *Tío* Gabriel. I've been worried about him too."

"You have reason to be. I shall be surprised if the shock of this revolution does not kill him. We hear about freedom of worship, just as we hear about freedom of the Press, and then comes an announcement that all Government officials will be forbidden to go to church. What kind of freedom is that?"

"It's a pretty poor kind. I think the new Government is just groping its way along. Ramirez told me at lunchtime that Miguel Maura walked into the Ministry of the Interior and said: 'There is no precedent for what I am going to do, so I shall merely say that I am taking control of this office.' Other leaders are floundering instead of grabbing. I think most of them really want to provide for some kind of arrangement like that existing in France, for instance, where there's separation of Church and State, but where most of the people are Catholic. But before they get it formulated there are bound to be disturbances. I don't even feel as confident as you do that convents are going to be perfectly safe. That's one of the things I want to speak to you about. I'm all alone here—Ramirez has gone out to the airport. So we can talk quite freely. By and by I'll go with you to your palace or wherever else you say. But I can't run off a second time without thanking Ramirez for what he's done."

"Thanking him for what he has done! Inciting rebellion and treachery! Did you know that the Socialists have issued a manifesto saying that they have a hundred thousand armed men ready for action? You may depend upon it, Ramirez has had a hand in this preparation!"

"I mean, thanking him for what he's done for me. And honestly, he's very sincere. He doesn't think he's a traitor, he thinks he's a patriot. And he's quite likeable. You'll see for yourself. . . . Anyway, we can't stand here for ever in this dark little hall. If you won't come into the *salita*, you can come into my bedroom while I pack."

"*Your* bedroom! Oh, my God!"

Nothing that had happened to Hans Christian so far had given him so completely the feeling that the world had been suddenly turned upside down as it did to see Sebastian in such a state. His very appearance was an anachronism in bourgeois surroundings. His beautifully cut clothes, the easy grace with which he wore them, his elegance of figure and refinement of feature—all these were incongruously out of place in the drab little flat. His lack of self-control was even more bewildering. Hansel had never visualized his kinsman otherwise than charming, suave and wholly master of any situation in which he might be found. That Sebastian should have lost his assurance was quite as incredible as that King Alfonso should have lost his crown. In the face of such a phenomenon an appeal to reason seemed fantastic, yet Hans Christian decided to attempt it.

"Sebastian, it's only two days since you told me you had stopped beating your head against stone walls, that you accepted them, knowing they'd either crumble of their own accord or prove impregnable. Isn't this a good time to put that theory into practice?"

"I'm not a German. I can't philosophize in the face of a cataclysm, any more than I can try to stop one by brute force."

"Well, in a way it's a relief for me to know your philosophy isn't impregnable after all," Hans Christian retorted. "On the other hand, if you simply stand there reviling me, instead of telling me more about what's happened, from your point of view, how am I ever going to get the other side of the picture? And I've got to, haven't I, somehow? I've got to know how best to stand by you. That's what I've been trying to find out, right along!"

"Are you sure you want to stand by me? This is a day of desertions, not of loyalties!"

"Sebastian, you know better than to ask me such a question or to say a thing like that to me—or you would, if you weren't beside yourself."

Everything in their respective positions seemed suddenly to have been reversed. It was Hans Christian this time who put a steadying arm around Sebastian, propelled him gently towards the small bedroom, and drew forth the two straight-backed chairs. Sebastian sat down mechanically in one of them. The first impact of his rage against Hans Christian had spent itself. But he went on talking frantically.

"Have you heard what happened at the Palace? All the grandees who were in Madrid, or who could get here, gathered in the Throne Room to bid their Sovereign farewell. Many of them were white-bearded old men who had known him ever since he was a baby—as my father did; he was in the Palace the night the King was born! They stood in a row, and embraced him, with tears running down their cheeks! And I was not there among them—neither I nor my sons! And now the Palace is empty except for poor old Aylar, the Intendente, who is packing up the King's belongings! The approaches are deserted and all the glittering guards are gone! One soldier, dressed in a field uniform, is at the only open gate! And exhausted revellers are lying asleep on the walls!"

"Well, at least the Palace hasn't been looted, at least the King's right to his personal property isn't questioned. And he'll be made very welcome in England. Remember, he's regarded as a member of the British Royal Family too. Besides, his exile may not be permanent. Perhaps he'll come back eventually, and everything will be as it was before."

"Nothing will ever be as it was before. If you were older and wiser you'd know that."

"You are older, and you weren't wise enough to see this coming. You felt sure it wouldn't."

"You remind me of that at such a time as this!"

"Only because I think that if you were mistaken in one way, you might be in another. Only because I'm so desperately sorry for you, Sebastian!"

Hans Christian drew his chair nearer Sebastian's and laid his hand on the older man's knee. He could feel it quivering under his touch.

"Have you seen the King's manifesto?" Sebastian went on, drawing a piece of paper out of his pocket. "No, I suppose not, since it hasn't been publicly printed—the people don't even know that their monarch has honoured them by his confidence! But I have a copy of the statement here. . . . Read it for yourself and tell me if you do not think it is one of the most touching documents you have ever seen."

" 'The elections which took place on Sunday have clearly shown me that I have lost the affection of my people,' " Hans Christian read, accepting the small slip from Sebastian. " 'In my conscience I am certain this disaffection will not be definite, because I have always done my utmost to serve Spain. . . . I am King of all Spaniards and I am myself a Spaniard. I could have employed divers means to maintain the royal prerogatives and effectively to combat my enemies, but I wish resolutely to step aside from anything that might throw any of my countrymen against others in fratricidal *war. I do not renounce any of my rights, because they are more than mine—they are the accumulated store of history, and I shall one day have to make a rigorous account of their conservation. . . . I am deliberately leaving Spain, recognizing in this way that she is the sole mistress of her destinies. Once more today I believe I am doing a duty which is dictated to me by my love of country. I ask God that all Spaniards shall understand their duty as deeply as I do mine.'"*

"I think it is beautifully worded," Hans Christian said guardedly, as he handed the paper back. "But just the same, Sebastian, I am surprised that Alfonso left. I don't believe you would have left under the same circumstances. You are not planning to leave as it is, are you?"

"Certainly not."

"I wish you would, of course. If the King's possessions can be sent to Bohemia for safe keeping, yours could be sent to Prussia. And I wish you would come to Germany with me. I've waited here on purpose to tell you that, Sebastian. And to tell you, too, that I want to marry Cristina at once. I don't want her to go back to the convent, even as a pupil. I'm afraid of it."

"You have no reason to be. It's the proper place for her at present."

"I don't agree with you."

"It makes no difference to me whether you do or not. I am her father. I must decide what is best for her without interference."

"But you can't. Because I'm going to interfere."

"You will never marry her if you talk to me like that."

"I shall certainly marry her, and I talk to you like that only because you force me into it."

He leaned forward again and put his hand on Sebastian's knee a second time. "Listen, Sebastian," he said urgently. "I'm fonder of you than anyone in the whole world except Cristina. I admire you more than any man I ever knew. I'm proud that you are going to be my father-in-law. I'd have been proud if—if you'd been my father. I want to do everything I can to follow out your wishes. I think I've proved that to you already. I agreed to every condition you made about Cristina and me. I'll agree to anything now in reason. But it isn't reasonable any more for you to expect me to wait for her two years. It isn't reasonable to expect me to go back to Germany and leave her behind. When I agreed to do that I didn't know that Spain was on the verge of a revolution. You didn't know it yourself. In fact, you kept assuring me that it wasn't."

Sebastian did not answer.

"You told me that castles in Spain were real, that I could have one for the asking any time I liked. I'm afraid I can't. I'm afraid the castles in Spain are crumbling, Sebastian. I'm afraid the convents

241

may crumble too. But my love for Cristina won't. That's enduring. Don't try to interfere with that because everything else is rocking around our feet. There's all the more reason for us to cling to that, because love is about all there is that can survive a real revolution."

Sebastian still did not answer. Hans Christian, feeling that his plea had failed, changed his tactics abruptly.

"What are you going to do next? This afternoon, I mean? When you leave here?"

"I'm going to my own house to spend the night. As far as I know, that hasn't been taken over by the Government yet."

"Of course it hasn't. I don't believe it will be. Well, I'm coming with you. And in the morning we can motor back to Granada together. Or I'll stay here as long as it suits you. I've had a wire from my grandmother. The heart attack has passed. Her condition isn't critical at all."

"It may be again at any moment."

"Well, the condition here is critical right now. I'm not going away, Sebastian, as long as it is. If you won't let me stay with you, I'll stay with *Tío* Gabriel or—or somewhere."

"I suppose you will tell me in a minute that you will soon storm the Convent of Our Lady of Perpetual Sorrows in the dead of night and carry Cristina away with you."

It was the first flicker of Sebastian's old spirit that Hans Christian had seen. He retorted almost gaily.

"I'd thought of it. But I decided I wouldn't tell you about that part. I was afraid if I did you'd spirit her off to some other convent, and I wouldn't be any better off than I was before."

"Of course I should—and of course you wouldn't. I must admit that you have basically sound sense, *querido*. And since that is the case, you must see that it is impossible for you to marry Cristina now. If she were even two years older, I might consider it—conditions, as you say, have changed greatly. But I have already reminded you——"

"Then at least bring her to Germany, where she will be safe!"

"And what makes you think that Germany is so supremely safe, Hansel? Are your reasons any sounder than mine were when I said the traditions of Spain were inviolable?"

"If they aren't there's no security left anywhere."

"Certainly there is. It still exists in America."

"Then take Cristina to America! Take her to my mother!"

Hans Christian had sprung to his feet. From the room beyond, the rumble of the radio continued to come persistently to his ears, and from the street below the roar of the populace still rose raucously. He was ready to defy them both, and all that they represented, to pour out a plan which had suddenly sprung, full-grown, from his brain, when he caught a warning look on Sebastian's face, and swung swiftly around to see what had caused it.

He had heard Sebastian's knock, but he had not heard Bautista's latchkey. Now he saw that Ramirez had come in, that the man who had befriended him was standing at the entrance of his room as unexpectedly as Sebastian had appeared at the entrance of the flat an hour earlier. Then he saw a gleam of enmity, vital as a living thing, flash quickly between his host and his kinsman before the two men bowed formally to each other.

"Señor de Cerreno does me too much honour," Ramirez said slowly, "in coming to my poor abode."

It was the first time that Hans Christian had ever known the customary salutation, "*Esta es su casa*," to be left out. He knew that its absence constituted a deliberate omission. He wondered how this would be taken.

"Your pardon, Señor. It was not so much to do you honour that I came here as in the hope that you might be able to satisfy my curiosity, which has been piqued. I have been wondering why I was not arrested."

"As to that, I can tell you easily, Señor. First, because the prosecuting attorney has not yet fully formulated his charges against you. Second, because your offences did not take place under the jurisdiction of the present Minister of Justice. And third, because we knew all the time where you were if we wanted you."

"I thank you, Señor. I am glad to have that point settled. It only remains for me to add that incidentally I also came here to reclaim my erring kinsman, who has apparently strayed."

"That can easily be explained also, Señor. If I am not misinformed, you had invited Señor de Hohenlohe to leave the shelter of your home. I invited him to accept the shelter of mine. That illustrates, I think, the difference of our respective methods. But I should say that our guest himself had been equally blameless in both cases."

Ramirez bowed to Sebastian a second time, and turned to Hans Christian. "Have you now decided what you would like to do next, Señor?" he asked.

"I should like to return to Andalusia tomorrow with Señor de Cerreno. But he does not seem to think that is desirable. Therefore I have no choice but to accept your offer of a seat in a northbound plane."

"It has been my pleasure to secure one for you, Señor. A special plane will leave at ten tomorrow morning, and your ticket will be held for you at the Cuatro Vientos Airport. If you will excuse me, I will go at once to make the final arrangements. Lest I should not find you here on my return, let me thank you again for doing me the honour of being my guest, and wish you a pleasant journey. Let me also add that I hope to see you in Spain again some time. You will always find a pot of coffee on the stove here, and a warm

243

welcome, if you care to accept it."

He shook Hansel cordially by the hand and bowed to Sebastian a third time. As the door of the apartment closed after him, Hans Christian spoke eagerly, his words coming in a rush.

"Don't you think I've had a good idea, Sebastian? Leave Doña Dolores at the Convent of Our Lady of Perpetual Sorrows, if that's where she wants to stay. She'll be near *Tío* Gabriel there, she can keep in close touch with him and go to him if he needs her. Leave Cecilia with her. Cecilia is sure to be all right anywhere! But don't try to keep Cristina there! And don't stay at the *caseria*—or the *Palacio* either—all by yourself! Don't you think it would be wonderful to take Cristina to my mother?"

The words were hardly spoken before he realized their double implication. The scar on Sebastian's face had grown livid, the corners of his mouth worked painfully. He turned his head away as if conscious that his face betrayed the fact that Hans Christian had put into words a yearning he had long held in leash, and which the revolution at last gave him a pretext for fulfilling. There was an interminable silence, and Hans Christian knew that when it was finally broken the threads of many interwoven lives would be severed too—or else knotted more closely together than ever before. But, though dimly, he knew also it would not be in this hour that he would clearly see the ultimate handiwork of fate.

"Yes," Sebastian said at last, clearly and steadily. "It will be wonderful for you to take her, by and by. But not for me to take her now. I am a Spaniard, and I must live in Spain. All of my duty lies here, even if all of my heart does not. When Isabella the Second fled, some of her nobles met her in France, thinking thus to show their loyalty. But when she saw them she said, 'It was not here I wanted to meet you again.' I must run no risk that my Sovereign will ever say that to me. Besides, it should be remembered that a Grandee of Spain does not go through a door ahead of his king, even to escape."

CHAPTER XXIV

"Convent of Our Lady of Perpetual Sorrows,
Cerca Granada,
May 2, 1931.

"Vida de mi vida,

"Your dear letter has been a long time in reaching me. But now I have it and I have read it over and over again. Every line is precious to me. First, because it tells me all is well with you and with your grandmother, that you were in no peril on your journey and that your homecoming was happy. Second, because it tells me that I have your whole heart, as you have mine.

"When my father returned from Madrid, he came at once to see us, and urged my mother to go back to the *caseria*, since he is now there to protect her. But she has preferred to remain here, at present, for meditation and prayer. I am sorry, because this leaves him so much alone. I am certain that after you and I are married, *querido*, I shall never willingly be absent from your side, for I am most loath to be separated from you even now.

"But *Tío* Gabriel tells me I must be patient under this affliction. He has come twice to the Convent since you went away and has talked at great length with my mother. I think he too has urged her to return to my father, and I believe he has spoken to her about our marriage. But she does not speak about it herself. I know she is displeased because I have decided not to become a nun. This displeasure would weigh heavily upon me if it were not that my joy in being betrothed to you is so much greater than any sorrow which she can cause me.

"Cecilia and I have resumed all our lessons. I wish that I might study German, and learn to speak to you in your own tongue. But, after all, there is no need for words between us, nor are there words in any language which would tell you adequately of my love.

"Besides being busy with our lessons, we are preparing for Ascension Day. It is one of our greatest feasts, and all must be in readiness to do honour to Our Lord. Reverend Mother has told me that had I wished, I might have begun my novitiate at this time. I have asked that instead I may begin to embroider my bridal linen.

"The Sister who supervises my singing also supervises my correspondence. But she is young and she has a kind face. It is my hope that she will let me send this letter exactly as I have written it. It goes to you with my fondest greetings mingled with my most fervent prayers for your happiness now and for our happiness together in the future.

"MARIA CRISTINA FIDELIDAD DE CERRENO Y ROMERO."

"CONVENT OF OUR LADY OF PERPETUAL SORROWS,
CERCA GRANADA,
May 12, 1931.
"MI CORAZÓN,
"This is a Day of Rogation and only by special permission am I allowed to write you. This permission comes from the Sister with the kind face, of whom I told you.

"I write because I am afraid you may be worried. Rumours have reached us that there have been sad happenings in Madrid and elsewhere, and possibly these same rumours may reach Germany. I wish you to know that in the sanctuary of Our Lady of Perpetual Sorrows tranquillity still reigns.

"Pupils at the Convent are not allowed to read newspapers and it is a habit my mother has never had. But that does not matter, for

245

my father and *Tío* Gabriel, who read them searchingly, say that all news has been suppressed or censored. The rumours of which I speak have all come by word of mouth, from travellers on the roads and on the trains. My father has seen some of these travellers, and after talking with them he has come again to the Convent, this time urging my mother not only to return to the *caseria* herself, but to bring Cecilia and me with her. Again she refused, saying that only by force can he compel her to do so, and naturally he will never use force against my mother. I think she believes that if she remains here, and talks to me daily on the subject, she can still persuade me to become a nun. She is mistaken.

"The sad happenings of which we have heard concern churches and convents. It is said that ten structures in Madrid alone have suffered. Among these are the Jesuit College and the Church of the Carmelite Fathers. A convent in Cordova has been stoned and two in Cadiz have been destroyed. The Episcopal Palaces in Alicante and Malaga have been burned. Of course Malaga is not far from here. Still we feel safe. We are sure that if there should be an attack it would be frustrated by the police, as it was in Saragossa. *Tío* Gabriel tells us that a very slight outbreak here in Granada caused great popular indignation, that it failed instantly and completely. A single guard stood at the door of the Cathedral and every time the mob approached he shook his head and quietly said, 'Not here.' Then the mob retreated again and finally it dispersed altogether. So you see there is nothing to fear.

"Nobody has been killed or badly hurt. The nuns and priests who have lost their schools and churches and cloisters have all been given homes by friendly families. We know that there are only small irresponsible elements that seek to cause trouble. Most of them are very young people. They will learn better. The crowds have shown respect to the cloth. I am sure they always will in Spain. And among the officials of the new Government there are many believers. The President and the Minister of Justice are both practising Catholics. They do not agree with the sectarian advances of their Socialist colleagues. We hear that the President confessed and received Communion on the very day the Republic was proclaimed; he was aware that it might be the last of his life and he did not wish to die unshriven. Señor Maura, like his father, Don Antonio, has a private chapel connected with his home, and has never concealed his devotion to the Church. Even Señorita Victoria Kent, the strange woman who has become Director of Prisons, has announced that nuns who customarily supplied prisoners' wants on a concession basis would be allowed a month in which to clear their accounts and turn their commissariats over to the officials who work under her. It seems sad that the nuns should lose their concessions. Still I believe that Señorita Kent means to be fair.

"So far I have said nothing about love. That is because my heart has been heavy with the thought of the sorrows which others have endured. But when I think of our joy it becomes light again. And so it is that I bid you farewell happily and not sadly.

"*Adios, mi Corazón.*

"MARIA CRISTINA FIDELIDAD DE CERRENO Y ROMERO."

"CASERIA CECILIA,
Ascension Day.

"ALMA DE MI ALMA,

"You see that I am at home again. And I am safe. We are all safe.

"Just after I had written you on Tuesday the great bell of the Convent began to toll. I was still in the school when I heard it, and then I heard a crashing sound, and saw stones come hurtling through the windows. One of them struck me, but it did not hurt me. The other girls had left the schoolroom already, so none of them was hurt either. I had stayed behind to write your letter.

"I ran out into the corridor, and the other girls were there, running too. But the nuns were not running. They were walking quietly along, telling the girls not to be frightened, not to lose their self-control and their faith in God. They made the girls stop running and march in an orderly way. Cecilia and I marched with the others. Cecilia is very brave, she did not cry at all. Some of the other girls did cry, at first, but they stopped, after the nuns had comforted and encouraged them.

"I did not see my mother with the nuns or among the girls, so I asked our Reverend Mother if I might go back and look for her. She had a little room to herself, on the second floor, between the girls' dormitory and the nuns' cloister. Reverend Mother hesitated a moment and then she said yes, I might go. She told me not to alarm my mother, but to give her a message that she was to come at once to the courtyard, no matter what she might be doing.

"I found my mother in prayer before a statue of Our Lady of Perpetual Sorrows. She had not heard the bell or seen the stones, she did not want to come with me. But I told her I had brought her a command. So finally she came. When we got to the courtyard everyone had gone out of it, except the Reverend Mother, who was waiting for us. The great doors leading into the street had been butted in, and flames were leaping all around them. We were scorched a little, because we were so late in getting through. But none of the others who went before us were burnt.

"The mob which had come inside the courtyard had built a big bonfire in the middle of it. When we went out we could see men throwing the beautiful old books from the library and the statues from the chapel and the vestments from the sacristy into it. Every time they cast something on to the flames and saw these leap higher and higher, they howled. They also jeered at the Reverend Mother as she went past, and one of them jerked at her veil. But outside the crowd was very quiet. Hardly anyone spoke at all. Except that as each nun went by someone came forward and said to her in a low voice: "Have you any place to go?" If she said yes, the throng stood aside to let her pass through it. If she said no, the person who had spoken to her took her home. It was the same way with the girls. If their own homes were not near by, other persons' homes were open to them. The Reverend Mother and the religious with the kind face of whom I told you, whose name is Sister Josefa, and four of my schoolmates have come home with us.

"Reverend Mother told us not to look back as we went along, so that we would not see the destruction of the Convent. But we could hear the licking sound the flames made and the howling of the mob. They were dreadful noises, and we felt very sad, but we obeyed our Reverend Mother and did not look back.

"It is a long walk from the Convent to the *caseria,* and we saw other sad sights along the way. We heard weeping in some rushes bordering a dry stream near the roadside, and when we went to see what it might mean we found several nuns and a number of little orphan girls huddled together in a cleft on the bank. They told us that early that morning they had been expelled from their convent. So they had made their way somehow to a large country house which was empty except for a caretaker. He gave them some milk and told them he was willing to shelter them if his landlord would give him permission. But presently the Communists came there also and set fire to this house. So then the nuns and the orphans wandered down the dry riverbed until they were so exhausted that they could go no further. We had no food with us that we could give them, and no water, which they needed even more. We told them that we would send help back to them if we could find any, and then we went in search of it.

"When we got to Santa Fe, we found that the convent there had also been burned that morning. The Alcalde had telephoned to Atarfe, and had told the authorities to lie in ambush for the destructionists as they came through. It was a well-meant warning, but it resulted in bloodshed. When a motor-car came in to Atarfe at high speed the authorities ordered it to stop because they thought it contained fleeing Communists. The driver, in his turn, thought that the order came from Communists and drove faster than ever. The authorities fired and then the occupants of the car fired too. One person in the car was killed and several in the crowd.

"I know you will be especially grieved to hear this, because the man in the car who was killed was Leopoldo. My father had heard about the destruction of our convent and had started out to seek us, taking Leopoldo and Leonardo with him. Of course, he would not

248

have stopped for anybody just then. But he is terribly unhappy, because Leopoldo had served our family ever since he was a little boy, and now he is dead and nothing will ever bring him back to life. We are afraid that Leonardo may die too, of grief for his twin, though his wounds are not serious in themselves.

"We stopped in Atarfe until the authorities were satisfied that this had all been a sad accident, and then my father and Leonardo were released, and finally we came home. Of course, we could not all come at once, because there was not room in one car, and we could not get another. So first my father took away the body of Leopoldo in order that it might be prepared for burial, and Leonardo because he was wounded, and the Reverend Mother because she did not shrink from the sight of blood. The rest of us waited in Atarfe until my father could return for us, and some of the good people there who saw that mother and I had been scorched gave us salve for our hands and faces and did what they could to make us comfortable until my father could get back. Cecilia went to sleep with her head against Sister Josefa's shoulder, and the other little girls slept also, on the floor.

"Today Leopoldo has been buried. *Tío* Gabriel conducted the services, and we all went to them except Leonardo, who is delirious with his wound. It is the saddest Ascension Day I have ever known.

"Sister Josefa has been talking to me. She has reminded me that nobody will talk to me any more about becoming a nun, because this will be impossible. It will be a long time before there can be new nuns in Spain. Once I might have rejoiced in knowing that this was so. But now, because I know the reason for it, I am sorrowful. We have never been able to find the nuns who had taken refuge in the rushes with the poor little orphans again.

"*Alma de mi alma*, I have written you a long letter, the longest letter I have ever written in my life, and this time I have not spoken to you of love at all. You seem so far away. Is it possible that I was mistaken, that we are not to have happiness together after all? God grant that this may not be so! Somewhere in the world, outside of Spain, there must still be joy.

"But whether in joy or in sorrow, I am completely your own.
"CRISTINA."

AUTHOR'S NOTE.—Hans Christian Marlowe von Hohenlohe did not receive this letter until long after it was written. Upon getting the one dated May 12th, but considerably delayed in transit, he at once started back to Spain, flying from Berlin to Paris and from Paris to Madrid. He reached Granada by car the morning of May 22nd. The following day he and Cristina de Cerreno were married by the Archbishop of Granada in the private chapel of the Episcopal Palace.

PART VII

"THE NIGHT OF LONG KNIVES"

1931-1934

CHAPTER XXV

THE only hours that mattered to Cristina von Hohenlohe were those she spent with her husband.

It was not that she was fretful or restless when they were separated. She could sit indefinitely in the garden or by the fireside, occupied, composed and contented, as she studied German or bent over her needlework or played her guitar. But these were merely periods of preparation and anticipation for her. They had no definite meaning of their own.

She arranged the flowers at Schönplatz because her touch with these was lighter than Luischen's, and Luischen had been the first to recognize this and to urge that the bride should take over the pleasant task. Cristina also had a way of giving loveliness to linen. The snowy sheets stacked in the Danzig chests, the bath towels, big as bedspreads, the crested cloths and damask napkins had never lain in such even piles, they had never been so smooth and sweet-scented as after she took charge of them. But when the flowers were fixed and the linen in order, her household labours were over for the day. When they were done she wrote long affectionate letters to each member of her family in turn, taking one a day, and wishing it were as easy to express herself to her mother as to her father. After that she sat and waited for Hans Christian.

He never left her for long, except when he was obliged to go to Berlin on Party business. He knew that it did not seem natural to her, as it did to Luischen, to range about the place alone, to visit the kennels and stables unattended, or to jump casually on a horse and gallop across the field. So he took her himself to see the foals and puppies; he walked or rode with her at some time every day that he was at Schönplatz. She never knew beforehand exactly when this would be. Hence there was all the more reason to be ready and waiting when he came for her.

She studied German because she knew her mastery of this would please him, though he never harassed her about her progress in it. She realized, too, that as his wife it was fitting she should be competent to converse with his friends and direct his servants; it was not hard for her to advance in it, partly because she proved to have a natural aptitude for such learning, and partly because she had such a powerful incentive for proficiency in it. But she preferred to sew, because while her fingers flew over the fine fabrics her thoughts were free to fly back over all the hours she had spent with Hans Christian.

First of all, they flew back to the May morning when he had come, unheralded and unhoped for, to the *caseria*. She had been sitting sadly in the patio, unmindful that birds still sang and flowers still bloomed there. Leonardo had died of his wounds as well as Leopoldo; and the Reverend Mother's burns were causing her great suffering. She did not refer to this or to the destruction of her convent and the loss of her school; but every day something more went out of her face which had been there before. Doña Dolores locked herself in her room, presumably to pray, and Don Sebastian stayed in the turret, turning over the leaves of books with unseeing eyes, or pacing the terrace which looked out on the land which at any moment might cease to be his. Even Cecilia no longer laughed. She studied, with unnatural industry. But when she had learned her lessons no one would hear them.

And then Hans Christian had come. Cristina had heard the door of the outer patio open and close, and footsteps coming swiftly through the garden. His footsteps. She had recognized them at once, and she had leapt up and run out to greet him, the sad world suddenly a different place. She had met him just as he reached the inner entrance, and he had caught her quickly in his arms and held her as if he would never let her go. It was a long time before he spoke to her at all. And when he did he still held her in his arms.

"I've come back for you, Cristina. I never should have left you. I'll never leave you again."

"What are you going to do?"

"I am going to marry you at once. Before any more sacrileges occur. I started back from Berlin the minute I learned of the destruction in Madrid. I ought to have known it was coming. I'd heard about the ten churches before, but I thought it was only ignorant prattle; I couldn't conceive that horrible arson could take place in a civilized country. Cristina, can you ever forgive me? I went to look for you at your convent first. I've seen what happened. . . . Darling, tell me how much you are hurt, how much you were frightened! No, never mind, don't talk about it yet. . . . You can tell me about it later on, but not now. I'll talk to you. I'll swear to you that you shall never be hurt or frightened again, if I can help it, never as long as you live."

After that he began to cover her face with kisses. He sat down on the tiled seat beside the patio and drew her on his knees and held her so close to him that she could feel his heart beating against hers. When he finally put her on her feet it was to ask her, almost abruptly, where he could find her father. He had seen her uncle, he said, already. He had gone straight from the ruins of the convent to the Episcopal Palace, he had spoken with *Tío* Gabriel. He had made it clear that all this talk about two years must stop. It had been folly from the beginning; now it was flying in the face of Providence. The Archbishop's duty lay in Granada, that was true; he owed it to his Church and to his people to stay with them, even though this cost him his life. And if Don Sebastian felt the same about his loyalty and his land, Hans Christian would not argue with him again. But nothing that either of them could say or do should keep Cristina in Spain another week. She must be married and go to her husband's home, where she would be safe.

It was pitiful—Cristina realized that—to see how little either her uncle or her father tried to do to keep her in Spain. It was only a few short weeks since they had bargained with Hans Christian, since they had told him what he could and could not do. Now they listened while he talked to them. Even Doña Dolores listened. Secretly she herself had already made a dress which she had hoped Cristina would wear on the day when her daughter became a nun. Now she took it from the fine linen in which it had been swathed, and dressed her in it on the day when she became a bride. Cristina went to the altar robed in dazzling white, carrying long lilies in her arms.

She and her husband reached Ventosilla that same night, for Hans Christian drove steadily and fast. He had bought a car within an hour of the time that he had landed at the Cuatro Vientos Airport in Madrid on his journey south; it was in this that he had come on, at breakneck speed, to Granada, and it was in this that he bore away his bride. A message had been sent to the servants at the old castle, which Cristina, like her father, loved better than any other they possessed; and though messages often went astray in these days, this one had not, and everything was in readiness to welcome the bride and groom. When they reached the ramparts they saw that hundreds of flickering lanterns had been placed there, and inside the *castello* the vast arched halls were illuminated with torches. Supper had been spread in the banquet hall, where, for hundreds of years, wedding feasts had been held; and in the vaulted chamber above, the bridal brocades, ivory with age, had been draped above the great golden bed.

Cristina had been in this chamber before, since it formed part of the State suite which was shown to visitors. But she had never seen it used, for she was the first bride of her generation. The myriad lights were missing here. There was only one large lamp, swinging like a censer above the bed, and small candles standing in the dim corners. She had thought beforehand that it would seem strange to see Hans Christian moving about her room, acting as if it were his

252

also; now she was thankful to hear his firm footsteps echoing across the dark stretches, to hear his happy voice ringing through the distances that divided them. He had ordered her belongings to be placed in the alcove, his own in the antechamber; and when they had come up from dinner he had said he knew she must be very tired, that of course she would wish to get undressed at once.

"May I help you? I should like to if you would let me. It would be like lifting your veil, to kiss you, as I did this morning after *Tío* Gabriel had married us. But if you would rather be alone . . ."

"I think I should rather be alone, for a few minutes."

He had said no more about it. He had put his arms around her, and walked with her to the alcove, and then he had kissed her lovingly, and left her there. Afterwards she was sorry she had sent him away. Her fingers trembled as she took off one garment after another, and when she slipped her nightgown over her head, she was shivering all over. If he had stayed with her he would somehow have saved her from this frightful fear. He would have made her feel, as he himself had said, that he was only lifting another veil, like the one he had lifted that morning, and not that he was affronting her modesty. He would have encompassed her with compassion, he would have comforted her. As it was, panic overcame her. She thought of coarse jests she had heard Catalina make, from which she had instinctively recoiled, though she could not grasp their full meaning. She thought of Doña Dolores saying in cold measured tones that since she had spurned the vocation of a virgin she must accept the suffering of subjection. She thought of her father telling her he would trust her to remember that her first duty lay in obedience to her husband and her second in the conception of children.

As she thought of all this she became more and more bewildered, more and more terrified. She no longer saw Hans Christian as her saviour and her lover; she saw him as her persecutor and possessor. She knew that now there was no escape from him; but there was always a refuge from every trouble in prayer. She knotted her dressing-gown around her and thrust her feet into her slippers. Then resolutely she crossed the dark empty space again, and knelt down at the prie-dieu beside the bed. There was a tiny vigil light there, which she had not noticed before, burning under a small silver statue. She lifted her eyes to this and prayed.

When she rose from her knees she saw that Hans Christian was beside her, looking at her with infinite loving-kindness, as if he had seen into all the secret places of her heart. He put his arm around her gently, and spoke to her gently too.

"Cristina, I want to talk to you. Are you too tired? Would you rather have me leave you again and let you sleep?"

"I would rather never have you leave me again. I was wrong to

253

ask you to do so before. And I know I shall never wish to sleep if you want to talk to me."

Although she spoke with an effort, she felt that what she was saying was true. And she did not shrink away from him when he seated himself on the edge of the great bed, drawing her down beside him and looking into her eyes.

"My darling, has anyone ever told you what marriage means?"

"No. Only that a wife should submit to her husband's will, even under compulsion. But this was mysterious to me. I could not understand why there should be either submission or compulsion, where there is love. But it does not matter. For now I know it would always be my will to yield to yours."

"I don't want you to yield to my will, Cristina. I want you to trust to my tenderness. Can you do that?"

"Yes—oh, yes!"

"Then nothing will be hard. Do you remember when I first held your hand, Cristina? And when I first kissed you? You knew that these caresses were acts of love. You were happy when you felt your fingers resting in mine, you were happier when you felt my lips pressed against yours. Isn't that so?"

"Yes, that is so."

"I shall never tell you anything that is not true, my darling. The closer caresses are, the more joy they bring. The greatest act of love merges two beings into one. That is what marriage means."

She remembered the joy that had suffused her soul when he had embraced her in the patio, and all her formless fears melted away. She yearned to feel his heart beating against hers again, and, as if he knew this, Hans Christian drew her nearer to him.

"I want to achieve this supreme state, Cristina. I want to take you in my arms and hold you fast until I have made you mine. Can you look into my eyes and say, 'I am ready for your love, I am not afraid of fulfilment, I can give myself utterly into your keeping'?"

"I am ready, I am not afraid, I can give myself utterly. . ."

Hans Christian rose and extinguished the brazen lamp above the great golden bed. Only the vigil light remained, under the silver statue, and soon that also flickered out. In the profound darkness, which now formed so kindly a cloak, Cristina could feel his arms encircling her again, his heart beating once more against hers, as she had longed to have it. She could hear him murmuring words of endearment and encouragement as his mouth closed down on hers. Adoration for him filled her being, and deep within her something suddenly stirred, demanding his dominance. She passed unflinchingly beyond resistance into realms of rapture. Then his passion poured through her in a rush of glory.

Eager as he was to be gone from Spain, Hans Christian did not suggest that they should leave Ventosilla the next day. They spent it languorously, without marking the flight of its golden moments; and when evening again enveloped them they welcomed its advent together. The consummation of their marriage had released them both. It was no longer needful that he should strive to save her from shock; he could rejoice, without restraint, in his prerogative. She was no longer bewildered by mysteries and bound by barriers; she could anticipate, with perfect pliancy, his every desire. The last veil had indeed been lifted, the last depth penetrated.

In her first flush of abandon Cristina was conscious of nothing except the floodtides of love. It was only long afterwards when she could reason again, that she recognized how unerring Hans Christian's instincts had been in all that concerned her. If he had precipitated their union, without preparing her for it, she could never again have given herself to him with such confident self-surrender; there would always have been lurking fear underneath her submission instead of rapturous response. On the other hand, if he had retarded the completion of his conquest, some of its glory would have been dimmed, some vital element deep within it would have been lacking. He had seen that her spirit could soar to meet his own, and had swept her along in the surge of his own passion.

They went from Ventosilla to Saragossa and from there to Carcassonne, lingering for some days above its matchless parapets. Theirs was no longer a flight from revolution, Hans Christian told Cristina; it was an excursion into high romance. They stopped in Nîmes and Arles and Avignon, Grenoble and Chamonix, beside the Swiss lakes, among the Tyrolean Mountains. Then they went to Vienna, where they stayed for some time, and where Cristina gradually became accustomed to having Hans Christian leave her from time to time, for he explained to her that he had work to do here, though he never told her exactly what it was and she never asked him. It was late summer when they finally reached East Prussia. And there they found a feudal welcome waiting for them, and Cristina stepped proudly into her predestined place as the young chatelaine of an ancient house.

They had been married for many months, and were already well settled at Schönplatz, before Cristina asked Hans Christian a question which she had been considering for some time. He was resting beside her, desire already drowned in sleep, when he became aware that she was still wide-eyed and wakeful in the darkness. He instantly turned to her again.

"Is something the matter, darling? Aren't you feeling well?"

"Nothing is the matter, and I am feeling quite well. But I have been wondering . . . When two people love each other as we do, doesn't that mean that by and by there will be a child?"

"Perhaps. Probably. . . . You would not be afraid if you found

255

you were to have a child, would you, Cristina?"

"Why should I be afraid?"

"Because childbirth brings suffering with it, my darling. I could not save you from that no matter how hard I tried."

"You know that I am not afraid of suffering. I am only afraid. . . . Would I know by now if I were going to have a child?"

"Yes, if it were the child of our first love. But it might not come until later."

"There is no chance, is there, that I might never have one?"

"Of course not. Of course you will have one. You have put it beautifully, darling. . . . When two persons love each other as we do they are certain to have a child. It is the natural result of their love. But often they cannot tell when this result will come about."

"Would you be glad to have a child, *querido*?"

"Yes. But I shall be just as glad if we do not have one too soon. I do not want to share you with anyone for a long while. I want you continually and unutterably."

Desire was no longer drowned in sleep. It was sweeping through him like a flame, threatening to consume him altogether. For the first time he forgot Cristina, except as the chalice for his passion, and thought only of himself, of his own craving and his own need. And, for the first time, she forgot him, though it was not of herself that she thought, as she lay in his arms throughout the long night. Later he remembered the words she had spoken, when at last he released her.

"I hope that now there will be a child."

But more than two years had gone by since their marriage, and this hope was still unfulfilled. Hans Christian had been sincere in saying that he wanted Cristina all to himself; his first feeling had been that a child would interfere with the closeness of their communion. But as time went on the primeval yearning for a son asserted itself, and he began to be conscious of frustration, even of slight shame. When his grandmother finally spoke to him on the subject of Cristina's childlessness, he flared up defensively.

"I really think you should take her with you to Berlin, Hansel, the next time you go, to see a doctor."

"I won't have her mauled around by some surgeon who treats her as if she had no more feeling than a machine. She is sensitive and highstrung. It would be a terrible ordeal for her."

"It's a great cross to her to go on like this. I know, though she has never spoken about it to me except once. But I shall never forget the night when Luischen's boy was born. You know that there were complications, in spite of the fact that both the little girls had come so normally into the world before that. There were several hours when the doctor was much concerned, when Luischen suffered horribly. Cristina was sitting in the next room with me, because we had been told we might be needed, that the doctor and nurse might not be able to manage alone. We could hear Luischen's cries quite clearly; I was afraid such sounds of suffering would unnerve Cristina. But when I looked at her to see how she was standing it then, she returned my glance calmly, though there were tears in her eyes. All she said was, 'I wish I were in Luischen's place.'"

"She ought never to have been in the next room to Luischen at such a time. I would have forbidden it, if I'd been here."

"Ah. . . . But you see you were not, Hansel. You were away at one of your Nazi meetings. As you so often are."

The Archduchess had never reconciled herself to his participation in the New Movement. While public meetings were still forbidden in East Prussia, Hans Christian had conceived the idea of holding private ones on his own grounds, since the authorities had not reached a point where they were ready to interfere with gatherings around a *Herrenhaus*; and there he had installed loud speakers so that all the neighbourhood could not help hearing what was said in the course of the speeches. Finding himself unmolested, he had next gone a step further; he had caused loud speakers to be attached to his automobile, and had gone boldly about in it, making speeches in various villages and towns himself. His ingenuity had resulted in many converts; now that the ban on meetings had been lifted, he already had a large nucleus on which to work. The doctrine of National Socialism was sweeping over East Prussia like wildfire, and among the younger men Hans Christian was its prime prophet.

His work took him away from home a good deal. That was his one regret, as far as it was concerned. Cristina meant more to him than any cause or creed, and he could not bear to be separated from her. But he believed it was his duty to go, and she never tried to hold him back. She took it for granted that whatever he did was right and necessary—even when he told her that he thought he should spend six months at a Labour Camp.

CHAPTER XXVI

HE was not forced to do so, he explained. Such service was entirely voluntary; he could get excused from it. Only men who intended to become teachers, or who wished to establish their eligibility for government positions, were actually required to undertake it. The unemployed, of course, were only too thankful for the chance to get free board and lodging. As far as he was concerned it was largely a question of good example. If he went, other Junkers might be moved to do the same, and the great strides toward equality of both fact and feeling would be made. That was the way the matter had been put to him, in the letter he received from those in high quarters. Personally, he felt the experience would be invaluable to him. He would never have been able to serve the Party so well if he had not left his comfortable quarters in the Margarethestrasse and gone to live in the Bomb Palast tenement. A six months' sojourn in a Labour Camp would certainly enable him to serve it much better.

She had never missed the revelation of details in regard to his work, but now she was touched that he should have told her all this, and her pride because he had done so helped her to hold her head high and to shed no tears until after he had gone. Then she went quietly to her room and locked the door. But when her mother-in-law tapped on this, two hours later, she opened it with her customary composure.

She was greatly attached to the Archduchess. There had never been any friction between Victoria Luise and herself, or between herself and Luischen. Harmony reigned at the *Herrenhaus,* and it did not seem to any one of the women there that either of the others infringed on her prerogatives. Besides, Cristina adored Luischen's children. In them she found an added occupation and an added joy. But she had always been careful not to separate them from their mother, and she had never said to Luischen what she had said to Victoria Luise on the night the baby boy was born and what she said again in substance now.

"I am glad you have come to me. I was wondering whether I should come to you, but I thought perhaps you would prefer to be alone. I did for a time. And as I sat here, I could not help thinking that if I had a child this would not be so hard to bear."

"Then our thoughts were much the same," the Archduchess replied, embracing her fondly. "Indeed, I have come to speak to you on that very subject. I think you should see a doctor, a specialist. I think you should go to Berlin for that purpose. I told Hansel so, months ago, but he declined to discuss the matter. He said he would not have you maltreated."

"Maltreated?"

"Doctors sometimes seem harsh in their methods. Modesty, as we understand it, means nothing to them. The more eminent they are, the more occupied they are, and they do not always take time to be gentle. I must admit that a visit to a gynæcologist's office is not a pleasant experience. They ask searching questions about the most delicate matters. They subject their patients to painful examinations. The click of their instruments makes a nerve-racking sound, even if these are not used, and, of course, often they are. It is from all this that Hansel has insisted on sparing you. Mistakenly, in my opinon. For such a visit might reveal the cause of your childlessness and indicate steps which could correct it. Why not take advantage of his absence to find out whether this is the case?"

"You know how hard it is for me to believe that he can be mistaken about anything. But if you really think that secretly he would like to have me go to a doctor, that his hesitation has been based on a wish to spare me——"

"I am sure of that, Cristina. So now that he is away I feel you should act. I do not need to tell you that this great and ancient house should not be left without an heir."

"No, you do not need to tell me. . . . Do you think I should start for Berlin at once? Would you be willing to go with me?"

"If you would like to have me, my dear child. I am pleased that you should wish me to do so."

Financial conditions at Schönplatz were much better than they had been. Hans Christian's self-sacrifice and initiative and Ernst's skilful service had both helped to put them on a better basis; and Don Sebastian had been determined that whatever his personal reverses might be, Cristina should not be the first bride to go undowered to the *Herrenhaus*. By sacrificing some of his foreign investments, on which he could realize money quickly, he had managed to send her a very substantial sum. It had never occurred to her to keep this for herself; she had turned it over at once to Hans Christian to use as he thought best. Now that in his absence Ernst was administering the estate, she went to him and asked for enough money to take the Archduchess and herself to Berlin, telling him candidly the reason why she wished to make the journey.

He gave her the cash without demur. Indeed, he encouraged her to feel that, since she was going there in any case, she might as well stay for a few days, and derive some pleasure from the trip. A little outing would do both herself and the Archduchess good. He was only sorry that he and Luischen could not come with them, but obviously they should not all leave Schönplatz at once. Besides, there were the children. . . . He smiled as he placed the necessary banknotes in Cristina's hand.

"You'll know how that is yourself some time, Cristina."

"Oh, Ernst, I hope so! Thank you for being so helpful. . . ."

The train trip across the Polish Corridor, with its many changes, was fatiguing; but lapped in the solid comfort of the Hotel Bristol, Cristina recovered from it quickly. She did not wish to postpone her visit to a specialist; as soon as she could get an appointment, she wanted to take it. She went through the examination without a murmur, and emerged from the gynæcologist's office white-lipped, but erect. He had found nothing wrong with her, she proudly told the Archduchess, who was waiting for her outside. There was no reason, that he could discover, why she should not have a dozen children, if that was what she wanted. He might like to see Hans

Christian also later on; but perhaps that would not be necessary. They might find, when they were reunited, that their separation had been of benefit. It was sometimes that way. He had congratulated her on her own courage and on her husband's exemplary patriotism. He believed both would be rewarded.

"We will hope he is right. If not, we will seek another opinion. You see, Cristina, that there is nothing unbearable about an experience of this kind."

"Oh no. But shall we go back to the hotel now? That is, if there is nothing else you would like to do this afternoon?"

It had been almost unbearable for her, though she would not admit it. She had never before been unclothed and manhandled, and the indignity, as well as the pain of it, had appalled her. When she was back in her own bed, safe and secluded, she found she was shaking all over, as she had not trembled since her wedding night. And this time Hans Christian was not there to comfort her and uplift her. Never had she longed for him so unutterably, never had she felt the gulf of time that separated them to be so interminable. She would gladly have given ten years of her life if she could have had him with her, even for ten minutes. She could not sleep, and finally, when she had controlled her quivering, she rose again from her bed and paced up and down her room until dawn. It was the first "white night" through which she had ever struggled. She was to struggle through a long succession of them before the next six months were over.

If the Archduchess suspected the inner conflict concealed by outward self-control she gave no sign. She suggested the next morning that they might do a little shopping and sight-seeing, that they might communicate with a few relatives. Cristina acquiesced willingly. Madrid was the only large city where she had ever been before; she was impressed by the stateliness of Berlin, and eager to see more of it. She strolled with delight up and down Unter den Linden at Victoria Luise's side, and drove with her in a state of fascination through the Brandenburger Thor and the Sieges Allee and into the Tiergarten. Later in the day, after they had made a round of visits, all of them pleasant, she agreed that, of course, they should leave cards at the American Embassy.

Hans Christian had told her about the Rhodeses and she was prepared to like them. But she had not foreseen that their proffers of hospitality would be so prodigal. The entire family immediately called in person, and it was actually with difficulty that she and the Archduchess resisted an effort to move them bodily from the Bristol to the Embassy. In the face of Victoria Luise's refusal to install herself there, Mr. Rhodes remained firm on other points.

"Remember what you told me about your traditions of hospitality when I came to Schönplatz, Highness! Why, you wouldn't let me leave, not on a bet! Now you and this pretty young lady must let Mrs. Rhodes and Trixie and me take you out on the town!"

His idea of taking them out on the town was expansive. It included a lavish luncheon and a highly official dinner at the Embassy itself, repasts at all the most famous restaurants, and two evenings at the opera. Every time the Archduchess mentioned the advisability of returning to the country, he argued with her vehemently. When she had been so long coming to Berlin, she mustn't run away from it the minute she got there! It was an exciting time to be in the capital just before an election. Had she ever been to a rally? Had she ever seen a torchlight parade? *What?* Well, didn't she want to?

"Mr. Rhodes, I have told you candidly that I'm not in sympathy with the present form of government in Germany. Like my son-in-law, Friedrich von Mitweld, I should like to see a return to the Empire. If that is impossible, then at least it should not be too much to hope that we might have some other kind of conservative and dignified government."

"I'm afraid it is, my dear lady, I'm afraid it is. The day of conservative, dignified government seems to be almost gone. I'm not in sympathy with what's going on here either—not that I can say so publicly, in my position, though I don't mind saying it to you. But that's all the more reason why I want to watch it. Don't you? . . . Don't *you*? he inquired, turning abruptly to Cristina and looking at her with appreciative appraisal.

"I should like very much to go to a rally. It would help me to understand better what my husband is doing."

She spoke as quietly as usual, but Mr. Rhodes did not fail to catch the longing in her voice.

"That's the idea. The Sport Palast it is then tonight, instead of the Winter Garden. It'll be a great sight and Göring's going to speak."

"He ought to diet, not talk," remarked Richard Eustis scornfully.

Cristina had not quite placed this personable young man. He appeared to be almost a perpetual guest at the Embassy. She supposed he must be a suitor for the hand of Beatrice. But then it appeared to her there was an endless number of such young men, with none of whom, as far as Cristina could discern, Beatrice was herself in love. Yet the Ambassador's daughter, whom Cristina secretly thought the loveliest-looking girl she had ever seen, was on terms of such easy friendliness with Richard Eustis that these seemed to bespeak a betrothal. Her curiosity, though not easily roused, was piqued, and she was pleased when Beatrice at last spoke to her spontaneously on the subject.

"I suppose that some day I shall make up my mind to marry Card Eustis. He's been hanging around for more than nine years now.

It will probably be the only way to get rid of him."

Cristina was increasingly puzzled. She had never heard the theory of marrying a man to get rid of him. And there was nothing in Beatrice's voice, any more than there had been in her manner, to indicate special affection. As if she divined Cristina's bewilderment, Beatrice linked her arm through her guest's, and drew her towards the ping-pong table.

"We can't all draw prize packets the way you did," she said gaily. "Some of the boxes at the church supper turn out to be duds. But we have to take a chance. Come on, let's have a game."

Her cordiality was clear, even though her speech was a mystery. Cristina, who was becoming more and more attached to her, decided to take her on trust.

The rally was certainly a great sight, as the Ambassador had predicted. His party reached the Sport Palast some moments before the programme was scheduled to begin, but the area surrounding it was already thronged with people waiting to listen to loud-speakers. The Brown Shirts on guard saluted respectfully at the sight of Mr. Rhodes, and the gates were instantly thrown open to permit the passage of the official car, which was waved forward so fast that the close-pressing crowd had to choose quickly between being run over or being crushed against the wall. But swift as this progress was, the distinguished guests could see a tall young man charging through the multitude, and plunging toward the gateway with every appearance of baffled rage. He began to argue with the guards, thrusting credentials in their faces. They answered with curt finality, which seemed to act as added fuel to his fury, and pushed him back. The next instant he was charging away again, and the Ambassador was following his flying figure anxiously.

"Too bad," he said, shaking his head. "That man's an American journalist, an able one. He's an angry one now too. I know what sort of a story will be sizzling over the wires within the next fifteen minutes. Incidents of that sort do a good deal to upset the balance of friendly feeling, and it isn't too steady at best. Well, I can't help just now, but I'll try to have a word with Hanfstängl tomorrow. . . . Come, we must get to our seats before this crowd gets any thicker. All right there, Highness? All right there, girls?"

It was the most remarkable spectacle Cristina had ever beheld. More than twenty thousand persons were packed into the vast arena, filling it to overflowing. Many of them, Mr. Rhodes told her, had been there since four in the afternoon, when the doors were opened. It was now after nine, and white-coated vendors of beer and sandwiches and chocolate moved slowly up and down the aisles. The audience patronized these vendors liberally, eating and drinking as they listened to the speeches, but this did not surprise Cristina.

who had already noticed that German crowds seldom stop eating and drinking, even in moments of tense excitement. That this was a moment of tense excitement she could not possibly doubt. Never had she heard such applause as that with which the Minister was constantly interrupted. Moreover, the twenty thousand kept rising as one man, with outflung arms and outstretched hands, which looked like endless flocks of birds suddenly summoned into flight. When at last Göring finished his speech, when the folded banners at the back of the stage were unfurled and swung out in full force of their scarlet splendour, when the band began to play "Hoch die Fahne" and every man and woman in the building began to sing, the sight, the sound, the surge of it all was almost overpowering. Even as an onlooker, even as an outsider, she was caught up in the vital current of force and feeling that flowed through the building.

What Göring actually said seemed comparatively unimportant, and Cristina could not understand why it roused such boundless enthusiasm. He attacked communism, parliamentarianism, pacifism, the German Supreme Court and the Catholic clergy. She was puzzled and a little troubled by his remarks about priests, but decided that perhaps her knowledge of German was not sufficiently thorough to enable her to understand him correctly. At all events, it was the unanimous force with which his remarks were greeted, rather than their own violence, which especially impressed her. That one man— even the Minister of a great country—should say what he did might have no portentous significance. That multitudes should applaud his words caused her to ponder deeply.

The following day she stumbled upon a gathering even more astounding. The Archduchess had insisted upon spending the election period secluded in her hotel suite. It was not until late in the afternoon that she consented to go out, accompanied by Cristina. Nowhere did the streets present the slightest sign of agitation. Indeed, except for a few casual Sunday strollers, these were entirely empty. At last, having traversed the entire length of Unter den Linden without any kind of provocative encounter, they turned towards the Lutheran Cathedral. Cristina might find a Protestant service interesting, the Archduchess said, if it was really true that she had never seen one. At any rate, they could sit at the cathedral quietly for half an hour and rest before walking back to their hotel.

Instead they were unexpectedly swept into the vortex of a throng of people who were streaming into the great building, and propelled into seats in a crowded gallery—the nave being already full to over-flowing. A black-robed verger had thrust an Order of Exercises into Cristina's hand, and she studied it as she waited for these to begin. It bore the heading "Gottesdienst der Deutscher Sendung" ("A Service of the German Mission"), and this service began with a gospel reading taken from Mark i. 15: "The time is fulfilled, and the kingdom of God is at hand." She was slightly startled at the obvious implication which had been given to this famous quotation, but she became very much more startled as the exercises progressed. For this reading from the Scriptures was followed by two extraordinary hymns. The first of these was sung with great feeling and fervour by the massed congregation accompanied by the splendid organ, and was entitled *The Time has Come, the Time of Times.* Though it was not actually offensive, it was permeated with *double entendre.* The second was sung by a male choir, which, clad in flowing white garments confined by twisted and knotted girdles, advanced up the centre aisle as it chanted slowly, without accompaniment and apparently with no sense of sacrilege:

> " Black is the cross that was borne by our Saviour,
> Black is the cross that God has laid on us.
> Take it upon you, Germans, without complaint,
> Carry it silently and strongly, as the Saviour carried his."

After these two hymns came numerous others, similar in type, as well as numerous other readings from the Scriptures. Cristina followed with amazement a passage from Matthew xxiv. 29-31, for which were given correlative passages from Mark xiii. 24-27 and Luke xxi. 25-26:

> "Immediately after the tribulation of those days shall the sun be darkened, and the moon shall not give her light, and the stars shall fall from heaven, and the powers of the heavens shall be shaken:
> "And then shall appear the sign of the Son of man in heaven: and then shall all the tribes of the earth mourn, and they shall see the Son of man coming in the clouds of heaven with power and great glory.
> "And he shall send his angels with a great sound of a trumpet, and they shall gather together his elect from the four winds, from one end of heaven to the other."

Even a person as inexperienced as Cristina, attending such a service on an election day, could not fail to be impressed by its extraordinary character. As they went down the steps of the cathedral, the Archduchess remarked, somewhat satirically, that the peculiar partnership with God which the ex-Kaiser so frequently voiced still seemed to prevail, that the German people had apparently never been more firmly convinced that the Almighty was for them and that therefore they might safely assume that no one could be against them.

"I suppose it is this conviction which permits them to make comparisons and use similes which are very close to blasphemous," she continued. "But they do not appear any less shocking to me on that account. Indeed, they seem to lack sanity as much as they lack reverence. I am really very much upset. I feel that I shall have to return to my own room and lie down."

They had already agreed to go to the Embassy for that strange period called the "cocktail hour," and the Rhodeses had sent the official car to the Bristol. In view of Victoria Luise's collapse, Cristina was obliged to take this alone; and after she had arrived at her destination she found that there were apparently no other guests. Her light step made no sound on the carpeted stairway, so no one was instantly aware of her presence. But she could hear Beatrice and Richard Eustis carrying on an animated conversation in the drawing-room beyond, and for a moment or two she was an involuntary eavesdropper.

"I always did think he had a screw loose, from the moment I heard about this crazy scheme of going away from Hamstead and making for Schönplatz. What man in his senses would leave a looker like Cristina to spend six months in a Labour Camp?"

"Lots of them. I don't mean that lots of them would leave lookers like Cristina, because there aren't so many in her class. But lots of them leave girls they're pretty fond of, just the same, when they think it's the square thing to do."

"Well, you must be taking leave of your own senses, Trixie. I never expected to see the day when you would stand up for a Nazi. And you know what those Labour Camps are like. It isn't as if you hadn't insisted on seeing one! Will you ever forget that hard-boiled sergeant that was detailed to take us out to the hideous 'hostel,' as they called it? . . . The dreariest, drabbest building I ever saw in my life! Why, he looked like a vaudeville caricature of a German—I couldn't believe he was real! And don't you remember that dismal swamp and the fields of half-frozen ruts he ran us over to show us the work of 'reclamation'? I was ready to drop in my tracks before I ever got to the hostel at all, and when I did get there I wished I hadn't."

"I do think it was sort of bare and musty. Except for the Common Room. You must admit the way the men had painted that was effective."

"Effective! I haven't forgotten the effectiveness of the plumbing—or rather the lack of it! No hot water and only one water-closet. Latrines and showers in an outhouse, and a limit put on the time you could use them!"

"Card, you're in a drawing-room, not a pullman smoker."

"All right, then; I'll never forget the expression on the men's faces—all of them sober, some of them frightened and sick! Why, not one of them cracked a smile the whole time we were there. Of course, I didn't see anything for them to smile about. But then I
265

thought the alleged object of these hostels was to teach the nobility of labour and promote comradeship. Well, I guess the poor devils who go there learn something about labour all right between five a.m. and ten p.m., what with ditch-digging and ground-clearing and tree-chopping! The whole system looks to me like a convenient form of slavery! And if I'm not at all wet they learn something about soldiering too. The only books I saw lying around anywhere were biographies of military big shots and manuals of drill—besides that everlasting *Mein Kampf*, of course. But comradeship! Well, all I can say is it was the dreariest bunch of buddies I ever ran into."

"I hope that's all you will say for the moment. You've monopolized conversation long enough. And, as I have told you before, I wish you wouldn't shout so when you're where the servants can hear you. We don't know how much of what they hear they repeat, or to whom. And whatever you do don't do anything that could upset Cristina. She's tops. What's more, she's happy. She's got hold of the best man in the world, and she knows it. If you so much as look at her cross-eyed I'll give you knock-out drops."

Cristina purposely waited a minute before she went on into the drawing-room. This was not only because she did not wish to distress Beatrice by betraying the fact that she had overheard Richard Eustis's remarks. It was also because she was thankful to catch at a chair, momentarily, for support. She was dreadfully dizzy. She had never fainted in her life, but she felt as if she were going to faint now. So this hostel which Richard Eustis had been describing was the sort of place where Hans Christian was voluntarily staying for six months! A dismal, dirty, evil-smelling spot where men slaved but never smiled! Hans Christian, to whom gentleness was a point of honour, and cleanliness a cult, and beauty a creed! It made her sick to think of him there, it revolted her to realize that there he must remain for months and months while she waited endlessly at home for him, wondering how much he would have changed when he was at last restored to her.

At first the change did not seem to be as great as she had feared, perhaps because she had schooled herself to meet it. She had gone back to Schönplatz the day after the disastrous episode of eaves-dropping, and she had never left it again. She had resumed her studying and sewing, her letter-writing and flower-fixing, and as the tranquil days flowed past she recaptured her lost composure. The memories of what she had heard and seen in Berlin became merci-fully blurred, and only the thought of Hans Christian remained clear. In her joy over their delayed reunion she was blinded to any essential change in the image with which she had lived so long.

Little by little she saw him more accurately as he was, but always through eyes of infinite love. If he seemed somewhat sterner, somewhat graver, in his general bearing, what did that matter, so long as his attitude towards her was still one of ardent adoration? If his muscles and his mind had both hardened, were these not added indications of virility? She was still separated from him a great deal, for he was constantly called for conferences at Marienburg, at Königsberg and at Allenstein; and when he was at home he spent endless hours over his correspondence, sitting at a huge flat-topped desk into which bookshelves were built along the sides. It was an inherited piece of great value and beauty, and, when he found that he could trust Cristina never to talk to him at times when he was harassed, he caused another precious heirloom to be brought into his study and placed beside the desk—a high-backed sofa, upholstered in crimson velvet, with drawers built underneath the seat and at the two ends, leaving shelves on top where lights and ornaments could be placed. He told her that it had once belonged to a waiting-lady of Queen Luise, who had doubtless slept on it in uncertain comfort at the foot of her royal mistress's bed, and kept her own belongings, as best she could, in the amount of drawer space it afforded. Probably she had felt cramped by it and had longed for a *Himmelbett* and a Danzig chest of her own. Cristina loved it, however. She reclined contentedly on it for indefinite periods, busied with her needlework or looking out at the lake. But she never failed to be conscious of Hans Christian's eyes when he glanced up from his writing in her direction, and if he rose from his desk and came over to her he always found her arms outstretched and her lips lifted as she made room for him beside her.

The intervals in the study were subject to frequent interruptions. Hans Christian found his contacts greatly expanded, both because of his Party pursuits and because of his marriage. More and more people came to Schönplatz in these days, not only to meetings but to dinners and dances. In their turn he and Cristina went to all the adjacent estates. The countryside had taken far more kindly to the bride on her arrival than it had to him when he came to East Prussia. Indeed, it was considerably impressed by her. She was gracious as well as beautiful, and her appearance caused something of a stir in a vicinity of dowdy women. She wore rare laces and rich brocades, high combs and ancient jewels, as no one in the neighbourhood had ever worn them before. She carried a painted fan as naturally as she did a fine handkerchief. There was always a flower tucked in the V of her bodice and another in the waves of her hair. She was a great addition to any gathering. She danced divinely, and the light tinkle of her guitar, rising above the sonorous sound of a grand piano, enlivened the stodginess of many a musical evening, and sent clear melody rippling through dark drawing-rooms and along silent stairways. Though she was completely contented alone, she proved to have a faculty for friendship. Everyone warmed to her sweetness because it was sincere, and she in return found herself happily disposed towards all she met, from the most important Junker to the humblest peasant.

There was only one exception to this rule, and Cristina reproached herself because this was the case. There was a young woman named Trüdchen in the village whom she instinctively disliked, and of whose covert disrespect she became more and more conscious. At first she did not see much of the girl, but, as the increase in Luischen's family gradually necessitated an increasing amount of extra service, Trüdchen was summoned on occasions to the big house, where, it appeared, she had worked before her own marriage. She was a capable chambermaid, and she took excellent care of the rooms entrusted to her. Cristina's was not among these, but now and then Trüdchen came in on some trifling errand, and eventually she brought a small basket of grapes, together with a little painted plate, and set them down on the bedside table.

"Why are you doing that, Trüdchen?" Cristina inquired. "I did not ask you for any grapes."

"I know you did not, Frau Baronin. But the Herr Baron likes to eat them at night, before he goes to sleep."

"What makes you think so?"

"I do not think so, Frau Baronin. I know it for a fact. When he comes in he will tell you so himself."

It was very late before Hans Christian came home from his meeting that night, and Cristina was already in bed when he reached their room. But as he moved about preparing for bed himself she was drowsily aware that he was standing beside the table, helping himself to grapes. Their pungent smell was still on his lips when he kissed her. She asked him a sleepy question.

"Why did you never tell me that you liked grapes at night, *querido*? I would have seen to it that they were always in readiness for you."

"I haven't thought of eating grapes at night for years. I used to do it, though. And when I saw them just now they looked good to me. How did they happen to be here?"

"A new chambermaid, or rather a former chambermaid who has come back, brought them in. Her name is Trüdchen. I suppose she used to take care of your room."

Hans Christian did not answer. Inexplicably, Cristina began to feel more wide awake.

"Did she?"

"Yes, I believe she did. A long time ago."

"Don't you remember her?"

"Yes, I remember her, now that you speak of her. I'd almost forgotten her until you did."

"She's rather a pretty little thing."

268

"Is she? It's so long since I've noticed anybody's looks except yours, darling, and you're so beautiful——"

"But you must have noticed, when she was working here before, that she was pretty!"

"I suppose I must have. But I'd forgotten about that too. . . . Cristina, you've hardly kissed me at all. . . . Aren't you glad I'm back?"

She was very glad he was back, and she kissed him instantly; not long afterwards she fell asleep. The next day Trüdchen brought grapes into the room again. Cristina said nothing, and Hans Christian did not touch them. So the next morning she asked him whether he wanted them or not.

"I don't care," he said curtly.

He had never spoken to her in that tone of voice before. She was so puzzled that she did not know what she should do, and therefore she decided to do nothing. Trüdchen continued to bring in the grapes regularly, and one evening, when she set them down on the bedside table, the painted plate hit the rosary that was lying there, and this slid to the floor. Trüdchen picked it up and replaced it with abject apologies.

"I'm so sorry, Frau Baronin. It is such a pretty thing. I have never seen anything just like it."

"You've never seen a rosary, Trüdchen?"

"No. Because I never had the honour of caring for Her Serene Highness's room. Of course I know she has one. I know that rosaries are used by Catholics. But she was the only Catholic here until you came. We are all Lutherans in the village. And the Herr Baron was a Lutheran also. There was never a rosary in his room when I formerly took care of him."

"The rosary is mine, Trüdchen. I do not think the Herr Baron ever uses one."

"Ah—then what they say in the village is not true. The Herr Baron did not become a Catholic when he married the Frau Baronin."

"Yes, he became a Catholic when he married me. My uncle baptized him and he was received quickly into the Church because it was necessary that we should be married at once."

"But the Frau Baronin did not have a baby!"

"I'm afraid you did not understand me, Trüdchen. It was necessary for us to be married very quickly because there was a revolution in my country, and the Herr Baron wanted to take me away from it to a place of safety. He became a Catholic because it simplified the arrangements for our marriage, and because it made me and all my family very happy to have him do so. But it did not mean much to him personally. I suppose that is why he never uses a rosary, as Her Serene Highness does, and as I do."

"I shall repeat what you have told me in the village, Frau Baronin. It will restore the Herr Baron to greater respect. I am sure that no one cares whether you and Her Serene Highness use rosaries. But for a leader in the New Party . . ."

Trüdchen's face had resumed its usual blank expression, and Cristina wondered why she had troubled to enter into explanations with an empty-headed little chambermaid. But all her life she had been used to the friendly familiarity existing between Spanish servants and their superiors, and it had not been easy for her to break away from it and to assume the habits of Prussian discipline. Because she was slightly concerned at her own lapse from correctness, she mentioned the matter to Hans Christian later in the evening. He had not been obliged to go to a meeting that night, and they were walking quietly beside the lake when she told him. To her infinite surprise he spoke to her even more curtly than he had when the subject of Trüdchen came up before.

"I can't imagine what you were thinking of, Cristina! You shouldn't even speak to a little slut like that. You, of all persons!"

"What do you mean, *querido*, me of all persons?"

"You can't understand because you're so different. I worship you because you are. Please do as I say."

"So different from what, *querido*? And what makes you think Trüdchen is not a girl of good character, merely because she seems a little silly and forward. Why do you use such a dreadful word in speaking of her?"

"I could have used a much worse one. I shall if she ever comes into our room again. See that she is dismissed tomorrow."

"But, Hansel——"

"You heard what I said. I won't have her in the house."

Cristina had never dismissed a servant; she had no idea how it should be done. She tried to speak very kindly when she told Trüdchen that they would not need her any more. But while she was worrying lest Trüdchen's feelings should be hurt, she saw that a sly little smile was playing around the peasant's lips.

"I did not mean to displease the Frau Baronin by coming to her room. But it seemed natural for me to do so. I used to be there so much. And of course it makes no difference to me whether I work at the Great House or not. Because the Herr Baron has never ceased to send money to my family. He has kept his promise to me, he has done so for many years. He has always paid for his pleasure. I know that he always will."

Trüdchen dropped a quick curtsey and was gone. Her sly smile was the last thing Cristina saw. Then she herself sat down unseeingly by the window and tried to be calm, tried to be composed, as usual. But she felt as if she had been cut to the heart, not by a clean swift dagger, but by a jagged knife which had stuck there, and which kept turning in the wound. All the flawless memories of her marriage to Hans Christian were suddenly smirched and stained. Now she understood why his approach to her had been so skilful. He had not been guided by the instincts of love, as she had supposed; he had been schooled by sensual experience. And he always paid for his pleasure. He had *paid*—for what she had gloried in giving him! How could she ever give him anything again? If only she could leave the Great House that very night and go to a convent —there must still be convents somewhere that were safe! If only she did not have to think of her mother's words, of which she had not thought since the wedding night, but which rose to haunt her now, that since she had spurned her vocation, she must accept her suffering! If only she already had conceived a child! Then perhaps she could reconcile her conscience to a withdrawal. But until she had given an heir to the Great House she could not choose but stay there, she could not evade her duty. She understood that other saying now too, that a wife must submit to her husband even under compulsion. Would Hans Christian use compulsion? Would he forget that he had said he did not want her to yield to his will, only to trust to his tenderness? She had trusted him unconditionally, and now her confidence had brought her to this pass. . . .

She heard his step, the step for which she had always listened with such eagerness, and which now she dreaded to find approaching. She shrank back in her chair, wondering what she would do when he came up to her, how she would greet him, how she would tell him. . . .

She did not need to try. He knew what had happened the instant he looked at her. He sank down on the floor at her feet, and took her hand, and covered it with kisses.

"My darling—if I could only have spared you this——"

"But why couldn't you?"

She had thought she would not be able to speak to him. But now the cry came straight from her soul.

"It happened long before I ever knew you, before I dreamed that I ever would know you. Cristina, this is what almost every man has to confess, sooner or later, to the woman he loves."

"Almost every man? But I thought you were different from every other man!"

"I'm not. That's what I hoped you'd never have to learn."

"Have you—— Was there ever anyone else besides Trüdchen?"

"Darling, do you have to ask me? Do you have to keep on torturing us both? Can't you say to yourself, 'I'm the only woman Hans Christian has ever loved, the only woman he ever will love. He's mine now, body and soul. This is all that matters.'"

"Could you say that, if before I knew you someone had . . ."

"No—no—no! But men are different, Cristina! It isn't the same

271

thing; you must believe me when I tell you it isn't."

Still clasping her hand, he laid his head down on her lap. She could feel him clinging to her, she could hear him sobbing. Until then she had leaned on him, she had relied on him. Now he was leaning on her, he was relying on her. The jagged knife ceased to turn in her heart. She knew that she could not repulse him now, that he needed her as he never had before, that he was indeed all hers. Their interdependence was complete.

It was soon after this that Cristina began to believe she was going to have a child at last. But she did not want to tell Hans Christian until she was sure, to raise his hopes only to dash them again. She was eager to let him know that out of their mutual suffering had come the blessing which had been denied them as long as they had known only rapture; but she waited until she herself felt secure in her certainty. Then she decided to share her secret with him the first night that she felt his mood was propitious for such joyful tidings.

It was late June when she concluded that she could not wait any longer, that her heart would burst with happiness if she did not unburden it. Hans Christian had been gone all day—a day of serene beauty, still and balmy. The roses were blooming in the garden, and the scent of them was lifted to her room. Early in the evening a young moon appeared in the sky, which was still blue as a sapphire; when the stars came out its colour seemed only to deepen. Entranced by the beauty of it, arching in sparkling splendour over the trees and the lake, Cristina left her room in darkness, to see it the more clearly, as she listened to Hans Christian's footsteps, her over-burdened heart pulsing so hard that she seemed to hear its beating.

At last she heard him coming up the stairs. In another instant he would have opened the door to their room, he would have caught her up and crushed her to him. She was sure of this, for he had never failed to do so, as soon as he came home. But this time he crossed the echoing hallway in the opposite direction, and rapped on Ernst's door instead. Ernst called out cordially from within, then came quickly to the threshold, flinging the door open.

"*Grüss Gott!* What can I do for you?"

"Ernst, wasn't your father in the War?"

"Of course, he was killed in the War. Near the very beginning, at Mühlhausen."

"And your mother, what about her?"

"She died too. I thought you knew. Of heartbreak, I've always believed. She was an Alsatian, you know. Wars are always hard on these border people."

"What was her maiden name?"

272

"Weiller. Johanna Weiller. It's a common enough name. What makes you ask?"

"And what was *her* mother's maiden name?"

"Let me see. . . . I've never known much about my forebears, never cared much. Poor people don't, Hansel, the way you Junkers do. But I think it was Bernstein—yes, I'm almost sure it was Bernstein."

"Oh, my God!"

"Hansel, I don't know what you're driving at. Why on earth are you waking me up at midnight to ask me what my grandmother's maiden name was?"

"Because I've been asked myself what it was by certain high officials. They think I should have asked you myself when I suggested that you should come to Schönplatz to take charge. . . . How many Aryans did you ever know whose name was Bernstein, Ernst?"

There was an interminable silence. Then Ernst began to speak again, very slowly and earnestly.

"Hansel, I don't know what to say. I swear to you that I never thought of this, that it never entered my head. I'd rather have cut off my right hand, I'd rather have died, than have made trouble for you. After all you've done for Luischen and me. After I've grown to care so for you."

"I know, Ernst, I know you're telling the truth. But——"

"Do you want us to go away? Do you want me to take Luischen and the children and go? If you do, we'll go at once."

"You'll go at once? You'll go where? Have you seen the signs posted in every village? If you were still living in Munich, if you'd never left there, you might be able to get away with staying. But to try to return——"

"We could go to Alsace. That's French now. We could take refuge among my mother's people."

"And what about Luischen? She isn't French, she isn't Jewish either. She's my own cousin. What about the children? You've got a son, he just escapes the three-generation ban. He'll grow up a fine German boy, he's a fine German boy already. He'll be fitted, in a few years, to lead the Schönplatz Jugend. I've been counting on it, since I haven't a son of my own, or any hope of one! He's my next of kin in the family of the future. . . . No, I won't have him go, I won't have any of you go, I'll keep you all here, no matter what's said to me. . . . I've given in on enough points, against my better judgment, against my conscience. . . . Surely this time—— How could I keep the place going, as far as that goes, if I didn't keep you? I can't be tearing from one end of Prussia to the other unless I've someone to leave here, someone that I can trust."

He stopped abruptly. His vehemence had spent itself. He spoke again shortly.

"I'm sorry I woke you up, Ernst, all for nothing. I was upset myself, it made me thoughtless. We'll find a way to fix things up. Don't worry. Good-night."

"Good-night, Hansel. And thanks again for all you've done for me."

Hans Christian was crossing the hall, he was coming to his own room, which was still unlighted. But in the dimness he could see Cristina standing there, waiting for him, numb with horror. He switched on the electricity and looked at her searchingly.

"What are you doing? Eavesdropping?"

"I didn't mean to, Hansel. I couldn't help overhearing. This is the second time I've listened, when I couldn't help it, to something I'd have given my soul not to hear."

"And when was the other time? You had better tell me!"

She told him, hesitatingly, haltingly, struggling to keep back the tears as she did so. Dreadful as the details about the Labour Camp had once seemed to her, she could not even keep her mind on them as she talked about them now. She could think of nothing but Ernst, who was so tireless and faithful, of Luischen, who was so comely and cheerful, of the three children whom she so dearly loved. *The children!* How could she tell Hans Christian now that they were to have a child of their own? If she did it might mean that after all he would feel he should send Ernst away, since his own line was to be secured at last. If she could only know that she would have a daughter, she might dare to tell him. She prayed that she would have a daughter. She who had prayed so long for a son. And distractedly she went on talking about something else while she prayed, until Hans Christian cut her short.

"Richard Eustis was always a damned fool. I'm sorry you ever saw him. He's filled you full of lies. I'll tell you myself what a Labour Camp is really like some time, since you're so curious about it. But not tonight. I've got too much else on my mind. And I'm tired, God, but I'm tired! If I don't get some sleep I'll go crazy myself, along with most of the rest of the world."

The next day he was called to Berlin. He did not tell Cristina why and she did not ask. After all, he had been called there often, now that so many dreadful things were happening in Germany. The Reichstag had been burned; all was not well with the Party; there had been suspicion of treason in high places. This much she did know, and it was enough; she wanted him to be free to serve, and she had never lost her faculty for waiting. But the only hours that mattered to her were still the ones which she spent with him; and she had decided that this time, when he came home, she would tell him about the child. She had resolved to do that no matter what happened.

His absence had not been protracted when he wired her that he would be home the next evening. All through the summer night she waited, thrilling to his approach. And still there was no sound of his car in the driveway or of his footfall on the stair.

When morning came she went with a haggard face to Victoria Luise, and together they tried to telephone. They could learn nothing. No one knew what had become of Hans Christian von Hohenlohe.

CHAPTER XXVII

The American Ambassador sat in the palatial headquarters of the Gestapo on the Prinz Albrecht Strasse, facing a high official across a polished desk. His manner was completely controlled. But his voice, though that was controlled also, was edged with anger and anxiety.

"This is a very serious matter, Herr Offizier."

The Herr Offizier shrugged his shoulders, so slightly that the movement was hardly noticeable. He spoke civilly, with almost imperceptible contempt.

"It is regrettable, certainly. But, as I have said already, there is nothing I can do about it."

"I believe it was Napoleon who said, 'If a thing is possible, it can be done. If it is impossible, it must be done.' I am asking you to accomplish something that must be done."

"Many of Napoleon's maxims sound impressive. But he died in exile, on a lonely island. It would seem, Your Excellency, as if escape from this would have been one of the impossibilities which he felt must be achieved."

The argument was unanswerable. Rufus Rhodes cursed himself inwardly for having laid himself open to it. He should have learned, long before, that he could not compete with men like this in adroitness. He had to try to cope with them otherwise.

"Hans von Hohenlohe is half American. His mother occupies a position of great power. She is very close to the White House, and the President has already protested, as you know. Now Senator Marlowe is on her way over here. I think it is highly advisable, from every point of view, that her son should be found before she arrives."

"Certainly it would be gratifying. Any mother is naturally anxious concerning the safety of her son; some mothers are over-anxious. But that seems to me slightly beyond the present point, in common with most of your remarks, if you will permit the observation, Excellency. It would have been easy enough for Hans von Hohenlohe to become an American citizen. His own father paved the way for

275

such an action. But he did not choose to do so. Instead he chose to come to Germany to take over his ancestral estates, and eventually affiliate himself with the Nationalist Socialist Party. I cannot conceive that if a man who was half German chose to go to the United States, establish himself on American soil, and become an active Democrat, the President of your country would consider our Chancellor responsible should this man be absent, without explanation, from his home. Neither can we accept responsibility for the case under discussion. As a matter of fact, our Government has tactfully refrained from any official comment on many cases of kidnapping, lynching, and other American atrocities which seem to us uncivilized, to say the least. In return, we should be much obliged if your Government would show similar restraint under much less provocation."

The high official picked up a folder which lay on the glass-topped desk, and glanced at a neatly tabulated file which it contained. Then he spoke gravely.

"I am sorry to say that the record of the young man in whom you are good enough to show so much concern is not altogether commendable. His moral character, for instance, leaves much to be desired."

"His moral character!"

"Yes. He had hardly arrived in East Prussia, when he seduced an innocent young peasant. Although she is now happily married to an honest villager, he still forces her to come to the *Herrenhaus*, ostensibly to work there. But the sums he continues to pay her are suspiciously large, and out of all proportion to his Party contributions."

"I know something about the case; I'd like to tell you the other side. . . ."

"I should be interested in hearing it some time. But for the moment, as our time is limited, suppose you permit me to go on. There is a young nurse in Nuremberg, whom Hans von Hohenlohe met when he first went there to a celebration of the *Parteitag*. Instead of attending its every function with fervour, he left his troop, whenever he could, to visit this girl. She is one of our most faithful followers. She noted down for us each of these lapses from grace."

"You mean she was deliberately set to spy on him? . . ."

"I mean that we do not countenance laxity of any kind, Your Excellency, in our code of discipline and training. The new Reich must be cleansed of everything carnal, and we are taking steps to see that it shall be. Hans von Hohenlohe has repeatedly disregarded our rules respecting this. His very marriage was an added affront to them. When he was given leave of absence to go to Spain this was to recuperate from a severe wound; it was not to court the daughter of

276

a decadent family. Yet he returned to it a second time, on the pretext of an emergency, and later it was revealed that this emergency was a hasty wedding. His attitude towards his wife is uxorious. He resents the slightest separation from her. And she is childless. By now she should have given three sturdy sons to the State."

"She's a beautiful, noble girl, who worships the ground he walks on!"

"I am not concerned with her beauty or her nobility or her senseless adoration. I am concerned only with her barrenness. And, I might add, with her religion. These Catholic women are usually a bad influence. Hans von Hohenlohe has been caught between two of them—one in her first and the other in her second childhood. The Austrian Archduchess is as bad as the Spanish princess. He also has an aunt who is a Carmelite nun in Cologne. And he has not had the sense to resist their wiles. He has become a Catholic himself! When, as he knew, we had millions of them to deal with already, to bring to heel, to exterminate!"

The official's expressionless face had suddenly become distorted. He brought his fist down on the desk with a bang. Then controlling himself quickly, he picked up the file again and went on reading.

"The fact that Hans von Hohenlohe is a voluptuary and a Papist is lamentable enough in itself. But there are much more serious charges against him. He has repeatedly questioned Party principles. He had begun to do this even before Horst Wessel died. It required endless effort on the part of his comrades to keep him in line. He has, on occasion, failed to carry out orders completely, when these involved the forceful methods which our Leader knows to be necessary. Worst of all, he has harboured a Jew in his own house. This Jew's wife is the sister of Karl Welder, an avowed Communist and a ringleader at the Liebknecht Haus. He and Hans von Hohenlohe have been seen talking together in the street. Moreover, this woman's father is an unreclaimed monarchist, who spends half his time at Doorn hatching plots for the restoration of the monarchy. The whole set-up could hardly be more damaging."

"Herr von Hohenlohe was completely unaware of Ernst Behrend's antecedents."

"He did plead ignorance on that score. But he was fully informed by the authorities, whom he next defied. They have been extremely patient with his shortcomings, because, to offset these, he had a powerful position and certain commendable qualities. He inspired confidence in our cause, and he awakened the affection of his men, though he had never commanded the respect of his neighbours. But there is a limit to such patience. Possibly this has been reached. It would seem to be conceivable, under all the circumstances. But be that as it may, I cannot tell you what has become of Hans von Hohenlohe."

"You mean that you won't?"

"I mean what I said, Your Excellency, that I cannot. It is possible, of course, that he may have been taken into protective custody. It is also possible that he may have met with some unfortunate accident. In the latter case his body will eventually be found and returned to his family by the authorities, with the usual recommendation that they should spare themselves needless suffering by refraining from opening the casket. In the former case he will eventually communicate with his family himself, if he cares to do so. Correspondence is censored at concentration camps, but it is stopped only in very unusual cases."

"It never begins at all, does it, after certain 'examinations'?"

The high official rose, replacing the file he had been holding neatly in the folder. He bowed from the waist.

"I am afraid Your Excellency has been reading extracts from the American Jewish Press, which makes up in hysteria what it lacks in accuracy. I am sorry that I have not been able to be of more service. Some other morning perhaps. . . . I know you will excuse me now. Unfortunately I must leave you to keep a pressing appointment."

Rufus Rhodes had never seen Faith Marlowe, though he had read and listened to countless stories about her, since she had become a legend on the American scene. He had heard that she was both lovely and beloved. But according to rumour, she had always been sought after vainly. Her marriage had been unhappy, her widowhood impregnable. In her youth she had been the inspiration of a great painter's genius, and he had immortalized her beauty without benefiting by it. She owed her political progress to an obscure and grotesque local "boss," named Caleb Hawks. All this was more or less hearsay, like the tales of her estrangement from her son. All that Mr. Rhodes actually knew was that she had resumed her maiden name with her American citizenship; that she had shown herself an able member of the group self-styled as the "greatest legislative body in the world"; and that she "stood in well" with the White House.

He felt poorly prepared to meet her, as he paced up and down at the airport, waiting for the plane to come in. She had made the quickest possible crossing, and had flown from London to Berlin. Trixie, who had gone out to the airport with him, did not seem to share his qualms. He often thought that if it had not been for her he could not have stuck to his post, that he would have sent in his resignation long before. Only her cheerful and courageous acceptance of conditions as they were in Germany at present made them tolerable for him. And this last week he had been worried about her. She was very pale, she did not smile or say much; he missed her lovely colour, her inconsequential chatter. But now, as she linked her arm through his, he felt vaguely comforted.

"I think we're going to like Senator Marlowe, Daddy. I believe she's going to be wonderful."

She was indeed wonderful. They saw that from the moment she stepped out of the plane. Inevitably, it was her beauty which struck them first, the beauty to which the thousands of pictures representing her had never done full justice. Her face and figure were both flawless in their perfection, and no hat could hide the glory of her red-gold hair. She was a woman in her middle forties, but she could easily have passed for twenty years less, if her expression had not lacked the softness and her carriage the suppleness of youth. Her lovely lips closed in a line that was almost hard; there was a suggestion of sharpness in the contour of her cheeks, a look of lost gentleness in her eyes. She held herself erect and moved with dignity; she had great presence. Nevertheless, some quality essential to supreme charm was missing.

"She's putting up a brave front," Rufus Rhodes said to himself. "She's beside herself with fear and grief, and she's determined not to show it. That's what gives her such a look." But even before the thought was fully formulated, he knew it was not wholly correct. Faith Marlowe's air of defensiveness was nothing new; she must have had it a long time. Such lines did not come overnight into a woman's face, nor such rigidity into a fine figure. He must seek further back for their underlying reasons.

"Have you any news for me at all, Mr. Ambassador?"

"No, none. But don't be discouraged—any more than you can help, I mean. I've got all sorts of lines out. And I've made appointments for you with several great personages tomorrow. I'll tell you as we go along. . . . Senator Marlowe, I nearly forgot. This is my daughter Beatrice."

They shook hands, regarding each other with covert appraisal. It was approving, on both sides. Trixie possessed herself of the Senator's dispatch case, speaking in a low voice as she leaned forward to take it.

"I'm driving the car myself; we'll have a chance to talk. A motor is about the only place where we can be sure we're not overheard."

Faith Marlowe nodded. She liked the way the girl faced facts, her brisk manner of walking, the effect of her clothes. Here, indubitably, would have been a desirable daughter-in-law, she reflected, as she got into the car, and felt it start off, swiftly yet smoothly. Tense as the moment was, she could not help wondering why she had not achieved Trixie as such.

"Cristina is not in Berlin?" she inquired, indirectly following her own train of thought.

"No. She could not leave the Archduchess. The poor old lady's heart is in bad condition, and this shock has been too much for it. She is completely prostrated, and the end might come at any time. Besides, the entire management of the estate has fallen upon Cristina. Ernst Behrend felt, no doubt rightly, that if he were no longer in the picture the situation might be eased at least. He has taken his entire family and gone to Alsace. Of course he has not been able to carry any money out with him, and his French relatives were in straitened circumstances already. But possibly a way can be found to cope with that condition at least."

"Yes, of course," Senator Marlowe said quietly. "Everything possible should be done for Ernst Behrend and it will be—— And possibly I may be able to help Cristina with the management of the estate and the care of Tante Luise. I have had a good deal of experience on my own farm, in Hamstead, and I have always been very fond of my mother-in-law. . . . You think it would be well if I went on to East Prussia myself, do you not, as soon as I have kept the appointments you have made for me here?"

"Yes, that would be the best plan. Candidly, I am afraid the appointments may not amount to very much in the end. The Ministers you meet will be extremely civil and completely inactive. Presidential protests from America do not move them at all."

Mr. Rhodes spoke with angry contempt and deep concern. Faith Marlowe answered him with the same calmness she had shown before.

"I know. And besides, President Conrad has always been bitterly opposed to the course Hansel took, and to my acceptance of it. He has been civil and correct in his behaviour towards me during this crisis, as you say the Ministers will be. But I have known that he was saying. 'I told you so!' to himself all the time."

There was not a break in her voice. But Mr. Rhodes found it hard to control his own as he took up the thread of conversation again.

"I'm sorry, but I'm afraid you're right. And I don't seem to get anywhere myself. Of course I've been to the *Polizeipräsidium*, to the Colombia Haus—in fact, everywhere—for long conferences. I really don't believe that your son is in any of these places, or at Plötzensee or Oranienburg, or a concentration camp of any kind, for that matter. I think he really has disappeared. What happened prior to the disappearance there is no way of telling. It is all the harder to trace the circumstances because he himself invariably said so little about his plans and orders. He never discussed them with his wife or his grandmother. He did not make mental companions of either one. He may have started for the pre-arranged meeting of the S.A. leaders at Wiesse, and never have reached there. Some men were arrested on the road in their cars, some at the railroad station as they got out of the train. Or he may have actually arrived, and come to

280

grief afterwards. On the other hand, he may not have meant to go to Wiesse at all. Our lack of knowledge is very complicating. But at least we know what precipitated his disappearance—which is more than many people do under similar circumstances. Often a man's family and friends can't even find out of what he is accused."

"Would you mind telling me just what you mean by 'disappearance.' Mr. Rhodes? I promise you that I shall not have hysterics. Do you mean that you think that Hansel is dead already?"

He hesitated, but he believed her; she was the kind of woman who could take the truth. He decided to give it to her.

"I don't know, Senator Marlowe. There have been a good many cases where men under arrest were 'accidentally' killed. There have been some where there was no pretence that there had been an accident, when there was open admission that they had been 'punished' on purpose. You know that this latest episode is boldly called a 'blood purge.' If it would help to harrow you with tales of torture, I would tell them to you. But it would not. Just now there is a reign of terror in Germany. It is horrible for its victims, and it is even more horrible for the nation. The Third Reich can never retrieve what it has forfeited during this so-called 'Night of Long Knives.'"

"Then the accounts of this have not been exaggerated?"

"I do not see how they could be. There are about eighty acknowledged dead. I should not be surprised if the real number were ten times as large."

"But a few have escaped, Daddy. You know that two or three have managed to get away somehow. I am sure that Hans Christian has."

"What makes you think so, Beatrice?"

For the first time there was a trace of tenderness in Faith Marlowe's voice. The answer to her question came clearly and instantaneously.

"Because I know Chris. There's something about him that Hitler couldn't kill."

Her conviction of this remained unshaken, at least outwardly. During the difficult days which followed she went with Faith Marlowe to one Ministry after another, driving the car herself, and sitting patiently in antechambers, while the Senator was closeted with dignitaries. She insisted that she rather liked "waiting outside with the weapons," and she admitted that she sometimes struck up conversations with guards, partly to pass the time and partly on the offchance of gleaning some valuable information. She also took Faith Marlowe to Friedrichshain, to the hospital which now bore Horst Wessel's name, to the Nicolai Friedhof, where "comrades" were constantly forgathering around his decorated grave, and to the Bomb Palast where the lost leader and Hans Christian had first met

281

each other. One never knew, she kept saying insistently, when some helpful hint might stray in their direction. She declined to be discouraged, even when Oskar Kraus rebuffed them.

"He is really a very kind person," she said as they drove unwelcomed away. "The first time I saw him was after I had been accidentally hit in one of those wild street brawls they specialize in here. I was with Chris, and Oskar Kraus asked us both to his lodgings. He took care of me as kindly as if I had been a baby and he had been my nurse. And when Chris was in the hospital—why, Oskar actually haunted it! . . . Well, it does give you a queer feeling when someone who's shown qualities like that practically slams the door in your face. But there's something behind all this. We'll find out what it is yet."

Days passed, and still they did not. But she declined to admit either deception or defeat. She merely suggested that they might as well go to Schönplatz.

"I'd love to drive you over there, I really would, Senator Marlowe. I've always wanted to go and Chris never invited me. Now this will give me a chance. And it will give us both something to do. There's nothing so bad as waiting around, is there, and feeling that nothing's worth while, while you go on pretending, buying new clothes, and making up your face and drinking cocktails before dinner? But Chris wouldn't want anyone to feel that way. He'd want us to make a stab at keeping up appearances. He wouldn't want these ruffians to have the satisfaction of knowing they'd got us down."

"I think you're probably right, Trixie."

"I know darned well I'm right. Besides, I know that the Archduchess and Cristina are simply counting the moments until you get to Schönplatz. In addition to worrying over Chris, they are grieving for Gabriel de Cerreno. His death wasn't unexpected, for he had been frail a long time, and he'd been through a good deal in these last years. Still, it came as a shock and they need comfort. Besides, I know they have a feeling that when you arrive and take charge everything will be better. Of course it will be too—— We could start tomorrow morning, if you like."

Faith Marlowe, secretly more sick at heart every day, agreed that it might be just as well, and neither Mr. nor Mrs. Rhodes put any impediment in their path. In fact, the Ambassador agreed with Trixie that Faith Marlowe was needed at Schönplatz, and that there was nothing she could do, momentarily at least, in Berlin. So they started off without further delay. Trixie drove through to Danzig without difficulty in a day, and, late as it was when they arrived there, insisted that they must go to Lauterbach's to dinner, that it was the best restaurant north of Paris, and that some *Danziger Goldwasser* would cheer them both up. The next morning she circled expertly around points of interest in the quaint old town before they took the road for Marienburg, deftly dodging various groups of Hitler *Jugend* which were on the march.

"Talk about being more Catholic than the Pope!" she remarked. "This place is more Nazi than Berlin. The *Free* City of Danzig! It's about as free as a convict. And the Poles are about as popular as polecats would be. I was waked up at break of dawn by those Hitler kids singing under my window, weren't you? And I'd just drowsed off again when along came two brass bands. Do you know what I think, Senator Marlowe? I think if you can manage to thrust a German into some kind of uniform—it doesn't much matter what kind—and start him off behind a band, he'll go anywhere. Do you remember that story about the Pied Piper? Well, it looks to me as if the same sort of thing was happening now."

Faith Marlowe glanced at her attentively, struck by the shrewdness of the comment, and increasingly convinced that as Trixie herself might have expressed it, here was a "great girl."

"Perhaps I wasn't very tactful to talk that way about Germans," Trixie went on. "I keep forgetting you married one. Of course you know a lot more about them than I do."

"I didn't, when I got married." Faith Marlowe paused for a moment and then went on, with a candour curiously contradictory to her controlled voice, "If I had I never should have married one, Beatrice. I like you so much that I can't help telling you I'm glad you haven't made the same kind of a mistake."

"The only reason I haven't married a German is because the one I cared about didn't want me. If he had, nothing would have stopped me. I did everything I could think of—I don't mean vamping, I mean trying to improve. It wasn't any use. And then I made a terrible mistake. The first time he confided in me, when he was just on the point of proposing, I argued with him. I thought I knew more about what he was saying than he did. I still think so. But he couldn't take it. He was terribly hurt and terribly angry. . . . After a long time we made up, sort of. But only because he was sick, only because I was careful not to get controversial and he was too weak to try. And right after that he fell for someone else. Hard, the way I had for him. Someone who'd never have a thought or a feeling that wasn't the same as his, someone who'd never try to find out what was on his mind unless he told her of his own accord, much less quarrel with him about it. Someone who'd just lie down and let him love her. I guess that's what Germans want out of girls, Senator Marlowe."

"I have often thought the same thing, my dear. And it is very fortunate you found this out before you married one, instead of afterwards. Though, of course you will never believe this."

"Of course I shan't. If I'd only had him just for a little while. . . . But never to have him at all—that's what hurts so, that's what I'll

283

never get over. I can't seem to put him out of my mind. I'd like to get married; I never was cut out for an old maid. I'd like a lot of children too, and I bet I could take them right in my stride, without losing my health or my figure. But every time I almost make up my mind to go ahead something stops me. I just can't do it. I've just written to a man who's been proposing to me periodically for ten years that I never want to see or hear from him again."

Faith Marlowe put out her gloved hand and lightly touched the bare brown one that held the wheel so firmly. There was affection as well as understanding in her voice when she answered.

"I know something about that too, Beatrice. Perhaps some day we'll talk it over—some day when we're surer we can keep calmer than we are just now. We're both carrying a pretty heavy load. But I believe we're going to help each other carry it. I believe we're going to be great friends."

She turned away, pretending not to see the tears that had fallen from Trixie's eyes to her own gloved hand. But she did not overlook the generosity and justice in Trixie's next remarks.

"What I said a few minutes ago wasn't fair, Senator Marlowe. The German I care about didn't fall for this other girl because she was a doormat. She did think he was perfect—she still thinks so. But he thought she was perfect too, and she was—she is. She isn't beautiful but dumb; she's beautiful and everything else besides—gentle and gracious and good. I mean really good, not just namby-pamby. You'll see—of course you know whom I've been talking about. But I can't help it. I had to tell you."

"I am glad you did, Beatrice—so glad and grateful. And I am sure you are right, sure that this girl of whom you speak is—almost irresistible. You see, I knew her father."

It was a beautiful midsummer day. They lunched at Marienburg, and Trixie, completely calm again, suggested that they should stop to see the Stronghold of the Teutonic Knights before they went on. She felt sure that both the Archduchess and Cristina took siestas in the early afternoon; there was no point in hurrying themselves; they might better plan to reach Schönplaz about teatime. Again Faith Marlowe agreed with her, and they made their way along at a rate surprisingly moderate for Trixie, talking to each other with increasing ease and intimacy as they went. It was nearly six o'clock when they skirted the vine-covered walls and turned in at the iron gateway leading to the *Herrenhaus*.

A young woman in peasant costume was standing at the door, evidently awaiting them. There was nothing strange about this, for Trixie had telephoned from Marienburg, announcing the approximate time of arrival. But there was something surprising in the smugness of the servant's plump and pretty face. Both Faith and

Trixie were conscious of it while she was still curtseying to them, before she had actually spoken.

"The Frau Baronin will be here as soon as possible to welcome Your Excellencies. But she may be delayed for a few moments. Something very sad has happened. Her Serene Highness has had another severe shock."

"What do you mean?" Faith Marlowe asked, almost sharply.

"Your pardon, Excellency. Will you not be pleased to enter the Great Hall? The Frau Baronin will be down at any instant, and Fritz will come to occupy himself with the car and the baggage. It is this way: Her Serene Highness has seldom cared to read the papers in recent years. But this afternoon, for some reason, the radio was turned on, and she accidentally heard an announcement concerning the death of the Austrian Chancellor—Dolfuss, was that his name? Her Serene Highness became convinced that he had been murdered. Nothing could dissuade her. She cried out wildly that this was the beginning of the end of Austria. It seems that this Dolfuss was a Catholic, that he did not receive the last rites before he died. Her Serene Highness cried out still more wildly that his murderers must have prevented his absolution. She was quite unreasonable, quite beside herself. She began to talk about the Herr Baron, to say she was certain his fate had been similar, that such would be the fate of all those who opposed the Leader. The Frau Baronin did everything possible to quiet her; the doctor came as soon as he was summoned. But unfortunately——"

"Trüdchen, what are you doing in this house?"

Faith Marlowe and Trixie both turned quickly, and through them both a simultaneous shudder ran. Cristina, dressed entirely in white, was standing on the dim stairway. There was something about her so closely akin to the supernal that neither of them could doubt for a moment that she had just emerged from a death chamber. But she did not seem to be bowed by grief. Celestial as she looked, she appeared more like an avenging than a sorrowing angel. She came slowly down the stairs without taking her eyes off the cringing servant. Then she took hold of her with slender hands that looked strangely strong.

"Have you forgotten that the Herr Baron gave orders that you were never to come here again?"

"No, Frau Baronin. But——"

"It appears that you did. It appears that you went into her Serene Highness's room by stealth this afternoon when I myself had left her for a few moments. It appears that you have done so before, since the Herr Baron went away. She told me so herself before she died. Now you have killed her by telling her truths from which I have shielded her. You talk too much, Trüdchen. You talked about the Herr Baron in the village and he disappeared. You talked to the Archduchess in her bedchamber and she is dead. The doctor will come to your cottage in a few moments and talk to you. I do not know what he and the authorities will decide to do with you, and I do not know yet what I shall decide to do myself. But I do know this. If you ever cross this threshold again you will be pursued by a ghost. Perhaps by more ghosts than one. The Hapsburgs haunt their murderers, Trüdchen. You had better remember that, and you had better go before they rise up against you."

She relaxed her grasp, and with a little whimpering sound Trüdchen scuttled off into the darkness. Cristina put her arms around Trixie and clung to her for a moment. Faith Marlowe saw, and marvelled in seeing, that there was no antagonism between the two, but deep affection. She saw too that this child of Sebastian de Cerreno had inherited his qualities of greatness no less than his qualities of grace. She put out her own arms as Cristina dropped quickly on one knee and kissed her mother-in-law's hand.

"I am grateful that you have come into this house of mourning, *madre mia*," she murmured. "My father has always told me that you bring comfort and radiance wherever you go."

CHAPTER XXVIII

FAITH MARLOWE did bring comfort and radiance to Schönplatz in the days that followed; but the unobtrusive foundation for these was the practicality of all her plans and the tactful efficiency with which she carried them out.

She did not commit the error, into which she might easily have fallen, of seeming to take over all the reins of government at the *Herrenhaus*. On the contrary, she deferred, and made it clear that everyone else must defer, to her son's wife. The Baroness von Hohenlohe was now the undisputed mistress of Schönplatz; her word and her wishes were law. But ready to reinforce and execute these, ready to shield her and smooth her path at every turn, stood Faith Marlowe. Cristina, so to speak, sat on the throne, and her mother-in-law stood behind it.

The result was order and harmony on every side. The respect which Faith Marlowe wrung from the neighbourhood was unreluctant. There were even a few admiring individuals who spoke of her among themselves as *echt Deutsch*, a true German, sincerely believing that they were paying her the greatest possible compliment, and complacently unaware that she herself would have recoiled from the designation. They marvelled at her perfect command of their language and her complete familiarity with their customs. Some of them recalled the time when she had first come to Schönplatz herself, as a girl of sixteen. How bewitching she had been then.

She had not possessed the supreme repose and refinement which characterized Cristina; but she had been dazzling. And after she married Rudolf von Hohenlohe, her conduct, both as his wife and as his widow, had been irreproachable, as far as any of them had ever heard. It seemed strange, to be sure, that she should have resumed her maiden name, that she should long have affiliated herself so exclusively with American affairs, that she should have so completely alienated herself from her son. *Ach ja!* This was perhaps largely his fault. He had always had a queer streak, and finally he had succeeded in getting himself into deep difficulties. But if anyone could extricate him from these, it would doubtless be his mother. There was really something dazzling about her still; she had lost some of her former exuberance, but that was a change for the better; she had gained in dignity what she had lost in glamour. She was *prachtvoll*.

The ceremonies attending the funeral of the Archduchess were imperial, and her burial, between her three sons who had fallen in the World War, and her husband, who had been one of its greatest heroes, was impressive in the extreme. The monumental marble and the iron crosses in the woodland cemetery were wreathed in revived majesty as another mound rose beside them; the stillness of the forest became doubly profound as it engulfed another presence. Beatrice, wandering into Faith Marlowe's room, as she had been encouraged to do, late in the day after the services were over, made one of the seemingly random remarks that never failed to prove arresting to the older woman.

"Do you remember what Cristina said the afternoon we got here? To the blonde bitch who was lying in wait for us? That the Hapsburgs haunted their murderers?"

"Yes, Beatrice. Why?"

"Well, I believe it's true. And maybe not just the Hapsburgs, but the Hohenlohes too. Maybe not only when there's been murder but in any case. Didn't you feel something strange, out there in the forest? Don't you feel something strange here in the house?"

"Yes . . . I think there may be truth in what you say. I think the Hohenlohes as well as the Hapsburgs . . . But as for your feeling in the woods, that might all be due to murder after all. Everyone buried there is the victim, directly or indirectly, of the World War."

"And you believe war is just like any other murder, only on a larger scale?"

"How can I believe anything else now? . . . As for your feeling about Schönplatz itself—well, you know:

> 'All houses wherein men have lived and died
> Are haunted houses.' "

"Yes, I know Longfellow said so. But Schönplatz is different from any other house I've been in. Listen!"

Shivering slightly in spite of herself, Faith Marlowe listened. The silence was even more profound, even more engulfing, than that of the forest had been. She knew that if any sort of sound had suddenly penetrated it, she would have been obliged to stifle a scream.

"I know what haunts this house," Beatrice went on inexorably. "It isn't just dead people. It's a dead tradition too. The tradition Chris thought was great. The one he was ready to give his life for. Maybe has."

Her lips were quivering, her eyes overflowing. Faith Marlowe put her arm around the girl.

"My dear, don't let it overwhelm you. Try to keep your heart and your manner both quiet. You may be right again. But don't forget this place has somehow survived for seven hundred years, through countless calamities. I hope it can survive still."

"I'd rather see a man survive than a house. I can't be quiet always when I think about Chris. Or Cristina either."

"Ah, yes, Cristina . . . I'm afraid we've been selfish enough to forget her temporarily. Do you know where she is, what she's doing?"

"I didn't forget her. I never forget her. She's in her room, lying down. She's terribly tired. She said she wanted to be alone."

"Very well, we will leave her alone for a time. But later, I think I had better look in on her. I'll be careful not to disturb her, in case she's asleep. But if she's awake, she might be glad to see me."

"No one could help being glad to see you, Senator Marlowe."

Faith's heart warmed to the girl's praise, as it had warmed from the beginning to her courage and sincerity. But, for the moment, her thoughts were preoccupied with Cristina. She was secretly worried about her daughter-in-law. It was natural enough for the girl to show signs of strain; but she had become abnormally pale, abnormally composed; there were deep circles around her eyes, and she seemed to hold herself erect with an effort. Faith wanted to see for herself whether Cristina was really resting. She continued to talk, in a friendly fashion, with Beatrice for another half-hour. Then she excused herself, and went softly into her daughter-in-law's room.

She was relieved to find that Cristina was indeed asleep on the ponderous bed which dominated its surroundings. Her parted hair fell in long braids over her breast, which was unconcealed by the fine laces that veiled it. Her hands were lightly clasped over the linen sheet with which she was partially covered. Her extreme pallor, enhanced by the whiteness of the linen against which she was lying, her complete stillness, and something about her posture sent a fresh tremor through Faith; she steadied herself, almost angrily. This was not death, or any semblance of it, at which she was looking, she told herself resolutely; it was a revelation of life and love. Cristina was only sleeping as a consecrated bride might slumber at last, overcome by the manifestation of erstwhile mysteries; she was only sleeping as a potential mother might slumber, burdened already by the expanding blossom within her. All day long, even while the earth thudded down on Victoria Luise's coffin, Faith had been obsessed with the conviction that she was confronted not only with the end of an era, but with the beginning of one. Now, as she sat looking searchingly at Cristina through the twilight, she became increasingly sure of this.

The girl stirred slightly, as if conscious that she were no longer alone. With a fresh pang, Faith saw her turn on her side, and stretch out her arms. As these reached only emptiness, she moaned a little under her breath, and half opened her eyes. Faith leaned over and spoke to her.

"It is I, *querida*," she said. "Hans Christian's mother. Have you had a good rest?"

Cristina sat up in bed, her eyes still heavy with sleep, her laces slipping still further from her shoulders. "I must have been dreaming," she murmured. "I thought. . . ." Colour came into her face, and spread slowly over her snowy skin. Then, as she remembered realities, she emerged from confusion into composure. "Yes, I am rested now," she said gratefully. "Thank you for coming to see me. But this is not the way for me to receive you. Let me. . . ."

"Please lie still, dear child. Let me go on looking at you, just as you are. I have been happy, merely doing so, as you slept. And happier still in thinking that my son's life has been beatified by yours. Wherever he is now, whatever he may be suffering, nothing can rob him of the memory of your bounty."

Cristina caught her breath, but she did not sob. And she lay still, as Faith had told her to do. Quiescence under control was still part of her creed, and she could hear her husband talking through his mother.

"If you are really refreshed, I should like to talk to you for a little while. But let us speak very softly. However still a house may seem its walls are sievelike. . . . Have you thought at all what you want to do now, Cristina? You cannot stay alone at Schönplatz."

"I could, if it were necessary, *madre mia*, and I would. But I hoped it might not be. I hoped, now that Tante Luise is dead, you would take me back to Spain."

"That I would take you? Back to Spain? Why, Cristina?"

"Because I am sure that when he is free, Hans Christian will seek for me in Spain. He will not try to come back here. That would be fatal."

"It might be dangerous. But are you sure that Spain is safe?"

"Can we be sure that any place is safe? At least, it is quieter now than in a long time. My father writes me that with the change of government, from Left to Centre Right, there has been much improvement in his opinion. And though he has lost both Ventosilla and the Castello Viejo through the passage of the Agrarian Reform Laws, he still has the *caseria*. I do not think he will be molested there. It is such a small property, and so simple, compared to the others."

"Yes—it is small and simple, compared to the others. Somehow I cannot seem to see your father shorn of those. Is it partly because you are sorry for him that you want to go back to Spain, Cristina?"

"Yes, but only partly. I have not seen him, you know, since my marriage. And we were always close to each other. Now that I have lost Hans Christian, it seems natural to turn back to him. So I am thinking of myself, partly, too. But I am also thinking of someone else."

"Yes, Cristina?"

"I am going to have a child, *madre mia*. And after what has happened, I could not bear that it should be born a German!"

Her words came with a rush now. "Hans Christian does not know it. I did not know it myself until just before he disappeared. And the last night he was here, when I meant to tell him—that was the night he found out about Ernst, the night he could think of nothing else. He did not think of me at all, for the first time. He was frozen with horror, there was no love left in his heart. How could I tell him, on such a night, that at last . . . after we had hoped so long, and so vainly. . . . No, no, I could not do it!"

"Of course you couldn't, Cristina. Of course you felt you must wait."

"Yes, and then I found I had waited too long. There was no other chance to tell him. And I did not know what to do. I was trapped. I could not leave Tante Luise all alone. I could not take her away with me, she was so old and ill. And still I felt that if I did not go before others knew how it was with me, I might not be able to go at all, I mean, allowed to go. But now she has died, and you have come. I am not trapped any more. I am free. I can go quickly. No one has noticed, no one has guessed!"

"I had guessed, *querida*, I had noticed."

Faith leaned forward and gently traced the circles around Cristina's eyes; then she laid her hand lightly on the veiled breast, finding, as she expected, that it was full and firm under her touch. "Someone else would see what I have seen, very soon, if you stayed here. I was afraid today that you might faint at the funeral, and then . . . It is a mistake to suppose that only a changed figure can betray you. But do not be frightened, dear child. You are not trapped, as you put it, any longer. You shall leave at once, or at least within a few days, after all the funeral proprieties have been observed. There must be no look of flight about your departure.

Now that the Archduchess does not need you any more, a visit to your father is quite in order. That is proper, that will arouse no suspicion. But as far as I am concerned . . ."

She stopped, and looked away for a moment. Then she went on, in a resolute voice, "I think I ought to stay here, Cristina. I think it is best that you should go, but I think it is best that I should stay. We must be practical. The dowry for which your father sacrificed is tied up here. It must be released. The sheep which have been the mainstay of the place for centuries—now that Ernst is no longer here, who would see they were shepherded, if I did not? And the horses—the beautiful white horses—what about them?"

"The beautiful white horses do not matter so much. But the dapple-gray mare—the only one Hans Christian has bred—I thought, *madre mia*, that perhaps I could take her with me."

"Take it with you? How?"

"I could ride it, easily enough, from here to Danzig. I should not ride much now, I know. But that is not far enough to do me any harm. And from Danzig I could go over the frontier into Poland. After that, anyone could take the mare safely into Spain. I thought, you see, that you and I could start together, as if we were out for the afternoon. The dapple-gray means so much. She's a symbol."

"Yes, dear, I know. I understand how you feel. But so is Schönplatz. It is not an estate, a valuable property. It is a legacy, a symbol too. If Frau von Mitweld would have stayed here, perhaps I might have trusted it to her. But, as you know, it was hard to persuade her to come to her mother's funeral; it was impossible to persuade her to linger, after this was over. She feels too keenly about Karl and Luischen. And who can blame her?" Faith stopped again, remembering what Beatrice had said of Schönplatz earlier in the afternoon. This was no time for repeating that to Cristina; but with the thought of Beatrice, another idea entered Faith Marlowe's mind. "I do not think that I should leave here," she repeated. "Besides all the reasons I have mentioned, there is still the chance that Hans Christian might come here, instead of going to Spain, or at least, that he might send a message. So one of us should be at Schönplatz on that account. Obviously you should not start out alone, however. Nor could you take the dapple-gray with you, if you did that. But perhaps Beatrice would go with you. The American Ambassador's daughter, jaunting about the countryside, accompanied by a friend —what could be more in keeping with Trixie's character? I doubt if the frontier officials would even stop her, strict as they are."

Again it was a beautiful day when Beatrice Rhodes passed through Marienburg. This time Cristina was with her instead of Faith Marlowe, and she herself was not driving her sporty roadster; she was riding a snow-white horse, and wearing linen breeches and a soft shirt open at the throat, a sleeveless scarlet jacket, black boots. Her mop of brown hair was uncovered, her face and hands sun-tanned, her teeth dazzling against the line of her lips as she laughingly greeted the *Kontrol Offizier* at the long bridge. He recognized her and gave her a gay salute.

"You are leaving us here in East Prussia, *gnädiges Fräulein? Schade!*"

"The Frau Baronin and I are dining with the High Commissioner of Danzig. We thought it would be amusing to go there on horseback. If we continue to have a good time, we may go further. It is so pleasant to ride in the summer!"

He glanced from her to her companion. The Frau Baronin—*Ach ja!* That would be the wife—or the widow—of von Hohenlohe, who had disappeared, along with so many others, the night of the Thirtieth of June. Well . . . it was not for him to question the omnipotence of the Leader. On the other hand, he had received no instructions about the Baronin, and her papers, which he inspected, were entirely in order. Doubtless she was bent on seeing the High Commissioner to intercede for her husband, though what could the Commissioner of the "Free City" do? The *Kontrol Offizier* would have shrugged his shoulders if the Baronin's bearing had not somehow precluded him from such a gesture. Her type was not so much to his taste as the American girl's—there was a *Mädel* to warm any man's heart!—but it commanded respect, touched by reverence. She was mounted side-saddle on a fine dapple-gray mare, and wearing a long gray habit, superbly cut. Her glossy hair was coiled in black braids under her gray beaver hat, her hands hidden in spotless gray gloves. And her eyes were gray too, clear and cool as crystal. She did not laugh, like the bare-headed, red-coated American; but she smiled and bent her graceful head as he handed her back her passport.

"*Glückliche Reise! Und auf Wiedersehen!*" said the *Kontrol Offizier*, saluting again.

Faith Marlowe sat alone among the stillness and the shadows of Schönplatz that evening. In a day or two, she knew, awkward questions concerning Cristina's absence might arise; she must be prepared to answer them convincingly and calmly. There were also endless problems to be settled concerning the estate. It was true enough that she had acquired experience on her own New England farm and in the management of her money; but was this wide enough to enable her to cope with endless acres, priceless stock, and tangled investments? She must not permit herself to doubt that it was. And when it came to the people who would surround her—"blonde bitches" like Trüdchen, silly snobs like Frau von Edelblut—could she handle them with a touch seemingly light as foam but actually strong as steel? Well, she had never faltered yet in any human relation. Why should she now?

Briefly, and without concern, she considered her own career. At present the Senate was not in session. When it reconvened, in December, the entire picture might have changed. If it had not, she could always resign. She was midway through her second term now, she had proven her mettle and redeemed her heritage, she had made the way easier for other women to follow, because of the trail she had blazed. It would not cost her anything to renounce an honour which had alienated her from her only child, and which had been empty from the beginning, as far as her personal happiness was concerned.

Her happiness! What happiness had life ever brought her? She could not answer that demand as easily as she had dismissed the question of a career. It became relentless, while the darkness deepened around the place where she was sitting. Her father's failure, her mother's disgrace, her shadowed childhood, the disillusionment of her marriage, the waste of her beauty, her renunciation of romance . . . She could not evade the mounting memories of these any longer. Was it enough for a woman, when she reached middle age, to know that her conscience was clear and her record remarkable? Bowing her head, since there was now no one left to see that it was bent, Faith Marlowe told herself bitterly that such knowledge was vain.

A board creaked queerly on the stairway, and through the open window strange sounds seemed to mingle with the rustling of leaves. She heard them without heeding them. The White Lady of the Hapsburgs might have glided past her, so close that her ephemeral draperies fluttered in Faith's face, and Faith would not have noticed. The graves in the woodland cemetery might all have opened, disgorging the dead they entombed, and she would not have seen the ghostly file these formed: Hans von Hohenlohe, the younger, killed at the first battle of the Marne; Heinrich von Hohenlohe, dead in a Flemish hospital from wounds received at Ypres; Rudolf von Hohenlohe, fallen before Verdun; General Hans von Hohenlohe, father of these three, broken in body and mind by their loss, stricken here at Schönplatz; Victoria Luise, Archduchess of Austria, mother of these three, bearing herself like the daughter and consort of kings through a long life, but breaking at last with the betrayal of an empire. What a procession they might have made! If they marched before her that night, however, Faith was unmindful of them. Her vision was fixed, not on the ranks of the dead, but on the image of Sebastian de Cerreno as he had looked on the night when she first saw him, with a scarlet sash around his waist and the Order of the Golden Fleece encircling his neck.

It was nearly thirty years since that night, it was more than twenty since she had last seen him. But this was a memory that had never been stilled, and therefore it was not like those lesser ones, merely awakened. How had she ever withstood him, the greatest grandee of Spain, the greatest gallant in all Europe? He would have defied every law of Church and State to make her his, and still he had not prevailed against her will. To the very end, her chastity had been stronger than his charm. Yet now, sitting alone in the darkness, she asked herself one more question. It did not matter any more how she had withstood him. What mattered was, why she had withstood him, since in the end she had come after all only to this extremity of frustration and isolation.

It was a long time before she even tried to control her weeping. But at last she rose, and resolutely went from the dim drawing-room up the obscure stairway and into her own chamber, determined that never again would she abandon herself to despair or say that all joy had passed her by. Not now, when she knew, beyond any possibility of doubt, that Cristina, riding the dapple-gray, had gone safely past the Polish frontier, and that Hans Christian's child would not be born in Germany.

PART VIII

THE STRONG STRAIN
1936

CHAPTER XXIX

ANTONINA sat in the kitchen of Bautista Ramirez's flat, with her apron flung over her face, rocking back and forth, and uttering low wailing sounds, like a wounded animal. Her own cries kept her from hearing the hum of the bombing planes circling over Madrid; they also made her oblivious for a long time to the noise of the bell buzzing above her own head. When she did hear it, she remotely remembered that the door of the house was unlocked in any case, since it no longer mattered whether this was fastened or not; if someone were seeking her, it would be easy enough to walk up the stairs and come down the corridor past the empty bedrooms and the *salita* where the radio stood silent, into the kitchen where there were no more live coals burning in the apertures on top of the blackened stove.

After she remembered this, she bothered no more about it. What if someone were seeking her out—or if no one were? What did anything matter any more? She muffled her ears, already covered by her apron, more closely by placing her hands over them, and resumed her moaning. It was not until she felt a touch on her shoulder that she dully dropped her apron and looked up.

She did not recognize the man standing beside her. He was a cadaverous-looking creature, and a month earlier she would have screamed at such a sight. But she was used to horrible sights now. This man was only one of many she had seen. What he wanted with her she did not know.

"You don't remember me, Antonina. But you were very kind to me once. I hoped you would be again. I thought perhaps you would make me some coffee, or a *refresco*. I'm terribly thirsty. I'm thirsty all the time."

As he spoke, the man tried to moisten his lips with his tongue, and seemed to fail. Antonina perceived now that he was not a Spaniard. He did not talk like one, although his speech was quite intelligible, and he did not look like one. His eyes, staring out of the sockets in which they were sunk, were blue. Possibly they had been a bright blue once, though now this was glazed. His hair was a queer colour, streaked and faded; but it had never been black. It might have been golden or even red before it became so drab. His skin, abnormally gray, was still untinged by brown; it must have had a clear red and white colour in happier times. In spite of her own grief, Antonina felt sorry for this stranger, who was suffering and thirsty, though still she did not recognize him.

"The fire is out. I have had no heart to light it. But if the Señor will wait, I will build it up, I will make him some coffee. And I think there are still two or three oranges in the larder. At least I can mix these with water at once for a *refresco.*"

She rose and set to work, forgetting to moan as she did this, so genuine was her solicitude. The stranger sank down on a chair and did not speak to her again until he had drained the last drop of the drink she had made him.

"Do you know when Señor Ramirez will be in?" he said at last. "I want very much to see him, the first moment I can."

Antonina shrieked, and began to cross herself, only to let her fingers fall quickly again to her side, as she tardily recalled that such signs, once instinctive to her, were now allied with evil in her mind. "Do I know when Señor Ramirez will be in?" she cried shrilly. "Where are you from that you have not heard? What did you want with him—not that it matters, now he is butchered! Who are you that you come here asking such questions, at such a time as this?"

The man sank down into his chair again, and covered his face with his hands, moaning in his turn. It was the sound of the moan that made Antonina glance at him; but it was the sight of his hands that riveted her gaze. She had never seen such hands before, in the midst of all she had beheld in Madrid—so disfigured, so maimed, that she marvelled he could still manage to use them. Pity welled up in her once more, drowning her own grief.

"It is a terrible story, Señor, but since I see that you yourself have suffered, I will tell it to you quickly—in order that you may be on your way to seek succour elsewhere. If my *patrón* had only stayed in Madrid, all might still be well—who can say? The bombs fall down, hitting here and there as they come, but there are many they never touch. It may be they would never have touched him. However, he was fearful for the safety of his mother, who lived in Badajoz. The fate of women has been worse than the fate of men, Señor, whether they be old or young."

The stranger struggled to his feet, putting one of his maimed hands to his throat, as if he were choking. "Tell me your story faster," he muttered desperately. "If Bautista Ramirez can't help me, I must find someone else who can—some friend of his, someone who would be friendly to me."

"I am friendly to you, Señor, I will help you, if I can. I am all alone, I have no *patrón* any more. I will put myself at your service. I am only an old woman, a servant, but I have a brother, and perhaps . . . It was this way at Badajoz, Señor—in some places it has been different. . . . Men and women have been herded into the cemetery and shot down during the night, in groups. My *patrón* and his mother fell side by side. There, I have told you, it is finished, my story. Will you tell me yours?"

"Antonina, don't you remember an unexpected guest to whom you were very good, you and your *patrón* both, at the beginning of the revolution? A young man whom such a story would fill with sorrow? A travelling German who——"

At the word "German" the woman recoiled, as she might have shrunk from a snake. She shrieked again, and crossed herself, completely and unconsciously this time. "A German!" she screamed. "Do I remember? That smooth-faced boy who was set to spy on us? Who went back to his own country and spread lies about us? There are thousands of Germans in Spain now, fighting under Franco! I know, and my *patrón* knew before he died, who sent them, who spread the poison, who the traitor had been. . . ."

"Antonina, you're wrong, you're mistaken. Please listen to me! That boy wasn't a spy, he wasn't a traitor, he never said anything except that you'd been kind to him. He didn't even know there were any Germans in Spain now, fighting for Franco. He's—he's suffered himself, at the hands of the same men who sent them. He was taken out into the woods, and told to run for his life. Then he was shot through and through; finally left for dead. When he came to himself, he managed to drag himself to a road. He was picked up by a passing car, borne away, nursed and hidden. Then he was found and clapped into a concentration camp and his rescuers with him. He escaped, but he was the only one that did."

"If he had died too, the serpent's nest would have been emptier! But we shall crush them yet; we shall kill them all, as they have crushed and killed us!"

"Antonina, you must listen to me, you must help me. I'm trying to get through to my wife in Granada. I have a little son I've never seen. I was born in Spain myself, my baby was born in Spain. My wife's a Spaniard, all her people are Spaniards. The Cerrenos have lived in Spain for centuries."

"The *Cerrenos!* The intimates of Alfonso! The arch-enemies of freedom! The people who are plotting, on the inside, to destroy the Republic and restore the Monarchy! The renegades who are shooting patriots in cemeteries and mowing them down with machine-guns in bull rings!"

She was beside herself with fury. There was more than menace in her manner now, there was murder. A kitchen knife would have served her purpose as well as anything. She snatched at one, as Hans Christian eluded her. When the street outside swallowed him up, she was still pursuing him. Then another bomb burst, and her pursuit was over.

297

The American Embassy in Madrid was in an uproar. The distraught secretaries were striving to cope with a situation which was entirely out of hand, in the midst of tumultuous conditions. The Chancery was filled with terrified tourists and enraged businessmen. One more man, amidst the scores storming the doors, inevitably passed more or less unnoticed. Winthrop Ayer's nerves were already beyond the breaking point, when one of these importunates actually took hold of him.

"What do you mean by doing that? What do you want?"

"I'm sorry, but I've been here two hours already, and I didn't have a minute to lose in the beginning. I've got to get through to the south, I've got to get to my wife."

"Are you an American citizen?"

"No, but——"

"Good God, what are you doing, then? Get the hell out of here!"

"I'm Senator Marlowe's son. I have a right to ask for your help. I intend to have it."

"Senator Marlowe's son! The Nazi volunteer, who was hoist with his own petard! So you escaped, did you, finally? And now you've come grovelling to get back what you gave up of your own accord! Well, let me tell you right here and now, there are plenty of men who've shown more sense and more grit than you did, who'll get help from this Embassy before you will."

"The American Embassy in Berlin didn't take that attitude. It was Rufus Rhodes who saw to it that I got this far. I believe he was your chief once. You must know something about his methods. He sent a wire to the Ambassador here."

"He sent a wire to the Ambassador here! Well, the Ambassador isn't here himself! He's gone over the border into France. And what do you think wires amount to, when civil war breaks out overnight?"

"We didn't any of us know civil war had broken out when I left Paris. We only knew that telephone service with Spain had been cut off, that radios weren't working. There were rumours that there'd been 'incidents' at Cuenca, a 'revolt' at Cartagena. But these were just reports. I didn't have any trouble about reservations. Then when I got to Hendaye, I couldn't get over the border. The trains weren't running and neither were the trolleys. Strikers were tearing up the rails. I lost a lot of time I couldn't afford to lose. But finally I heard that eight buses flying red flags as a badge of safe conduct were taking refugees from San Sebastian to Biarritz. They were supposed to go back empty, but I persuaded the driver of one to let me hide in it. The usual method of persuasion still works, though the rates are higher. I've used it all the way to Madrid. But apparently I got out of San Sebastian just in time. There are rumours that the Insurgents are upon it already."

Winthrop Ayer had begun to regard the interloper with reluctant admiration. Hans Christian, conscious that he had produced the effect necessary to galvanize the Secretary into action, went on more tersely.

"All this is beyond the point. The point is that I'm going to rejoin Mr. Rhodes in France as soon as I can get back there. I'm sailing for America on the same boat with him and his family. They're waiting for me at Versailles until I can get back. I'm taking my wife and child out of Spain with me. If there's any avoidable delay in carrying out his plan, you'll be responsible. You'll answer for it, eventually and officially, to the Secretary of State. And you'll answer for it to me personally right here and now and again after I become an American citizen. That won't be so long either."

Hans Christian drew a deep breath. A different look came into his sunken eyes as he spoke. Winthrop Ayer, shrinking back from the sight of the hands laid upon his own, tried to shake himself free. But he knew he was caught and cornered. He knew that whoever else waited and for what, this escaped exile who held him in his mutilated grasp must get through to Granada that night.

It was two hours later still before the *salvo conducto* from the War Office was actually in Hans Christian's possession. By that time the last scheduled train had left Madrid for the south, and in any case no trains were running on schedule. Winthrop Ayer mentioned this, unresourcefully, as he and Hansel went down the steps of the Ministry together.

"Will you lend me your car? If I stop to buy one, that'll involve still more delay—even supposing I don't run into fresh complications in trying to make the purchase!"

"I'll be very glad to, of course, but you see——"

Hans Christian did not wait to see. He had always been a rapid runner, and weak as he was, he had no trouble in gaining the bottom of the steps before Winthrop Ayer grasped his purpose. The Secretary's car, bearing diplomatic licence plates and flying the American flag, was parked at the kerb. It was veering around the corner, with Hans Christian in it, by the time the outraged Bostonian had reached the sidewalk.

Hans Christian had been over the road from Madrid to Granada only once, when he had made the trip in Sebastian's "glorified gypsy waggon." lying down all the way and sleeping a large part of it. So he had nothing but instinct now to guide him in getting out of the city. But the sense of direction which comes with habitual driving stood him in good stead; he did not make a single false turn as he steered his way southward through the tortuous streets. He was determined not to stop, of his own accord, to ask the way, and thus lose still more time, if he could help it; and nobody attempted to stop him.

There was no disorder in this quarter of the city. The populace was preoccupied, the police recognized the number plates, and a few Spanish soldiers actually saluted the flag, He gained the open highway without opposition or impediment.

As he sped over it, he drew deep breaths of relief and refreshment. A glance at the gauge had shown him that the tank was full of petrol; it would be hours before he would require more. He could afford to disregard the problem of refuelling until it arose. It was hours since he had eaten, but he was not hungry, and he was conscious of no pain in his hands as these rested on the wheel. The summer night was bountiful in its beauty. The warm air stirred slightly; there was freshness in it, and fragrance. Stars shone overhead, and a full moon. The fields were filled with released radiance, the road was a silvery band between them, leading to Andalusia, "the land blessed by God"—"*tierra de Maria Santissima.*"

By this time Cristina would have had his messages—oh, long before this! He had sent her one the moment he had been over the Belgian border, another as soon as he had reached Paris, still another from Hendaye. She would be expecting him, waiting for him, watching for him. Probably he would see her as soon as he reached the outer courtyard, standing at the grilled gate leading to the patio, with a flower in her hair and the baby in her arms: his son, whom he had never seen, but whose birth had brought about his deliverance.

Pressing down harder and harder upon the accelerator, drinking in deeper and deeper draughts of the scented air, he put together the pieces which formed the pattern of this deliverance. He knew now that Cristina had kept in close touch with Trixie after she had gone back to Spain; and Trixie, in her turn, had kept going at regular intervals to the Bomb Palast. The first time, when Faith Marlowe had been there with her, Oskar Kraus had slammed the door in her face. But the second time, when she had gone alone, he had grudgingly consented to let her in . After that he had come to take her visits as a matter of course, eventually to look forward to them. Apparently she had been very tolerant and very tactful. She had managed to keep their conversations impersonal over a prolonged period. And when she had finally spoken of Hans Christian she had done so almost incidentally but very appealingly.

"I had a letter from Sebastian de Cerreno today—you remember, the Spaniard of whom I told you, who has suffered so much from the Communists. But this letter was almost happy. He has a little grandson—a real Christmas *Kindlein*. I do wish there were some way we could let Hansel know—if he is still alive. Don Sebastian says the baby looks exactly like him—golden hair, blue eyes, fair skin, all that. And at this season—— If any of us only knew how to reach Hansel, or whether it was worth while to try again——"

After that she had spoken of other things. But when she had risen to leave, she had suggested that perhaps Oskar would come to the Embassy on Christmas Eve.

"Now that Hansel is not here to cook your dinner and trim your tree I am afraid it is dismal for you at the Bomb Palast. I should like to try to give you a good time myself, since he can't. I have never forgotten how kind you were to me when I was hit on the head, the first time I met you. You have a very gentle touch, Oskar. You would be wonderful with children yourself. Well—— My father and mother told me to say that they would also be very pleased to welcome you and Max on Christmas Eve. *Auf Wiedersehen.*"

"*Auf Wiedersehen, gnädiges Fräulein.*"

Oskar and Max had been genuinely touched by Trixie's invitation and they accepted it. As the party was drawing to an end, Oskar whispered to Trixie in saying good-night.

"Hansel is alive. He has been very ill, but he is better. He was lost for a long time, but I know where he is now, and I have found a way to send him a message about the *Kindlein.* Since it came at Christmas-time, and since it is so like him, with golden hair and blue eyes, I felt——"

"I knew you would, Oskar. I can't tell you how grateful I am. You've made my Christmas a happy one too."

She had asked no questions, either then or later. When Oskar told her, eventually, that he thought he might get into closer touch with the prisoner, she had not pressed him for details. She had only nodded, and said she was very glad. More than a year had gone by, after that, before Oskar had asked her, without preamble, if she would be afraid to take a long ride with him at night, in her car, and whether she had large sums of money easily available. She had answered almost nonchalantly that she would be pleased to go out with him at any time, in her own car or any other, and that she always had large sums of money lying around and was always wondering what to do with them. As if to prove the point, the catch to her handbag had come unclasped, and a roll of bills had fallen to the floor. She had not picked them up.

All this Trixie had told Hans Christian herself, in her own words, on the night they met in the woods, and now he recalled every syllable she had spoken. It was not such a night as this, balmy and beautiful. A cold unseasonable rain had been pouring down, and the wind had lashed the trees about, and both wind and rain had stung them in the face. But Trixie had not seemed to mind. She was caped and hooded in scarlet cellophane, from which the water poured down, and she did not trouble to shake it from her face. She carried a big bag and a smaller one, both encased in waterproof covers, and she did not seem to mind the weight of these either. She talked quickly, but without any show of excitement.

"You must get into some of the clothes I have here. They're your own, they'll fit you all right. You'll get soaking wet, but that can't be helped. You can change into dry things on the train."

"What train?"

"The night express to Cologne. I have your tickets here and a compartment reserved for you. We've got plenty of time to catch it, if we don't dawdle. There's a passport in the envelope with the tickets—an American passport. We doctored up an old snapshot I took of you on the boat and had it rephotographed, and I copied your signature from one of the letters you wrote me when you first got to Schönplatz—just the Christian Marlowe part, of course. It's a pretty neat piece of forgery, if I do say so. . . . Please don't try to talk, Chris. There really isn't time. Just one thing more. I won't say it before Oskar, then it will be true he never heard anything about your plans. I don't think you'll have a bit of trouble if you take a train at Cologne for Brussels. But if you'd feel any easier, go to the American Consul. He's a good scout, and I know he motors over into Belgium every day or so to buy vegetables. He'll take you with him. By the time you get to Paris, we'll be there too—Mother and Daddy and I. Meet us at the Meurice. We'll have a room engaged for you and your reservations all made to Madrid."

Again he tried to speak to her, and again she interrupted him.

"I'm going back to the car now to wait for you. Here's a flashlight I brought for you in case you couldn't feel for your things. But don't use it any more than you have to."

Oskar was waiting in the car as well as Trixie when Hans Christian came up to it. They greeted each other briefly.

"Did you have any trouble getting out?"

"No. It was surprisingly simple—at the end. I won't go into all the rest. But finally it was merely a matter of *Trinkgeld* for a couple of troopers, and 'leave of absence' for an hour's rendezvous. They agreed, by the time they were half drunk, that even prisoners needed to have one occasionally." He could not have made such a statement before Cristina, but with Trixie it was easy and natural. "You're sure you're not going to get into trouble, Oskar, for your share in this?"

"I haven't had any share, beyond locating you in the first place and getting a few messages through to you. Fräulein Rhodes has done everything else."

It still proved futile to try talking to Trixie, so Hans Christian went on talking to Oskar instead, though nothing they said to each other was of much consequence. When they reached the station they said good-bye in the car, so that they would not be seen together going through the waiting-room or crossing the platform. But Trixie boarded the train with him and saw him safely into his compartment. He put his arms around her and clung to her, shaking all over, with tears of weakness and emotion streaming down his cheeks. For a few moments she steadied and supported him, until he had regained some measure of self-control. Then without apparent effort she disengaged herself.

"Good-bye, Chris; I have to go. The train will start in a minute. But remember, I'll be in Paris when you get there. I'm going to take the morning plane. Don't worry any more than you can help. And whether you worry or not, don't break down or back down."

He had done his best to meet her challenge, and on the whole he had succeeded. He sped along now with no sense of shame and with one of increasing exaltation. At every village and crossroad he was stopped by guards, but the delay they caused him was brief. They raised their fists in the salute of the People's Front and said, "*Salud!*" They asked to see his credentials and gave these a cursory glance. Usually this was all, before they waved him on his way again. He made good time, for the road was almost empty. Then suddenly it was choked with soldiers. They were a sorry-looking lot, ill clad and ill armed. Most of them were clad in the dark smock of the Spanish peasant. Some might have come straight from the fields, others direct from small shops. Several looked sick, a few really ruffianly. Scattered women, wearing rumpled blouses and dangling ornaments, marched beside them, and among these were girls, hardly more than children—younger than Cristina had been when Hans Christian first saw her, almost as young as Cecilia. Gay, impudent, rollicking Cecilia! How good it would seem to hear her laugh again!

The soldiers were going south, like himself. As long as he crawled along behind them, they paid almost no attention to him. But he could not afford to continue at this snail's pace. Neither could he take the risk of running one of them down, if he tried to cleave his way through their ranks without warning. He blew his horn, hoping against hope that they would part of their own accord and let him through. But he was instantly called upon to halt. The soldiers closed in around the car with a certain show of ferocity. Several shouted to him simultaneously to show his credentials and explain his errand. One of them raised a dilapidated musket in a threatening gesture. Hans Christian shut off his engine and spoke with the serious politeness to which he had never failed to find a ready response in Spain.

"*Buenas noches, amigos!* May I give three or four of you a lift? We seem to be all travelling in the same direction. You will see, *Señor Capitán*, by this car and these documents, that I am an American. And you will sympathize with my errand, I am sure of that. I have a Spanish sweetheart, whom I have not seen in some time.

303

Since we parted, there has been a *niño*. I am hurrying to her, to assure her of my undying love, and of my eagerness to clasp our child in my arms."

The ferocious frowns changed to smiles; the man with the musket cheered. The ragged individual whom Hans Christian had addressed as *Señor Capitán* handed back the extended papers with a flourish. He had recognized both the seal of the War Office and the flag flying in front of the radiator. He did not even glance at the passport.

"*Por favor, camarada.* If you are in earnest, four of us will accept your offer and ride with you as far as Valdepeñas. I will do so because it is imperative that I should reach there as soon as possible, and my friend Felipe, because he is lame and it pains him to march While if two of these ladies who are with us and who are very tired——"

"It will be my pleasure, *Señor Capitán.* Let us be on our way. I too am in a hurry to reach Valdepeñas. Can I buy petrol there, and a drink?"

"As to the drink, that is certain. But the petrol—I do not know. You will understand, *camarada,* that it is necessary to commandeer and conserve it. But I have a cousin who keeps a small garage there. He might be able to help you, in return for favours received."

They were off, shouting their farewells to the rank and file left behind. The Captain had seated himself in front, beside Hans Christian. Felipe, his lame leg extended, sat in the rear between the two "ladies," a steadying arm around each. One of them was a woman of thirty, with intense eyes and an aquiline profile. She spoke very little, and that through compressed lips; but the gaze she turned on Felipe was tender. The other was the very young girl who had made Hans Christian think of Cecilia. She had the same careless laughing manner, the same dark vivid beauty. There was nothing coarse or common about her looks. She had the basic refinement which Hans Christian had noticed in nearly all Spanish women. But she was plainly pregnant, and he marvelled that she should have started out on such a march, when her hour must be so near. She must be passionately attached to her lover, indifferent to suffering, oblivious of danger. This also was the way of Spanish women, as Hans Christian knew.

He questioned them about the war. Did they know how far the Insurgents had penetrated already? The Captain became voluble. Cadiz had fallen first; that was where Franco, the Insurgent General, had landed with his foreign legions when he flew over from Morocco. Since then it had been bombed. General Queipo de Llano, commanding the garrison in Seville, had joined the Revolutionists. Indeed, he had sent an enthusiastic message to Franco saying that all the garrisons in Andalusia were going over to him, as well as the Navy. The message had ended with the words, "No earthly power

304

can check our triumphant movement."

"So he says," the Captain concluded almost gaily, "which shows how little he knows about the matter. For we shall check him—the men and women like those you have with you, *camarada*. What if Cordoba has been taken too? We shall recapture it. What if half Malaga is in flames? The other half still stands!"

"And Granada?"

"We are still holding Granada, though the Insurgents are very close. At any minute they may enter it. Was it to Granada that you were going, *camarada*?"

"Not into the city. To a *caseria* some kilometres this side of it."

"Ah, then all may be well. Let us trust that all may be well."

Hans Christian noticed that the Captain did not say "Let us pray that all may be well." But he himself prayed, silently mingling his petitions with assertions which he tried hard to believe. O God, keep them safe!! Don't let anything happen to them! Of course they're all right. The Insurgent lines haven't spread to Granada. Even if they have the Cerrenos will be safeguarded. The only difficulty will be in getting through. The Safe Conduct will be of no value then. On the contrary, I shall have to hide it, it will be incriminating. But the American flag, the diplomatic licence plates, the Special Passport —Christ, those are all any man would need! Christ, grant that they may be!

Felipe went to sleep with his head against the curving breast of the woman with the great intense eyes. She put her arm around him protectively, and gazed steadfastly ahead of her. Every now and then the young girl leaned forward to exchange a lingering embrace with the Captain. Their lips met hungrily and repeatedly, and finally he drew her forward and held her on his lap until they reached Valdepeñas. Still holding her, he directed Hans Christian how to reach his cousin's shop, and when he descended from the car he did not release her, but kept her close to him while he talked about the petrol. There was a difficulty, as he had anticipated; indeed, cars as well as petrol were now subject to commandeering. But he told the story of the American's kindness, and of his purpose, graphically and sympathetically, and the cousin was much moved. It was forbidden, of course. But still—— Enough petrol to get to Granada, was that the requirement? Well, probably it would never be missed. Motioning Hans Christian to drive inside the shed, where their movements could not be seen by idle and curious passers-by, the man opened a large tin can and began to pour its contents into the tank. Meanwhile, the Captain and his sweetheart entered an adjacent house, and, returning to the shed, brought with them beer and bread, cheese and olives.

Hans Christian had not known that he was hungry. Now he devoured the food ravenously and drank down the beer at one draught.

305

It was necessary to wake and dislodge Felipe before he could proceed, but the cripple tumbled out philosophically. When Hans Christian climbed back into the car again, the older woman touched him gently on the arm.

"If I could be of service to you, *camarada*, I will go on with you. You have helped us so much—— I know the road to Granada well, and the crossroads guards know me, and so do all our soldiers. You will not be stopped if you meet more troops, and you can go faster if you do not have to watch the way."

"But Felipe? Who will care for him while you are gone?"

"He will not lack for care, *camarada*, you may be sure of that."

The younger girl had spoken proudly. Hans Christian knew she was telling the truth. He tried, tactfully, to offer her a little present, "for the need she would soon have of it," and after she had looked at the Captain questioningly, she accepted it with a flash of white teeth and a volley of grateful words. When Hans Christian last saw her she was standing with her arm linked through her lover's, shaking her curly hair back from her laughing face.

The moon had melted into the sunrise. The heat of the day had fallen early. It came and went in waves around the speeding car. The woman at Hans Christian's side was very quiet, completely controlled. Though there was no physical resemblance, something in her manner made him think of his mother, almost as poignantly as the young girl had made him think of Cecilia—his mother whom he had so tardily remembered. It had been only Cristina of whom he had thought, with any degree of concern, throughout the horrors of his imprisonment. Yet he had learned from Trixie, in Paris, that Faith Marlowe had come to Germany at once when she heard of his plight, that she had moved heaven and earth to secure his release, and that she had stayed steadfastly at Schönplatz until she had been literally dispossessed.

"As long as no one knew where you were she had the upper hand," Trixie explained. "The Gestapo chiefs were telling the truth when they said they couldn't give any information. Of course, their original instructions had been 'Shoot to kill!' When the murderers returned to the scene of the crime and found the 'corpse' missing, they were pretty puzzled. It wasn't until they had tracked you down in your hiding-place and dragged you off to prison that the *Regierungspräsident* of the Schönplatz area could write to your mother to tell her that your property was *sichergestellt*. Did he send you a duplicate document? I believe that's supposed to be the correct thing, when the government becomes a 'benevolent custodian, prior to confiscation."

"Yes, I had the document, but I never heard from my mother, and I suppose none of my letters reached her. Is—is Schönplatz confiscated?"

"It must be, by this time. Confiscation seems to be automatic, if a prisoner flees the country. That and loss of citizenship. You're not a German any more, Chris."

"No, I'm not a German any more."

Trixie had said nothing further about that, knowing how it would hurt, and neither had he; but she handed him the letters which Faith Marlowe had sent him in her care at the Meurice. It would be only a matter of days, perhaps of hours, his mother wrote, with characteristic brevity and reserve, before she would be called upon to surrender Schönplatz, now that his escape was known. The buildings and grounds were in good condition; she had kept them in the best possible repair. She supposed that the stud would be very valuable to the government; it might serve to supplement Trahkenen. And of course there were always the sheep. She hoped he would not reproach her for failing to save the property for him. She had staved off usurpation as long as possible. And she had become attached to the place herself, in the long quiet months she had spent there. She would regret to leave it. But she felt sure she could at least assure him that the woodland cemetery would always be respected.

Remembering the mocking laughter of Max, with whom he had once passed Stresemann's tomb in the St. Nicolai Cemetery, Hans Christian felt less certain of this, and his heart contracted. But this was not only because of the dead. It was also because of the living. He could see his mother, unshielded and unsupported, confronting the confiscators with the same courage which had enabled her to keep them so long at bay. He knew that she would have done it with firm lips and an unbent head, even at the very moment of turning over the keys. She must have gone through the paddocks and the pens, one last time alone, and through the fields and the forest, as well as from the top to the bottom of the house. But if her eyes had been blurred with tears as she walked, her step would still have been steady——

"She'll be at Hamstead waiting for you when you and Cristina and the baby get there," Trixie said, as if she had read his thoughts. "She'll feel better when she gets home. She sent me a letter too. About something I said to her once when she and I were talking about you. I told her I'd rather see a man survive than a house. She wrote to say I'd been right. I was, too, that time, anyhow, Chris."

"There was another time when you were right, Trixie. The time when you talked to me in the Spreewald. I haven't forgotten."

She had not forgotten either, but she did not say so. She only urged him on, paving the way for his departure. Nothing that she could do had been left undone. But even Trixie had not been able to foresee the explosion in Spain.

As he thought of all this, Hans Christian turned to look at the

307

woman beside him and was again struck by her spiritual resemblance to his mother. She had not spoken to him once, on her own initiative, since they left Valdepeñas. But she had responded, sympathetically, every time he spoke to her. He felt increasingly drawn to her.

"Have you a son, *Señora*?" he asked impulsively.

She smiled, and as she did so her face became beautiful. "*Sí, camarada*," she said in a glad voice. "He is a good son and a great toreador. I love him deeply and I am very proud of him besides, with reason. He has filled my home with joy and honour. A mother is blessed in such a boy."

"I shouldn't have thought that you were old enough to have a grown son, *Señora*. Is it your only one?"

"Yes, it is my only one. But you know what the lioness said to the jackal who taunted her: 'It is true that I have a cub instead of a litter. But that cub is a lion.'"

"I'm an only son too, *Señora*. I wish I thought my mother had reason to feel about me as you feel about your son."

"You may be sure she does, *camarada*, whether there is reason for it or not. That is the way with mothers."

She smiled again, and, as if in afterthought, suggested that he should let her out at Jaen. She had relatives there, she could rest before she started back to Valdepeñas. The rest of the way would be clear. There were no more troops on the march, and it was evident now that there would be no lines to pass through. She wished him well, and thanked him for his kindness. He thanked her a hundred times for hers. They kissed each other and parted as friends and allies, with the expressed hope of meeting each other again in happier times. He felt sure that from that time forward he would never instinctively regard a Communist as an enemy.

The perfumed patio had never looked more lovely than when Hans Christian entered it. Even the flow of the fountain seemed more musical than before, and on the bench beside it lay Cristina's guitar, carelessly laid down. But the patio was empty. Hans Christian called, and only the echo of his own voice answered him. He walked through the *galeria* and found it empty also. Then, frantically, he began to go through one room after another. Their vacancy mocked him as he passed along.

It was not until he reached the winding stair leading to the turret that he heard a small smothered cry. A great tapestry hung on the wall there, and underneath it was hidden a door leading to a small secret space. He wrenched down the drapery and flung the entrance open. Inside the hideaway Catalina was crouching, holding a child in her arms.

He needed no one to tell him that this was his son. Wide blue

308

eyes looked up at him trustfully under a tangle of red-gold curls. He snatched the boy from the servant and hugged him hungrily to his heart. But at the same instant he asked a desperate question.

"What has happened? Where is everyone? What has become of your mistress?"

"*Disculpe, Señor Baron*. A detachment of the Red Forces has been this way. It was Doña Cristina herself who first saw them as they approached, who hid me and the *niño*. After that, I do not know. She made me swear by the memory of my mother that I would save him, whatever happened."

"And what has happened?"

"How can I tell, Señor? If the house is empty, everyone else is gone. But I have kept my promise. You see that the child is safe."

The old woman was crying bitterly. A puzzled expression came into the child's trustful eyes. Then he smiled, and, crowing, leaned forward from his father's arms to pat her face. Her tears fell on his small rosy hand.

"You've done all you could, Catalina, I know that. But now you must help me search. We must find Doña Cristina, we must find them all."

"Have you been to the library yet, Señor Baron? You know that Don Sebastian is often in the library. We can look. He may have hid the others himself."

"No, I haven't been to the library yet. Yes, we can look."

He was already on his way up the stairs again, carrying his son. Something told him that he would find Sebastian there, and he was not mistaken. His father-in-law had not been mercifully killed. He had been bound hand and foot and left to starve. He was still conscious when Hansel reached him. But he was beyond speech.

"Where is Cristina? What has become of her?" Hans Christian was past coherent words himself. But Sebastian had collapsed utterly as he was released, and had fallen to the floor in a huddled heap. With mounting frenzy, Hansel stooped over him. "Sebastian, you must talk to me, you must tell me! Where shall I go? What shall I do?"

"It is too late. If you had only come yesterday! Cristina had your message. She watched for you all day. But now you can't go anywhere. You can't do anything. They have all been taken away."

"All? Not just Cristina? Cecilia and Doña Dolores too?"

"Yes. Cecilia and Dolores too. Cristina was playing her guitar, Cecilia was reading a funny story. Dolores was still at prayer when they took her from her prie-dieu. They were all brought in here after I was bound, stripped and raped before my eyes. Afterwards they were dragged away to the parish church. Don't go there, don't try to see the end. Take your child—the child Cristina saved for you —and flee before it's too late."

"Sebastian, you're beside yourself, you don't know what you're saying. Where is this parish church?" And as the only answer was a groan, he struggled to his feet again, and spoke sternly to the weeping woman beside him. "Catalina, you must tell me where this church is. Clearly, so I can find it without delay. And then you must stay with Don Sebastian and the *niño* until I return. Do you hear? Doña Cristina trusted you and I do too."

"Señor Baron, do as Don Sebastian has said. Take the child and flee. I will stay here with Don Sebastian and care for him faithfully as long as we are allowed to live. But do not go yourself to the parish church. It will be like the Church of Santa Maria at Baeza."

"And what happened at the Church of Santa Maria in Baeza?"

"It was there, Señor——"

"Yes, Catalina, tell me quickly!"

"We do not know for certain. But we heard that there all the women who resisted were butchered. May God have mercy on their souls and on us!'

He found the church fast enough. It was not far away. Its doors stood wide open. But they were blocked by corpses. Hans Christian stumbled over them and found the floor strewn with many, as he searched for one.

It was Cecilia he saw first. Then Doña Dolores. They were close together, and though many of them were mutilated, they still retained in death a little of the look they had possessed in life. Horror had closed down so quickly upon them that Cecilia had not lost all her childish charm, or Doña Dolores all her pious precision. He could believe the one had been laughing, the other praying, when she was overcome. There were some vestments lying near them, that had been torn asunder and trampled under foot. He picked them up, smoothed them out, and placed them reverently over the mother and daughter. Then he went on through the crowded nave.

It was not until he reached the altar that he found Cristina, lying on the steps. The crucifix and candlesticks had toppled over, but the altar cloth was still in place. He drew it off and laid it lightly over her. As he did so, he saw her eyelids flutter, Instantly he was on his knees beside her, calling to her.

"Cristina, I've come for you, I'm here. My darling, it isn't too late!"

Her eyelids fluttered again, her lips moved slightly, forming his name.

"I knew you would come, *querido*. It is never too late for your coming."

He put his arms around her, drawing her head against his breast, and as he did so, he saw a stain on the altar cloth grow brighter and deeper. But he saw too that she was still trying to speak, still trying to smile. He bent over more closely to catch the words.

"The child and the horse—they're both safe. I saved them for you —the strong strain."

"Yes, darling, I know. I know. I'll keep them both safe. I'll take them with me to America. But don't try to talk about them. Tell me that you love me. Let me hear you say that again."

"I'll say it over and over again, until the end comes. But there is something else besides——"

"Yes, Cristina?"

"There is my father. Promise me you'll make him go too."

"I promise. I'll make him go too."

"And ask Beatrice—if she would help you. She is so strong—I won't be afraid—for you—or the boy—if I'm sure——"

"I promise you. I'll ask for her help. And take it. As much as she'll give me."

Cristina closed her eyes. The red stain was not spreading any more. She lay very still. But she spoke to Hans Christian once more, with her lips against his.

"It was like this—in your arms—that I found life—*alma de mi alma*. And now—in your arms—I meet death. What does it matter— that one follows the other? You have made them both—so sweet."

PART IX

MORE SACRED STILL
1936

CHAPTER XXX

"OF course I never talk about it without being pressed, but I went over on purpose to be presented at Court. The Secretary of State suggested it to me himself, one evening when he took me in to dinner at the British Embassy. You know that's very exclusive in Washington nowadays, not at all like the French, where congressmen and writers and all sorts of queer people like that are invited. Well, as I was saying, Mr. Estabrook seemed to make such a point of it that I felt I couldn't refuse, though what I should really have enjoyed would have been a nice quiet summer in the country—one of those quaint villages in Vermont, for instance, where all the old houses have been reclaimed from the natives. Michael Trent, a great friend of the Secretary's, is our Ambassador to England now, and he and his wife, who is simply charming, did *everything* to make my stay in London pleasant. I went to the Royal Enclosure at Ascot, and to tea on the terrace of the Parliament Buildings, and—oh, everywhere! I didn't have a free moment, it was almost as hectic as Washington. I really think I'll have to go to a nursing home for a few weeks before the season there begins, because I've been rushing all around the Continent too—Deauville and Carlsbad and places like that, so exhausting! And finally the usual siege with Paris dressmakers. They certainly are the most unmitigated thieves and liars in the world. I was disappointed in almost everything I bought, and still I don't know how I'm ever going to get through the customs. They're more arrogant and unreasonable every year, aren't they? Naturally I wouldn't really smuggle, but——"

"I think I've kept pretty well within my hundred dollars. I don't expect to have much trouble. I don't go to the big houses—I've found the little ones so much more satisfactory. That's the way the French feel about it themselves, of course. And then I never waste much time on shopping. Our stores in Texas have all the latest styles, and besides, there are so many more important things to do in Europe than to spend days and days getting fitted. I came over as one of the delegates to the Biennial of the Women's International League for Peace and Prosperity. In fact, I don't like to brag, but I've just been elected one of its Vice-Presidents by the largest vote any American's ever received for such an office. We had our meeting in Vienna this year, and I think it's simply ridiculous to talk as if any sort of trouble were brewing there. Why, everything was just as pleasant as possible! The little sidewalk cafés all crowded, and orchestras playing, and nicely dressed people enjoying themselves. I've always heard it was one of the most delightful cities in Europe, and now I'm convinced of it. I took a wonderful side trip too, down the Danube to Budapest. There were special rates for the delegates to the Congress, and the Hungarian women gave us a marvellous welcome. I think it's very inspiring to realize how women from all parts of the world are coming closer together in these days, don't you? It makes one so hopeful for the future. Now there was an Estonian lady I met—a most superior person—who explained to me all the reasons why the Baltic States would cling together and prevent aggression. Not that I believe there's going to be aggression. I think all those reports are greatly exaggerated. But I mean just in case——"

"Yes, I suppose so. I've never taken much interest in club work myself. You see in Washington there's such a constant round—why, last winter I didn't dine at home alone for six weeks running! And, as I said, London's just as bad. Of course, I've always had a great many English friends; in fact, one of my cousins married a member of the nobility. He's the most charming man you ever saw. His clothes have that *sculptured* look that make American men seem so unkempt. These cousins of mine have an enchanting place in Sussex, and I spent a weekend there—Thursday to Tuesday, you know. The English certainly understand the arts of leisure better than we do. They make you feel it's vulgar to go tearing after money. Two English ladies—I mean real ladies—who had been presented at the same time I was, were at this house party, and it was pleasant to talk over the drawing-room with them. All the little details. For instance——"

"You don't suppose we're going to be alone at this table all the way over, do you? Of course I understand that the Captain never appears before the second or third day because of his duties, but certainly all the others he's asked to sit here can't be sick already. I wonder who they are, don't you? Frankly, as I looked around the deck this morning I didn't see anyone whom I thought would be likely to receive such an invitation. I've crossed ten times now, in connection with my Peace and Prosperity Work, and I'm always struck with the ordinary appearance of most people on shipboard. I often wonder what becomes of all the distinguished persons who travel. But perhaps——"

"Good morning. I'm sorry to be a little late. My father and mother asked to be excused. They're rather tired, so they're lunching on our verandah. But they'll be down to dinner."

The girl who had spoken so cordially slipped into one of the

313

vacant seats at the Captain's table and began to study the menu, apparently oblivious of the fact that her two table companions were avidly studying her. It was painfully evident to them both that she had been having no trouble with dressmakers and that she had not been patronizing little houses either. Her powder blue flannels were exquisite in both cut and colour, and the moulded felt hat, finished with a simple silk cord, which she wore with them, matched them perfectly as to shade and style. There were aquamarine clips at the neckline of her dress, and she had on a single ring which was also set with one large aquamarine. She looked up at the hovering steward with an agreeable smile.

"Can you recommend the caviare?" she inquired. "Yes, I'm sure it's delicious. I'll have that first, please. Then partridge, and lettuce with pâte de fois gras. A glass of sherry, very dry. Black coffee afterwards."

She laid down the card, and turned again to the women beside her.

"This is Mrs. Delmaine of Washington, isn't it?" she inquired. "And Mrs. Brice of Fort Worth? The Captain told us we would have the pleasure of being with you—he's just dropped in to see us for a few minutes. He'll be here for dinner too. I'm sure you'll like him. We've crossed with him two or three times and we do, tremendously. Oh, I must introduce myself! My name is Beatrice Rhodes."

Mrs. Brice beamed. Mrs. Delmaine purred. Both spoke almost simultaneously.

"Miss Rhodes! Why, I hadn't heard! I've wanted so much to meet your mother and somehow I've just missed her several times. Is the Ambassador going home on leave? I hadn't seen any announcement——"

"Yes, Father's on leave rather indefinitely. We've been in Versailles more than a month, waiting for friends to join us. Their plans have been very uncertain, so ours have too. There hasn't been any announcement."

"But how wonderful that everything has turned out so pleasantly, and that you're on this boat! It's such a privilege——"

The caviare had come, beautifully embedded in ice, surrounded by lemon delicately sliced. Beatrice soothed the solicitous steward, assuring him of its perfection in her eyes. But after she had tasted it appreciatively, and broken into a piece of melba toast, she laid down her fork.

"Everything hasn't turned out as pleasantly as we'd hoped. Will you forgive me if I tell you a little about it? On such short acquaintance and all? Because I think perhaps it will be easier all around if I do. Especially as two of the persons whom the Captain invited to sit at his table may not feel that they can. I hope they will, but perhaps they won't. So I think you ought to know why—in a general way."

She picked up her toast again. She did not eat it, but neither did she crumble it. She held it firmly in her shapely tanned fingers.

"When Father and Mother and I left Germany," she said, "we joined a great friend of ours who had just gone over the frontier. You may have heard of him. He's quite well known. Some people call him Hans von Hohenlohe. Some people call him Christian Marlowe. It doesn't matter what you call him. He's one of the grandest persons in the whole world."

She was speaking quietly, attracting no attention at the surrounding tables. But there was a ring in her voice which had a strange effect upon her hearers. They both felt spellbound as they listened to her.

"We all came to Paris together and then Chris went on to Spain. His wife and his little boy were there, with his wife's family in Granada. He was very eager to get to them as soon as possible, and bring them back with him. The day after he left us, civil war broke out. He didn't even know it had started until he was almost to Madrid. By the time he could get to Granada, terrible things had happened. His wife's family had been practically wiped out—her uncle, her sister, her mother. She—died herself, just after he got there. But her father and her baby were still alive. Chris brought them back to us. They're on this boat with us now."

Beatrice Rhodes paused and her listeners both managed, this time, to murmur something unintelligibly sympathetic as she did so. She went steadily on.

"The baby has an old Spanish nurse. He's well and happy; he's stopped crying for his mother already. But Chris—and Sebastian de Cerreno—I'm sure you'll understand why you may never see them, why it's better I should tell you the truth before all sorts of wild stories start circulating around the boat. You could both be a great help to me, if you felt like it. You could repeat what I've said to you, just as I've said it. Then other passengers would understand, they'd be kind and merciful. In what they said and what they did too. It would be good for Chris and Don Sebastian if they could get out on deck, knowing they wouldn't be molested. It will be terrible for them if they have to stay in hiding, all the way across the ocean. Not only because of what has just happened, because they've lost everyone that belongs to them except the baby. But because they've both been in hiding so long."

"Miss Rhodes, you know I'm very much honoured——"

"My dear, if there is anything on earth I can do——"

"Thank you so much. I felt sure I could count on you.—But I mustn't go on talking about this all through luncheon. I didn't want to depress you. Just to enlist you. . . . Tell me about your presentation, Mrs. Delmaine—I understand London was unusually thrilling this year. And I want to congratulate you on your election, Mrs.

Brice. Is it true that there are nearly a thousand new members in the International League of Peace and Prosperity?"

Beatrice Rhodes smiled and began to eat her toast again.

When luncheon was over, she sat on the verandah for an hour with her parents. Then she went across the corridor to the cabin which Christian Marlowe and Sebastian de Cerreno were sharing, and knocked on the door. It was Don Sebastian who opened it.

"I came to see if you two wouldn't come up on the boat deck with me for a while. We could walk, or lie around in the sun, just as you like. And later on we could have a swim. The pool's very nice. I was in it this morning."

Hans Christian, who was standing by one of the portholes, neither turned nor answered. Don Sebastian, after glancing towards him, replied gravely:

"Thank you very much. It is thoughtful of you to suggest it. But not today, I think."

"Well, perhaps tomorrow."

"Yes, perhaps tomorrow."

When she returned the next day, however, the same episode was repeated. But the third time, after Don Sebastian had glanced towards Hans Christian's unresponsive figure, he made a different answer.

"It is very kind of you to think of us so constantly. I shall be glad to go up on deck with you, if you can find a secluded spot."

"I have one picked out already. I'm certain you'll like it."

When they reached it he assured her that he did, and he spoke sincerely. Two big lounging chairs had been drawn up high in the bow, and the place where they were had been roped off and marked "No Admittance." There was a small table between the chairs, on which a thermos jar stood, and a few books and magazines were scattered about. Beatrice poured out two glasses of orangeade, offered one to Don Sebastian, and sipped slowly from the other herself, making a casual comment from time to time. Then she picked up a book and began to leaf it through in the same desultory fashion. Eventually she read a few paragraphs aloud. When she stopped tentatively, Don Sebastian asked her if she would not go on.

It was nearly two hours later that she closed the book, glancing at her wristwatch.

"I have to go down. I can get into the stable about this time for a few minutes. And I always stay with the baby while Catalina has her supper. Don't you suppose you could persuade Chris to come up here when he finds there won't be anyone here but you?"

"I will try to persuade him, Be-atriz. So you stay with the baby every night while Catalina has her supper?"

"Oh, yes! We're great friends. He bounces around on my lap until

316

he gets tired. Then he curls up and goes to sleep. . . . Will you meet me up here tomorrow afternoon at three, Don Sebastian? I won't bother you by coming to your door and knocking first."

"I shall do so very gratefully and gladly, Be-atriz."

He was waiting for her when she reached there, and this time it was he who poured out the orangeade and made the initial remarks as they sat sipping it and smoking cigarettes. When Beatrice set down her empty glass she asked if she should read to him again.

"The book is very interesting and you read well. Your voice is perfectly suited to reading aloud. But perhaps today we might go on talking for a time, Be-atriz."

"I should love to go on talking with you, Don Sebastian. And I love to hear you call me 'Be-atriz.' "

"Do you know the meaning of your name?"

"No—names do have meanings, don't they? What does it mean?"

"It means 'making happy'—I believe you are well named. I believe you have acquired a gift for making people happy, Be-atriz."

"Oh, Don Sebastian, if I only thought so, I'd be the happiest person in the world myself! If I could only bring some happiness to Chris! But I can't reach him at all. He won't speak to me. He won't even look at me."

"Not yet. But some day he will. You must be very patient with Hans Christian, Be-atriz."

"Don Sebastian, I—I have been. I am. But——"

"When you remember what he has gone through——"

"But, Don Sebastian, haven't you gone through just as much? And you speak to me, you don't shrink away from me!"

"No, I don't shrink away from you. I am thankful for your thoughtfulness, thankful to talk to you. But I have not been through as much, Be-atriz. Or rather, I've been through it in a different way. Though my grief is great, it is untinged by any sense of guilt. I have made many mistakes in my life, but none of them has destroyed my own standards or brought down destruction on those I loved. I am upheld, in a certain measure, by the knowledge of this, whereas Hansel has not even that cold comfort. Sincerely as he acted, he cannot escape from the consciousness that if he had been ruled by reason instead of swayed by impulse, he would never have become enmeshed in the Nazi web. He cannot forget that having made his initial mistake he might still have retrieved it. If he had returned to America, when I first urged it, he would have redeemed himself and saved Cristina. He cannot forgive himself because this is so."

"Don't you think he ever will?"

"No, never, any more than I shall ever recover from the desecration of my country and the slaughter of my family. I have terrible moments too. But I am not a young man any longer; I have learned

317

more than Hans Christian. I know that I have not reached the end of my endurance. Hans Christian believes that he has. That is the supreme tragedy for him just now."

"And you think it always will be?"

"No. I think that some day he will learn, as I have, that the only way to go through life is to keep beginning it over again. That is the one sure sign of vitality, the capacity that Americans, especially American women, have to such an ultimate degree. Even the revolutions in Europe are inspired by remembered wrongs. Americans may sometimes stumble in going ahead, but we Europeans stumble because we are always looking back. When Hans Christian forgets that he ever imagined himself a German and is conscious only of his Americanism, he will reach out again towards the realities of which you are a part."

"Don Sebastian, you said I had acquired a gift for making people happy. I believe you must have been born with one."

Sebastian de Cerreno shook his head. "No. On the contrary. I have failed in most of my efforts to create happiness. But for that very reason, it will mean the more to me if I have given you a glimpse of it. All I have really done is to make you understand. When you do that, you do the rest yourself. The youth of Europe has been sacrificed, Be-atriz, to those remembered wrongs of which I just spoke. In Germany, this sacrifice has taken one form; in Spain, another. Both are horrible, and Hans Christian has been caught in the toils of both. He has a dual holocaust from which to rise. But he will—if you never fail him, if he comes to realize that you are standing by, whatever happens."

"I'll—I'll never fail him, Don Sebastian."

It was true that Beatrice and the baby were very great friends. Very often, after he had gone to sleep in her arms, she put him to bed herself without really rousing him from the comfortable torpor into which he sank after he had exhausted himself by bounding up and down on her lap. A crib had been set up for him beside Catalina's bed, in the small cabin that adjoined the one occupied by Hans Christian and Sebastian. Beatrice always stayed beside this crib until Catalina came back from her supper, and sometimes she sang as she sat there, looking down on the sleeping child, and glancing across, every now and then, to the closed door leading into the next cabin.

It was not until they were almost across the ocean that the door finally opened, and Hans Christian came into his son's room while Beatrice was sitting there singing to the baby. He walked over to the crib without a word, and stood looking down at it himself, still speechlessly. Beatrice rose and came to stand beside him.

"Don Sebastian wants us all to be very careful to talk Spanish to him, so he won't forget it, so it will always come naturally to him," she said without artificial preamble. "When I found this out, I asked Don Sebastian to recommend some books for me to read, some that would help me with idioms and conversation. I've studied Spanish before, but of course that wasn't the same. He told me about several. One of them is by Benavente—the man who won the Nobel Prize, you know, who wrote *The Kingdom of God*. There's a line in it that keeps running through my mind, every time I sit here looking at the baby. May I tell you what it is? It may hurt you at first, but after you've thought it over, it will comfort you."

"Nothing will comfort me, but nothing will hurt me any more either. You may tell me if you like."

" 'There is something more sacred than a grave: a cradle. There is something greater than the past: the future.' "

Hans Christian winced, but otherwise he gave no sign that he had heard her. She waited for a moment, and then she spoke to him again.

"Chris, won't you come up on the bridge with me for a little while? The Captain told me to go there whenever I liked. No one will speak to you, no one will disturb you. And it's so beautiful up there, between the sea and the sky."

"We can't leave the baby alone."

"I think Don Sebastian would stay with him until Catalina comes back. I think he'd like to. I'm going to ask him, anyway. And I'm going to ask him if by and by he won't join us, when she's finished her supper. I think he'd like to watch the stars come out too, after the sun's gone down."

"Very well. Ask him."

Don Sebastian did not decline. Beatrice had felt very sure he would not. He answered her with characteristic courtesy when she inquired whether he would be willing to sit with the baby while she and Chris went up on the bridge.

"Certainly, if that will release you, Be-atriz. You have been faith-fulness itself to our little boy."

"I think he's the most beautiful baby I've ever seen. It's all I can do to tear myself away from him. But I want Chris to come out in this glorious air with me. I want you to come too."

"Since I know you mean that, I will join you, when Catalina has returned."

"I always mean what I say."

"That also I know, Be-atriz."

She opened the outer door of the cabin and held it ajar for Hans Christian. Then she went swiftly down the long corridor and up a succession of gangways, at last leaping lightly over the barrier guarding the bridge. The officer on duty nodded, smiled and stood back. He did not speak to her and Hans Christian as they went by, and Hansel did not speak either, for a long time. When he did, it was to say something sad again.

"Do you remember the Captain on the other ship, Trixie? The one we came over on? He's lost it."

"Yes, I heard. But some day he'll get another."

"It won't be the same."

"It may be better. And the Captain of this boat won't lose his ship, Chris. He'll keep it, unless he does something disgraceful himself. He's an American. It's an American ship."

Again Hans Christian winced, and again Beatrice gave no sign that she had noticed this. She went on talking as if there were nothing unnatural about his silence, as if no strain existed between them.

"I think Don Sebastian is beginning to look better, Chris. I think he's beginning to realize what it will mean to find your mother waiting to welcome him, when the ship gets in."

"How can he think of such a thing? He wouldn't be coming, she wouldn't be waiting for him, if——"

"You told me yourself once, Chris, that a great scholar said there weren't any ifs in history. Perhaps there aren't any ifs in love. Anyway I don't believe there ever have been for your mother. Even if Don Sebastian isn't glad he's going to see her, he must know how glad she'll be to see him. That must mean something to him."

"I don't believe it means much."

"Well, it will when he sees her, even if it doesn't now. And I don't agree with you. I believe it does already. We ought to hope it does, with all our hearts. Because, whatever else he's lost, he hasn't lost everything, as long as he's got her."

Hans Christian turned around at last and looked at Beatrice. There was no joy in his gaze, no radiance, no eagerness. But at least he did not flinch from her eyes, he faced her squarely and searchingly. He did not speak, and neither did she. But despite this, in one long triumphant moment, a question was asked and answered for all time. As they looked from each other out towards the sea again, their hands, clasping the railing, accidentally touched. Neither one drew away. They continued to stand, side by side, confronting the far horizon.

THE END

The following pages contain
a list of titles which have
been reprinted in this series

PORTWAY & NEW PORTWAY

NON-FICTION

Anderson, Verily	Beware of children
Anderson, Verily	Daughters of divinity
Armstrong, Martin	Lady Hester Stanhope
Arnothy, Christine	It's not so easy to live
Asquith, Margot	The autobiography of Margot Asquith
Barke, James	The green hills far away
Bentley, Phyllis	The Pennine weaver
Bishop, W.A.	Winged warfare
Blain, William	Home is the sailor
Brittain, Vera	Testament of experience
Brittain, Vera	Testament of friendship
Brittain, Vera	Testament of youth
Buchan, John	The clearing house
Cobbett, William	Cottage economy
Crozier, F.P.	Ireland for ever
Day, J. Wentworth	Ghosts and witches
Dunnett, Alastair M.	It's too late in the year
Edmonds, Charles	A subaltern's war
Evans, A.J.	The escaping club
Falk, Bernard	Old Q's daughter
Fields, Gracie	Sing as we go
Firbank, Thomas	A country of memorable honour
Gandy, Ida	A Wiltshire childhood
Gary, Romain	Promise at dawn
Gibbons, Floyd	Red knight of Germany
Gibbs, Philip	Realities of war
Gough, General Sir Hubert	The fifth army
Grant, I.F.	Economic history of Scotland
Hart, B.H. Liddell	Great captains unveiled
Hart, B.H. Liddell	A history of the world war 1914–18
Hart, B.H. Liddell	The letters of private Wheeler
Hart, B.H. Liddell	The other side of the hill
Hecht, Hans	Robert Burns: the man and his work
Holtby, Winifred	Letters to a friend
Huggett, Renee & Berry, Paul	Daughters of Cain
Jones, Ira	King of air fighters
Jones, Jack	Give me back my heart
Jones, Jack	Me and mine

PORTWAY & NEW PORTWAY

FICTION

Albert, Edward	Herrin' Jennie
Aldington, Richard	All men are enemies
Aldington, Richard	Death of a hero
Anand, Mulk Raj	Seven summers
Andersch, Alfred	Flight to afar
Anderson, Verily	Our square
Anderson, Verily	Spam tomorrow
Anthony, Evelyn	Imperial highness
Anthony, Evelyn	Victoria
Arlen, Michael	Men dislike women
Arnim, Elizabeth von	Elizabeth and her German garden
Arnim, Elizabeth von	Mr. Skeffington
Ashton, Helen	Doctor Serocold
Ashton, Helen	Family cruise
Ashton, Helen	Footman in powder
Ashton, Helen	The half-crown house
Ashton, Helen	Letty Landon
Ashton, Helen	Swan of Usk
Barke, James	Bonnie Jean
Barke, James	The land of the leal
Barke, James	Major operation
Barke, James	The song of the green thorn tree
Barke, James	The well of the silent harp
Basso, Hamilton	Pompey's head
Bates, H.E.	The purple plain
Baum, Vicki	Berlin hotel
Benson, R.H.	Come rack come rope
Benson, R.H.	Lord of the world
Bentley, Phyllis	Love and money
Bentley, Phyllis	A modern tragedy
Bentley, Phyllis	The partnership
Bentley, Phyllis	Sleep in peace
Bentley, Phyllis	Take courage
Bentley, Phyllis	Trio
Birmingham, George A.	General John Regan
Birmingham, George A.	The inviolable sanctuary
Blackmore, R.D.	Mary Anerley
Blain, William	Witch's blood

Blaker, Richard	The needle watcher
Bottome, Phyllis	Murder in the bud
Bromfield, Louis	Early autumn
Bromfield, Louis	A good woman
Bromfield, Louis	The green bay tree
Bromfield, Louis	The rains came
Bromfield, Louis	Wild is the river
Brophy, John	Gentleman of Stratford
Brophy, John	Rocky road
Brophy, John	Waterfront
Broster, D.K.	Child royal
Broster, D.K.	A fire of driftwood
Broster, D.K.	Sea without a haven
Broster, D.K.	Ships in the bay
Broster, D.K. & Taylor, G.W.	Chantemerle
Broster, D.K. & Forester, G.	World under snow
Buchan, John	Grey weather
Buchan, John	The Runagates club
Buck, Pearl S. *(Trans.)*	All men are brothers (2 vols.)
Buck, Pearl S.	Fighting angel
Buck, Pearl S.	The hidden flower
Buck, Pearl S.	A house divided
Buck, Pearl S.	Imperial woman
Caldwell, Erskine	Place called Estherville
Caldwell, Taylor	The arm and the darkness
Caldwell, Taylor	The beautiful is vanished
Caldwell, Taylor	The final hour
Caldwell, Taylor	Let love come last
Caldwell, Taylor	Melissa
Caldwell, Taylor	Tender victory
Callow, Philip	Common people
Chandos, Dane	Abbie
Chapman, Hester W.	To be a king
Church, Richard	The dangerous years
Collins, Wilkie	Armadale
Collins, Wilkie	The dead secret
Collins, Wilkie	The haunted hotel
Collins, Wilkie	Poor miss Finch
Common, Jack	Kiddar's luck
Comyns, Barbara	Our spoons came from Woolworths
Cookson, Catherine	Maggie Rowan
Cookson, Catherine	Mary Ann's angels

Riley, William	Laycock of Lonedale
Roberts, Kenneth	Arundel
Roberts, Kenneth	Oliver Wiswell
Roche, Mazo de la	Delight
Roche, Mazo de la	Growth of a man
Roche, Mazo de la	The two saplings
Sandstrom, Flora	The midwife of Pont Clery
Sandstrom, Flora	The virtuous women of Pont Clery
Seton, Anya	The mistletoe and sword
Seymour, Beatrice K.	Maids and mistresses
Shellabarger, Samuel	Captain from Castile
Sherriff, R.C.	The Hopkins manuscript
Shiel, M.P.	Prince Zaleski
Sienkiewicz, Henryk	The deluge (2 vols.)
Sienkiewicz, Henryk	With fire and sword
Sinclair, Upton	Boston
Sinclair, Upton	The flivver king
Sinclair, Upton	The jungle
Sinclair, Upton	Oil!
Sinclair, Upton	They call me carpenter

WORLD'S END SERIES

Sinclair, Upton	World's end
Sinclair, Upton	Between two worlds
Sinclair, Upton	Dragon's teeth
Sinclair, Upton	Wide is the gate
Sinclair, Upton	Presidential agent
Sinclair, Upton	Dragon harvest
Sinclair, Upton	A world to win
Sinclair, Upton	Presidential mission
Sinclair, Upton	One clear call
Sinclair, Upton	O shepherds speak
Sinclair, Upton	The return of Lanny Budd

Smith, Betty	A tree grows in Brooklyn
Smith, Eleanor	Caravan
Smith, Sheila Kaye-	The children's summer
Stone, Irving	Love is eternal
Stone, Irving	Lust for life
Sue, Eugene	The wandering Jew (2 vols.)

PORTWAY JUNIOR

Armstrong, Martin	Said the cat to the dog
Armstrong, Martin	Said the dog to the cat
Atkinson, M.E.	August adventure
Atkinson, M.E.	Going gangster
Atkinson, M.E.	The compass points north
Aymé, Marcel	The wonderful farm
Bacon, Peggy	The good American witch
Baker, Margaret J.	A castle and sixpence
Blackwood, Algernon	Dudley and Gilderoy
Coatsworth, Elizabeth	Cricket and the emperor's son
Edwards, Monica	Killer dog
Edwards, Monica	Operation seabird
Fenner, Phyllis R.	Fun, fun, fun
Haldane, J.B.S.	My friend mr. Leakey
Hill, Lorna	A dream of Sadler's Wells
Hoke, Helen	Jokes, jokes, jokes
Hoke, Helen	Love, love, love
Hoke, Helen	More jokes, jokes, jokes
Hoke, Helen & Randolph, Boris	Puns, puns, puns
Hourihane, Ursula	Christina and the apple woman
Lemming, Joseph	Riddles, riddles, riddles
Lyon, Elinor	Run away home
Parker, Richard	The sword of Ganelon
Pudney, John	Friday adventure
Pullein-Thompson, Christine	Ride by night
Pullein-Thompson, Diana	The secret dog
Pullein-Thompson, Josephine	Janet must ride
Pullein-Thompson, Josephine	One day event
Pullein-Thompson, Josephine	Show jumping secret
Manning-Sanders, Ruth	Children by the sea
Manning-Sanders, Ruth	Elephant
Saville, Malcolm	All summer through
Saville, Malcolm	Christmas at Nettleford
Severn, David	Burglars and bandicoots
Severn, David	Dream gold
Severn, David	The future took us
Sperry, Armstrong	Frozen fire
Sperry, Armstrong	Hull-down for action
Sperry, Armstrong	Thunder country
Stucley, Elizabeth	Springfield home

Abbott, W.C.	Colonel Thomas Blood
Abrams, Mark	The condition of the British people 1911–45
Adams, Francis	History of the elementary school contest in England
Andrews, Kevin	The flight of Ikaros
Balzac, Honoré de	The curé de Tours
Bazeley, E.T.	Homer Lane and the little commonwealth
Bowen, H.C.	Froebel and education by self-activity
Braithwaite, William J.	Lloyd George's ambulance wagon
Brittain, Vera & Taylor, G. Handley	Selected letters of Winifred Holtby and Vera Brittain
Cameron, A.	Chemistry in relation to fire risk and extinction
Clarke, Fred	Education and the social change
Clarke, Fred	Freedom in the educative society
Caldwell-Cook, H.	Play way (1 map, 14 illustrations)
Crozier, F.P.	A brass hat in no man's·land
Crozier, F.P.	Angels on horseback
Crozier, F.P.	The men I killed
Dewey, John	Educational essays
Dewey, John	Interest and effort in education
Duncan, John	The education of the ordinary child
Fearnsides, W.G. & Bulman, O.M.B.	Geology in the service of man
Ferrier, Susan	Destiny (2 vols.)
Galt, John	The provost
Gates, H.L.	The auction of souls
Gilbert, Edmund W.	Brighton old ocean's bauble
Glass, David V.	The town — and a changing civilization
Gronlund, Norman E.	Sociometry in the classroom
Geological survey	The geology of Manchester and the south-east Lancashire coalfield (H.M.S.O.)
Hadow report 1933	Report of the consultative committee on infant and nursery schools (H.M.S.O.)
Harrison, G.B.	The life & death of Robert Devereux Earl of Essex

Smith, Norman Kemp	A commentary to Kant's "critique of pure reason"
Smith, P.W., L. Broke	The history of early British military aeronautics
Smollett, Tobias	The adventures of Sir Launcelot Greaves
Stocks, Mary	The workers' educational association— the first fifty years
Strutt, Joseph	Sports and pastimes of the people of England
University of London Institute of Educ.	The bearing of recent advances in psychology on educational problems
Wall, W.D.	Child of our times
Watson, Francis	The life and times of Catherine de Medici
Watson, Francis	Wallenstein — soldier under Saturn
Wells, H.G.	Crux ansata
Yoxall, Ailsa	A history of the teaching of domestic economy